THE TROUBLES WITH HEARTBREAK

BOOK THREE: THE HEARTBREAK SERIES

BRITTANY TAYLOR

THE TROUBLES WITH

Heartbreak

BOOK THREE: THE HEARTBREAK SERIES

DEDICATION

To Nana
Losing you was unexpected and painful.
Thank you for loving me as your own and for supporting me.
This one is for you.
I love you.

SYNOPSIS

Trouble #1: Levi Hawkins. Always…
Levi Hawkins has been trouble since the first time I saw him through the lens of my camera our senior year of high school.

He was the star quarterback.
I was the yearbook photographer.

Although Levi's hatred for me was no secret, I spent the entire school year fighting my feelings for him, counting down to the day of graduation.

When that day finally came, I foolishly thought I'd seen the last of him. Until five years later, when he walked into the same newspaper I worked for. Only now, he was no longer a football star. He's the paper's newest reporter.

Disguised by a grand opening of a hotel on the shores of South Padre Island, Levi dragged me on an assignment. His college football reunion.

But just when I thought he'd roped me in enough trouble, he asked for one more favor.

Pretend to be his fiancé… for the entire reunion.

I knew he had dragged me along to get a story, but it wasn't long before I realized there was more written between the lines.

And then I remembered… Levi Hawkins has always been trouble.

PROLOGUE

Five years earlier . . .

HATE IS A PRETTY strong fucking word. Reserved only for the most extreme cases.

Or so my father has always told me since I was a little girl.

Although I've never outright stated I've hated someone, there's only one person who's ever come close.

Levi Hawkins.

Quarterback of our school football team and the bane of my existence.

Not that I've ever held a decent conversation with the guy. He's only ever muttered all of a few sentences to me since he transferred here at the beginning of the year. I'm basically invisible to the same man who is everything but to the rest of the world.

Instant football star. Instant popularity.

Still, I know how Levi Hawkins truly feels about me. Between the constant glares and backhanded comments to his other teammates, it hasn't been hard to miss. The only times I've ever heard him speak about me are under his breath whenever he's forced to be near me.

Sometimes, I swear I hear him call me *Nasty Cassidy*. But I could be wrong.

I don't know where his contempt for me comes from. How can you possibly hate someone when you've never actually spoken to one another?

Being the photographer for the school yearbook requires me to have a certain level of interaction with our varsity football team. Especially in a state like Texas. Where football is as sacred as the iced tea in their glasses and the barbecue on their plates.

On the days when I've been forced to stare at Levi for the sake of my yearbook duty, I've considered all possibilities of why he seems to curl his full lips and narrow his piercing blue eyes in my direction every chance he gets.

Maybe he considers me an inconvenience to the team, always sticking a camera in their faces. Football games and team photos. I've been there, camera in hand, snapping shot after shot.

Or maybe it's because, for guys like Levi, it's impossible for them to bother to associate with anyone who isn't on the team or shaking those obnoxious black and gold pom-poms. And if you aren't a cheerleader or a football, you don't get any sort of attention from Levi Hawkins.

None.

But even with those reasons why Levi despises me, the same could be said for me. I can't stand him. Staring at Levi through my lens has only made my chest burn and my legs tighten even more.

He's impossibly gorgeous and I fucking hate it.

I *loathe* it.

I loathe the times where my eyes are forced to look in his direction. Only because of what it does to me.

Too many times I've imagined what it might feel like to have his mouth press on mine or how it would feel to see his eyes looking up at me as he buries his face between my legs.

Square jaw. Soft, yet strong lips. Large hands cupping me in all the places no one has yet to explore.

In all honesty, I can't stand the power he has over me. It's incredibly frustrating to want the guy who gives you absolutely no indication he has any interest in you at all.

My only saving grace is graduation in eight months. In eight months, I'll be off to college and far away from here.

Eight months and I'll never have to see him ever again.

But I know even then, I'll remember how Levi Hawkins has always been trouble.

Trouble #1

Levi Hawkins. Always.

ONE

Cassidy

I've always hated social gatherings.

The whole idea of placing myself into a situation where I'm surrounded by a large group of people is enough to make my armpits sweat, my stomach wobble with nausea, and my throat swell.

But here I am, standing in the middle of the backyard, staring out at nearly all my coworkers. And when I say all of them, I mean *all* of them.

They litter the entire backyard, standing in their cocktail dresses and pent-up ties, fancy drinks perched in their hands.

I look down and stare at my toes. The black nail polish coating each of my nails peeks out from my black sandal wedges. There's a chip on my pinky toenail and I cringe, hating that I'm only noticing it now. It shouldn't be a big deal, but I can't help how out of place it looks compared to the rest of the crowd surrounding me.

Everyone here is perfect. It looks like they walk around with a social media filter on them all the time.

I stare at the two inches between the tip of my sandals and the edge of the swimming pool in front of me.

The water laps back and forth, splashing against the inside wall. It's a bright, clear blue and even through the small, subtle waves, I can see straight to the bottom.

Lights illuminate from underneath. Mixed in with the deep blue are bright spots of yellow. Part of me wishes I had my camera, the other part wonders if the water is warm or cold. I fight the temptation to jump in, not caring if I'm the only one swimming. I won't care if I ruin my entire outfit. It at least would be better than standing here by myself, listening to the constant mindless chatter of the entire staff of *The Austin Daily News.*

I slide my toe forward, nearing the edge.

"Thinking of taking a swim?"

I slide my foot back and swing my gaze up to find my friend Vada. Her purple painted lips are spread into a wide smile. An empty martini glass is pinched between her fingers.

"Do you think Nate would be pissed if I did?" I laugh, darting my eyes over her shoulder.

She turns her head, following my gaze. Her long brown curls are swept up in a high ponytail. They bounce up and down like a loose coiled spring. The ends dance across her bare back. When she turns back to face me, she lets out a light giggle. "Maybe. It looks as if no one has ever actually gone swimming in it. If they have, it's very well taken care of."

"What's the point of having a pool if you never use it?"

"They look nice," Vada says matter of fact, shrugging one shoulder.

"Do you want to go get another drink?" I ask her, shifting our conversation.

She looks down at the empty glass still in her hand and shakes her head. "No. Colton and I were about to head out."

"Really?" My shoulders immediately drop in disappointment.

This is why I hate social gatherings. If your friends leave, you're left by yourself. I can feel my armpits sweating already.

"Yeah," she says. "Colton has work early in the morning, and then he's taking Jonah to that fancy hotel with the water park inside."

"Oh, right." I nod, remembering how they were taking my nephew Jonah to a resort a few hours away. "I forgot you were going tomorrow." Colton's brother tragically died in a car accident last year. It wasn't until a few months ago that Colton found out Jonah is his brother's son. Only his brother never knew about him, since my sister never shared her secret relationship with Ryan.

Despite the sadness that comes with knowing Jonah will never meet his father, I'm so grateful that Jonah has family outside me and my father. Most of all, I'm thankful Colton uses every chance he gets with Jonah. Even including Vada.

"Well, I'm actually not leaving for another couple of days," Vada says. "I have some things I need to finish up at the office before I can go."

"Vada . . ." My voice fades as my eyebrows knit and I tilt my head, unconvinced. She has a bad habit of allowing herself to get swept up in her work. I think a part of her is still in fear that she'll lose her job somehow. Much like the last paper we were at. Or when she was working at her brother's bar after his wife passed away.

In a way, I understand her. Being here without my camera wrapped around my neck is killing me. Utterly killing me.

"Don't worry," she says. "If I don't go, I won't hear the end of it from Colton. I just need to make sure my office is good to go after Nate clears out the last of his files tomorrow."

"Good."

I look back over her shoulder in the same direction I was earlier and spot Nate standing on the opposite side of the lawn from where we are. This isn't even his house. Honestly, I'm not even sure who owns it. Everything about this place feels fake. Fake smiles, fake decorations, even the pool seems fake.

It's as if I'm standing in the middle of a stage, surrounded by hundreds of actors and props.

Our old boss, Nate, is transferring to a paper in Lubbock to reunite with his family. Yesterday was his last day at our newspaper before Vada took over his position. Technically, she's my new boss, but I think of her more as a friend than anything else. It's a strange position to be in, but my respect for her will never change. Being a couple years older than me, Vada has been an incredible mentor. We may work in different departments, but she's had my back ever since we started working together.

I'm still watching Nate over Vada's shoulder. He's standing with a group of reporters from the office. His movements differ slightly from usual. You can tell he's had quite a bit to drink. There's a beer in his hand and it's a foreign sight. I've never seen him with alcohol.

My attention is pulled away when I see someone crossing the yard from the corner of my eye.

Levi Hawkins.

On instinct, my heart leaps at the sight of him. It's not as if I'm surprised to see him here. I knew he would be, and I also know Levi would never miss the opportunity for a party such as this one. It's the perfect setting for him.

Since we were seventeen years old, I've always known Levi to be the center of attention. Even when he didn't appear to be asking for it, he got it. Because all throughout high school, that's what he got. Exactly everything he ever wanted. Sure, there were a few years where we were hundreds of miles apart, attending different colleges, but the day I saw him walk into our newspaper as the newest reporter to be hired, I'd known he hadn't changed. No amount of time can change a person that much.

Levi lifts his hand and loosens the tie around his neck, tilting his head from side to side. He looks frustrated as he swings both of his arms at his sides. His long fingers curl, his hands forming into two tightly clenched fists.

He's wearing a black collared shirt, the sleeves partially pushed up, revealing his perfectly toned and sculpted muscles. Between his shirt and his dark jeans and the black leather belt around his waist, he sticks out in this party like a neon sign. His outfit alone sets him apart from the rest of the office cronies.

The thick muscles of his arms stretch the sleeves of his shirt as he crosses the yard, from one corner to the other. My eyes move in an invisible line, following back to where he came from inside the house. A woman stumbles behind, a good distance away from Levi, but she veers off course, turning her attention to another group of people. I can't tell if she's involved with Levi, or was a few minutes ago, but knowing him, it wouldn't surprise me.

Levi has never been one to shy away from fucking any woman that looked his way. Well, every woman except me. Or at least that's the way he was in high school. During our senior year, he had a different girl drooling on his every word nearly every week.

I'm not entirely convinced he's changed much since then.

I look back to Levi as he finishes the last few feet before finding the small bar set up near the back for all the guests. Nate spared no expense in hiring a catering service to hand out hors d'oeuvres and an endless open bar. Looks as if Levi isn't wasting the opportunity to use it.

From where I'm standing several dozen feet away from him, I'm able to see his mouth move as he mutters a few words to the bartender. When he turns around, he leans his arms on the edge of the counter and hangs his head for a few seconds. The bartender places a small glass filled with clear liquid in front of Levi, causing him to bring his head back up. He thanks the bartender, then lifts the glass to take a sip.

"Anyway," Vada says, bringing my attention back to her, "I better grab Colton before he spends all night getting caught up in conversation."

She tilts her head toward the other end of the yard where Colton is standing with two other guys from our office.

"Okay." I give her a reassuring smile. "I think I'm about to head out as well."

"Drive safe."

"You too."

She turns on her heel and heads toward Colton.

I watch her as Colton wraps his arm around her waist, then guides her to the gate off to the side of the yard, leading to the front.

I inhale a deep breath as I look around at the remaining party guests. There's no one here I have any interest in sparking conversation with, so I adjust the strap of my purse on my shoulder and step away from the edge of the pool.

The urge to jump in has completely left me.

I look down at the half drank mojito in my hand. From two hours ago. Mashed mint leaves are packed inside, mixing with the alcohol.

I scrunch my nose and look around the yard, not seeing a designated place for me to place it other than the bar. I turn on my heel and head to the bar. My throat bobs with nerves the second I catch Levi staring at me. His dark brown eyebrows are knitted above his sharp blue eyes. They're narrowed on me and the image of them takes me straight back to high school, when I'd catch him staring at me exactly like this. Only this time, I don't have my camera lens to hide my flaming red cheeks or the bob of my throat as I swallow my nerves.

Levi absolutely hates me.

We work together, a fact I never thought I'd face in the five years since high school. I thought then was the last time I'd see him. I hoped it would be. But fate couldn't have proved me any more wrong. Because here I am, strutting through some random fucking stranger's lawn with black wedged heels and a half-empty mojito in my hands, staring straight into the eyes of a man that's hated me since we were teenagers. See? Levi hasn't changed since high school. He still hates me as much as he did back then.

I'm halfway to the bar when the corner of Levi's insatiably delicious mouth curls in the corners, the creases of his cheeks deepening. I hate how many times I've imagined how his mouth might taste when he kisses me, or how it might feel to have his tongue slide between my folds, pressing against my clit.

My mouth goes dry, his sneer barely fazing me. I'm used to it. I've had to get used to it since we started working together.

When I reach the bar, I place my glass on the counter. The glass clinks on the hard surface, but I don't bother looking in Levi's direction.

I've never fully understood his hatred for me and I'm sure as hell not going to figure it out tonight.

I just want to go home.

The bartender spots me and moves to stand in front of me. He eyes my glass, bringing his gaze up to mine with furrowed eyebrows. "Can I get you something else to drink?"

"No." I give him a smile, feeling Levi's stare burning the entire right side of my body. I ignore him, biting on the inside of my cheek.

He stays silent, listening to my exchange with the bartender who grins, taking the glass. He dumps the contents into a large black bin behind the counter. I can feel Levi's stare and the longer I stand here, the more my heart races. It pounds in my chest and deep down I know it's because of how I feel about him. I've always been attracted to the one man I annoy without managing even a single glance.

I hate it. I detest it. I will the sensation brewing inside me to go away, watching him from the corners of my eyes. He's still leaning over the counter, his sleeves rolled up to his elbows. A bright light shines from the top of the counter, what I'm assuming can only be his phone.

I clear my throat, then turn my head slightly, enough to chance a glance at him. I immediately regret it.

He snaps his head up from what he's doing and his eyes stare straight into mine. His sharp eyes have deepened in their color. They remind me of a flickering blue flame. I don't stare into them too long before I look off to the side, anywhere but at him.

"Leaving so soon?" he asks, and then his shoulders quake as he laughs under his breath. "Shouldn't surprise me, though."

"What is that supposed to mean?" I ask him, coolly. Heat presses against the back of my throat, simmering across my tongue. I'm shocked he's even bothering to talk to me. He speaks to me more now than he ever did in high school. But I know that's purely for work purposes. This is not.

"Nothing really." He casually shrugs, turning off the screen to his phone and shoving it into the front pocket of his black slacks. "I never took you as the kind of girl who'd enjoy parties like these."

"From the looks of it, you don't seem to be enjoying it either." I nod my head toward the group of people standing to my right. The same group of people that woman joined a few moments after stepping out of the house after Levi. I shift my gaze back to Levi, narrowing my eyes as I adjust the strap of my purse on my shoulder. "Besides, you don't know me, Levi. So don't bother trying to pretend to."

He pushes off the counter and moves to stand closer to me. I try not to breathe in too deeply, unsure of how I will react. Instead, I take a step back.

He matches me, step for step. He comes closer. His chest and arms are as sculpted as they were in high school, as if he still spends a good hour of his day working out. His arms are relaxed at his side, but he lifts one, scratching at the shadow of stubble lining his jaw. "It's hard to pretend when I know exactly the woman you are, Cassidy."

I swallow down his words as they shoot straight to the core of my chest. I can feel his voice wrapping around my heart, then piercing it with his disdain for me. It's confusing because Levi doesn't know a single thing about me. I wish I could say the same for him. But I can't. I know exactly the man he is and has always been.

"I don't even know what that's supposed to mean. If anything, I know the kind of man you are. You haven't changed a single ounce since high school."

"Hmm." He frowns, intrigued. His eyes flare. "I'm interested to hear what hasn't changed in five years."

I inhale a deep breath, contemplating on indulging him. He's laying out the bait, begging me to take it. Regrettably, I do. If only for a moment. "Let's see . . ." I tap my finger on my chin and look up, pretending to think. "Arrogant. Egotistical. Player."

He simply stares at me when I arch an eyebrow. "Does that sound about right?"

"Sounds typical," he says evenly. There's no emotion or reaction from his eyes roam over me. The music playing over the party fills in the widening silence between us. My patience wears thin the louder the piano notes get and the brighter Levi's eyes spark under the bright lights.

"Have a good night, Levi. Be safe." Not wanting to deal with him any longer, I give him the most artificial smile I can muster.

Without waiting for a response, I spin on my heel, already digging inside my purse for my car keys. I push through the gate and walk through the side yard of the house before reaching the street. I press the unlock button on my key fob, ready to get out of this dress and these wedges. The rubber of my wedges scrapes against the asphalt with each step I take closer to my car. I shove every thought of Levi out of my head.

It hasn't been difficult to do, a task I've accustomed myself to. Ever since the first time I saw him our senior year. He was the hot new quarterback everyone absolutely fell head over heels for. And Levi didn't shy away from giving them what they wanted. Everyone ate that shit up out of the palm of his hand. His popularity skyrocketed while I stayed hidden behind my camera.

When I reach my car, I immediately sit in the driver's seat and stick my key in the ignition. My headlights turn on, even before my engine, shining their golden beams on the back of the car in front of me.

I twist the key, attempting to start my engine, but nothing happens. The engine tries to turn, whining repeatedly. I turn the key back, then try again. The same sound pours out. It struggles to start and the red battery light flashes on the dash.

My father has taught me enough about cars to know the basics. Essentials, as he called them. The battery is dead.

Even so, I try a few more times before falling back against my seat, deflated. I rest the back of my head against the headrest and allow my shoulders to fall, deciding what to do.

"Dammit," I mutter, slamming my palm against the steering wheel.

"Rough night?"

"Shit." I sit up in my seat as my heart sinks to the bottom of my stomach, catching my breath. When I look up, Levi is standing on the other side of my door. The window is shut, and his voice is muffled coming from the other side. He's bent down, peering through my window. His tie hangs down, swinging between his chest and my window.

I roll my eyes and reach out for the handle, opening the door and stepping out. I shut it behind me and lean against the door.

"What are you doing out here?" I ask him.

"Looks like you need help." He lazily waves his hand out toward my car. "Or that you need a jump."

"I don't." I quickly shut down his weak attempt to offer help. "Besides, you didn't have to go out of your way to offer to help me or come out here for me."

"I never said I was going out of my way. Or that I was out here for you."

"Right." My cheeks heat, flaming with red. "Of course not. That wouldn't be like you to come over here simply out of the kindness of your heart."

He ignores me and clamps his mouth shut as he tightens his jaw, nodding toward the hood of my car.

"Is the battery dead?"

"I'm pretty sure that's the problem." I refuse to give in to Levi or this conversation he's half attempting to have, knowing he isn't simply offering out of kindness. He's doing it out of arrogance.

"Okay." He walks over to the hood of my car, sliding his sleeves even farther up his forearms. "Pop the—"

"No," I tell him, cutting him off. "I'm fine. I can figure it out on my own." Again, I'm too stubborn to give in.

"So, what?" he asks me. "You're going to stand out here all by yourself?"

"No." I pull out my phone, ignoring Levi's sudden presence. "I can call for a rideshare." I'm not entirely sure why he's out here. I'm at least fifty feet from the house. Did he follow me out here after I walked away from him?

The lights from the party shine a subtle glow around his silhouette. Shadows cover his face, accentuating all the sharp angles of his face.

I bring the rideshare app up on my phone, requesting for a car.

"Listen," Levi says, pulling my attention away from my phone. "Let me look under the hood and then I'll leave you to it."

"Why do you care?" I ask him, narrowing my eyes. Suspicion tingles underneath my skin, heating me from the inside out.

Deep down, I know Levi doesn't truly care. There's another explanation for his offering to quote unquote help.

I've already clicked on the button confirming to have someone pick me up in about ten minutes by the time he answers.

"What's with all the questions? We work together and I heard you having trouble starting your car all the way from the front lawn."

I pause, still unconvinced. The party is too loud for Levi to hear my car if he were standing on the front lawn. But I don't bother analyzing him any further. With a deep groan, I roll my eyes as I reach down below my steering wheel and lift the lever to pop my hood.

It gives a loud metal pop sound and Levi is quick to lift it. I don't move from where I am, crossing my arms over my chest as I wait. My feet hurt, standing in my heels. I lean against my car and tip my chin up to stare at the sky. It's pitch-black, all the stars washed out by the surrounding city lights.

I'm lost in my thoughts as I'm staring up at the sky when I jump at the sound of my hood slamming shut.

I tip my head to the side, watching as Levi makes his way around my car.

"Well?" I ask him.

I catch a quick glimpse of small grease stains on the tips of his fingers before he shoves his hands in his pockets.

He doesn't seem to notice, or care.

"It was your battery. One connection was loose, so I tightened it up." He nods toward the driver's seat. "You should try it now."

I sit in the seat and insert my key into the ignition. The engine immediately turns over, roaring to life as usual.

Dammit.

I'm thankful my car is working but I hate that Levi was the one to fix it. I leave my engine running and stare up at him from where I'm sitting with my legs outside of my car, my heels resting on the asphalt.

Levi's eyes move from my toes all the way up my body to my eyes. I hold my breath and give him a weak smile. "Thanks. I guess I'll see you at work."

"Yeah." He nods once, his features settling back into their normal place. Hardened jaw and narrowed, brooding stare. All of it turns my body to mush and I still fucking hate it. "And to think, you were ready to call a rideshare when all you needed was a simple tightening of a cable."

"I said thank you, Levi. Can't we leave it at that?"

"I guess." He shrugs.

"Sorry to pull you from your night." I point toward the house. "I could tell you were having a good time."

All lies. I saw the frustration dripping off him as he stormed out of the house earlier, but I don't tell him. I keep it to myself.

"I was." He nods, twisting his mouth in thought. He backs away from me, spinning on the heel of his brown leather dress shoe. "See you at work, Cassidy."

My palms sweat and my heart thrums inside my chest, replaying the sound of his voice in my head, repeating the way my name sounded passing his lips.

When he's already across the street and crossing the yard to head back into the party, I look down at my phone. I close out the rideshare app and swing my legs inside, closing my door behind me.

I can't describe it, but as much as I'm curious about Levi helping to fix my car tonight, something isn't settling with me.

It isn't until I'm turning out of the neighborhood do I realize the reason. I just accepted help from Levi Hawkins, and something tells me it's a fact we'll both never forget.

TWO

LEVI

"Mmm. You taste so fucking good." The voice vibrating down my cock should bring me closer to my orgasm, but it's doing the complete opposite.

I slide my hand away from her long hair and tilt my head back against the headrest of the driver's seat in my truck. She continues sucking on my cock, twisting her tongue near the tip before bringing her mouth back down to the base.

I squeeze my eyes shut, telling myself I should enjoy this. Meeting a woman and bringing her back to my truck isn't exactly new. It's not something I do all the time, but it's nothing out of the norm for me. But this time, I can't seem to shut my mind off.

All I can see is blonde hair instead of black and all I can smell is vanilla instead of the wine coated mouth sucking on my cock. "Mmm." She hums. "I've been wanting to do this ever since I saw you back in the house."

"What?" I ask her, catching my breath. It isn't that it doesn't feel amazing. I mean, she has her mouth wrapped around my cock. But the more she talks, the more I'm beginning to second guess my decision to take her back to my truck. "We only met an hour ago."

The woman I met inside is working her tongue along my length, puckering her lips when she reaches the tip. Her head bobs in my lap and I groan, frustrated that I'm not enjoying this.

She notices my lack of energy in reciprocating what I'm sure she thinks is a spectacular blow job and sits up. She presses her hands on my thigh, pushing herself back up. She swipes the back of her hand across her mouth, wiping my pre-cum from her lips and sneers. "What's your problem?"

I smile, unsure myself. I rest my elbow on the top of my door and swipe my thumb across my lip, staring outside. I parked my truck farther down the street from the party, out of view from everyone else. The party is still in full swing. I don't plan on going back.

"Nothing's wrong," I tell the woman sitting in the passenger seat of my truck. "It's just been a long night."

I look back over at her as she leans forward, swiping a fresh coat of lipstick on her mouth. She's leaning forward in the seat, bringing her face close to the visor.

I watch her in silence as I zip my jeans and buckle my belt. I shove my key in the ignition, starting my engine. It roars to life, rumbling the inside of my cab.

She applies coat after coat of lipstick, painting her lips a bright red and for a moment, I'm worried she'll never leave.

I don't even know this woman's name and I don't intend to ask her for it. I met her when I first showed up at Nate's going away party tonight. I was walking to the bathroom when a door in the hall suddenly swung open, slamming into me. Next thing I knew, a champagne glass was flying out of her hand, shattering at my feet. Champagne immediately soaked my shirt all the way down to my boots. Women and bathrooms at parties. An equation that seems to always land me in trouble.

After helping her to clean it up, I headed straight for the bar where I, unfortunately, ran into Cassidy. I knew she was going to be here at the party, I was just hoping to avoid her. As usual. I've always tried to avoid her. Ever since we were teenagers.

But I couldn't avoid her when she walked away from the bar and out onto the dark street. I didn't exactly follow her. I wanted to make sure she made it to her car. She did and when her car didn't start, I was reminded of every reason I keep my distance from her.

The conversation between us was enough to make me regret it.

After she left, I headed back into the party and found the woman I met in the hallway. Somehow, we made it back to my truck where she immediately unzipped my jeans and put her mouth around my cock. I didn't stop her, determined to end this miserable night on a high note. But it's looking like it won't.

"You know, I was hoping we could have taken this a lot further." She snaps the visor shut and shifts in her seat to face me. Her lips are swollen, but she looks nearly the same as before her mouth found its way to my cock. Only slightly.

"I'm not in the mood anymore." I wave her off. I'm now convinced it's simply exhaustion pulling me away. I've been spending the past six days working nonstop on my next article. Even though I turned it into Vada this morning, I can feel the pressure and stress of the past week hitting me like a ton of bricks.

I rest my elbow on the door of my truck and pinch the bridge of my nose.

"Fine," the woman says. I open my eyes as soon as I hear her opening the passenger door. "I'll just head back inside to see if someone else can show me a better time."

"Okay." I resist the urge to laugh.

"Considering how this went, I'm sure it won't be difficult."

She hops down from the seat with her heels dangling from her fingers. Her bare feet land on the asphalt.

She slams the door shut and walks around the front of my truck, back toward the house and the party.

I shift into drive, ready to head home. I'm about to press my foot onto the gas when my phone rings through my truck. I press the green button on my steering wheel to answer.

"Hey, Zane. What's up?"

"Hey, man. Are you still at your work party?"

"No." I shake my head and turn my steering wheel all the way around, turning onto the next street out of the neighborhood. "I just left."

"Awesome," he quips. "Meet me at the Barley House for a few drinks."

I rest my elbow on the center console and run the pad of my thumb across my bottom lip, considering Zane's offer. Ending this night with my best friend sounds infinitely better than mulling over the details of what's happened tonight. Before I've even answered him, I've turned back around, in the direction of the Barley House.

"Be there in ten," I tell him.

"Fuck yeah."

I hang up with my best friend and readjust in my seat, relieved to know the night isn't a complete waste.

As soon as I pull into the parking lot of the Barley House, I hop out of my truck and find Zane standing on the front patio. The Barley House is a large brick building set apart from the shopping malls surrounding it. Wrapped around the entire square building is a small black wrought iron fence, creating a clear divide between the sidewalk and the restaurant. Wooden tables of all sizes are scattered across the patio, some with small fire pits built into the middle. Zane isn't seated at one. Instead, he's standing near the back door with a beer perched in his hand, inhaling a draft from his vape.

He sticks the tip of the long black cylinder into his mouth and breathes in. He pulls it away, blowing out a large white cloud.

I hop the fence and walk toward him, not bothering to walk around to the gate. A few of the people sitting at the tables turn their heads in my direction, surprised.

Zane pushes off the wall and grins when he sees me.

"About fucking time," he says.

I nod my head, giving him a grin in return. "I told you ten, I came in ten."

"Felt like longer." He shrugs, laughing.

"Whatever." I walk past him and reach for the door leading into the bar area.

"How was the party?"

I run my fingers through my hair, pushing it off my forehead. It's thick from the moisture lingering in the night air. I don't mention the girl I met or my run in with Cassidy. "It was fine. I'm sure my boss will be happier once he's back home in Lubbock with his family. Party was still pretty fucking sick considering he'd rented out the house specifically for it."

Zane massages his beard with his fingers in thought. "Doesn't surprise me. Corporate functions are staged like that. Usually in the most lavish bullshit way possible."

"How would you know?" I genuinely ask him, amused.

He gives me a sly grin. "Movies."

"This is why you're forever single."

"Hey, man." He frowns. "Same could be said for you. You're never with a woman long enough to even get her name."

"Not going to lie. You have a point there." I inhale a deep resolving breath, thinking back to the woman who I took back to my truck only twenty minutes ago. "I think I need a beer."

He winces before he slowly grins. "You will after what I'm about to tell you."

I stop in my tracks, allowing him to pass me when we step over the threshold. He pauses when he notices I'm no longer moving.

The bar is dark on the inside, almost every wall painted a rich, dark black. Metal sheets are nailed to the ceilings and the lower half of the walls. The only light is coming from behind the bar and through small lamps above each table. Everyone is covered in a seamless blend of shadow and dull amber lights.

I narrow my eyes on Zane as he slides his vape into his front pocket.

Zane's been my best friend since college. We were room-mates freshman year, even both rushing the same fraternity our sophomore year. Not to mention, we were both on the football team together. Well, until junior year at least. Zane stayed on the team, whereas I didn't.

It's a decision I haven't stopped thinking about for over two years. Even though I still think about football more than I care to, I believe shifting to a career of writing was the best decision I could have made for myself.

I'm staring at Zane with a quirked eyebrow, wondering what he's planning on telling me. "Don't tell me you bribed me with having a few drinks with you just so you could talk to me."

Zane combs his fingers through his beard in thought, a mischievous grin spreading across his mouth. "Not exactly. But maybe you should get that drink first."

I sigh and slide the sleeves of my shirt farther up my fore-arms. The smell of auto grease wafts in front of me and I see a few grease stains streaked across my fingers from when I helped Cassidy with her car.

Fuck. This is why I try to steer clear of Cassidy Walsh. She's always been trouble. Leaving her mark long after I want her to. Like these fucking grease stains. I flex my fingers back and forth, foolishly hoping it will help them disappear, but it doesn't. My thoughts float back to earlier with her in her fucking miniskirt and black painted toes. I stop my thoughts before they get carried away, ready to get a drink. I leave Zane and head toward the bar as I intended when I first got here.

After I grab my beer, I meet him in the same spot I left him. We both make our way back out to the patio, this time sitting at an empty table in the corner. I drink the first bit of my beer before leaning back in my chair, turning my attention to the parking lot. The city lights of Austin flicker in the distance. It's only been a few months since I moved back here, shortly before I landed the job at The Daily News.

I didn't grow up here in the city, yet I'm familiar with its luster. Living on the outskirts of the state's capital forces you to live with a life of yearning. I always knew there was more to life than the dirt country roads and tight-knit communities of the towns surrounding the city. Towns like the one I grew up in. College gave me a reprieve from the constant pressure I'd grown up around long enough to lure me back in. I was satisfied with a taste of a different life. But even when I returned last year, I didn't want to move back home to my parents' house. The same house where my three siblings still live. Here, in the heart of Austin, I'm not completely hiding from my roots, but I can keep my distance enough to make me feel as if I'm living on the opposite side of the country.

I bend my leg, resting the ball of my boot on one of the supports under the table. I lean back, turning my attention back to Zane. With one hand, I wrap my fingers around my beer glass, ready for when I want to take another sip.

"So, what did you really bring me out here for?" I ask him, curiosity eating away at what little patience I have left.

"Miles Deacon."

Zane uttering Miles's name immediately catches my attention. I snap my head up from my beer and my eyes widen.

"What about him?" I keep my anger at bay. The history between Miles and I goes all the way back to our junior year of college. Back when we were teammates. Back before he'd betrayed me. It's a period in my life I try not to let myself revisit.

Zane leans forward, crossing his arms on the edge of the table. The end of his dark beard dances across his skin and it makes me wonder how he keeps up with it. Especially given the fact he's a high school counselor.

"Well, you know Miles got drafted last year to play for some minor league football team over in El Paso, right?"

"No, I didn't know that."

"Really?" Zane asks, pretending to be surprised.

"Yes, really," I tell him, flexing my fingers around my beer a little tighter. "I don't keep tabs on him, if that's what you mean. There's an infinite number of other things I'm more interested in than keeping up with that asshole."

"My bad." He casually leans back in his chair. "I didn't think you would, but I figured I'd ask anyway."

I lift my beer and take a long sip, the bubbles popping and cracking their way down my throat. I swallow and look back at Zane. "So, why are you bringing him up?"

He pauses for a few seconds before sighing and tapping his finger on the table. "Not only does Miles play for a minor league team, but he's also inheriting his family's hotel business. He's been appointed CEO. They have locations all over the country, but they're opening an entire chain along the gulf. The first grand opening is out at South Padre Island."

"Okay." I shrug. "Good for him, I guess. What does this have to do with me?"

"Well," Zane's voice trails, "Jimmy Thayer emailed me a

week ago and told me Miles wants to invite everyone who was on the football team in college. The original team anyway. I guess he wants to make it a reunion of sorts."

"No way." I immediately dismiss Zane, knowing where this is going. Zane's going to convince me to go. "To start, I highly doubt Miles meant for me to be included when he told Jimmy to invite the entire team. Plus, aside from the bad blood between us, I wasn't even on the team during our last year of college. I haven't played in over two years." I swallow back the nerves running through me. I can't decide if I should be annoyed or simply that I shouldn't care at all. Why should I? I've moved on with my life and I'm happy with what I've built with it.

Right?

Zane shakes his head. "No, Jimmy specifically mentioned your name. He said he emailed you as well, but he didn't get a response."

I straighten my back, pulling myself up from the back of my seat, dropping my foot back to the ground. I lean my elbows on the table and stare at my now empty beer glass. I think back to my emails, knowing I check them all the time, especially considering I'm a reporter. I have my emails connected to my phone. Maybe it didn't go through or went to a different folder.

"I never got an email from him."

"Regardless." He waves me off. "What do you think?"

"What do I think about what?" I laugh. "You don't seriously think I'm going to go."

"Come on." Zane grins, his eyes swimming with hope, as I knew he would. "I figured enough time has passed now where it wouldn't be that bad. We'll get to see all the guys from the team. Plus, Miles is paying for everything. Hotel, food, every single event."

"It's only been a year since we graduated from college," I

say. "I thought reunions were usually at the ten-year mark, five tops."

"I told you," he says. "He's tying it into the opening of the hotel chain in South Padre."

I scoff and look away from Zane, tapping my finger on the table. I think back to earlier tonight when I was listening to Cassidy object to every ounce of help I was offering her. Even when she begrudgingly allowed me to figure out what was wrong with her car. Somehow Zane has me questioning which situation is worse. Listening to Cassidy insult me or listening to him relentlessly try to convince me going to this bullshit reunion is a good idea.

"You know," I tell Zane, "I'm surprised *you* want to go at all. I thought you couldn't stand Miles as much as me. We both know he's the biggest asshole after that shit he pulled our junior year."

"Oh." He laughs. "I hate the asshole with nearly every fucking muscle and bone in my body, but I'm not one to pass this up. As much as I hate Miles, I still like everyone else that was on the team. I figure it'll be good to see them. Not to mention, we get to stay at the hotel and eat for free."

"Ridiculous." I rest my elbow on the arm of my chair and scratch at the stubble lining my chin.

"Listen," Zane says, pulling my attention back to him. "Even if you don't want to go for your own personal reasons, I figure you could use it as an opportunity for work."

"Opportunity?" I arch my eyebrows, unsure of where he's going with this.

"Miles taking over his family's company and opening up this chain is a huge deal. I'm talking huge. Every newspaper and blog will cover the event. All week long. Come on, man." Zane sits up, leaning over the table with his finger pushed into the top. "Every other news outlet will scramble for a story. But you,

you'll have an automatic in. You'll be in a prime position to cover it."

I wince and turn my attention back to the parking lot. I spot my truck parked two rows over, thinking back to the girl I'd met at the party and how I ended up with her in the front seat, her mouth wrapped around my cock.

I've never cared what others thought of me. My life has been more about doing whatever the fuck I wanted in whatever moment I was in. That's part of the reason there's a rift between me and Miles. My tendency to live in the moment hasn't always been the best decision for me.

Where Miles couldn't stand my free spirit, I couldn't stand his arrogance. Miles Deacon lives by the code that he's above anyone and everyone else. Always believing he was better looking and that he was the best on the team.

But I knew the truth. I've always known the truth.

It's been over a year since I last spoke with Miles, but a pulse in my body tells me he hasn't changed.

Nothing's changed.

"I don't know." I shake my head, uncertainty continuing to run through my mind.

Even if Zane had a point about the opening of hotels becoming a major story, one other reporters would salivate over, stories don't always fall into my lap. Each day differs from the one before. But if there's one thing I know, it's that Vada is always up for a new story. This I know she'll take up in a heartbeat.

"Come on, man," Zane says. "Pitch it to your boss. With a story like this, I'm almost certain she'll agree to it."

I stare at my best friend, awaiting my decision. I imagine a scale, weighing my choices.

On one side, I can completely write Zane off and come up

with a different story for work. On the other, I can grab hold of it and use it to my advantage, catapulting my career.

But I know deep down, there's more to it than a simple tipping of the scales.

In truth, I need to decide whether a killer story is worth the trouble that will certainly follow it.

THREE

Cassidy

Part of me hoped I would never see Levi Hawkins again after high school to make my life easier. Like ripping off a Band-Aid. The quicker and cleaner the separation, the less painful in the long run.

But then there was the one day in college, when I'd seen him at a football game between our schools. I didn't speak to him that night and he never saw me, but I still haven't forgotten it. My heart jolted at the sight of him, reminding me the Band-Aid removal was anything but quick and clean. It was agonizing and painful.

The last time Levi had laid eyes on me was after our graduation ceremony. I saw him standing across the football field with his family. His mom was taking an endless number of pictures and his younger brothers were playing a game of frisbee with his cap. I couldn't look away from the way his brown hair caught the sunlight or how his cerulean blue eyes seemed to be brighter from a distance. He couldn't stop lifting his hand, fingering the smooth medal resting on his chest, the gold and black ribbon draped around his neck.

A medal for football.

The gorgeous asshole I'd hopelessly had a crush on the past year was awarded a medal at graduation for bringing the team to the state championship that year.

High school football and Texas. I've never understood the obsession.

But after we went our separate ways that summer, I'd vowed to never think of Levi Hawkins again.

I should have known back then he wouldn't go away that easily.

I'm sitting at my desk, resting my chin in my hand as I stare at my computer screen. And Levi's face.

It's as if my eighteen-year-old self has betrayed me.

Bypassing my worktable, I headed straight for my computer when I first showed up this morning. I haven't looked up since.

I can't explain it, but my conversation with Levi last night has spurred on this new curiosity. I've fallen down a rabbit hole and held out on diving in until I walked in the office this morning. My eyes caught his empty cubicle and took the opportunity to do a bit of research.

Levi's picture is staring back at me on the screen. It's a picture he posted on his Instagram several years ago. His hair is cut shorter than it is now and his face is closer to the one I remember from high school.

After combing through a few news articles from a couple of years ago when he played for his college, every article that was written about him turned into articles written *by* him.

It's as if there are two versions of Levi's life. Blatantly and obviously cut apart by an invisible line.

There's no transition.

"Don't you have about a million pictures you should edit or whatever it is you do with that red crayon of yours?"

I jump back in my seat and gasp for air. My chest stills and squeezes as my chair slides backward a few inches. I look up to find Levi standing on the other side of my computer. He looks the same as he usually does when he comes into the office. Tie, button-down shirt that seems to fit impeccably in all the right places. His light brown leather bag is strapped across his shoulder and, as always, his face is set into a scowl. Just for me. I narrow my eyes and lean forward in my chair, gripping onto the edge of my desk with my fingers. I pull myself back into my original spot and roll my eyes, quickly clicking out of the social media page I've been scrolling through. The picture of Levi's face disappears on the screen, but when I look up, I find him still standing in front of me.

I fight the way my chest squeezes at the sight of him. "Don't you have some article to write or something? Anything that involves you bothering anyone else but me?"

"Maybe." The corner of his mouth curls into a grin and my heart can't decide if it hates it or wants to see more of it.

I inhale a deep breath and pull myself to a stand. I walk over to my worktable and pretend to sift through the photographs splayed out across my desk. "Well, you should probably get to it instead of staring at me like a creep."

"Huh." He sneers. "Speak for yourself."

"What does that mean?" I look up from my photographs. He's already turning to walk away.

"Nothing," he says, pressing his mouth into a flat line. He isn't forcing it, he's simply relaxed. But his eyes move along my face as if he's studying every inch. They dance around, moving from my lips to my eyes, back down to the photographs I'm holding.

My eyebrows arch across my forehead. "Is there something I can help you with?"

He inhales a deep breath, steeling his gaze. "I was wondering if you were finished with the photos from the protest. I need to turn in the article to Vada this morning and kind of need them."

I drop the photos I have in my hand and move farther down my worktable to where I keep a stack of all the photos I've completed. The protest images are on the top. I lazily drop them in front of him, unable to get last night out of my head. I hate to stoop as low as to thank Levi, but honestly, if it weren't for him, I would have been forced to ride home in a rideshare. And I hate that.

Levi silently flips through the photos and steps back away from my table. He doesn't lift his head up from the pictures when he turns around. He doesn't give me so much as an acknowledgment or even a look of appreciation.

Yet my need to thank him more sincerely overrides my irritation.

"Thank you again for last night, by the way."

"What?"

"I wanted"—I clear my throat—"to thank you again for fixing my car last night."

He presses his smooth lips together, the corners creasing as he mulls over my words. I can see them working behind his eyes, as if his bright blue irises have transformed into gears. Spinning with thought.

Silence surrounds us despite the sound of the morning newsroom. The clicking sound of keyboards and hushed conversations lies over us like a blanket. A suffocating one.

As soon as the words leave my mouth, I regret them. Nearly every word I've ever spoken to Levi has been an immediate regret. If only because of the way he makes me feel afterward. My chest burns as if a hot iron has been pressed against it. My heart hammers beneath flesh and bone. Sometimes it beats so fucking hard, I think Levi might hear it. The blanket of sound suffocating the air between us now swells like a balloon ready to burst.

As if Levi lifts his hand, bursting the balloon with the tip of a needle, the tension between us releases when he turns and walks away. Without a single word. Without a single acknowledgment of my gratitude for what he did for me last night.

I'd say I'm surprised, but I'm not. This is how it's always been between us.

I stare at his back until he crosses the newsroom and disappears behind the short wall of his cubicle.

Sighing, I return to the photos I was sifting through earlier, the ones I was using to pretend I was more focused on work than the way Levi's Adam's apple slid across his neck every time he spoke.

My phone vibrates across my desk, the humming sound echoing from the hard surface to the worktable.

"Hello?" I rest my elbow on my desk and realize Levi's social media page is plastered across my computer screen. My cheeks heat as I scramble to exit out of it, wondering how it managed to pop back up when I'd clicked out of it earlier. Maybe I only thought I did. I peek up, hoping no one else saw the screen before I closed out of it and click my mouse more times than necessary.

"Hi, Cassidy, this is Joni."

"Oh, hi, Joni." I massage my fingertips across my forehead and breathe out, leaning back in my chair, keeping my phone pressed to my ear. "How are you?"

"I'm good."

It's been a few weeks since I'd heard from Joni. She's one of my father's physical therapists. She and Rebecca, the other physical therapist, have been working with my father ever since he received his knee surgery last year. His rehabilitation has taken a while longer than expected, even affecting the way he's been able to take care of Jonah. Most days he's well, but other days I know it's a struggle for him to walk more than a few feet without his knee throbbing. Joni and Rebecca are supposed to split the days they visit with my father. However, for as long as Joni has been with us, she's worked more than her typical schedule, offering to work for Rebecca when she's scheduled. I've never questioned it, nor felt the need to. Until now. Maybe.

"Is everything okay?" I ask Joni, a twinge of concern tugging on me. She hardly ever calls me.

"Um, sort of. I'm calling to ask you if your father has mentioned my transfer? I'm supposed to be leaving next week."

"Oh." I straighten my back. "No, he hasn't."

Joni sighs, then pauses. "I had a feeling he hadn't. He hasn't indicated he wants to continue physical therapy once I leave."

"What?" I ask her, my eyes widening in surprise. "Is he finished with his sessions? Does he not need them anymore?"

"Well, that's the thing." She clears her throat. "He needs them, but he's been very insistent these past few sessions that he doesn't want to continue once I leave."

"I'm sorry." I groan, resting my head in my hand. My elbow is resting on my desk, the bone of my elbow digging into the solid surface. "What about Rebecca? She's still going to be working with him, right?"

"Um." Joni pauses before confiding in a rush of words. "At first, he told me he wouldn't want to continue physical therapy unless I stayed. I've been working on convincing him to continue with Rebecca, and I'm not sure how well it's working."

"Does he not like her?" I sigh again, the pressure of my father's stubbornness getting to me. "I thought he liked Rebecca."

"Oh," Joni's quick to add, "from what I understand, he does. Rebecca's told me their sessions always run smoothly, so I'm not sure where this is coming from."

"I'll talk to him."

"Thanks." Joni's voice sounds relieved. "But don't worry too much. I have a couple more sessions with him before I have to move onto my next patient. I'm hoping I can have him stick with Rebecca."

"Okay," I tell her. "Thanks again for calling."

Once Joni hangs up, I open my thread of texts with my dad. I hover my thumb over his name, ready to ask him why he wants to back out of physical therapy without Joni, but I don't. I drop my phone on my desk and figure I'll talk to him when I get home.

I leave my desk and head back over to my worktable, continuing to pour over the mound of photographs I laid out. I need to get these photos done before Vada leaves for her trip tomorrow.

I spend the next hour examining and editing. When I'm done, I clean up my work area and grab my camera bag, ready to head out on my next assignment. Another reporter in the sports department is writing a story on one of the local high school football teams.

Ever since I started working here, I've taken countless photos of numerous sporting events. Especially football.

But today I'm shooting a golf tournament. It's a nice break from what can sometimes feel like monotony.

"Oh, Cassidy, good timing."

I'm nearly to the elevators when I pass Vada's office and her voice stops me. The main wall dividing the rest of the entire news floor is made entirely of glass. I catch her standing behind her desk in a tight black pencil skirt and matching blazer. Underneath, she's wearing a mustard yellow silk blouse. I internally sigh, catching myself admiring her bold choice of colors.

Today I'm simply wearing a loose-fitting black tank and dark jeans. Photo shoot days are the only exception as to why I can get away with wearing jeans. Otherwise, I'd be wearing a similar outfit to the one Vada is wearing today. Minus the condiment-colored shirt.

"Hey, Vada." The second I stop at the threshold of Vada's office, my eyes shift to her left. Standing on the other side of her desk, with his hands shoved into the front pockets of his black slacks, is Levi. He's half turned toward me and then he wastes no time before his eyes are immediately all over me. His ice blue stare burns every inch of me from my head all the way to the thin spaghetti straps of my black tank. He avoids meeting my gaze, keeping his eyes anywhere but on my face.

I step inside Vada's office when Levi breaks his attention away from me, turning back to Vada. She's standing behind her desk with her hands on her hips. "You aren't busy, are you?" she asks me on a breath.

I point behind me, hitching my thumb over my shoulder. "I was just on my way out to shoot the golf tournament."

"Oh, right," Vada says, nodding in acknowledgment.

I shrug my shoulder. "I should be back in a couple hours if you need me."

"Not really. Or at least not right this second," Vada says, shifting her eyes toward Levi. Her expression tells me this isn't going to be a single question or even a quick request.

Vada doesn't know the history between me and Levi. In fact, not a single soul inside this building knows Levi, and I went to the same high school or that we even graduated the same year. Or that we can't stand to be around one another. We've been successful so far, playing it off. As far as I know, no one suspects a thing.

In the beginning, I'd wondered whether Levi told anyone we knew each other, but the more time passed with us working together, no one seemed to let on they knew anything.

And they still don't.

Works for both of us, I guess.

"What's up?" I ask Vada, confused as to why she called me in here.

"I have an assignment for you starting this weekend."

"Oh?" I feel my eyebrows lift across my forehead, intrigued. I'm always interested when Vada has a new story idea for me.

Levi's deep voice groans and rumbles beside me. I snap my head toward him, wondering what my assignment has to do with him.

Noticing his groan has grabbed Vada's attention, he clears his throat and pulls his hand out of his pocket. He nervously scratches at the stubble on his chin. "If you want, I can take photos myself. Cassidy doesn't need to come."

"Are you kidding?" Vada asks him, a hint of a smile ghosting her lips. "What would you use? Your phone?"

"Well, yeah," Levi answers, shrugging his shoulders.

"No." Vada laughs, shaking her head. Her smile fades when she sits down in her chair. She crosses one leg over the other and leans back. "This kind of story definitely needs professional photos done and Cassidy is the best. She'll get what we need."

"Um." I press my lips together and hum, still confused. My lips pop open when I open my mouth to add. "What story?"

Vada leans forward with her elbows on her desk. This time her grin is stretching from one ear to the next, the dimple in her cheek deepening.

I chance a glance at Levi. He's avoiding me, keeping his focus out the window behind Vada.

Vada nods her head toward Levi.

"Levi has scored a great position on a story in South Padre."

"You mean South Padre Island?" My eyebrows arch across my forehead again, this time in shock. I've never been sent out to the gulf coast for a story. Part of me wonders why there and how Levi has scored a story in one of the most popular vacation spots in the Texas Gulf. South Padre Island is out of our typical area to be considered local news. Which is usually the types of stories Levi covers.

"Yeah." Vada waves her hand in Levi's direction, clearly wanting him to explain our assignment.

"Oh." He clears his throat, finally turning to face me. The times when we speak to each other in front of our colleagues are the only time he's ever civil with me. According to Levi, it's fine to be civil as long as it's work related. His blue eyes shift to the side briefly before they swing back to face me. "My old college football team is having a reunion . . . of sorts and I've been invited."

I trade glances between Vada and Levi, surprised she'd want to cover a silly college reunion. Maybe Levi went to one of the larger colleges in Texas. After high school I never heard from him again so I'm unsure exactly which college Levi ended up going to.

My mind wanders thinking of all the big colleges in Texas that Levi could have gone to when I realize one small detail about this supposed reunion.

"Wait," I say. "Your college team is already having a reunion? Hasn't it only been a year since you graduated?"

I ignore the tiny bit of question written on Vada's face and keep my focus on Levi.

His piercing eyes twitch with my question. "It has." His tone is slow and calculated. "I said it's a reunion of *sorts*."

I cross my arms over my chest, trying not to let Vada on to my tone. But this is how I usually talk to Levi. Words laced with venom disguised with a hint of sweetness. "And what exactly does that mean?"

The second my eyes meet Levi's sapphire blue ones, I feel like I'm back in high school with him. His face hardens and his jaw pulsates.

"Miles Deacon," he explains, his stare hardening, "was our

second string quarterback, and he's opening a chain of beach-front hotels. This weekend is the grand opening, and he's invited the entire team."

"Ah," I say, tilting my head back. "Okay, I see." I cross my arms over my chest, ignoring the way his shoulders tensed under his collared shirt.

"The reunion is scheduled to last ten days."

"Ten days?" I trade glances between Levi and Vada with widened eyes. "What kind of reunion lasts for ten days?" The strap to my camera case slips off my shoulder. I quickly unravel my arms to catch it before my thousand-dollar investment falls to the floor.

I skip a breath and once I quickly recover the strap on my shoulder, I catch Levi staring at me again.

"Miles Deacon's," Levi says. "Apparently." The tone in his voice has shifted slightly. As if he can't understand it either.

"Ten days is a long time."

"It is," Vada says. "But it's an incredible opportunity to catch this story. It'll be a great feature piece. A first for Levi since I'm charging him and solely him on this."

"Oh." It's the only word I can think to say before I chew on the inside of my cheek, mulling it over. As if I technically have a choice.

Silence fills Vada's office. Levi is looking out the window. Vada's focus shifts between the two of us.

"So, what do you think, Cass?"

"About what?" I snap my head toward Vada. Her tan, slender face is filled with hope. She knows this is a good story. Even if I wanted to, I wouldn't say no to Vada. This is my job, and I would never let the odd history between me and Levi come between us.

"About going to South Padre for the reunion," Vada explains. "What do you think?"

"Oh." I blink, nodding. "I think it'll make for a great story, but I'm actually not—" I wince, worried about the phone call I had earlier this morning with Joni. I need to speak with my dad and figure out what's going on with him.

"I know, Cass." Vada rests her elbows on her desk and leans forward. "I'm sorry I won't be in the office, but I could really use you on this project. I'm usually not one to guilt trip, but you're seriously the best I've got, and I need the best I have on this story. That's you and Levi."

I drop my shoulders, wanting to tell Vada I can't. I try not to let my opinion of Levi cloud my judgment. If I didn't hate him and he didn't hate me, would I jump at this opportunity? Probably.

Still, I'd rather spend this time with my dad and helping him the best way I can.

But the pleading look in Vada's eyes rips at the resolve I have inside me. Apparently, this is big for her and will put her at ease knowing I'm going. She's worked hard to get where she's at and with her now settling into her new role, I don't want to let my editor in chief down. Especially when she's one of my closest friends.

I avoid looking at Levi when I give Vada my answer. "Okay, I'll go."

"Awesome." She claps her hands and shifts back to face her computer. "I'll let you two coordinate the best way of getting there and all those sorts of details. I assume you're staying at your friend's hotel, Levi."

I briefly shift my eyes to my left, catching Levi standing beside me.

He clears his throat. The muscles on his forearms flex as he stretches his fingers. "Um, yeah, I believe that's the plan."

"Perfect." Vada keeps her focus on her computer. "Check in

with me now and then. I'll be out of the office, but I'll have my phone on me."

"Sounds good," Levi says.

"I won't keep you any longer, Cass. I know you have that photo shoot you were heading out to."

"Thank you." I clench my hand around my camera strap, the fibers grating against my palm and fingers. "I'll let you know when I'm on my way back to the office, so I can see you before you head out."

I spin on my heel, the stiff air of Vada's office heating my throat. Something about agreeing to this trip with Levi has my body scorching on the inside and my stomach wobbling.

Ten days with a man who can't stand my presence. This should be interesting.

My feet land with more force than usual, attempting to put as much distance between me and Levi as possible. I stop halfway to the elevator when I realize I've forgotten my keys. By the time I make it to my desk, Levi is already standing on the other side of me.

"Ugh." I groan, shaking my head. "I can't deal with you right now. I have to go."

"I didn't ask for you to come."

Immediately, I shoot him a glare with narrowed eyes, my irritation with him carrying over from what just happened in Vada's office. The pressure around my eyes builds and I clench my hand impossibly tighter. "What?"

He rolls his eyes. "Do you ever hear what I say? I feel like I always have to repeat myself to you."

"It's because most of the time all I hear come out of that mouth of yours is utter bullshit. I have to make sure I heard it correctly." My eyes instinctively fall to his mouth, my mind betraying me.

"It's not," he whispers, slicing his eyes as narrow as mine

were a few seconds ago. "I'm simply saying that I didn't ask for you to come to the reunion. That was all Vada."

Without moving, he shifts his eyes to either side of me, clearly checking to see if anyone can hear us. We've never spoken to each other for this long in front of our colleagues. Thankfully, there are only a few people in their cubicles, with their heads down.

"I can't believe you seriously followed me over here to tell me this," I whisper back. "Of course I know you didn't ask for me to be there."

He straightens his back. "Well, I needed to set the record straight."

"Right, of course you did." I cross my arms over my chest. "Because what a shame it would be to actually be cordial and civil to me. You always have to have the upper hand, don't you? I can see absolutely nothing has changed about you since high school."

"Well—"

"Let's get this straight." My cheeks flame red. "I went out on a limb to agree to go to this stupid reunion of yours. I actually have a life, you know, both in my career and outside of it." I point to my chest, swallowing. "But that's beside the point. All you need to do is tell me when and where this silly reunion of yours will be. That's it. Otherwise, stay away from me."

I snatch my keys from my drawer and move around the desk, giving Levi one last direction to ensure he doesn't get this confused. "You've done a pretty good job of that since we've known each other. Shouldn't be difficult for you to handle."

FOUR

LEVI

The revolving door to the entrance of Miles's hotel moves painstakingly slow. It takes almost an entire minute for me to push my way through. My laptop hangs from one shoulder and on the other, my backpack. I tried to fit as many items as I could into the small bag, hoping it would last me the entire trip. I didn't know what kind of shit Miles was going to pull this weekend, and the last thing I needed was to bring more baggage.

Metaphorically and literally.

I even emailed Jimmy Thayer to double check Zane hadn't lied to me about this whole reunion. I mean, Miles's last name is slapped onto nearly every sign around this place. I know he isn't lying about inheriting this business. But that still didn't mean that the reunion didn't truly exist. I wouldn't put it past Miles to create some bullshit story for the sake of boosting his image.

But Jimmy was right, and so was Zane. Within minutes, I'd received a reply from Jimmy, ensuring me there was a reunion. And I was invited. He even asked if I was bringing anyone else, claiming Miles needed to know so he could figure out how many rooms to book under my reservation. I told him only one, not bothering to explain who.

I remove my sunglasses when I finally emerge from the revolving door. The lobby is massive. Ridiculously, fucking massive. Every inch of floor from one corner to the next is blindingly bright. A mixture of brown marbles covers the walls, spilling onto the floors. Touches of gold contrast against the white countertops. Part of me thinks this hotel seems out of place for being on the coast and one of South Padre's most popular beaches, but I'm not a designer. There must be a reason behind it. Miles does nothing without a purpose. Most likely, he did it to show off. Wouldn't surprise me.

For a hotel that hasn't technically opened yet, there are quite a few employees and what I guess are guests, like me. I don't recognize any of them, all strange faces. Maybe this is one of those exclusive stays before the actual opening. I type a few quick notes on my phone about my first impression of the hotel to use when I write the first draft of my article.

When I finish, I glance around the lobby, looking for Zane or Jimmy, fuck, even Cassidy. But I find no such luck. I haven't spoken to Cassidy since that day in the office when she'd told me to stay away from her. Her request wasn't unreasonable and unattainable. She was right when she'd said it's what I've always done. I remember it. The day I decided I couldn't stand to be around her was the day I first saw her out on that football field. It was also the day I decided to stay away from her, the camera held between her hands, and her endless questions. It's been about five years, and she hasn't changed one bit.

I push my annoyance with Cassidy aside long enough to call my best friend.

He picks up on the second ring.

"Hey, Levi."

"What's up, Zane? I just arrived at the hotel and am about to check in. Want to grab a drink or some lunch? I drove straight here without stopping, so I'm fucking starving."

"Sorry, man," he answers in a hesitating voice. "I'm going to be a few days late to the reunion."

"What?" I lift my hand and shove my hair back. The ends run through my fingertips as I let out a heavy sigh.

"Yeah, my sister went into labor last night, so I'll be spending a few days in San Antonio before I'll be able to make it out there."

I sigh again, knowing this reunion will already be tense. I was hoping Zane would make it more bearable. Instead, I'll be riding out most of this trip without him. "Oh."

"I'll be there for the last two nights, though. I wouldn't miss the final celebration for anything. Even for my new baby nephew." He laughs.

"I guess." I cross the lobby and drop my backpack onto the floor, sitting in one chair near the front window overlooking the beach.

"Hey, I'm sure you'll be able to find someone to keep you company. You always do."

"You know"—I lean forward and scratch at the stubble on my chin—"somehow you manage to make a point even when sounding like an ass."

"I'm not wrong though."

"No. You aren't." I swallow, my eyes roaming across my view of the beach. Waves crash onto the sand in the distance as the water shifts to a darker shade caused by a cloud rolling overhead. It's large, dark, and heavy. It feels like an omen for this trip. "Congratulations on the new nephew, by the way. And to your sister."

"Thanks. I'll let you know when I'm headed that way."

"Don't worry about it," I tell him. "You have enough on your plate. It might be cool to see some of the guys and I won't lie, this whole week *will* make for a great story."

"That's right," he says, firmly. "My man always writes the best ones."

"Great," I tell him. "Inflate my ego a little more." I'm only half-sarcastic. It feels good to hear others say they think my work is good.

I didn't exactly receive words of affirmation growing up. Life was only about football and if you didn't have football, your life was basically wasted. Without football, there was no future.

"One more thing," Zane adds, "just try to not fight with Miles."

I tighten my grip on my phone, now realizing I'm not only spending the entire week with Cassidy, but I'm also spending it around Miles.

"All that shit between me and Miles is in the past, man. You don't have to worry about it. As for Miles, that's up to him."

"I'm going to be honest with you, man. I don't believe a word you just said."

"I guess you'll have to wait and see."

"I guess so." He chuckles. "I'll talk to you later."

"Sounds good." I press the red button and pull my phone away from my face in time to see Cassidy walking into the hotel. She used the regular automatic door off to the side of the revolving door. The one I should have used.

I swallow, heat suddenly reaching the back of my throat. I can't tell if it's the frustration from earlier resurfacing or it's from the sight of her.

It's as if Cassidy heard the words *South Padre Island* and ran with the whole concept of vacation.

She's wearing a simple pair of black sandals and jean shorts. They fray near the tops of her thighs, exposing her smooth legs. Cassidy isn't the tallest woman, but these shorts make her legs look as if they go on for miles. They aren't as golden as you would expect them to be for someone vacationing on the beach.

Tucked into her shorts is a tight, bright blue spaghetti strap tank top. The elastic fabric accentuates the curves of her waist and every peak and valley in between. As usual, her camera is hanging around her neck, the woven strap pressing into her cleavage. My cock twitches and I curse under my breath.

Where the fuck did that come from?

I blame my reaction on the fact that I've never seen Cassidy wearing anything resembling what she's wearing now. Even in school, she always dressed more modestly compared to other girls. Which never bothered me. But now as I'm standing here, watching Cassidy, I'm reminded of another reason I haven't been able to stand Cassidy Walsh all these years.

For this exact reason.

I close my eyes, blocking out the sight of her long enough to calm my cock down. Within seconds, it softens enough for me to open my eyes again. This time I find her looking up at the ceiling. Her camera is held between her long, slender fingers. I look up, following what she's staring at. The ceiling.

It's covered in mirrors. Hundreds and hundreds of mirrors are screwed into the seamless ceiling. She lifts her camera and snaps a few pictures before she lowers it again.

She continues looking at it, slowly bringing her gaze back down. She stops when she catches me in the reflection.

The part of the ceiling we're standing under is closer than the rest. The farther you step into the lobby, the more it opens up, exposing every level of the hotel. We're only standing about twenty feet apart, so when she brings her gaze to mine completely, I close the distance between us. I grip onto my backpack still hanging from one shoulder, and tightly wrap my fingers around the strap.

"You're late," I firmly state.

She arches an eyebrow and tilts her head to the side. One side of her neck is exposed as her blonde hair slides away, falling back off her shoulder, cascading down her back. "Actually, you're the one who is late."

"I am not." I point to the door behind her. "I literally just saw you walk through the door."

"Yeah." Her chest vibrates as she laughs. "That's because when I first got here, I couldn't find you. It doesn't help that the reservations for the rooms are under your name. It's not as if I could have called you either. I don't have your phone number."

"How long have you been waiting?"

"Only about an hour." She shrugs. "I went down to the beach and looked around. Took some pictures." She shakes her camera at me.

"Okay, that's good at least."

"I guess you could say that." She shrugs again, only this time she diverts her eyes away from mine.

"Come on." I tilt my head back, ignoring her comment. "I'll get us checked in."

"Fine." She sighs, dropping her camera. It gently falls against her stomach. "But you're grabbing my bag from my car."

I roll my eyes when I turn away from her and start making my way to the reception desk.

When I reach the desk, the receptionist greets us with a large grin. "Hi, welcome to Deacon Hotel and Resort. How can I help you?"

"Yeah, I'm here for the reunion. Miles should have put in a reservation for Hawkins."

"Okay." The receptionist straightens her back in piqued curiosity, quickly typing into her computer. "Wonderful. Miles has booked you one of our best rooms. It's one of our two deluxe suites, just below the penthouse level. You get complimentary room service and a spectacular view of the beach. The drinks in the refrigerator and at the minibar, however, are not included in your stay. If used, those will be charged at check out."

"Really?" I'm confused. Zane said Miles was covering everything about the stay. I guess he was wrong. But still, suspicion peppers its way under my skin. I narrow my eyes, feeling the pressure behind them build. Maybe I'm overreacting or thinking too much into it, but I can't help thinking there is something behind Miles's invitation for me to come. Regardless of not including all the amenities in our room, I'm surprised Miles is being this generous. It's not as if he's gone out of his way to greet me. But I can't help wondering why he invited me here. And now he's given me one of the best rooms in the hotel. Considering our history, I simply find it odd he would treat me this well.

"Excuse me."

I turn my head as Cassidy's voice interrupts my conversation with the receptionist.

The receptionist shifts her attention to Cassidy. "Yes?"

"Did you say one room?"

The receptionist's smile fades and her eyebrows dip in confusion. "Um, yes. That's what Mr. Deacon instructed to put in for your reservation."

"Oh." Cassidy shakes her head. "That's okay. I won't be needing to stay with Mr. Hawkins here." She gestures in my direction.

"I told one of the guys to let Miles know I was bringing someone with me."

"I apologize." She frowns. "Mr. Deacon must have been under the impression you were sharing the room then."

"You said there were two deluxe suites, correct?" Cassidy asks. "Can I book that room, then?"

The receptionist winces, hissing between her teeth. Her eyes fill with regret. "I'm sorry. That room is already reserved."

Cassidy's face flashes with disappointment. I can practically feel it dripping off her.

Same with me. My chest twists and my head aches, thinking of spending ten days in a room with Cassidy. I clear my throat, resting my arm on the desk and leaning forward. "Maybe another one? A regular room?"

I'm cursing myself for not asking about the room situation sooner. It's not as if I had enough time to prepare or even think about every detail of our trip, but still . . . I blame myself for it.

"I'm sorry." The receptionist apologizes again, this time shaking her head. "All of our rooms are booked."

"What? I thought this place hasn't even opened yet," Cassidy argues. "I thought it was just the football team staying here this week."

"There's more than the reunion, ma'am," she explains. "Mr. Deacon has invited many guests to stay at the hotel this week. He's given his old teammates here the best rooms." She turns to me as if her explanation will be enough to put Cassidy at ease.

It doesn't.

"Fuck," I mutter the word under my breath. If Cassidy heard it, she doesn't let on. Her eyes are looking down at the marble desk between us and the receptionist, her eyes shifting in thought. She's thinking of other possible scenarios.

"How many beds are there in the room?"

"One king size bed, ma'am."

Twenty seconds pass where Cassidy stands in awkward silence. I move to open my mouth, but she stops me.

"I see," she says. "Thank you, anyway."

"Of course," the receptionist says. Her smile returns. "If either of you need anything, don't hesitate to call room service or come down to the desk." She slides two of the cards into a paper sleeve and hands them to me over the counter. Afterward, she turns around and grabs two paper bags from the table behind her. "These are complimentary welcome bags for staying here at Deacon Resorts and Hotels. Inside is a bottle of water and a few snacks. There are also menus to our room service and to the restaurants here in the hotel."

"Thank you," Cassidy and I both say at the same time. I avoid glancing in her direction.

It's not that I'm exactly thrilled to be sharing a room with her. If it wasn't for Vada, Cassidy wouldn't even be here.

In all the years I've known Cassidy, even through the four where we separated after high school, I never imagined spending ten days with her. Much less sharing a room with her.

Just when I thought this week couldn't get any worse between seeing Miles and the team again, I'll be sharing a room with Cassidy Walsh.

She inhales a deep breath while sticking her tongue out and swiping it across her mouth. She wets her lips and just like when she walked in the front door, my dick twitches. Only this time the sensation emanates, reaching the lower part of my stomach.

What is happening to me?

The feeling subsides when Cassidy grabs her bag and steps away from the front desk. I grab my bag and follow her, heading toward the elevator.

When I catch up to her, she has her arms crossed over her chest.

"So," I say. "What are you going to do?"

"Me?" She spins around. "What do you mean *me*?"

"I don't know." I shrug. "You looked as if you had another idea for this room situation. I can tell you aren't thrilled with the idea of us sharing this room for the next week."

"Well, no. I'm not. Are you?"

"No." I shake my head. "Of course not." I shift my focus to the lobby, keeping an eye out for anyone I know. I'm obviously not expecting to see Zane, but I look for Jimmy or anyone else. Shit, I even find myself looking for fucking Miles.

When I come up empty yet again, I look back at Cassidy. "Did you have a different plan in mind?"

I ask her this question, already knowing there probably isn't a way out of this. I want to fight this situation tooth and nail, but I'm also practical.

"Not exactly," she says, pursing her shiny lips. They're wet from where she licked them. "I was thinking of maybe staying at a different hotel nearby or something, but I don't know."

I fight the urge to jump on the idea. I already know she can't do that.

"You can't," I quickly tell her, pushing my hair off my forehead in frustration. "You need to be here for every photo opportunity. You could miss something by staying in a different hotel."

Her eyes twitch as she studies me. "I guess you have a point."

"I do," I agree with her, attempting a small smile. A. Small. One. I'm not remotely happy about this living situation, but I get a tiny ounce of satisfaction out of being right. "It'll be fine."

When I've reached the elevators, I press the call button.

Cassidy stands beside me, her arms crossed over her chest. The doors open.

She keeps her chin tipped up and her focus straight ahead. "So much for staying out of my way."

When the words slip between her still wet lips, I realize she has a point.

FIVE

Cassidy

The deluxe suite Levi booked is absolutely insane.

A mix of marble tile and gleaming, rich hardwood planks cover one side of the suite to the other. Every room from the entryway to the bathrooms has multiple pieces of furniture to sit on. Aside from the usual bed in the bedrooms and sofas in the sitting areas. Each piece is unique. They're round and plush and out of place all at once. In some instances, even pointless.

Why would there need to be a red velvet upholstered stool placed next to a toilet?

Every inch of the room smells like fresh laundry and pineapples. The scent filters out all the way to the enormous balcony where four glass French doors are propped open. The sound of the waves crashing onto the beach mingles with the bright orange and purple setting sun.

I can't quite put my finger on this hotel. It's different from what I expected of a beach style hotel, yet it somehow fits. I know absolutely nothing about the owner. Other than that he used to play football with Levi back in college. Otherwise, absolutely nothing. But then again, it isn't my job to know more.

That's Levi's job. I'm just here to capture as many photos as possible.

Still, curiosity picks at the back of my brain. I can't help it. I want to know the story between Levi and Miles. I want to know why his face stiffens and the corded muscle in his arms swells when he talks about college. Or why football doesn't seem to be a part of his life anymore. Not even a little bit.

I'm sitting on my bed, cleaning a camera lens as the click of the front door closing echoes throughout the room.

The sound of Levi leaving. Headed out to dinner. I didn't care that he left me here on our first night in the hotel. I told him to stay far away from me and I meant it. Even if we are forced to share this extravagant room.

I'm glad he left. It gives me a chance to call my dad and check in on him. I tried earlier when I explored the beach before Levi had shown up at the hotel. But he didn't answer. Instead, I texted him to let him know I would call him when I was all settled in my room. Once we got settled and Levi took a quick tour of the room himself, he announced he was heading out for dinner with his old teammates, insisting I didn't need to be there.

I didn't argue. I headed straight for the bedroom, claiming the bed, and set on keeping myself busy until he left.

When I'm done cleaning the lens, I put it back in the case and head over to the minibar. I bend down and survey the minifridge. In the back corner, I catch a stash of four small readymade cocktails. I grab the bottles filled with a bright blue liquid and carry them out to the balcony, cracking one open with a grin. If I'm forced to stay here all week, the least Levi could do is pay for food and drink.

Starting with these beautiful bright blue drinks.

I settle into one of the wicker patio chairs facing the beach, crossing my legs underneath me. The beach is so far down I can see the horizon in the distance. The water seems to stretch on for miles before it abruptly ends, drawing a clear distinction between it and the sky. From what I've heard, the gulf coast has always had a bad reputation for not being as pretty as either ocean surrounding the states. But honestly, I think they're wrong.

This place is beautiful. I'm only six hours away from home, but it's as if I've been transported to a completely different world. The shore stretching out from my left to my right is covered in beautiful near white sand and the water is a deep blue-green color. It doesn't quite match my drink. I twist the cap on my bottle, listening to the sizzle of the carbonation getting lost in the sound of waves hitting the sand. Seagulls fly across the perfect, cloudless blue sky.

Maybe this trip won't be terrible after all.

At first Levi didn't hold up his end of the deal about staying out of my way, but I must admit, he's doing a pretty good job now.

I have this whole suite to myself. At least for the next several hours. I sip on my pineapple coconut blue cocktail and decide it's the perfect time to call my dad.

I prop my phone against one of the unopened bottles and lean back in my seat to video chat with my dad. A breeze floats across the balcony, wisping the ends of my loose hair across my face. I quickly brush them back and press the call button on my phone.

This time, he answers nearly right away.

"Hello, daughter. I'm glad to see you made it safely."

"Hi, Dad." I smile. "I called earlier, but you didn't answer."

"Oh, I know. I was out in the backyard fixing the railing on the deck."

"You're kidding," I tell him, frustrated he didn't ask me to do it before I left.

"As much as you don't want to admit it, Cass, I'm still very capable. It just needed a couple of nails and a few whacks of a hammer."

I set my bottle in the space between my legs, twisting the neck with my fingertips. I hate making my dad feel as if he isn't capable of working around the house or even taking care of himself while I'm gone. Sometimes the words leave my mouth before I'm able to understand what they truly mean.

Almost like me agreeing to come on this stupid little assignment disguised as a vacation with Levi. I didn't truly know what I was agreeing to until now. I glance over my shoulder and spot his backpack sitting on the floor beside the bed. I'm not sure where he intended on sleeping, but I know there's no way in hell it'll be with me.

I've always known there's a deep, innate piece of me that wonders what it would be like to touch Levi. I can't help it. My eyes always find their way, dancing between his eyes and his mouth. And don't get me started on the way his long fingers stretch to push back the hair that always falls into the lashes of his eyes.

The way his fingers move across his own skin only makes my heart flutter more when I'm around him. I don't need to tempt how far I'd be willing to go by letting him sleep in the largest bed I've ever laid eyes on with me.

"Cass?"

"Yeah." I snap my head back from the bed and focus on my dad. He's sitting in his favorite recliner, a glass of sweet tea in his hand. Typical.

"I told you," he explains. "You forget that I'm fully capable of taking care of myself."

"I haven't forgotten. I can't help but worry about you, especially when Jonah and I aren't home with you. Which reminds me . . ."

My dad rolls his eyes. He sits up in his chair and sets his glass on the end table beside him. He rubs his eyes with his fingertips. "What is it?"

"I talked to Joni yesterday."

He immediately shakes his head and waves his hand in front of his phone. He leans back in his chair with a huff. "I don't want to talk about this with you, Cass."

"I think we should talk about it." I hate talking to my father as if he isn't capable, but at times I feel as if I have every right to worry. Ever since my mother died when I was barely able to walk and my sister disappeared after the birth of my nephew, Jonah, I worry my dad will be alone.

"There's nothing to worry about."

I ignore him.

"You can't blame me for worrying about you. It's my responsibility to take care of you and Jonah."

"No." He shakes his head again, disagreeing. He tilts his head, anger settling on our conversation. "When did we cross this line, Cassidy Jean? When did we get to this point where you treat me the same as Jonah? I'm not a seven-year-old boy. I'm your father and you do not need to watch over me."

"We crossed that line when Lyla decided to leave her son. We crossed that line when she left all of us." Silence falls between us and tears spring behind my eyes. The topic of my sister has always been a sore subject between us. Even after all these years. I bite down on my lip, trying not to let the tears spill over. This is not how I wanted this conversation to go.

My voice wobbles and the sun sears every inch of my skin, drying the tear that spilled from my eye before it slid all the way down my cheek. I swipe at my face anyway.

"Listen." My dad sighs. The sight of him through my phone screen has blurred. "You don't need to worry about me. Do you understand? I don't want to argue with you when you're in such a beautiful place. I want you to enjoy your trip. All I will tell you is that Joni and I have an understanding. I know I told her I don't want her coming by anymore, but I need you to trust me when I make my own decisions about my health."

"I do trust you," I tell him, leaning forward to make sure he knows I mean every word.

"Good." He nods, picking up his sweet tea again. He brings it to his mouth but doesn't take a sip until he adds, "Now it looks fucking beautiful there. Show me where you're staying."

"It is beautiful, right?" I arch my eyebrows, relief settling over me. My heart already feels a smidge lighter. Not completely, since he still intends on not having Joni come by for physical therapy anymore, but I do trust him. I remind myself that I have to trust him. Because if I don't, what do we have?

I sit up from the wicker chair, unraveling my legs and pick up my phone, giving my dad a tour of the suite. I start with the bathroom, pointing out the overstuffed stool beside the toilet. He laughs before I move on to the bedroom.

The camera on my phone is pointed away from my face as I scan the room, pointing out the large bed.

"Isn't this amazing, though?" I ask him, in awe of the beauty that's woven itself into its eccentricities.

"Whose bag is that?"

"What?" I ask him, showing him my suitcase resting on the bed. "That's mine."

"No." He points downward. "The bag on the floor."

"Oh." I clear my throat, switching the camera back to where he can face me. Shit.

"Is someone staying in your room with you?"

"Dad, I'm almost twenty-four years old." It's true. Not that I have much of a love life, but still, those types of conversations have never been a part of our father-daughter relationship.

"So," he says. "It is someone else's bag. Do I know him? Have we met?"

"Oh my god, Dad. I'm not talking to you about this." I can feel my cheeks warming. "I have to go."

We never talk about my love life because, ever since my first year of college, it's been basically nonexistent. That and he's never asked before. I didn't think he noticed.

The only semblance of a relationship I had in the past six years was with a guy I'd met at one of our college's football games. He didn't play for our team, but he was there on the sideline as an assistant. Our relationship didn't last more than a couple of weeks. I could never make him a priority, nor did I want to.

"You know I have to give you shit, Cass." The laugh rumbling from his chest warms mine.

"Apparently."

"Wait, you really aren't going to tell me?"

"It's no one." I wave him off. I'm not completely lying. Levi really isn't anyone to fuss about. Especially not to my dad. "Listen, I want to grab some shots of this boardwalk I saw when I first got here, so I have to go before I lose the sunlight."

"Fine," he mumbles. His shoulders deflate. I internally sigh with relief, thankful he's conceded.

I may be in my twenties but it's still awkward to be talking relationships with him.

"I'll talk to you tomorrow, okay?" I raise my eyebrows, heading back out to the patio.

"Okay, as long as you promise to drop the whole Joni situation. I need you to trust me."

"I trust you if you trust me."

He presses his mouth into a thin line and nods once. "I do."

"Good." I grin. "I love you, Dad."

"Love you too."

When I end the call with my dad, I slide my phone into my back pocket and pick up my half-empty blue drink. I take a sip before grabbing the other three and heading back into the room.

I consider calling Vada and checking in on how Jonah is doing with his minivacation with his uncle, but I decide against it. I know Jonah is loving spending time with his aunt and uncle. That and it's barely been a day since I've been gone.

I glance over my shoulder once I reach the bed. The sun is slowly reaching the horizon, drawing out more orange and purple hues. The water sparkles and shimmers, almost as if a bottle of glitter has been dumped all over it. I seriously don't want to miss it.

Maybe I'll shoot a text to Vada before I head to bed.

I quickly pack up my camera bag and stuff my wallet into the side pocket. I originally planned to order room service to irritate Levi, but I figure I might find something farther down the beach.

And who knows?

Even if I grab dinner while I'm out, I'll still order room service. You know, for the satisfaction it will bring.

SIX

LEVI

My stomach grumbles as I stand outside the hotel restaurant. But I can't tell if the pain roiling in my abdomen is from lack of food or nerves.

Truly ridiculous. I've never let nerves get the best of me. Even moments before football games, my body and mind remained calm and focused. Even when I've waited until the last few hours and minutes of a deadline, scrambling to finish up a story. Nerves have never gotten the best of me.

But sitting at the bar in the hotel restaurant, waiting for the rest of my old teammates to arrive, I know I'm no longer the same man. It's definitely nerves.

"Levi fucking Hawkins!" I hear a voice booming across the bar from the entrance to the restaurant.

I grin and stand as Jimmy Thayer crosses the dining area, immediately reaching his hand out the moment he's finally standing in front of me.

"I honestly didn't think you'd come." He grabs onto my hand and pulls me in for a quick hug, slapping me on the back. It reminds me of the nights we'd win games and congratulate each other on our victory.

"Seriously?" I ask him, laughing off my confusion. I sit back in my seat and take a swig of my beer.

"Yeah." He laughs, running his fingers through his long wavy blond hair. Seriously, this guy hasn't changed since the last time I've seen him. "We all know you and Miles can't stand each other. Especially after what went down between you two."

"Fuck." I scratch at the stubble on my chin. "I forgot the entire team knows. But seriously, I was just as confused as you when Zane told me he'd invited me."

"I'm glad you came, though. I can't wait to see everyone. Feels like forever."

"Dude." I laugh. "It's only been a year. Who does reunions when it's only been a year?"

"Apparently we do." His smile reaches his eyes. "I'm thankful for it, though. Gave me the opportunity to take a break from my wife."

My eyebrows shoot up, arching across my forehead. "You're married?"

"Yep." He lifts his hand, quickly showing me the black ring around his fourth finger. "I married Michelle. Remember when I started dating her?"

I narrow my eyes in thought. "Oh yeah. You met her that night we dared you to go to that taco place and order a hundred tacos because you missed the winning field goal."

"Yeah." He laughs. "Lucky for me, I didn't scare her away with my ridiculous order. By the time I got to the eightieth taco or something like that, I'd asked her out. Best missed field goal ever."

"I guess so." I nod toward his hand. "Congrats, man."

"Thanks."

I keep quiet about the main reason I'm here for this reunion. To grab a story. It's not that it's a huge secret, and maybe closer to the end of the trip I'll mention the article I plan on writing.

But not tonight. Tonight I'm just Levi Hawkins. Former quarterback for the Black Canyon Panthers.

"Oh, here comes Ty."

I follow Jimmy's gaze. Tyler, one of our defensive ends, walks in, followed by Caleb. I give them a small wave over when I catch Cassidy crossing the lobby from the corner of my eye. There's a considerable amount of distance between us. Guests and tables scattered around, filling the space dividing us.

She looks the same as when I left her in the room earlier. Her loose blonde waves hang over her shoulders and back. She's wearing those same fucking shorts. The kind that cut so close to the bottom curve of her ass cheek, they cause my cock to twitch with excitement. I was hoping she'd taken the time to change. But it's clear she didn't.

She bites down on her bottom lip as she pulls her phone out of her back pocket, using her other hand to grip onto the strap of her camera bag. She must be going out to take photos. A piece of me feels guilty for leaving her so quickly after we got into the room. But the frustration of all the circumstances surrounding this trip became too much. I couldn't stay in the room and face Cassidy. I needed time to think. I needed time to think about what the fuck I was going to do about our sleeping arrangement. I wasn't above sleeping on the floor or on one of the many sofas and chairs, but in a way, this is a vacation. And I sure as fuck don't want to be sleeping like shit on vacation.

Jimmy's text letting me know the team was meeting for drinks and dinner down in the hotel restaurant came at the perfect time. I didn't want to dwell on it too long, thankful to have a shift in focus. This fucking joke of a reunion and getting my story.

When I left, I told Cassidy where I would be and to not wait on me.

I took her silence as her acknowledgment.

She must have heard me because the moment she passes the restaurant, she turns her head, almost as if she's looking for me. I catch her eyes quickly scanning the bar as she continues walking. For a second, I think I see a smile curling up around the corners of her mouth, but I'm probably wrong. It's hard to tell from this distance.

"Holy shit, Hawkins. Is that you?"

I snap my head to my left, recognizing the voice calling my name. Tyler meets us at the bar, followed by the rest of the guys he came here with. I greet all of them and for the first time since I heard about this reunion, I'm having a good time. It's like I've slipped back to the time we were all still a team. The time in my life before it all crashed and burned into a pile of nothing but memories. Memories I've been trying to forget for the past two summers.

I'm listening to Jimmy and the other guys shooting the shit, waiting for Miles to show up. I never know what to expect with him. He's always been the kind of guy who was like a bomb waiting to go off. One wrong word or one wrong move and he seizes the opportunity. Whatever that might be.

"I figured Miles would have been here by now," Ty says.

Jimmy tilts his head and picks up his fresh beer from the counter. "Fucker is never on time. Remember when he would show up late to practice and preseason games?"

"Yep," Randy, who played wide receiver, answers. "Back when he played second behind Hawkins."

My discomfort rises with Randy's comment. It burns and moves throughout my body like hot lava. I clear my throat as everyone's eyes turn to me. They talk about it as if the truth of what happened back then doesn't still burn. Bringing up my failed college career feels like a hot branding iron, searing all the parts of me that used to value the sport.

I open my mouth to call them out for bringing it up this

early. I mean, we aren't even five minutes into this dinner. But I stop when Miles walks through the entrance to the bar. He's wearing a dark blue suit and a bright red tie. His arms are spread wide with an equally as wide shit-eating grin on his face and his blue eyes are piercing with fire. He's clearly excited about tonight.

"Fuck," I mutter under my breath, wanting to get this over with. I could kill Zane for leaving me to deal with Miles on my own. The closer Miles gets to our group, the more fragile my promise to keep things civil becomes. I find myself wishing Cassidy were even here with me. She'd make a decent buffer.

"What's up, motherfuckers?" he yells, shaking hands with the guys standing on the outside of the group. The rest of our old team shows up in small groups. Eventually, nearly the entire bar is filled.

The crowd hoots and hollers, cupping their hands around their mouths. I keep my hand wrapped around my drink, not sharing in my teammate's sentiments. They don't feel the same way about him that I do.

Despite how he nearly derailed our entire season when he became first string quarterback.

"Jimmy, what's up, man?" Miles shakes Jimmy's hand and pulls him in for a hug. The same way he did with the rest of the guys. Surrounding us are hushed conversations, but I can tell everyone is keeping one ear glued to whatever Miles is saying.

"Not much, Deacon. Thanks for inviting us here. Your hotel is incredible. Congrats."

He nods. "Thanks. There are still a few kinks to iron out, but I think everything will smooth out on its own. I'm glad you were able to take the time to come out here. You said Michelle couldn't make it, right?"

"Yeah." Jimmy nods. "She couldn't break away from work or else she would have come."

"That's okay," Miles says, patting him on the shoulder. "Maybe next time."

I take a drink from my glass and the ice slides against my lips as Miles finally sees me.

"Hawkins." My name uttered between his lips churns my stomach. His tone has changed. If the other guys notice, they haven't let on. But still, I can practically hear all of them holding their breath, all while keeping up the pretense.

"Deacon," I answer him back. His eyes spark with enjoyment. I only ever called him Deacon when we were on the team together. When he was my backup quarterback.

"I'm surprised you made it."

"Well, I'm here." I hold out my hand and shrug.

"I heard Zane had to convince you to come."

"Not really," I disagree, shaking my head.

He gives me a conniving grin, as if he was expecting me to immediately feed him a lie.

Shit. Miles isn't wasting any time.

I clench my hand into a fist, resisting the urge simmering inside me. Hearing his voice and seeing his face brings back every single memory I have of Miles. Every second of our fallout slams into me all at once. Pressure builds in my chest, and it feels as if I've been tackled by a defensive lineman.

"Wow, Hawkins," he says, gripping onto my shoulder. He's acting as if we're best friends. "If that's true, then I appreciate that, man."

"Yep."

"Right." Miles rubs his hands together, stepping back and away from me. He lets his eyes linger on me longer than is necessary. Creepy fucker. He looks around at all the guys. "I'm treating everyone to dinner tonight and I've reserved the entire restaurant for the rest of the night. Let's get this party started!"

Miles lifts his arm into the air, among the other guys surrounding him, signaling to the bartender to grab him a drink.

I stay seated where I am and wait until everyone filters out to the tables arranged in the dining room. Jimmy lingers, hanging around me.

"Be sure to grab another drink before heading in there," he mutters, tilting his head toward the dining room. Some of the guys have already claimed their seats. "Something tells me we're going to need it."

"I think you're right." I turn around, signaling the bartender to bring me another beer.

Jimmy leaves me at the bar as I wait for the bartender to make his way over to me. I stay on my barstool and glance over my shoulder. The large table situated in the back, reserved for the team, is starting to fill up.

Part of me wishes I could head up to the room. I have no idea how long Cassidy planned on staying out, but it didn't matter. Maybe if I get back to the room before she does, I can take one half of the bed. Let her figure out whether she wants to sleep in it with me. The idea of playing that kind of game with Cassidy thrills me. It's not that I get off on irritating her, but it's the way we've been as long as I've been around her. And it only seems to grow the more time we spend together.

Either way, when it comes to Cassidy, I try not to think about it too much. I have enough going on in my life. The last person I've ever wanted to waste another thought on is Cassidy Walsh.

I'm considering leaving when Miles leans on the bar beside me. He rests his arms on the edge of the bar and twists to face me. He shoves his right hand into his pocket and grins.

"So, Hawkins." Fuck, I know exactly where this is going. "How's life been since graduation?"

"Fine." I nod, biting on the inside of my cheek. The delicate flesh stings as I try to think of what to say. "You seem to be doing fine as well. I guess you didn't quite make it to the NFL, did you? At least you have all this."

He presses his mouth into a thin line. There it is. I've struck a chord.

My grandfather always taught me to never throw the first punch. I've always taken that saying literally. I may not have physically touched Miles, but I can tell I've struck a nerve regardless.

This shot was one to his ballooned arrogance.

His forehead creases as he lifts his hand, scratching at his chin. I can see the words working behind his eyes as he considers how to answer me.

"The same could be said for you though, right, Hawkins?" He clears his throat. "Last I heard, you were writing half-ass articles for some shit paper in Austin."

And there he is. The true Miles Deacon. The one I've always been at odds with. The one who stole my career out from under me. The one who turned my whole world upside down because he's an arrogant, selfish asshole. The one who constantly tries to hold me down to push himself up.

"Nah." I shake my head. "I think you were misinformed."

"Oh." He scratches his chin, frowning while shrugging his shoulders. "You're right. Maybe I was."

I don't believe him.

I bite my tongue, not wanting to cause a scene on the first night we're here. I wasn't foolish enough to believe Miles had dropped what happened between us, but I hadn't expected him to say anything on our first night. Especially when the entire team is only feet away from us.

I'm tempted to say more, but I keep my thoughts to myself.

Miles pauses and his eyes move past me, looking over my shoulder. He's looking out at the table full of our old teammates, considering what to say next. He inhales a deep breath, cutting his eyes back to me. "How's Lindsay doing?"

I slide out of my stool, cutting him a hardened stare. If I wasn't angry before, I certainly am now. I thought I could hold it together for the sake of the rest of the team. But the longer I stare at Miles, the more I'm questioning his intentions for me being here. The more I'm thinking he brought me here to test me. Humiliate me. Or in his words from the night my life completely changed, *"I'll never forget this, Hawkins. Fuck with my life. I'll fuck with yours."*

He was telling the truth.

I slide my hands into my front pockets to hold myself back. "Tell me something, Miles. How long have you been waiting to ask me that question? Since the night you fucked up my entire career? We both know what you did."

He narrows his eyes even more. "Come on, man." He reaches out, gripping onto my shoulder as if we're best friends. "I'm only giving you a hard time. I figured you and Lindsay weren't together anyway. That's not how you work."

He removes his hand and moves to walk around me, heading toward the rest of the guys waiting on us.

I spin around, not entirely believing him. "What do you mean, that's not how I work?"

"Oh." He smiles. "Come on. You, Levi Hawkins? Everyone knows you can never stay with a woman longer than one night. I mean, look at what happened with Lindsay. We all know you'll never settle down and hey, if that's how you want to live your life, then by all means, Hawkins." He holds his hand out in front of him as if his reasoning makes perfect sense. "Live your life that way."

I never put much stock into what Miles has ever said. But I wonder if there's truth in his words. I think back to all the relationships I've ever had and come up with zero. I've never had an actual relationship. Not that I've ever considered it a terrible quality of mine. I'm still only twenty-three years old. Big deal if I've never been in a serious, committed relationship. But the more I stare at Miles, staring back at me with that fucking smug expression of his, the more tense my fingers get as they stay clenched tightly in the pockets of my jeans. I hate that I'm allowing him to get under my skin so easily.

"Anyway," he adds, nodding his head back, "I think we should get back to the rest of the team. Don't you think?"

With that, he spins back around and heads back to the dining room. I watch him walk away, staring at the back of his obviously overpriced suit.

I turn and grab my beer, wishing I'd taken a shot of whiskey before deciding to follow Miles back to the table. But the bartender is busy. I grab onto my beer and start making my way back over, wondering why the hell I'm letting Miles's words get to me. Maybe it's because his attempt to ruin my life and my career was nearly successful had it not been for my love of journalism. And maybe it's because ever since that night where one mistake I'd made changed everything has put me in a constant battle with Miles Deacon. A constant competition of who's the better player. A competition to see who is more successful in life.

Before heading over to the table, I glance over my shoulder, checking to see if I glimpse Cassidy crossing the lobby. I only linger for a few minutes before giving up.

I'm walking toward the table flexing my fingers to release the tension built up inside me.

Because from what I've been able to tell in my first ten minutes with Miles is that he's exactly where we left off a year ago. He's playing the same game and we've merely come back from halftime, setting up our first play of the third quarter.

"So, there I was, at this holiday party at my parents' vacation home in Miami, last December." Miles lifts his whiskey to take a sip and swallows before continuing. "My parents had invited about five hundred guests. Most were people my father had done business with in the past, some I'd met over the years as well. About an hour into it I was still mingling around when I ran into this random guy who'd sparked a conversation with me. We talked for several minutes about absolutely nothing. Mostly, I had to listen to him ramble on about this short trip he'd taken to Maine one time and how he'd absolutely hated it and how it was nothing like Miami." Miles leans forward, resting his elbow on the table, turning halfway in his seat. He's speaking to the table, and I shift my gaze, watching as everyone is hanging onto every word this asshole spits out.

I lean back in my seat and keep my arm outstretched, keeping my fingers loosely wrapped around my glass. I spin it between my fingertips, thinking of any possible scenario I could come up with to get out of this miserable dinner. So far, Miles hasn't said anything worth salt. At least not enough information for me to gather a story about how this hotel was even started.

I give up on the idea that I'll be able to leave when I look around at the rest of the guys. Jimmy gives me a brief glance before turning his focus back to Miles. I do as well.

"Right? I mean, the fucker was clearly drunk and didn't understand what he was saying or he seriously had no clue.

Anyway, after about twenty minutes of him talking to me, he walks away, leaving me standing in this hallway. Next thing I know, I'm being grabbed by the lapels of my suit. The woman who was holding onto me stood on the tips of her toes, pulled me down, and kissed me." He slaps his hand on the table. "Bam. Just like that. I'm telling you, full on, open mouth kiss." He laughs. "And when she was done, she smiled, pointed up to the single piece of mistletoe we were standing under, then walked away."

"So," one guy says from the other end of the table. "What happened after that? Did you ever see her again?"

Miles cuts his gaze toward me before swinging it back to answer the question. "Well, I've always considered myself a loyal guy and truth be told, when I want something, I'll get it. One way or another." He taps me on my arm, then leans back in his chair. "Hawkins knows what I mean."

While he may ignore how every eye has now turned on me, I can't. Everyone stares at me with a mixture of both confusion and surprise. Usually I'm all for the attention, but this isn't the kind I'm a fan of. This feels different.

I swallow down the irritation that's resurfaced from earlier. I add it onto the pile resting at the top of my throat.

"Right." Miles continues. "I ended up tracking her down later in the night and the rest is history." He pauses, allowing silence to fall on the group. "I was going to wait until she gets here later this week to tell you guys this, but we got married three months ago."

The entire table explodes into praise for Miles, congratulating him. It almost feels endless, and I sit back, unsure of what to think.

Miles. Married.

The two things together are a contradiction.

Once the conversation dies down and the servers hand out

our food, Miles turns the conversation to me, keeping his voice lower than when he was speaking to the whole table.

"You know what's funny, Hawkins?" he asks. "For some reason I always had it in my head that you would be the one to get married first. But here we are."

I bite the inside of my cheek, finding the same spot as before. A sharp metallic taste hits my tongue and I know I've made myself bleed. I drop my fork on my plate. The metal knocks against the porcelain. Avoiding his stare, I lift my glass and down the rest of my drink. I set my empty glass down, the ice swirling around the bottom.

"What makes you say that?" It's a stupid question, but I ask it anyway. If the motherfucker keeps this conversation up, I truly might knock him out. But only once before I would decide to leave and head back to Austin. Even without a story.

"I don't know. For the longest time you always got what you wanted and given how many times we all saw you with a different woman"—he inhales a deep breath and shrugs—"I figured you were bound to stumble across the right one at some point. The odds were guaranteed to be in your favor."

I narrow my eyes and clench my fist under the table. Every word out of Miles's mouth has been nothing but an insult disguised by a false pretense of interest in my life.

It's a shame because at one point in time I considered him a friend of mine. But those days are long gone. Consider me a fool, but ever since the day Miles was made second string quarterback and I became first, we've had it out for each other. If I ran a faster time in practice, he'd beat me in distance. If he threw so many yards, I'd throw double.

I'd say it's always been that way between us, but I truly never felt competitive with Miles until that day he'd single handedly destroyed my life. Up until then, I considered it typical competition between teammates. But Miles took it to the next level, and I've never forgotten it.

Since then, every word out of his mouth is adding salt to an open wound. Even one I've ignored this past year.

The only fact that keeps me holding out for this trip is this story and knowing if I can write it, my career in journalism will go further than football could have ever taken me.

But even if I'm willing to stick it out on this trip doesn't mean I'm willing to put up with Miles's bullshit. That is one trait I haven't lost this past year. If Miles wants to spend the entire reunion trying to get the upper hand, I won't let him.

Trouble #2

**A favor is never simply a favor.
There are always loopholes.**

SEVEN

Cassidy

I caught the sunset.

It was as beautiful as I thought it would be. The orange and purple hues that peeked through the clouds when I left only deepened. Eventually the orange faded into the purple and the purple transitioned into a light blue. When the light blue had faded into the darkness creeping in, I finally put my camera down. The seemingly endless number of colored lights emanating from the shoreline is tempting me to dig my camera back out of my bag, but I don't. I want to enjoy the rainbow of colors shimmering on water that is so clear it looks like a plane of glass.

Scattered along the shoreline and boardwalk are small beachside shops selling souvenirs and bathing suits. In between the shops are all different kinds of food stands. I consider grabbing a taco from one of the food trucks parked along the sidewalk, but I decide to order room service when I get back to the hotel.

Not because of Levi. More so because I didn't realize how far down the beach I'd walked until I'd lowered my camera. Walking back to the hotel, it still seems far in the distance. At this point I'm exhausted. The inner arch of my foot rubs against my sandals, burning my skin, and I can already tell I'm going to look like a fresh steamed lobster in the morning. I lift my hand and touch my shoulder. It's hot, the familiar feel of a midsummer sunburn making its mark.

But this isn't midsummer. It's early fall in southern Texas. Where it feels like midsummer all year round.

I continue walking down the shore, switching to the sand. I remove my sandals and let them hang from my fingertips before continuing to trek toward the hotel. The sand feels good on my feet, and I dig my toes in a little deeper with every step.

It truly is beautiful here. The warm salty air adds to my already dampened skin. Standing this close to the water gives me a reprieve from the stifling weather of the day. I'm hoping I'll be able to come back here tomorrow, during the day. I'm unsure of the schedule Levi will give me but I can't imagine he'll have me around all the time. He didn't even want me here in the first place so knowing him, he'll only ask me to be somewhere if he absolutely needs me.

Which, to be truthful, makes it a tad easier. If only because I'm realizing the more I'm around him, the more I imagine what it would be like if he cared about me. What the world would look like if Levi didn't hate me at all. And that is a slippery slope I'm not prepared to fall down.

I finally make it to the hotel as some of the shops and restaurants shut down. One by one, the lights begin shutting off, bringing us closer to the night. The music blasting across the boardwalks fades before drowning out completely by the sound of the tide crashing onto the shore.

When I reach the steps, I drop my sandals on the concrete and slide my feet in, trying not to rub it along the blister. I test it out before walking up the steps and pushing through the revolving door. It moves slowly and I'm cursing myself for not going through the door I'd used when I'd first arrived at the hotel. While I'm waiting for the door to move, I reach into my pocket for my room key. When I don't find it in the first pocket, I try the other.

Nothing.

I pat the pockets on the back of my shorts and again, nothing.

Shit.

I sigh and close my eyes, realizing Levi never left me a key before he left for dinner.

I push through the rest of the door and step into the lobby. I consider heading to the front desk to ask for another key, but the woman Levi and I checked in with earlier is no longer there. It's someone else and I doubt they'd give me a key when I'm not on the reservation.

I cross my arms over my chest, at odds with what to do. There's no way I'm hanging out in the lobby, waiting for Levi to finish with dinner.

I don't have his phone number, so I can't even text him to meet me out here. The longer I stay here, the more the blister on my foot burns and the more my patience wears thin. I cross the lobby, hitching my camera bag higher on my shoulder, stomping my way over to the restaurant.

In the front of the restaurant, to the left of the host stand is a long bar. Its glossy black counter reflects the warm golden lights hanging above it. I expect to find Levi sitting on the same stool I'd seen him on earlier, but I don't. The bar is completely empty.

Mingling with the typical piano music playing throughout the hotel lobby, I hear a sudden roar of laughter coming from the back of the restaurant. The sound is deep, rumbling across the otherwise empty dining area. I follow the sound and step inside. The front is dark, every chair at every table turned upside down, the seat resting on the edge.

I almost feel like I'm in one of those movies where I'll emerge to find a secret group of mobsters gathered in the back room playing poker and puffing on fat cigars, surrounded by a thick cloud of smoke.

I'm weaving in and out of tables until I reach the corner of the dining area. I immediately spot Levi sitting near the end of the table. He's leaning back in his chair, resting his elbow on the wooden arm, running his thumb back and forth across his bottom lip.

Only he isn't a mobster, and he isn't gambling with a cigar sticking out of his mouth. He's surrounded by more than twenty of his old teammates. I don't recognize any of them except maybe the one seated at the head of the table, next to Levi.

His dark blue suit is sharp and crisp, standing out against some of the other men. They look underdressed next to this man. He must be the one who owns this place. I can tell from the way he's leading the conversation. It's almost as if the entire table is hanging on his every word. Except Levi. The leader of the table must have told a punch line to a joke. Everyone erupts into laughter. And once again, it's everyone except Levi.

I continue stomping my way to the back. Levi's focus immediately shifts to me when I step into the lighted area of the dining room. It's as if I've emerged from the shadow dividing them from the rest of the otherwise lit hotel.

A few of Levi's friends sitting beside him notice me. The rest are too deep in their conversation or digging into the food on their plates to bother looking my way. The few that see me only look at me briefly. Until Levi slides his chair back and leaves the table to meet me. He stops me before I have a chance of getting too close.

"What are you doing here?" His eyes are spread wide apart and the muscles in his jaw tick, clearly irritated I've come down here. But I don't give a shit. I'm tired. I'm hot. I'm sticky. And I could really use one of those bright blue coconut flavored cocktails I left back in the room.

I slice my gaze to his, narrowing my eyes. "I can't get into the room. You took both key cards."

"Shit." He sighs, closing his eyes. Not with relief. More like he's internally kicking himself for not leaving one with me when he'd left the room.

"Yeah." I hold out my hand, flicking my fingers open and closed, begging him to hand it over. "So, can I have one of them?"

He stares at my open hand, then flicks his gaze up to mine. I immediately furrow my eyebrows, unsure why his expression has changed. He stares at my hand longer than a reasonable amount of time.

"Not yet," he says, his eyes flickering. They've shifted from annoyance to near excitement.

"What?" I arch my eyebrows, confused. My heart hammers in my chest, not understanding where he's going with this.

Most of the guys that were watching us, still are. A few have given up and turned their attention back to their food. I don't blame them. It looks fucking delicious and more interesting than the conversation Levi and I are having. I watch one of them take a bite of pasta covered in pesto and my mouth waters. My stomach grumbles, but Levi pulls me back before I completely lose myself to hunger.

"I'll give you the room key, but I need you to do something for me first." He's speaking in a low and hushed tone. But somehow his words are falling from his mouth so quickly, my mind is racing to keep up.

"You need me to do something for you first?" I ask him, baffled. "I thought I was already doing that by agreeing to come here."

"I'm not talking about that one." He rolls his eyes, sighing with as much effort as he did when he realized he hadn't left me a key.

"Then what favor are you asking me, exactly?"

"I need you to trust me."

I snort. "Trust you?"

"Yeah, trust. It's something people have in others from time to time."

"Not us," I say.

"Look," he says, stopping me from making a scene, "I know we don't exactly have much of that between us."

"You mean none."

"Sure." He sighs. "I'm asking you to go along with me, okay?"

His piercing blue eyes are begging for me to agree.

"Fine." I groan. My heart hammers and thrashes inside my chest. Every nerve and feeling inside me is multiplied, watching him this close. I've never stood this close to him before. The toes of his boots are touching the ends of mine. He reaches up and grabs onto my hand. The one still held out, waiting for the key card. Only he doesn't drop the card into it. Instead, he places his hand on mine and my lungs nearly collapse.

It may sound dramatic, but it's true. I'm finding it hard to breathe as my entire body heats as his fingers wrap around mine. His fingers that I've imagined touching me for so long curl around my hand, nearly covering it, and before I know it, he drops our joined hands between us. He tugs me toward the table.

I follow him, not understanding what he's doing. I nervously look around. One by one, another one of the guys pops his head up, noticing there's a new guest that's joined them. My stomach lurches. I'm out of place. I'm the only woman at a table full of twenty men and something about the way Levi's hand is holding mine gives me a foreign sense of comfort. Especially when I see the man sitting at the end of the table. The one Levi was sitting next to. His unwavering gaze follows us as he tears off a piece of bread, popping it into his mouth. He smiles as he chews, watching as we approach. Levi stops in front of the seat he was sitting in when I first walked into the restaurant.

"Oh," the man at the end of the table says. He stands up, holding his tie against his stomach as he leans forward to shake my hand. "Nice of you to join us . . ."

"Cassidy," Levi quickly blurts out, placing his hand on the small of my back. "Miles, this is Cassidy. My fiancée."

Miles's eyebrows shoot across his forehead at the same time I snap my head to my left. Levi's face is directly beside mine and he's staring directly at me. His bright blue eyes are impossibly brighter than before. An insatiable electric blue. Even though his expression is firm, I can see the truth hidden behind it. It's a mask. Underneath, he's begging, pleading with me to go along with what he's saying.

He doesn't move. Not a single breath passes his lips. His broad, hardened chest stills as he simply stares at me without a word.

I swallow past the lump in my throat. I don't know whether it's realizing that Levi wants me to pretend to be his fiancée or if it's the realization of how close he's standing to me.

Levi's never stood this close to me. Ever.

"Wait, what?" I whisper between my teeth. I'm hoping Miles doesn't catch the surprise in my voice. My eyelids spread wide open and for a moment I'm certain my eyes are going to pop right out of my head with shock. I clear the ringing in my ears, forcing myself to utter a response. A single word. A string of words put together to create a sentence. Anything to kill the silence in the room.

Every single eye is pinned on me and Levi. I'm struggling to catch my breath. Like a bubble, the oxygen is caught between my stomach and my throat, unsure where to go. It twists and aches until I'm able to look at Miles long enough to come up with a coherent string of words.

Words that I know will inevitably seal the deal on this arrangement Levi has created.

"Yes." I nervously swipe my tongue across my lips and inhale a deep breath, turning back to Miles. "I'm sorry I'm late. I planned on coming down to meet you all earlier but got caught up taking some photos down the beach and didn't realize how far I'd gone."

"No shit, Hawkins," Miles says, leaning over the table. He rests his elbows on the surface, clasping his hands in front of him. "Why didn't you mention this before? Here I was giving you shit earlier."

"Yeah, well," Levi says, not bothering to look in my direction. Probably because he knows I'm angry at him for springing this on me. "I didn't want to overshadow the reunion and all that."

"That's kind of you, Hawkins," Miles says, bringing his attention back to me. "With a fiancée who looks as gorgeous and kind as this one, I bet you wouldn't have kept her a secret for long."

"Of course not." I can feel Levi uttering those words through gritted teeth. "Cass is staying for the whole trip."

A large part of me wishes I'd stayed on the beach. Or fuck, at least taken a chance and asked the receptionist to give me another key. I would have been willing to pay her my entire paycheck to get one, so I wouldn't have to deal with the tangled web I've caught myself in. Or I should say the web Levi has tossed me into.

Miles examines me, his eyes roaming up and down my body. They stop on my camera wrapped around my neck. "You're a photographer?"

"I am." Somehow, I get the sudden inkling this will probably be the only truth I speak for the rest of this reunion.

"Interesting." Miles grins, displaying his perfect teeth.

I have no idea why Levi wants me to lie about us being engaged, but I'm guessing by the expression on Miles's face and the way Levi pulls me closer that this has something to do with him.

Miles has been kind, but it's the sort of kindness you can't help questioning whether it's real.

"Would you like something to drink?" Miles waves to one of the servers standing against the wall.

"Um." I hesitate, knowing a drink will only keep me here longer. "Maybe just a glass of water. I've been out in the sun nearly all day."

Levi's fingers graze against the small of my back, sliding around to my waist. He pulls me tighter against him, the tips of his fingers pressing into my flesh. I'm wishing I hadn't spent all day in the sun, covered in sweat. Of the times I imagined Levi touching me, this definitely was not it. I can only imagine how sticky I might feel or how frizzy my hair is.

"Why don't you join us?" Miles waves to the empty seat beside him. The one Levi was sitting in when I'd shown up.

"O-oh." I look down as if I'm surprised to find a chair there. "I was just about to head up to our room. I'm actually pretty exhausted."

"Yeah." Levi shrugs, hitching his thumb over his shoulder. "Cass and I have had a long drive plus her photographing the beach and all . . ."

I nod my head, agreeing with Levi. The quicker I can get out of here, the better. Mostly so I can figure out why the hell he's wanting me to play as his fiancée.

But hearing him call me Cass instead of Cassidy has turned my insides to mush.

"Bullshit." Miles waves us off. "Hang out for a while. Drinks are on me."

"Um, okay," I mutter. "Is there maybe another chair we can . . ." I look around, considering taking any one of the chairs in the dining room. But Levi sits down in his empty chair and grabs onto my hand, tugging me onto his lap.

Okay, yep. We're doing this. No need to dip our toes in. We're heading straight for the deep end.

Headfirst.

All in.

I slide onto his lap awkwardly, not knowing what to do. His thigh is between both of my legs, and I part them enough to make sure I at least have both feet on the ground. Having Levi's thigh between my legs causes my heart to pound. Deeper and heavier with every breath. It's incredibly distracting. I glance around the table, getting familiar with the faces who haven't stopped looking at me since I walked in here.

"I'm Jimmy." The man across from me reaches his hand out to shake mine. He's softer looking than both Levi and Miles. His sandy blond hair is cut short at the sides and longer on top. His soft brown eyes soften even more as I return his gesture. "It's nice to meet you. I was the kicker for the team, but Levi and I roomed together sophomore year. I don't know if he ever mentioned me or talked about the team."

I nod, unsure of what to say. I hate lying, especially to someone who looks as nice as Jimmy does. But alas, here I am.

"He did." I grin. "It's nice to finally meet some of Levi's old teammates."

Jimmy smiles in return, shifting his eyes between me and Levi.

My breath catches in my throat as Levi's hand moves from beside him to the top of my leg.

His fingers graze over my thigh. He draws invisible circles. All I can focus on at this moment is his fingertips. Is he writing letters against my skin? Is he trying to write me a message? Maybe he's lazily drawing nothing. Either way, it leaves me gasping for air every time his finger completes another circle. Part of me wonders why he's bothering when no one can even see under the table.

I try to reason away what he's doing. Maybe he's committed to making this look as real as possible. Leave no stone unturned. Don't give this Miles guy or anyone else any reason to doubt our "engagement."

Guilt builds inside me, knowing Levi and I aren't anything close to what we're putting on. Little do these men know that deep inside, Levi and I hate one another.

"How long have you two been together?"

Levi's hand stops. We both turn to Miles.

"A year."

"A year."

We both say it at the same time.

I internally sigh with relief. At least we both said the same amount of time. Levi's hand is still paused on my leg, but now he's dug his fingers into my thigh. He only presses them in long enough for me to notice before he relaxes. He's relieved we answered the same time as well.

"Cass is the photographer for the newspaper I work at."

"Oh, so that's how you two met?" Jimmy asks. I hadn't realized he'd been a part of this conversation.

This time I don't answer. I don't know how to. I can't keep lying. Instead, I take a sip of lemon water sitting in front of me and allow Levi to take this one. It's his fault anyway.

"Yep." He lies. "We both started about the same time. Cassidy graduated the same year as us."

After I take a long sip of water, I set it down and place my hand on Levi's knee. I'm hoping I can do the same to him that he's doing to my thigh. Use it for signals.

"That's great," Jimmy says. "How is it working with your fiancée? Does it make it harder since you see each other all the time?"

"No," Levi answers. "We don't see each other as much as you would think. Cassidy works in a separate department from mine in a different area of the office. Besides, we get along so well, it doesn't bother us."

I clench my fingers, grasping onto Levi's knee. His leg twitches, noticing my grip tightening. The tips of my fingers turn white, finding the irony in Levi's answer.

We get along so well.

Fire returns to my chest, remembering the true relationship between us. It's not as if I'd ever forget, but I realize how sidetracked I've become since Levi dropped this bomb on me. I've forgotten how Levi has pushed me away and spoken to me in a way that's reminded me I've only ever been *in* his way since we were both seventeen.

I've only ever been an inconvenience to him. Except tonight. Tonight I'm a convenience.

Only I'm clueless as to the reason he suddenly needs me.

I swallow down the anger and frustration roiling inside me. The rest of the table has already returned to the conversations they were having before I walked in. The only ones who seem to care about Levi and his fiancée (a.k.a. me) are Miles and Jimmy.

It doesn't take long before the conversation shifts away from getting to know our fabled history and onto other topics.

I'm still sitting in Levi's lap and by the time the conversation has shifted again, Levi's hand has stopped and I'm now leaning forward with my elbow resting on the table. I don't know how much time has passed considering my phone is shoved into the back pocket of my jean shorts.

"Who's ready for another round?" Miles lifts his glass in the air, speaking to the whole table.

I straighten my back, my eyes growing heavier every second I'm sitting here. I have my hand gripped onto Levi's knee and the moment I hear his breath shift and feel his chest expanding, ready to answer Miles, I tighten my grip.

There's no fucking way I can sit here through another round. Especially when I feel as if I've been fed to the wolves and forced into this arrangement.

Levi gets my message and rests his hands on my waist, signaling for me to get up from his lap. He clears his throat before standing. "Actually, Cass and I are going to head up to our room."

"Oh, man." Miles frowns. The alcohol he's been drinking has made his eyes turn glassy. "That's too bad."

"Yep." Levi sighs, then nods to Jimmy. "I'll see you tomorrow."

"Sounds good, Levi." Jimmy stands and reaches out to shake my hand again. "It really was nice meeting you, Cassidy."

"You too." I muster enough energy to return his gesture with a smile.

"Listen," Miles says, "I've reserved a stadium in the city for us to play a game if you're feeling up to it. It doesn't have to be anything too serious, but I figured the team can toss the ball around. You know, nothing crazy."

Levi pauses, working his jaw. The muscle under his stubbled skin flexes and twitches. "Sure, I'll be there."

"You're coming too, right Cassidy?" Miles laughs, and he lifts his hand to scratch his chin. "Hawkins won't keep you hidden from us again, will he?"

I glance over at Levi. I want to stare at him with daggers, but instead I hold them back. They're merely butter knives at this point. I turn back to Miles. "Of course, I'll be there."

"Perfect." Miles sits back down in his seat.

Levi quickly waves to the rest of the table before he wastes no time ushering me out of the restaurant. I hold my breath the entire way, and I know by the time we make it to the room, my butter knives will have sharpened into daggers.

EIGHT

LEVI

My boot stops the door before it slams in my face.

Cassidy hasn't uttered a single word since we left the restaurant. But she hasn't needed to. I've already known she would be angry with me since the second I introduced her to Miles.

As my fiancée.

I follow her inside our room, allowing the door to shut behind me.

She storms across the room, making sure every step lands with more effort than the last. I toss the room keys onto the table and stand near the end of the bed, facing the ocean, watching as she crosses to the bar.

She spins around and opens the minifridge in the corner of the counter. Her back is to me as she grabs a cocktail from inside, slamming the door behind her. She opens several drawers and slams them shut before she finds what she's looking for. A bottle opener.

She places the opener to the cap, but before she pops it, she pins her eyes on me.

She's staring at me with daggers. Her usual wide eyes have narrowed to two tiny slits and her cheeks are flamed red.

The bottle cap pops off, rolling along the counter before it finally lands several inches from her.

I slide my hands into my pockets and tilt my head to the side, watching her.

Admittedly, she's even more attractive when she's angry.

Keeping her eyes on me, she lifts the bottle full of bright blue liquid to her lips and takes a giant swig before slamming it back down on the counter.

She leans on it and spreads her arms out, straightening them.

"Are you feeling better now?" I ask her. I know what I'm saying isn't helping, but I'm not going to stop talking to her the way I have in the past simply because she's now my fake fiancée.

"No." Her voice is low and methodical. She lifts the drink again, takes another gulp, and puts it down. "The only thing that's giving me any sort of enjoyment right now is knowing that every single one of these isn't included with the room. You're paying for them." She gives me an evil sneer before taking another sip.

I flex my fingers back and forth, frustrated. She likes to push my buttons. All of them.

"What do you want me to say?" I hold my arms out.

She shakes her head. "I don't want you to say anything right now."

"Okay, fine." I raise my eyebrows and head back over to the bed. I dig through my bag, looking for my plain black T-shirt. The one I didn't plan on using to sleep in but will anyway considering Cassidy and I are sharing our room. I find it and set it down beside my bag. I grab onto the hem of the shirt I'm currently wearing, ready to lift it over my head. Cassidy stops me.

Her arm stiffens as she stretches it out, pointing toward the door. "I want to know what the fuck that was all about. I want to know why all of a sudden I'm now your *fiancée*."

"Right." I nod, ignoring the part where she didn't want my explanation. Now she wants it. I twist my mouth in thought. Truthfully, I knew she would demand an explanation after we left the dinner. But I didn't know exactly how to answer her.

I don't want to tell her about the history between me and Miles. Aside from the fact it would require me to speak the truth out loud, I'm too exhausted.

I'm too exhausted to explain a story to Cassidy where she wouldn't exactly see the truth for what it is. She'd see it from Miles's perspective. Because no matter how I told the story, she'd always see me as the man she knew in high school. Nothing else.

I decide to give her the shortened, cliff note's version instead.

"You're going to think it's ridiculous."

"That's a given. Everything you say is ridiculous." Her expression is angry, and her eyes are sending me daggers.

"Miles and I have a history. We aren't exactly friends." I start to explain, reminding myself to keep my story short and to the point.

"What?" she asks, her anger changing to surprise. "If you and Miles aren't friends, why are we here? Why did he invite you to the reunion?"

I lift one shoulder and shake my head, stuffing my hands into my pockets. "I'm still trying to figure that out."

She takes another sip of her drink. She carried it over with her and she's already near the bottom. "Still doesn't explain how I became your fiancée"

I avoid her sharp stare and walk around her, headed toward the bar myself. I reach for a bottle of water and twist the lid off.

My stomach aches. The drinks I had from earlier are overpowering the small dinner I've managed to keep down.

"Miles and I have a history of competition." I dance around the topic, keeping my story short, hoping to fucking hell Cassidy doesn't read more into it. Or ask for me to explain more. "He was droning on and on about his success since college and how he recently got married. I don't know. The second you walked in, demanding me to hand you one of the keys, the idea came to me. It sounded like a good one at the time."

She scoffs, her near perfect eyebrows arching across her forehead. She closes the distance between us, taking several steps forward, meeting me somewhere between the bed and the bar area. The room is only dimly lit by a few lamps. Her face is covered in shadows and her blonde hair glows as bright as the moon reflecting off the gulf below.

"Well, it's a terrible idea, Levi." She plants her hands on her hips. "How are we supposed to go through this entire reunion pretending to be engaged? We can't even pretend to be friends."

"We'll figure it out."

"No, we won't figure it out," she argues. "You'll just tell them tomorrow that we aren't actually engaged."

"Can't do that." I immediately shake my head.

"Yes, you can," she says. "I don't know. Tell them you were drunk or something and it was a joke."

"Nope." I shake my head. There's no fucking way I'll admit I'm lying about being engaged to Cassidy. "Once I put it out there, I can't take it back. Besides, it's only while we're here."

"We hate each other," she says.

"You're right. We do." I bite the inside of my cheek. I have to admit this lie is pretty big and will take a lot of convincing over the next few days.

She runs her hands through her hair, tucking a few loose

strands behind her ear. She crosses her arms over her chest and takes another step forward. "Maybe I'll head back to Austin. I'll tell Vada you don't need me or something."

"You'd risk your job for that?"

If there's one thing I know about Cassidy, it's that she values her job.

"I wouldn't risk my job." She shrugs. "Vada would understand."

"I don't know," I tell her. "She seemed pretty adamant about you coming along. Besides, you kind of owe me."

Her anger immediately flares back up. She steps closer to me again. She tilts her chin up, staring up at me with those daggers again. Her expression is filled with confusion as she speaks with her pineapple coconut scented mouth. "I owe you?"

"Yeah." I lift my hand and swipe my finger over my bottom lip in thought. "Think of this as a way to pay me back for fixing your car the other night."

"I didn't ask for you to fix my car."

I wince and release a hiss between my teeth, disagreeing with her. "You didn't, but you clearly needed my help."

"I want to make one thing clear, Levi." She stomps toward me, closing the gap between us. There's no more space keeping us separated. I lean back, surprised by her shift in attitude. Fire burns in her eyes. "I've never once asked for your help, nor have I ever needed it. And I will *never* need you. I don't owe you shit. I'm only staying for Vada, who happens to be one of my closest friends. The last person I'm doing this for is *you*." She tilts her head, bringing her face close to mine. The light shining in through the windows casts her face in white shadows. Her eyes flicker in the light, two small white dots in the center. The moon is reflected in them and for a moment, I forget she's angry with me.

Under this moonlight with her chest pressed against mine, she's fucking stunning. Again, I fight the urge my cock has to spring to life. It threatens to turn hard as a rock. I know if I allow it to, if I don't think of anything else right now, it will perk right up and press against her lower stomach.

She's standing with her body pressed against me and her chin tipped up. I imagine what it would be like to bite into her pale pink lip, what her skin would taste like if I were to drag my tongue across it. How it might feel to wrap my arms around her waist, slam her hips into mine. She's obviously been kissed by the sun today. She's golden in some places, bright red in others.

My cock is tingling, threatening to spring up if I don't take care of it soon. It strains against my jeans, begging to be free. But I won't let it.

"Does this mean you're still going to be my fiancée?" I try to play off my question as a joke, but Cassidy doesn't flinch. Her entire body is as stiff as a statue. It's odd seeing her this way. Cassidy has always been the kind of woman who's carried a softness and light with her. It's part of the reason I've pushed her away since the moment I saw her walking through the halls of our high school. I keep the other reason for my distance buried as deep as the truth of what happened between me and Miles.

Those are two truths I've always kept to myself, and I don't plan on changing it.

"You are unbelievable." She closes her eyes and breathes out. She backs away then marches over to the bed. She grabs my backpack and tosses it on one of the many couches scattered throughout the suite. "I know thinking of anyone other than yourself is out of the ordinary for you and a trait you have clearly never possessed. At least, to my knowledge. But it might come as a surprise to you that I actually have a life. Not that you ever cared or will ever care to know anything about it. But I had to put mine on hold so I could come to this stupid fucking reunion of yours only to be dragged into it even deeper." She cuts me an icy glare, piercing the darkness surrounding us. "So for that, *future husband,* you can sleep on the couch. There are plenty to choose from. Take your pick."

NINE

Cassidy

He called me by my nickname.

It's a ridiculous fact to be thinking of this early in the morning.

I'm sitting on the balcony, sipping on the latte I made using the oversized espresso machine in the room. I ordered breakfast and according to the man who'd taken my order, it should have arrived twenty minutes ago.

I told him to add it to my fiancé's tab.

Fiancé.

The word sounds odd coming out of my mouth. Like it doesn't belong there. Probably because Levi isn't my fiancé.

I've been sitting in this metal patio chair since before the sun rose from behind the horizon. Looking over my shoulder, I think about how last night, after Levi had announced me as his fiancée, he called me by the shortened version of my name.

Cass.

A name reserved for only those who I love and love me in return. A name my dad calls me by.

Half of Levi's body is hanging off the velvet couch in the center of the living room. He isn't wearing a T-shirt. The black one he'd been wearing last night is crumpled on the floor beside his hand. It's hanging off the edge and hovering an inch above the carpet. Every now and then one or two of his fingers twitch as if he's in a deep dream.

When I watch his chest rise and fall or the corner of his mouth curl into what looks like a smile, the anger from last night resurfaces.

Aside from the fact that it is wrong on more levels than one, lying being the biggest one, I've realized my anger comes from the simple fact that I now don't know what to expect from this trip.

At no point was I under the assumption this trip would be easy. Not when I'm staying in the same room and spending every single hour with Levi. But this fake engagement brings this trip to a new level. A level of astronomical potential for disaster.

Pretending to be Levi's fiancée requires me to touch him. Him to touch me. His hands to draw lines on my skin like invisible ink. The very thought is enough to squeeze the air out of my lungs. Those thoughts bring back every single feeling I've ever felt for Levi in the time I've known him. What it felt like to watch him through the lens of my camera. What it felt to feel him brush past me as he walked through the tunnel to the locker room at halftime. What it felt like when he'd glare at me, swiping the pad of his thumb across his bottom lip in a sneer.

And how all of those simple things put together made my body go numb and my throat run dry with heat.

It's a realization that hadn't fully sunk in until this morning when I saw the muscles in his arm flex as his long fingers twitched one inch above the carpet.

Don't get me wrong. Levi is fucking gorgeous, and he's always been easy on the eyes. His muscles are more defined than I ever thought they could be. The defined curves and valleys of the muscles of his hips that peek out from the top of his jeans are enough to make me clench my thighs together. More than once.

I look away from Levi again and turn my attention to the beach. I'm wondering when I might be able to go back out there again. I'd love to take more photos.

The breeze gliding over my skin tells me it won't be as hot as it was yesterday. I'm hoping I'll be able to at least sneak away later. It's the only silver lining to this trip.

Doubt in that possibility only grows the longer I realize what this reunion has turned into.

Today is all about Levi and football. Another combination of circumstances taking me back to when we were in high school.

With my empty coffee mug, I head back inside to make another cup. I'm going to need the caffeine if I'm going to make it through today.

This time, the sound of the coffee machine wakes Levi up.

"What're you doing?" He groans. His voice is muffled into the small pillow buried under his head.

He shifts on the couch, stretching and rubbing his eyes with the heels of his hands. His hardened abs flex as he lifts himself up, the long thick muscles on his back stretching with him. He stays sitting with his back to the arm rest and tilts his head to the side, watching me while resting it on the back.

"I'm making coffee," I mutter.

"Why is it so loud?" he asks, still groaning.

My back is turned to him. I glance over my shoulder long enough to catch the way his hair is tousled and stubble peppers his jaw. It's thicker than it was yesterday.

"It's an espresso machine." I turn back to my coffee. He really needs to put on more clothes.

"It sounds like I'm sitting in the middle of a coffee shop."

I don't respond. I grab some cream from the refrigerator and pour it in. I spin back around, lifting the cup to my mouth, and nearly spill it all over my chest. Levi is standing beside me.

"I got a text from Miles. We need to be at the field in an hour."

I resist the urge to roll my eyes. I'd probably have to be at the field even if I wasn't pretending to be Levi's fiancée. But still. All the thoughts I've had about him this morning lodges itself into my chest. My face flushes, heat blooming under my skin. I duck around him, carrying my mug with me as a proverbial shield.

Psh, as if coffee could somehow hide the thoughts clearly running through my mind.

I sit in the chair opposite of the couch Levi slept on last night and crisscross my legs underneath me. I adjust the top of my tank top, ensuring it isn't dipping too low.

"How did you sleep last night?" I hide my smile behind my mug. My shield.

"Like shit." Levi's head bobs up and down as he moves around the bar, searching for a mug. He finally finds one and sticks it in front of the coffee maker. "I'm sure that couch wasn't worth what it cost. I might as well have slept on the floor." He bends his legs, trying to figure out how to work the machine. He fiddles with buttons and knobs, sighing each time it doesn't work.

I unravel my legs and set my mug on the coffee table. I meet Levi at the bar, grab a pod of coffee and stand beside him, holding it between my fingers. "Here," I tell him, "I'll do it."

"I can figure it out. Just tell me where the coffee goes." He sticks his hand out, waving it across the machine.

"It goes in here." I point to the metal cup at the top, twisting it off. I drop the pod in, then close it.

"How did you figure this thing out this morning? It looks like it belongs on a spaceship."

I stifle a laugh. "I worked at the coffee shop down at the square back in our hometown for a few months one summer. They had a machine similar to this one."

Three lines crease each one of his cheeks as he gives a small smile.

"What?" I ask him.

"Nothing." He shakes his head, frowning. "It's hard to picture you putting your camera down long enough to make and serve cups of coffee."

"I'm capable of other things, Levi." I plant my hand on my hip. I move to the side, allowing him to stand in front of the machine. I consider telling him the reason I'd gotten a job at the coffee shop that year. I decide against it.

"I know that," he argues.

I cross my arms over my chest. "Tell me something." I chew on my bottom lip, wondering if I'm opening a can of worms I even want to open.

"What?" he mutters. His dark eyebrows are furrowed in concentration as he hovers a finger over each button, deciding which one to push.

"Have you told Miles you're wanting to write a story about his hotel?"

"No." He sighs, still not looking at me.

"Don't you think you should tell him? I mean, it's going to be in one of the state's biggest newspapers."

He stops, dropping his hand. He squeezes his eyes shut and, with a heavy sigh, rolls his head to look at me. "Two things, Cassidy. Not that I necessarily need to tell Miles I'm writing this story, I haven't decided whether I want to tell him. I figured I'd cross that bridge when I got to it. And second, we're not talking about this before I've had at least one cup of coffee.

Okay?" He bends his knees once again, studying the machine. "Is there already water in here or do I need to put more in?"

"Levi. Move." I lean to my left, brushing his side with my arm. I pop my hip out, nudging him. He moves, but I immediately feel his eyes on me. He's watching me as I slide my hand to the side of the machine, lifting the lid. I clear my throat, the fire returning to my cheeks. "There's water already in here."

"Right," he says, nodding as if he knew all along.

"And my answer is yes, by the way."

"What?" He turns to me, that same look of confusion plastered on his face as before.

"I understand. No talking before coffee." I press the start button, then head back over to the coffee table, picking up my cup. I don't turn around, heading directly for the bathroom. I take my coffee with me. "I'm going to take a shower, so we aren't late for this game."

By the time I turn on the water, I swear I hear him say this wasn't a game.

💔

"What's the game plan?"

"I told you," Levi says, shutting the engine off to his truck. "This isn't a game."

"No," I say, grabbing my camera bag from between my feet on the floorboard. "I meant for us. What are we doing?"

"Oh yeah," he says, resting his elbow on the top of his door.

He stares out of his window, watching some of the other guys pulling into the driveway and stepping out of their cars. They don't waste any time walking down to the field. Unlike us.

He shrugs, then grabs onto the handle. He gives me one last look before opening his door. "I don't know. Act like you actually like me."

He pops open the door and hops out of his truck, slamming it behind him.

I tuck my bottom lip between my teeth and bite down. Nerves bundle inside my stomach. I'm queasy and force myself to take a deep breath. It's not that it'll be difficult for me to pretend to like Levi. The difficult part is knowing the moment I step out of this truck, everything Levi does will be a lie. Every touch. Every word. All of it is fake, protecting a lie we can't go back from.

I'm still taking a breath when Levi opens my door. He holds his hand out for me and it takes a moment for me to grab onto it. His truck is lifted and there's no running board for me to use as a step. I'm about to slide out myself when his hands land on my hips. He lifts me up and pulls me out of the truck.

I'm holding my breath. It twists and tightens. I'm seeing Levi in an entirely different light. He's being nice and kind. When he would normally have left me in the truck only to be forced to catch up to him, he waited for me. He held his hand out.

I tell myself this is the fake Levi. The one putting on a show for everyone else. I might as well do the same.

"This will take some getting used to."

"Tell me about it," he mutters, sliding his hand into mine. He weaves our fingers together and closes my door behind me.

I finally inhale a deep, resolving breath. Levi's crisp, clean scent surrounds me. He's dressed in a plain shirt and shorts. It's been a long time since I've seen him dressed this relaxed.

When I catch the person walking through the parking lot, I understand why Levi pulled me out of the truck.

Miles crosses the lot. His hand is gripping a football.

His gaze shifts to us for a few seconds. Miles and I both wave. He lifts his hand, and a grin breaks out across his face. He's clearly as competitive as Levi.

I'm unsure how long Miles is watching us when Levi pulls my attention back to him.

"Oh yeah," he says, "I want to do this before I forget." He reaches behind me, pulling my phone out of the back of my shorts. His face is close to mine.

"What are you doing?" I ask. My breath passes my lips with heat and weight. It's unfamiliar, but I find it exhilarating all the same.

He swipes the screen, ignoring my question. "You should really put a passcode on this or the fingerprint lock." He types a phone number in, presses the green button, lets it ring once before tapping on the red button. Satisfied, he clicks on the number and adds it to my contact list.

World's Best Fiancé.

"Don't you think that's overdoing it?" I ask him.

"No." He grins, reaching forward and returning my phone to my back pocket. His mouth is less than an inch away from mine. "Don't all women put their partner's numbers in their phone like that?"

"How would I know?" I laugh. "Some might. Some might not."

"Okay, I amend my question then." He adds my name to his contact list.

Cass.

I think my heart stops for a beat or two. Or three.

"Have *you* ever added your partner's number into your contacts that way?" he asks.

I pause, looking past his shoulder. Miles is gone, but Levi's face is still near mine. Hearing Levi ask if I've ever put my partner's number in my phone makes me want to snort. My love life has never been deep enough or active enough to get to a point such as adding them to my contacts list. Levi and I have completely skipped about ten stages of dating, and we've only been fake engaged for one day. "I have now."

"What made you think this is what engaged couples do?"

Levi shrugs nonchalantly. "My parents did that for each other before my dad died."

"Your dad died?" I ask him, swallowing. I never thought to ask him about his personal life. I remember seeing him after our graduation day ceremony.

It was just his mom and his brothers.

"Yeah." He clears his throat. "He died of a stroke the summer before our senior year of high school. That's why we ended up moving."

"I'm sorry to hear that. I didn't know." I swallow, a heavy wave of sadness coming over me. I couldn't imagine a life without my father.

"Thanks," he mutters. "Well, it was a long time ago so . . ."

I can tell he wants this conversation to be over.

I think back to last night and how I was so angry with Levi for dragging me into this lie with him. I'm frustrated, knowing I'm only a pawn in this game of his. Yet, somehow being here with him, seeing him show a new side of himself to me, has made it more bearable than I thought it would.

I grab my camera bag before Levi scoops up my hand, wrapping his fingers between mine. I follow his lead as he takes us toward the same entrance the rest of the guys were going into when we pulled in.

I inhale a deep breath, reminding myself of the main reason I'm here. To take pictures of the reunion. Already having taken pictures of the main areas of the hotel and the surrounding beach, I tell myself this is the first opportunity to snap images of all the guys together. Doing what they all have in common.

We walk inside the stadium and down to the field. A large group of the guys are already huddled on the fifty-yard line. A large gray wolf is painted in the center, the home team's name wrapped around it.

We've almost reached the group when Levi pulls us to a stop. A few of the men in the huddled group pop their heads up. They wave to both of us, then wave Levi over.

Levi spins around. He releases my hand, but wraps his hand around my waist. His eyes search the area around us. I'm assuming to ensure others are watching.

"Some of the guys are watching," I mutter, trying not to move my mouth too much for them to read my lips.

Jimmy calls out a quick greeting as he passes us on his way to join the rest of the guys waiting.

"Hey, Jimmy. I'll be over there in a minute," Levi says.

We both smile, then Levi's eyes are on mine. The sun beams across his tan face, the brown strands of his hair already sticking to his forehead. It seems he's already let the heaviness of our conversation in the parking lot dissolve.

His eyes dance between mine and my mouth. It's as if they can't decide where to stop. Before I know what's happening, his hand slides down my lower back to my ass cheek. He presses into my flesh, tugging me toward him. My hips slam into his as he lowers his face to meet mine.

And then his lips are on mine. They're warm and soft as he presses them against me even more. He presses into my flesh even harder, pulling me impossibly closer. My camera bag is strapped around my shoulder, and I keep my hand wrapped around the strap. I clench my fingers, using it to remind myself I haven't stepped into a dream or some alternate reality.

Levi keeps me pressed against him longer than I expect him to. A tingling sensation courses through my body and heat travels to my center the more his hand massages my ass cheek, but he doesn't open his mouth. He doesn't part his lips to his tongue against mine. He doesn't take it a step further.

He simply kisses me on my mouth. Then, as suddenly as he was there, he's gone.

My entire body feels as if it's on fire when Levi steps backward and away from me. His cheeks are flushed red as well, but it might be from the sun that's been beating on his skin all morning.

My fake fiancé gave me the best fake kiss I could ever dream of.

"Just, um," he says, pointing to the sideline, "remember it like high school."

"What?" I clear my throat, unsure what's going on. My mind is clouded with fog and the memory of Levi's mouth on mine. "Remember what like high school?"

"You can take your pictures from the sideline. Just try to stay out of the way."

He spins around, leaving me standing where we kissed. I stare at his back the whole way over to the middle of the field. Once he joins everyone, I make my way to the sideline.

My entire body is conflicted. One half feels like it's floating away into the galaxy, the other half is deflated, wanting to disappear right onto the fake grass beneath my feet. My thighs are on fire, and I'm wet between them. I know my panties are soaked already. All from a simple kiss.

But the other half of me feels heavy as my chest squeezes, aches with the words from Levi.

This fake engagement is already a complete mess. And all he's done is kiss me.

Scratch that. It's been messy ever since Vada convinced me to come.

I inhale a deep breath, reminding myself I have a job to do. I set my bag down on the white painted line along the side of the field. I'm the only one standing out here. I pull my camera out and adjust the lens, peering through it before pulling it away from my face again.

I snap pictures of the field itself before moving onto the guys. When I feel I've taken enough, I move on. They're still standing around, in a circle. It's clear they're discussing the rules of the type of game they're going to play.

Levi and Miles are standing in the middle of the circle as everyone surrounding them hangs on to every word they say.

Miles points to some of the guys. I snap a picture.

Levi points to Jimmy. I snap a picture.

Miles points to Jimmy again. Then the goal post. I snap another picture.

Levi's staring directly at me, still surrounded by everyone else. I snap a picture.

Click, click, click.

I lower my camera when I realize the picture I've taken. The moment I've just captured. It's true what Levi said after he'd kissed me.

This felt like high school all over again.

As if the memory of his kiss has already been seared into my brain, my mouth tingles. My legs are humming, wishing Levi had done more than place his mouth on mine.

It's terrible to know the true nature of our relationship, yet somehow, I'd enjoyed Levi's kiss.

It's as if that one kiss has told my body it wants more. I feel a pull toward him, my body betraying what I know to be the truth.

Levi only kissed me because he knew it's what couples do in

those types of situations. Remembering high school brought me back to all the times I'd seen him with different girls. Ninety percent of the time, they were cheerleaders or on the school dance squad. Levi was familiar with public displays of affection.

As for me, it's been over a year since I've been with a man. Even one as close as Levi just proved himself to be. My life hasn't left much room for even a single date. When your sister leaves her newborn baby with you at the age of fifteen and your father's health is slowly declining, your love life is as desolate and dry as the Sahara Desert.

All the men line up. They crouch down slightly, bending their knees low enough it looks like they're on the brink of bursting out into a sprint. Directly into each other.

Seven of the men stand on one side, seven on the other.

A few of the men are scattered on the sideline, including Jimmy. He's bending down in the same position as the men on the field. His hands on his knees, eyes narrowed with concentration.

I snap a picture of him with the others. Keeping my camera to my face, I focus back on the guys lined up on the field. They shout to each other. Some laugh. Some keep their faces set as hard as stone.

I move my camera back and forth, searching for Levi. I'm expecting to find him standing behind the center, where the quarterback usually is. But he isn't. Miles is.

Instead, I find him at the end of the line where the tight end stands.

Strange since I've never known Levi to play any position other than quarterback. As far as I know.

The first play moves quickly. The center tosses the ball back to Miles and, although Levi is wide open as he runs down the field, Miles throws the ball to another guy. Paul, I think, is his name.

I snap a couple pictures before I get sucked into watching the guys play. Until I snagged the job of becoming the yearbook photographer, I was never into sports. I didn't even understand what any of the plays meant or what the names of the positions were. But having spent months on end with the football team, I'd learned the basics enough to understand what was going on.

After Miles's team scores a touchdown and Jimmy runs out on the field long enough to score a field goal, the men switch. They rotate through several plays before taking a break.

Levi jogs over to me and grabs his bottle of water from the backpack he brought with him.

"I thought you would play quarterback," I say. He's standing beside me, tipping his bottle back. Sweat drips along his jawline, down the sides of his neck. His Adam's apple bobs and the veins in his neck swell as he catches his breath. When he's done drinking, he swipes the back of his hand along his mouth.

I can't explain it, but when his eyes meet mine, they're a shade darker than usual. They're heavy and clouded, piercing me even more. But this is a weighted stare. A stare that, for once, isn't directed toward me.

"It's been a while since I've played." He shrugs, keeping his answer short.

"How long?" I ask him, lowering my voice. I don't need the other guys to overhear and wonder why I wouldn't know this. You know, since I'm supposed to be his fiancée and all.

Levi sighs, raking his fingers through his damp hair. He shoves it back and off his forehead. "Not since junior year of college. I stopped the summer before senior year."

"Oh." I raise my eyebrows, surprised. "I didn't know it's been that long."

"Yeah, well . . ." He keeps his attention on the field before stopping it on Miles. He stares at him for a few seconds, then turns to me. "Quarterback has always been my favorite. But sometimes I like mixing it up. Keeps me on my toes. It's nice to play with these guys again."

I stare up at Levi, wincing against the midday sun. He closes the gap between us. "Did you get enough pictures?"

His eyes search my face and for the first time, his question seems genuine. There's no play behind his stare, no teasing. He's genuinely asking.

It's a foreign sensation. His words bounce around in my chest. I can't distinguish between them and my own beating heart.

"I did," I say, picking up my camera. I show him some of the images I've grabbed using the small screen on the back side of my camera.

He nods his head, not speaking a word.

"You ready to head back out there?" Miles joins us and stands beside me and Levi, peeking his head between us. He eyes my camera. "You have some talent there, future Mrs. Hawkins."

I turn to look up at him. "Thanks."

"No problem." He pats me on the back, turning his attention back to Levi. "You want a round of taking quarterback? For old times' sake?"

Levi doesn't immediately answer. Instead, his eyes fall to his hand resting on my back. Miles lets his hand fall away.

Levi shifts his gaze back, this time the muscles of his neck twitch. Another drop of sweat slides across his skin. "Sure."

"Great." Miles pats me again and then signals to a few of the men standing down the line. "Let's head back out there."

I let my camera fall back against my stomach. Levi wraps his hand around my waist as he did when we'd first gotten here. His hand lands on the small of my back.

As if my mind is remembering our kiss from before, my

mouth tingles and heat blooms in my legs. My stomach dips, knowing what's coming.

Levi's kiss for show.

This time it's short and quick. Straight to the point.

He presses his lips to mine quickly before he runs off.

And then as he makes his way over to the center of the field, my heart slows, settling into disappointment.

Disappointment that now that I'd had a taste of what it would be to be with Levi, I'd wanted more.

Dammit, I'm in trouble.

TEN

LEVI

It's the first time I've played football in two years and it's the last thing I want to do at the moment.

Long lashes, blonde hair, green eyes.

Smooth, soft lips. My mouth on hers. My fingers pressing deeper into her flesh. My hand molding to her body so effortlessly.

It's the only thing I've been able to think about since I stepped onto the field.

Fake fiancée. That's all she is.

I repeat the words over and over in my mind.

Although we'd only been playing as an engaged couple for twenty-four hours, being with Cassidy this way was easier than I expected it to be.

Normally, I find myself pushing her away as far as humanly possible. For reasons I've never spoken out loud.

But being with her in this way has fucked up my head. It's as if I can't tell what's up and what's down anymore.

"What the fuck, Hawkins?" I look up from the field. Miles is staring up at me. He's crouched down in front of Paul, who's playing as center, waiting with ball in hand. "Are you going to play or not?"

I tilt my head, confused as to why he's now playing defense. Sure, plenty of us play multiple positions. But never like this.

I don't think I've ever seen Miles play defense.

"Yeah," I tell him. "I'm ready." I reach down, waiting for Paul to pass me the ball. I call out the usual signals. He's spot on.

After a few plays, the sun is eclipsed by a large group of clouds. Now, I can get a better view of Miles.

We set up for another play, but I stop when Miles speaks again. "I have to say, Hawkins, I'm liking that fiancée of yours."

Fire hits my chest the moment the words fall from his mouth. He's barely crouched, not even in full position. A few of the other guys laugh under their breath, assuming what Miles is saying isn't serious. But I know better. I know the shit he's capable of.

"Let's make the play," I mutter.

"We are." He smirks. "Just having a bit of fun."

A drop of sweat slides down the side of his face.

I press my lips together, releasing a hot breath. Then it's as if something inside me has triggered. A spark, a fuse has been lit and the anger of the shit Miles pulled back in college resurfaces.

"Ready . . ." I yell. "Set . . ."

The ball snaps, I catch it. I'm looking for an opening to throw the ball. But then suddenly, a heavy weight slams into me. I fall onto my back and my head slams into the green turf. I wince, a pain shooting down my spine to my toes. When I open my eyes, I'm staring at a clear blue sky.

I groan and turn my head to the side, catching my breath. Cassidy is walking toward me, concern in her expression. I turn back to the clear blue sky. Miles is standing over me, holding his hand out.

I don't grab it. I ignore it and stand up as he pats me on the shoulder. "Didn't mean to hit you so hard, man. Bad habit, I guess." He glances over his shoulder to Cassidy who's walking over to us. He grins, amusement in his expression. "You're a lucky man. She's talented, that one. Well, taking photos at least."

"What the fuck is that supposed to mean?" I seethe, anger ripping out of me. "And what the fuck was that all about?" I point to the line on the field where he'd tackled me.

I know deep down Miles is talking shit. I still don't understand what he meant by his comment about Cassidy.

He laughs. "Did you forget how the game is played, Hawkins?"

"We aren't playing like we're in a league." I grind my teeth. "It's one thing to tackle, it's another to slam someone to the ground. I can tell the difference."

"You must have misunderstood me." He holds his arms out. "I didn't mean any harm. It was all in good fun."

"Holy shit, Levi." Cassidy is walking toward me, coming from behind Miles. He turns, watching her walk up to me.

She presses her thumb to my temple. "What happened to your eye?"

Confused, I lift my hand, touching where her thumb is placed against me.

"Ouch." I hiss. When I pull my hand away, there's blood on my fingers.

"It's nothing," I say to Cassidy. I avoid looking at Miles, knowing he's probably enjoying this. Humiliating me.

"It's not nothing," Cassidy says. "You're bleeding."

"I'm sorry, Levi," Paul says, his eyebrows dipping in apology. "You went down right on my foot. I think you caught the metal on the end of my shoelace."

"Really." I hold my hand up to him. "It's fine. I didn't even realize I'd gotten cut."

Paul gives me a reassuring smile.

"Listen," Miles says, clapping his hands together. "I have practice with my team later today and then a business meeting for the hotel after that. Why don't we all meet back up tomorrow night? I'm planning a little bonfire out on the beach. Dinner, music, drinks. That sort of thing." He swipes his hand across his forehead, soaking up the sweat. He plants his hands on his hips and catches his breath, like the rest of the team seems to be doing.

Cassidy lowers her hand as she steps back, standing beside me.

All the other men standing around us look between me and Miles. I can tell they're unsure of what's going on between us. Most are silent, but a few agree with Miles, heading back toward the sideline to grab their things.

Zane is the only one on our team who knows the truth of what happened between me and Miles that summer. The rest have no clue. They only know I was forced to step down and allow Miles to take over my position.

"We'll be there," Cassidy agrees, not caring whether I do or not.

I hold back my frustration.

"Perfect." Miles grins at Cassidy.

She nods, then wraps her fingers around my wrist, pulling me in the direction of the stadium exit. "We should get this cleaned up."

"I'm okay, Cass," I say, touching the bloody spot again. "It's not that big of a deal."

I wave to the rest of the guys, not bothering to say goodbye to Miles. That fucker doesn't deserve one.

"You don't need to take care of me," I add.

Her eyes soften and her steps slow. I slow my own to match hers. Don't want anyone to wonder why we're walking back to my truck separately.

"That's not what I was doing. Sorry, I guess it's a habit of mine." Sadness fills her pale green eyes.

My chest squeezes realizing what I said seems to have struck a chord I didn't know was there. Usually, when I'm short with her, she sends it right back at me, returning the pitch.

But this is different. It feels different.

I've never asked Cassidy about her personal life. In school, I never went out of my way to find out too much about her life. All I knew were the rumors that were talked about among our class. Mostly about her sister and how she'd ran away from home, leaving Cassidy behind, without a word.

My curiosity is piqued as we pass through the exit and enter the parking lot. I inspect my dirt and sweat covered hands.

"Habit of what? Taking care of people?"

"Maybe." She bites down on her bottom lip and shakes her head. "It's what I've done my whole life. I know you and I are different."

"It really isn't that bad," I say again, telling the truth.

Her fingers are warm, pressed against the base of my wrist. The sensation moves up my arm and to my neck, spreading across my chest. It's a small familiar feeling, one I've tried to ignore whenever I'm around Cassidy. Her touch seems to awaken a piece of me I don't recognize. A piece I didn't know existed. And it's a piece that's only been awakened since last night when I pulled her into my lap.

"I would ask if you've always been this stubborn"—she blinks those long lashes of hers, brushing off our conversation—"but I already know the answer."

"I *have* always been that way." I smirk. "Or at least that's what my mom always told me."

"Your mom sounds like an intuitive woman, then."

"She is."

I follow Cassidy out to the truck, knowing when we get back to the room, I'll need a large pain pill and a stiff drink.

Only I'm not sure if it's in the hopes it'll help me forget about the bullshit Miles pulled today. Or Cassidy.

When we're inside my truck, driving back to the hotel, I glance in the rearview mirror. Blood is dripping down the side of my face. I wanted to wipe it off before we headed for the hotel, but my chest twisted at the thought of giving Cassidy another reason to touch me.

The truth is, there's a perfectly good towel folded under her seat. I use it on the days I go to the gym and don't want to ride the whole way home dripping with sweat.

I don't want to give Cassidy another reason to touch me. Not when we aren't in front of the others.

Okay, scratch that. I *do* want Cassidy to touch me. I just don't want it stirring whatever the fuck those feelings were inside me. Every single touch makes me want to take it further.

I'm still confused.

Once again, I can't tell the difference between what's up and what's down.

We drive the rest of the way back to the hotel in silence. Cassidy scrolls through the photos she took on the football field.

At one point, she even yawns. Her eyelids droop and grow heavy. Her chest swells, her breasts lifting as her mouth spreads wide open. The silhouette of her peaked nipples is visible through her tank top.

Suddenly, I'm imagining my fingers pinched around them and my mouth pressed between her legs, my tongue sliding across her clit.

The familiar fire settles in my lower stomach. The same one from when I pulled her into my lap last night at dinner. My body hums with the memory of her soft, round and full cheeks pressed against me. My cock wants to spring to life and break free from the confines of my shorts.

I keep my focus back on the road and turn my body as much as I can until we pull into the parking spot. Thankfully, my erection has subsided, and I can step out of the truck without Cassidy noticing.

She follows me to the room and once we're inside, she's already heading toward the bed.

She looks over her shoulder, dropping her camera bag on the table in the living area. Her arms lazily sway back and forth. "Unless you have anything else you wanted to do, I'm going to take a nap."

"No." I clear my throat, grabbing a bottle of water. "I'm going to shower, then probably head down to the front desk to see if they have some headache medicine."

"You said it wasn't that bad." She yawns again, walking over to the bed. "Now you need medicine?" She drops herself onto the bed. She climbs up onto the edge then lies on her stomach, bending her arms under her head, using them as a pillow. The bottom curves of her cheeks are peeking out of her shorts.

"It's not bad," I tell her. "But any time I take a hit like that I take some kind of headache medicine. It's something you learn early on to prevent the pain from hitting you later."

"Okay," she mumbles against the mattress. Her eyes are already closed. "Wake me up when you're back."

I don't answer her. Her breathing has already slowed, and her lips separate, allowing a bit of her breaths to pass through them. She's already asleep.

I head straight to the bathroom to start the shower. While the water heats, I look in the mirror. Two streaks of dried blood reach the top of my cheekbone. I shove my hair aside, looking at the cut that's caused this large amount of blood to spill. It's a decent sized cut but nothing to worry about. I've had worse.

When I step into the shower, I'm thankful to have the hot water washing over my aching back. It's been a while since I've played football to the caliber that I played today. All without pads.

I wash the blood from my temple first. Then, I stand in the middle of the shower, taking a moment to remember the true reason I'm here. To get a story. I haven't even told Miles about me wanting to write a story about his hotel, but I'm figuring I can save that for the end of the trip. If we even make it that long.

But thinking about work makes me think about Cass. I think about her and the kiss we shared outside my truck. I think about her hand wrapped around mine.

My thoughts start to spill, one into the next. They're like a stack of dominoes. The memory of her mouth on mine leads to her hand. Her hand in mine leads to her hand on my head. And then all the times in between when I've felt her skin touch mine.

Fuck.

My hand is already wrapped tightly around my cock, stroking it. I slide my hand to the tip, adding pressure before moving it back to the base. I lean forward and press my free hand against the tiled wall. Water splashes from my mouth as I release a heavy breath. I tighten my grip and the muscles on my forearm swell.

Long lashes.

Blonde hair.

Green eyes.

My cock pulsates under my hand when I reach my orgasm. I press my hand into the wall, moving my hips back and forth. My cum spills out onto the shower floor, quickly swirling down the drain with the water.

My legs and arms are vibrating as I tilt my head back and look up at the ceiling. I take a moment to catch my breath, knowing I'll have to see Cassidy when I step out into the room.

When I look back down and see my still swollen cock relaxing, I realize Cassidy is more trouble than I thought. In fact, she's always been trouble. And I've only made it worse.

ELEVEN

Cassidy

Me: Have you ever wondered who came up with words for certain things?

World's Best Fiancé: What do you mean?

Me: You know, like the word banana. Who thought to name a banana, banana? Or a spoon, spoon. Such a weird word for something you put in your mouth.

World's Best Fiancé: How late do you stay up thinking about these types of things?

Me: I don't. I mean, I've thought about it before, when I'm lying in bed and can't sleep. But it doesn't keep me up at night. I'm just bored over here and started thinking about it. Paul keeps talking about this car he bought in Canada and plans on fixing up to resell it.

World's Best Fiancé: Yeah, he told me he started a car flipping business.

Me: It's such stimulating conversation. Truly.

Me: What do you think about when you can't sleep?

. . .

. . .

Three dots float across my text exchange with Levi, waiting

for his response. I'm standing with Paul on the edge of the water, where the tide rolls in and meets the sand. The water rolls out and then back in, covering the tops of my feet. I hold up the bottom of my long dress to keep it from getting wet, listening to Paul go on and on about flipping a rusty old truck from the fifties.

If he hadn't been so sweet when he started a conversation with me fifteen minutes ago, I would have walked away already. All I wanted to do was dip my toes in the warm water. Now I'm stuck and completely regretting my decision.

I look down at my phone as the three dots are finally replaced with Levi's response.

World's Best Fiancé: You should come over here and act like my fiancée.

I smile at Paul, nodding in acknowledgment to part of his story before quickly typing out a response to Levi.

Me: Exactly how does a fiancée act? I thought I was playing my part by mingling and chatting with your old teammates.

I look up from my phone and give Paul another smile. He's changed the subject, now talking about how he loves living in New York. I focus my attention over his shoulder, searching for Levi.

The air in my lungs comes to an abrupt halt in my throat when I find him sitting in one of the wooden beach chairs opposite the fire. The flames of the fire crack and pop, sending sparks flying into the cooler night air. Behind it, Levi is staring directly at me. His face is painted in a subtle orange color mixed with the shadow. His piercing blue gaze shoots me straight in the chest.

He isn't smiling. He isn't even waving me over. His phone is resting in his hand as he stares at me. His eyes are pinning me in place, squeezing all the air out of my lungs.

It's the fourth night in a row where Miles has arranged a bonfire on the beach. None of the team was complaining, considering dinner and drinks were free, along with a different live band every night. I didn't understand why Miles was throwing these get togethers every night or why it's even a ten-day reunion. I'm not entirely sure Levi does either.

For the past three days since the day of the football game at the stadium, Levi has kept his distance from me. When we're with the other guys, he's in full fiancé mode. He keeps me close, clasping my hand around his and placing his lips on mine. But that's the farthest he's ever taken it. He's careful to never go too far up my leg or too low down my neck.

Half the time we end the night when I feel I'm on the brink of internally combusting. I go to bed alone with my body still humming from his touch. The sight of him half naked, stretched out on the crushed velvet couch is the last thing I see before my eyes shut.

Levi's been teasing me by treating me as his fiancée. It's torture.

He keeps his intense stare on me from behind the fire. He raises his phone and only looks down long enough to type out a response. His eyes snap back up to mine.

My phone chimes in my hand. I break our trance to read the text.

World's Best Fiancé: Come over here and I'll show you.

If I wasn't already deprived of all the oxygen in my lungs, I would be now.

I turn to Paul, listening to him, and walking toward the bonfire and where Levi is sitting. Paul follows me. The sand slides along my feet, sticking to them the more I walk farther up the beach. The fire is circled by the same kind of chair Levi is sitting in, but only half of them are filled. The bonfire has been going for several hours, easily pulling us past midnight. Not everyone who originally showed up is still here. Half have gone to bed and some have left, heading out in different directions. Each bonfire hasn't been exclusive to the football team either. The guests Miles invited for this week have spent about as much time out here as the rest of the team.

Behind the bonfire, closer to the boardwalk is the edge of the hotel and resort. Between the palm trees lining the property, lights from the cabana and pool are shining bright. The band Miles hired to play tonight is on stage, the song echoing down to us.

The mixture of the muffled music and the fire flickering in front of Levi causes my stomach to flutter.

"It was nice talking to you, Paul." I turn to Paul as we continue walking, gently placing my hand on his arm with a grin.

"You too, Cassidy. We'll catch up later." He heads up the stairs leading back up to the cabana.

I move to stand in front of Levi. He relaxes back into his seat, looking up at me. The corner of his mouth curls. It's the first expression he's given me all night.

"About time you came up here and sat with me," he says with an even tone. It's a contradiction to the playfulness written all over his ridiculous gorgeous face.

I playfully kick some sand at his feet. "You could have come with me. I was dipping my toes in the water. You should try it some time."

His mouth turns into a frown as he shakes his head. "I've never been a fan of the ocean. I'm more of a pool guy myself."

"Oh." I nod slowly, smiling. I can't help it. I know Levi hasn't changed his feelings about me. Deep down, I know he still detests me. His feelings simply haven't changed overnight because I'm pretending to be his fiancée.

The past few days have become a bit routine. Keep me close when other eyes are on us. Push me away when they aren't.

"Come sit with me." He sits up enough to hold his hand out.

There are empty chairs on either side of him, but I take his hand anyway.

I sit on his lap and turn to the side, keeping my legs together and hanging over the side of his. He wraps an arm around my lower back, the other he rests in my lap.

Disappointment eats away at me for deciding to wear a long summer dress today. The fabric nearly touches the tops of my toes. Although, I'm thankful there's a slit that runs up to the top of my knee. Levi finds it, inching his finger underneath the fabric to find my bare skin. I break out in goose bumps and swallow.

"No camera today," he says, his eyes falling to my chest. My beach dress is a wrap style dress, tying around my waist, just under my breasts. Levi's eyes roam over me before he brings them back up to mine.

"No, I haven't brought it since the first bonfire."

"That's surprising."

"There are only so many pictures I can get of a bonfire slash pool party. Trust me, you and Vada will have plenty of photos to choose from for your story."

"Mmm." He hums, pressing his mouth into a tight line.

He slides back into his seat until his back hits the wooden slats of the chair. I arch my eyebrow. "I thought you brought me over here to show me something."

"I did." He lets out a half laugh, his chest vibrating. He moves the hand resting on my lower back to my hip. He presses his fingers into me, directing me where to go. He turns me, pivoting me while I'm sitting in his lap. Keeping my legs together, I swing them to my right, stopping them over Levi's legs. He relaxes his knees, allowing for my legs to sit between them. It reminds me of the first night we were here at the hotel. When he'd pulled me into this charade of his.

"What was it you wanted to show me? How a fiancée is supposed to act?" No one can hear me ask him this question over the myriad of sounds surrounding us. Music, small talk, and a crackling fire.

"I don't think a fiancé would enjoy watching another man flirt with the other all night. Especially when the other is forced to watch."

"I—" I open my mouth, not understanding whether he means hypothetically or if he's talking about me and Paul. Logic tells me he isn't talking about me and Paul. He's never cared about me enough for it to bother him whether I was talking to someone else.

"Do you?" he growls. His voice is impossibly deeper than usual.

"No." I turn my head slightly, hoping he can hear me under my hushed words. "But we're pretending, so it doesn't count."

"You might be right."

"I am?" I ask.

I gasp as I slide backward, farther onto Levi's lap. My dress slides up my thighs, exposing more of myself. The slit that usually only goes up to my knee is now cut up to the top of my thigh.

My back slams against his chest and my head falls back onto his shoulder, exposing my neck.

I'm gasping for air when his mouth hovers over the hollow of my ear. "I said *might*. Now, this is what a future husband would do to his future wife."

A shiver breaks out across my body, heating the space between my thighs. I fight to hold myself together as his fingers dance along the top of my thigh, growing dangerously close to the top part of the slit of my dress.

"I still don't think I understand." I'm staring out at the near pitch-black ocean. The only color is the white waves crashing onto the shore.

His fingers keep dancing along my skin. He bends his fingers playfully, eventually pulling back the fabric of my dress far enough to reach the hem of my bathing suit bottom.

He breathes in my ear again. "What's not to understand, Cass?"

Fuck. Hearing him say my nickname into my ear is enough to make me orgasm right here. I can't help but rock my hips. It's a subtle movement, one I try to contain. But the closer he gets to the top of my thigh and the heavier his hot breaths caress my ear, the harder it is for me to hold back.

I wiggle on top of him, unable to stop myself from moving forward. Underneath his jeans, I can feel his hardened cock. Every time I move, his erection becomes more obvious underneath me. My eyes flutter shut, and I count my breaths, forcing myself to keep them even.

The group surrounding the bonfire may not be large, but there's a decent number. Enough for others to notice if I start panting and writhing against Levi.

A few of them glance in our direction. I offer them a weak, most likely unconvincing smile before they look away.

I still haven't answered his question, but my mind is becoming muddy. I can't remember what he asked or even what we're talking about. All other thoughts have narrowed down to his fingers and the rising heat inside me causing me to soak my bikini underneath my dress.

"You haven't answered me," he says. I fight back a moan as he continues whispering in my ear.

"Wh—" Heavy breath. Swallow. Close eyes. "What did you ask me?"

His fingers move up again. He's close to my hip bone now. "I asked you what you're not understanding."

"Oh."

"Maybe I should make myself more clear." His voice is hard as steel. He edges the tips of his fingers on the waist of my bikini bottom. It's tied around my hips by a thin strap.

My chest stills as I hold my breath. He hooks his finger under the strap. For a moment I worry he might pull on it, unraveling it right here.

We've never gone this far and now that he's taking it here, my heart hammers inside my chest. I can't think straight.

He ghosts his mouth across the curve of my neck, never allowing himself to bring it directly to my skin, before he brings it back to my ear. With one finger hooked onto my bikini bottom, he pulls it up and away from my hip.

"When the party's over . . . And everyone is gone . . ." His deep velvet voice vibrates through me. I hold my breath, anticipating what he's going to do next.

"Meet me at the pool." He pulls on the strap even tighter before letting it go. It snaps against my skin, and I bite the inside of my cheek, fire igniting in my belly.

"Okay." I breathe out.

TWELVE

Cassidy

I've spent the last two hours in complete and utter agony.

All one hundred twenty minutes have been spent with a few of the guests who aren't a part of the reunion. And Paul.

Paul sought me out again when I was ordering a drink from the bar near the pool. This time he talked about how when he wasn't working on flipping cars, he was out hiking in the mountains of Washington State. His conversation was more interesting the second time around, but I couldn't help keeping one eye focused on Levi.

I don't know what to make of our conversation earlier. But with each passing second and with every guest I see leaving the pool area, my stomach does another somersault. In the best way.

I'm sitting on the edge of the pool with my legs hanging off into the deep end. The water is cool as I slide my legs back and forth. It reminds me of Nate's going away party. The night Levi followed me out to my car, claiming I'd been lucky to have him there.

I lifted the bottom of my dress and set the train behind me. Half of my ass cheeks are pressed onto the cool concrete.

The bar is now fully closed, and the last person left in the pool area walks out. Lights surrounding me shut down, one at a time. Soon, all that's left are the lights from inside the pool and the moon hanging over the horizon in the distance. The sky is near pitch-black. White dots sprinkle the sky. The teal blue of the water of the pool pops, creating a spotlight from below. I lean back on my hands, looking around for Levi. I saw him head into the hotel earlier. But I'm unsure if he ever came back out. I was expecting him to return by now. Especially since he said for me to meet him here when the party was over.

At least it appears to be over. I'm the only one here.

"It's good to see you know how to listen to directions." Levi's voice cuts through the darkness, coming from the opposite end of the pool, closest to the beach. We're surrounded by endless palm trees. I'm sitting on the edge of the largest pool. At the opposite end is a smaller pool with a small waterfall, a hot tub beside it.

I narrow my eyes, searching for Levi in the darkness.

He's sitting in one of the poolside chairs in the corner. The pool is surrounded by palm trees, almost making this a private oasis. The only sound between us are the waves crashing onto shore and the water lapping against my bare legs.

It's just the two of us.

My stomach is twisted into knots and my heart pounds to the same beat I'm becoming familiar with.

I tip my chin up, leaning back on my hands. Pretending my nerves aren't scrambling to calm down. I continue swinging my legs back and forth in the water. "I've always been good at listening to directions. You just don't know me very well."

"Hmm." He stands from his chair and rubs his hands together as he walks along the edge of the pool. Toward me. "You always say I don't know you well, Cass."

Still haven't gotten over him calling me Cass.

"But," he continues, growing closer, "I think you'll see I know more about you than you think I do.

"You hate me," I say. Maybe it's the empty rum cocktail next to me or maybe it's that I suddenly have the courage to do so. I tell Levi the truth.

He stands beside me and crouches down, resting his arms on his knees. His eyes meet mine as he quirks an eyebrow, firming his stare. "*You* hate *me*."

He pulls himself to a stand. He lifts his shirt and tosses it aside. He unbuckles his jeans and steps out of them. He's left only in his boxer briefs. Staring down at me.

Fighting every urge in me to not look, I give up. I look all over his body, taking in every inch of muscle. I swallow as my eyes roam over the hardened planes of his abs to the dips of his hip bones, creating a perfect *v*. The outline of his cock is clear to see under his boxers. My stomach twists again and the heat I'd felt earlier sitting on his lap returns.

Without a word, he jumps into the pool. He disappears under the surface. When he comes back up, he wipes his hands across his face and pushes his hair back. He gives his hair a quick shake, then swims over to me.

I hold my breath as he wraps his hands around my calves, parting my legs. He moves himself between them.

The string to my wrap dress is on my left side, just below my breast. Levi lifts his hand and pinches the end of one of the strings. He starts to slowly undo the tie.

I hold my breath, unsure where this is going. Levi has spent the past five years hating me. In a matter of four days, it seems his opinion has changed. Slightly.

I don't get my hopes up, knowing we're only in this together for show. But then again, we're alone. None of his teammates are around. None of the guests are around. Miles is nowhere to be seen.

I dampen the spark of hope in my chest, allowing Levi to take this however far he's willing to take it.

Once he has the tie undone, my dress slips apart, exposing me. I'm wearing a bikini underneath. I have yet to go swimming in the pool or in the water down by the beach. Still, every night I wore one in case I'd decided to.

It's a simple dark blue bikini. Two triangles of fabric cover my breasts, held together by a tie around my back and another around my neck.

My nipples have already peaked into two small pebbles. They're silhouetted the same way Levi's cock was under his boxer briefs.

His eyes fall straight to them before moving back up to mine.

"I don't hate you," I say, narrowing my gaze down to him. "I strongly dislike you."

He chuckles under his breath. "It seems we know more about each other than we think we do."

I tilt my head to the side and study him, trying to figure him out.

He continues to kick his feet under the water, keeping him afloat enough for his shoulders to be exposed. Water dots his hardened tan frame and, like a sudden craving, I want to lick them away.

A breeze blows across my chest and my nipples harden even more. Levi's hands are now back into the pool. He wraps both of them around the back of my legs, starting with my ankles. His fingers curve across my bone and muscle. The water makes his movements effortless. When he reaches the back of my calves, he lifts each leg over to rest on his shoulders.

Reaching outside of the pool, with my legs over his shoulders, he reaches behind me, grabbing onto my lower back. "Scoot yourself to the edge." He instructs.

I do as he says, not questioning him. I let my dress slide off my shoulders, falling to the concrete. I'm now left in my bikini. I look around us again to make sure we truly are alone.

"Levi, I'm not sure . . ." I try to zero in between the palm trees, closer to the gate leading to the hotel. There's no one.

"Come on, Cass." Levi smiles playfully. "Are you going to be the good girl forever, or are you going to live a little?"

"I don't have room to live a little. Besides, I haven't always been a good girl."

"Really?" He quirks a brow. "Prove it."

I look around the secluded area we're in again. Anyone could walk by at any moment. Part of me is surprised no one urged us to leave, telling us the pool was closed for the night. No one bothered to make sure the area was cleared out. The only conclusion I can come up with is that the hotel isn't technically even open yet. The staff has more to worry about than checking to make sure all of Miles Deacon's special guests have cleared out of the pool.

When I'm satisfied knowing we truly are by ourselves, I decide to prove Levi wrong. I sit on the edge, waiting for him to take the lead. Anticipation simmers across my body.

He turns his head to his left, placing his lips against the inside of my thighs. I gasp, my throat seizing.

He keeps his eyes on my legs, never breaking focus. I want to ask him a million questions. The overly analytical part of my brain wants to know why he's doing this with me when no one is around to watch. Or even why he's doing it when he *strongly dislikes me.*

I pinch the tip of my tongue between my teeth, keeping my thoughts to myself. The vision of Levi in between my legs, his eyes matching the teal blue of the water. Drops of water continue to spill from the ends of his hair as he moves to my other thigh. He kisses it again, this time opening his lips a little more. With each kiss, I'm left gasping for air again.

He works his way up my thighs and I already know I'm soaking wet for him. He stays in the same position for a moment as he looks up at me with hooded eyes.

"I think we both know the truth here, Cass."

Before I'm able to respond, his mouth is on me again. Only this time, he drags his tongue across the inside of my thigh. I moan and tilt my head back, swiping my tongue across my lips. "What truth?"

He pauses, sucking and pulling on my flesh. A tingling sensation shoots straight to my center. I rock and roll my hips, hoping it will bring some sort of relief. But it doesn't. My body is begging for Levi to rectify the situation he's put me in. I'm igniting into flames for him, and he's barely done anything yet.

My eyes are closed, and my head is tilted back when I feel the tie on the side of my bikini bottom loosen. Then the other one. I look down, attempting to catch my breath. My chest rises and falls quickly.

"What truth?" I ask him again.

"The truth that you've been wanting this since you met me." He drags his tongue across the other side, biting down the same way he did on the other leg. I let out a sharp hiss between my teeth, relishing in the pleasure it gives me. "The truth that you've imagined me tasting you . . . fucking you."

With my bikini bottom completely undone, he pulls down the front, completely exposing me.

"I know your truth," I tell him.

My pussy is on the edge of the pool, in perfect line with Levi. He pulls himself closer, bringing his mouth above me. He blows across my folds, wrapping both his arms around my thighs. He goes under them, wrapping them around to rest his hands on the top.

"What's my truth?" he asks me.

It's there that I see it in his eyes. As much as Levi Hawkins has hated me over the years, he's wanted this. The excitement and anticipation are clearly written in his expression.

"To taste me and fuck me." I let the words spill out of my mouth, not missing a beat. I don't know if it's the truth. Much like I've never truly known much about Levi and what goes on in that stupidly gorgeous head of his. Stories, articles, one-night stands with women he barely knows. Those are the thoughts I've always thought were running through his mind.

But this is different.

My words burn my chest as if I've now thrown them out into the world, exposing them to the entire universe. The truth in this moment settles between Levi and me like a sinking anchor, landing with weight to the bottom. Without hesitation, he brings his mouth to me, separating my folds slowly with his tongue.

"Oh my god." His tongue reaches my clit. He's warm and soft, yet there's a sense of urgency to him. He doesn't waste any time, making it known what he wants to do to me. He swirls the tip of his tongue around my clit before sucking on it.

I latch my legs tighter onto his shoulders, pressing my calves into his back. He draws impossibly closer as I sit up, using one hand to support me. I grab onto the ends of his hair, clenching my fingers with every pass he makes with his mouth.

All the times over the years that I've thought of this moment. How it would feel to have his mouth sliding and sucking on my clit as I buried my fingers into his hair. He groans against me, and my entire body bursts into tingles. They climb their way to the ends of each finger, shooting like an arrow to my toes.

"Mmm." He hums against my clit. "There's one truth I have gotten the answer to."

"What's that?" I pant, my throat running dry. He holds my legs down as his large hands spread across the top of my thighs. I'm subtly rolling my hips back and forth, moving with the motion of Levi's mouth.

"I know exactly how you taste now."

He laps his tongue and mouth all over me. He removes one of his hands from my legs, bringing them between us, keeping his tongue pressed against my clit as he buries one finger inside me. Then two.

"Oh god, Levi." I grasp onto the ends of his hair a little tighter. Heat expands across my chest. "I-I'm . . ."

The sound of my legs writhing in the water causes Levi to lift his mouth off me long enough to press his hand against my lower belly. He lightly presses his palm against it. A small whimper escapes my chest, a new feeling spurring inside me. The two movements of his mouth on me and the pressure inside me intensify what he's doing to me.

"Shh." His mouth brushes against my folds as he speaks. "You need to be quiet or else you'll get the both of us in trouble."

His mouth finds my swollen clit again. I bite down on my bottom lip and moan as I watch Levi move against me. He laps his tongue back and forth, in and out, never letting his hand up.

He keeps the subtle pressure in the spot above where he is, and I start to feel it.

"Levi, your tongue . . . your mouth . . ." I tilt my head back, trying to keep my voice down. "I'm going to come."

"Come then," he growls, dragging his tongue across me. He's firm, yet there's something deep and primal in his voice that lets me know he wants me to come. He wants to watch me come undone under him.

He presses his hand harder against me. His tongue moves faster.

My legs tense around his shoulders and back. I grab onto his hair and let out a small cry. "Fuck, Levi." My hips roll faster before I reach the top of my orgasm. Then when my orgasm hits me, spreading across my body, my body pulsates against him. Goose bumps and little fireworks burst across my skin, like tiny, delightful pin pricks.

When I slow down and my breathing has somewhat returned to normal, Levi pulls away from me, letting my legs fall lazily into the pool. I look down, seeing my undone bikini strings lying beside me.

I'm half expecting Levi to jump out of the pool and leave me here, but he doesn't.

Instead, he gently brings my knees together and presses each of his hands beside me.

I'm catching my breath when he pulls himself up, lifting himself high enough to be in line with my face. Water drips down his face and now his entire body is soaked. Half of his body remains in the pool as he holds himself up, long enough to bring his face closer to mine.

His muscles strain to hold himself up. They take a new shape and a few veins I haven't seen before pop up underneath his skin. He's still incredibly strong, even if he hasn't played football in two years.

"Have you ever tasted yourself after you've come before?"

Shallow breaths escape my rapidly deflating chest. "No."

"Hmm." He hums, his eyes falling to my mouth. "Seems we have a few things to rectify during this reunion."

Pushing himself up more to meet me, he crashes his mouth to mine. He immediately parts my mouth with his tongue. It's the first time he's kissed me this way. It's all consuming, quickly clouding my thoughts. I wrap both of my legs around him, keeping him against the wall. He slides it along every inch of my mouth, making sure every inch is coated. I'm about to reach up and wrap my arms around his neck to urge him to keep going, but he pulls back before I even get the chance.

"Do you taste that?" he asks me.

I swipe my tongue across my mouth as he falls back into the pool. Heat blooms in my cheeks as a sweet, unfamiliar taste settles in the back of my mouth. "Yes."

"Good," he says, dipping underneath the water. He stays under and his body stretches as he kicks his way back over to me. But this time he doesn't come back over to me. He reaches the wall beside me. He emerges from the water, pushing his hair back. He plants his hands on the edge of the pool, pushing himself up and out of it.

Water splashes onto me as he climbs out. He bends to pick up his dry clothes. I watch him in stunned silence, unsure of what to say. Or do.

I start with the ties on the side of my bikini.

"I thought you were going to show me how a fiancé treats the other."

"I did." He pauses. "I told you I preferred the pool to the beach." His face is settled into a blank, unreadable expression. He finds a towel folded on the edge of one chair. It must have been left over from the party and no one has come out here to pick it up yet. He wraps it around his waist and passes me on his way over to the hotel entrance. "I'll see you back in the room."

I close the top of my dress and stay sitting on the edge of the pool, trying to decide how to feel. My body is humming with the orgasm he gave me but somehow, my heart is left a tiny bit cracked. A slight twinge of regret seeps into the crack.

I'm unsure whether I'm getting the fake fiancé Levi. Or the one who's found a loophole to our agreement.

Either way, I have a feeling what happened won't change a thing.

Trouble #3

**Over time, the more you tell yourself a lie, the
more you believe it.
Until all that's left is the truth.**

THIRTEEN

LEVI

"How's the reunion going?"

"Oh, um . . ."

"Wait, more importantly"—Vada holds a flat hand up, stopping me—"how's your story coming along?"

"Well, the reunion has been going okay." I lean forward and rest my arms on my knees, nodding. "I've only written a few starting lines to the first draft. I'm sorry, I—"

"No," she says, waving her hand. "That's okay. You still have about five days, right?"

"Yeah." I sit back on the couch and rake my fingers through my hair, the realization of my assignment coming back to me. I'm here for a story and nothing else. Or at least that's the way it's supposed to be. And until Vada requested a video chat this morning, I had nearly forgotten it was the motivating reason for me being here. "We'll head back this weekend. I don't know why Miles stretched this out so long."

"It might not be a bad thing," Vada says. "It gives you plenty of time to get great content. Well, you and Cassidy. Where is she, by the way? I tried to call her, but she didn't answer."

"I haven't spoken to her yet this morning, but I think she's in the shower."

I avoid looking up at the off chance I'll spot Cassidy stepping out of the shower. I haven't spoken to her since last night in the pool, when we'd displayed our truths between each other. We laid them out and devoured them. Exposed and raw, we'd both spit out the truth we've known for the past five years.

We simultaneously hate one another while wanting each other.

By the time she'd made it up to the room behind me, I was already lying on the couch that's become my bed the past few nights.

Guilt for ignoring her and leaving her at the edge of the pool has stuck with me all night. My chest still aches, knowing it's not exactly my best move. But the thoughts going on in my head haven't worked themselves out yet.

I won't lie, pressing my mouth to her skin and giving her an orgasm like the one she had has been living rent free in my brain since I was eighteen years old.

Until last night, my plan was working. Keep Cassidy at a distance. Play by the rules of fake engagement.

Only touch her and kiss her in public. Treat her the way I've always treated her when we were alone.

But something inside me last night snapped and I let my guard down. Now I don't know how to deal with it.

"I'm right here," Cassidy yells from the bathroom door.

On instinct, I look up, catching her as she makes her way across the room, sitting down beside me. She doesn't allow herself to sit too close to me. Only enough for Vada to see the both of us on the computer screen.

Her damp hair is pulled into a high bun resting on top of her head. A few stray pieces hang loose, framing her face. Black eyeliner is drawn above each of her lash lines, her lids are brushed with a bright pink, and her lips are painted a pale magenta color. The sun catches the gloss on her mouth, highlighting them. She's wearing a simple floral sundress, the flowing fabric stops above her knees, exposing her long legs. The same legs that wrapped around me last night, keeping my mouth pressed against her.

I chew on the inside of my cheek, reminding myself I need to keep it together. This isn't how this reunion is supposed to go. I need to keep Cassidy at arm's length.

"Hey," Vada says to Cassidy. "I was hoping to catch you."

"I'm sorry I didn't text you back last night," Cassidy says. It's a quick, flash movement but I can catch her eyes shifting in my direction before going back to Vada. "I was tired and went straight to bed."

"Okay." Vada smiles. "No worries, I mainly wanted to check in with you and Levi. I know you've been messaging me and calling to talk with Jonah, but I haven't heard much from either of you about the story, so I wanted an update. Are you having a good time at least?"

Cassidy clears her throat. Her cheeks flush a pale shade of pink. "I am."

Two words is all she gives Vada.

"Colton and I are taking Jonah to the movies later, so I'll have my phone on me. Feel free to send me any photos you have."

"Jonah loves going to the movies. Tell him to order some popcorn with extra butter for me." Cassidy grins wide. It fades when she changes the subject. "And besides, you know I hate sending you photos before I've edited them."

Vada rolls her eyes. "I know, but sometimes I can't wait to see them. These I know will be amazing."

"Thanks," Cassidy says.

"I'll let Jonah know about the popcorn." Vada turns to me

and inhales a deep breath. "Aside from all this work talk, Levi, I hope you're having a good time with your old teammates. Keep up the good work and please keep me updated on all the progress you're making with your rough draft."

"I will." I nod.

"What do you have planned for today?" Vada asks.

"Miles is taking us to a winery he has over at one of his other properties."

"Good," Vada says. "Be sure to include that in your story. I'm interested in understanding all of his investment properties surrounding the hotel."

"Of course." I agree, knowing this will require me to get more information out of Miles.

Once we hang up with Vada, Cassidy stands, moving to the table near the bar. She rifles through her purse, then grabs her camera. She loads all her memory cards.

"I didn't know you had a nephew." I surprise myself by asking her this question. I've never once asked Cassidy about her personal life. My defenses must be down.

"Really?" she asks. I immediately hear the sarcasm in her voice. "I'm surprised since you always claim to know so much about me."

"I never said that." I'm lying.

"You're lying." She scoffs. "You've always said multiple times that you knew me more than I thought you did. This just proves it."

I watch her finish getting her bag together in silence. Something about her words hits me right in the chest. It aches and twists, stopping me from saying anything back to her.

Her words have never affected me before. Of all the times I've seen Cassidy, I've actively worked against letting what she does and says affect me. It's worked out perfectly. Until now.

"Hey, Cass," I say, nerves climbing their way up my throat. I try to come up with a way to bring up last night. I want to tell her what I truly wanted to happen. I know she's waiting for an explanation. And I owe her one.

I walk over to stand beside her. She smells like roses and coconut.

"Yeah?" she asks, zipping her bag closed.

She takes her time looking up at me. Her soft green eyes stay on me as her eyebrows arch across her forehead. It's there that I see it. She's been afraid to look me in the eye, knowing I walked away last night. I only wish I had the guts to tell her exactly why. I wish I could tell her that everything I've ever said and done is the complete opposite. A way to shield her from the truth.

I push the nerves back down, reverting back to old habits.

Fuck, this woman has me completely messed up.

"Let's go," I say instead. "We can't be late, and I have a story to write." I pass her on my way to the door, avoiding her. Mostly because I don't want to be tempted again. It's hard to pull myself out of my usual brush off with Cassidy. It's hard to admit the truth I've always kept deep inside me.

"Right." She nods, pursing her pink lips.

The disappointment evident on her face stabs me in the chest, the familiar ache and twist only getting worse.

I thought if I'd gone back to treating her the same way, this feeling would go away.

💔

Cassidy hasn't spoken one word to me since we left the hotel room. Every time I walk down a row of grapes, I can feel her stare burning a hole in my back.

I've been walking through the tour with Jimmy at my side. Other than Zane, he's the only friend I feel I truly have here. All the other guys are great, but I've never been close to any of them. Not in the same way, at least.

I've been listening to him go on and on about his wife and the life they've built in Lubbock. I'm thrilled for him, but I can't bring myself to get my mind off Cassidy long enough to keep up with our conversation.

Miles leads us through his field of grapes. The harsh rays of the sun have been beating down on us ever since we got here over an hour ago.

The farm we're touring is massive. If I didn't think Miles was already obnoxious with his money as it is, this would definitely top it. I keep in mind that I'm here for a story. Even if I don't want to hear about the three different styles of wine he plans on producing and selling exclusively to his hotel, I suffer through it. For the sake of my job.

I have yet to tell Miles I'm writing a story about his family's hotel empire and how he's expanded on it, slowly taking over the tourist industry here in South Padre. But like I told Cassidy, I'd cross that bridge when I got to it.

We've been touring the grape fields for the past thirty minutes. All thirty of those minutes Cassidy has been walking several feet behind me, near the back of the line, avoiding me at all costs.

While Miles has taken to staying near the front of the line, I figured my safest place has been to stay in the middle with Jimmy. Still, I haven't been able to stop thinking about Cassidy and the way we've been ever since last night. She's all I can think about.

Not just that she's angry with me. But all of it.

The way she tasted and how my tongue slid across her swollen clit. The way her legs shook and quivered around me, reacting to my touch.

She'd given me every signal I'd ever wished for her to give me.

That she wanted me.

"I haven't seen you talk to Miles much since the football game," Jimmy says, shoving his hands into his pockets.

I do the same and shrug. "I don't know. You know how it is between us."

"I know." He nods, agreeing. "I don't blame you for not letting it go. I just figured I'd ask."

"No." I sigh, blowing out a hot breath through my nose. "You're right though. I need to talk to him."

"Might be a good idea before our last night here. It's going to be a massive dinner and ball. The last thing you need is dredging up old shit."

I give Jimmy a mock laugh. "Right."

"Kind of strange to bring us here, though. Am I right?" Jimmy asks.

"What do you mean?"

"I don't know. Everything about the hotel, I understand. But this feels a little out of context from the reunion. Like he's showing off or something."

"Are you surprised?" I ask him, fighting the urge to laugh. "I've known this ever since he mentioned coming out here."

"Yeah." Jimmy shrugs, laughing. "You're right."

I keep my focus on Miles, wondering when I might talk to him when someone passes me on my right.

Cassidy bumps into my elbow as she passes me without a word, making a straight line for Miles up front. He's stopped talking and is now taking us out to a row of barns along the outer edge of the farm. Where the wine tasting, and restaurant are.

"Are you guys okay?" Jimmy asks me. I look over at him with furrowed brows. Even he notices Cassidy and I aren't in a good place.

"Yeah." I look over at Jimmy. "Of course we are."

"Just thought I'd ask. I obviously haven't known her that long, but from what I can tell, she usually isn't this quiet. Or at least she hasn't been."

When I turn back to face forward, I stare at Cassidy's back, watching her as she strikes up a conversation with Miles. Jimmy has a point. Until now, she hasn't really spoken with anyone. I wonder why she's chosen to speak to Miles out of everyone here.

Heat spreads across my chest and I curl my hands into fists. They're buried in the pockets of my jeans. The tension spreads from my hands, all the way up to my arms. I'm not liking the way it's making me feel watching her talking to that fucking asshole. He's the last person that should be talking to her.

Miles is the kind of man who believes he can have anything or anyone he wants. Even when it isn't for him to take.

The entire walk over to the restaurant, I watch Cassidy as she talks with Miles. Every now and then she tilts her head back in laughter. Moments from last night flash in my brain. The same way she's tilting her head in laughter is the same way she tilted it back in pleasure as my mouth sucked on her sweet center.

She swipes her tongue across her mouth as she lifts her camera, showing Miles some photos she's taken. He leans in, lifting his hand and pointing to a few of them. Probably giving her some bullshit compliment he doesn't mean. It wouldn't surprise me.

I can feel the heat building inside me, spreading to the ends of my fingers down to my feet with every step we're taking.

When we finally reach the restaurant, we form one large group, the line thickening with us coming together. Everyone makes their way up the small steps, heading straight for the table Miles had his employees set up for us. The table is already set with linens, plates, and silverware. Bottles of wine are lined up.

But I don't follow the crowd. Instead, I follow Cassidy.

She places her hand on Miles's arm, muttering words I'm unable to hear before giving him a smile. She drops her hand from his arm, allowing it to fall away as she heads off to the barn in the distance.

Memories of college flood back to me. My blood simmers beneath my skin, pressure building behind my eyes. Aside from the fact that Miles is now married and obviously flirting with Cassidy, it shows me he hasn't changed since college. He's still the same fucking asshole.

The barn is a few hundred feet from the restaurant, set off behind the rows of grapes. The red paint is faded and peeling, somehow fitting in with the area, as if this winery has been here for hundreds of years. Miles might have said that on his tour, but I can't remember. I wasn't listening.

I follow Cassidy, wondering why she's wandering over to the barn when everyone else is sitting down for lunch. Part of me wonders if she even cares where I am. What does she plan on doing inside the barn?

She opens the door on the side of the building, and I follow her in, hoping to set the record straight between us.

FOURTEEN

Cassidy

Being surrounded by a dozen men while in one of the worst moods hasn't exactly been my idea of fun. I wish I could say my first wine tour was more exciting, but I'd be lying if I said otherwise.

Aside from the familiar feeling of being an outcast, I haven't been able to stop thinking about Levi.

My mind and my body have been in complete contradiction since last night. I don't know whether my feelings for Levi have bloomed or if it's hatred sprouting more thorns. As if his mouth has branded my skin, I think about every swipe of his touch and every inch he covered with his long fingers. Every inch he's touched has scored my skin. It's all I've been able to think about since he pulled himself out from between my legs.

But despite Levi and I laying out our truths, I can't get over the ball of frustration in the pit of my stomach since he left me sitting on the edge of the pool.

I need a moment to breathe. I need a moment away from staring at Levi's back, wondering if anything will ever change between us. I need a moment to remind myself it's Levi I'm talking about. Nothing ever changes.

I step farther into the barn, pushing my way through one door off to the side of the larger main door. My eyes widen when I take in what's surrounding me. Endless rows of wooden barrels, stacked neatly along the wall. Each barrel is supported by a beam. It's quiet in here and I'm thankful for the silence, allowing the warm sun to pour through the only window near the front door and the cracks between the wooden slats.

I close my eyes and breathe in, unsure of how I'm going to make it through the rest of this trip. I consider calling Vada and telling her I want to leave early. I've taken all the pictures I need to take.

But I can't. Something inside me is telling me to stay. Like an anchor tossed into the ocean.

Taking photos of the winery has helped only slightly at distracting me from the truth I've known all along. One touch from Levi would only draw out the feelings I have for him. The same ones I've suppressed for over five years. It's not as if I've pined over him during college. But seeing him again reminded me of how intense my silly high school crush was and what it turned into now that we're twenty-three.

"So, was it your plan to ignore me all day and then spend the rest of the tour talking to Miles? Or are you kind of winging it?"

"Holy shit, Levi." I gasp, placing my hand on my chest as I spin around. I stumble backward, nearly rolling my ankle and falling back against a barrel. I steel my gaze and tighten my fists at my sides. "What the hell is wrong with you?"

"I'm going to ask you again," he says, stepping closer. His voice is deeper. Smoother and drawn out. His eyes are a perfect storm, drawing me in. Somehow they still appear dangerous, as if I allow myself to get any closer I'll somehow only hurt myself. "Was it your plan to ignore me all day?"

I inhale as he steps closer. I take a step back. He takes one more.

My back hits one of the barrels. I lean back into the barrel, moving my arms behind me to grip onto the edge. I hold my breath as his large frame towers over me. My chest is pushed up in his direction. I tip my chin up, challenging him to finish his sentence.

He takes the bait.

"Answer my question, Cass."

I pause, pressing my mouth into a thin line. I'm attempting to gather enough courage to push back and not give into him so easily. But I'm weak when it comes to Levi. It's a fact I'm willing to admit.

"Maybe." I quirk an eyebrow, hoping that answer will be sufficient. "What if it was?"

"Well." He lifts his hand, drawing his finger across my cheek. He stares at his hand as he traces an invisible line down my neck. He removes my camera from around my neck, carefully placing it on top of the barrel behind me. "I think you know by now that I don't like being ignored."

I breathe in. Then out. "I told you."

"You told me what?" he asks against the hollow of my ear. Goosebumps break out across my skin.

I lean my face into his, bringing my mouth to his ear. I'm standing on the tips of my toes, lifting my hips out and against him. "I told you I've always known what kind of man you are, Levi."

"Maybe with some things," he whispers back, dragging his hand down the center of my chest. He traces a line along the curve of my breast, pulling the top of my tank top down. He pulls the cup of my bra down with it, freeing my breast. My nipple peaks and tightens with the change in air.

"Like being possessive?" I ask him.

He twists my nipple between his fingers, the sensation prompting a whimper from my throat.

"I don't like it when others threaten to take what's mine."

"But I'm not yours." I make the point as my eyes flutter closed at his touch.

"Some would disagree," he whispers again.

I swallow down the nerves bundling inside me. I'm not sure what he means by his admission, but I don't press him any further.

"I wasn't ignoring you, by the way," I say, forcing myself to get the words out.

"Tell me what you were doing, then."

He brushes the pad of his thumb over my nipple. I gasp, this time, the heat between my legs growing more intense. I buck my hips, rolling them into his, pinning me against the barrel.

"Listening to Miles talk about wine." I bite on the inside of my cheek, wanting Levi to keep going. I want him to keep moving his hand over my skin, re-marking the areas he touched last night, while exploring new places.

"Is that what he was talking to you about before you came in here?"

"No." I breathe in.

"Mmm." He hums before clicking his tongue. The sound alone sends a shiver down the back of my neck.

"Does it bother you when I talk to Miles?"

"Maybe."

I tilt my head to the side, surprised by his answer. He grabs onto my chin, pulling my gaze back to his.

His fingers are firm yet soft as he grips my chin in his hand. I can practically feel the jealousy coursing through his veins. Knowing me talking to Miles has sparked a new feeling from Levi, thrills me. My heart hammers in my chest, pulling me toward him.

"You haven't been a very good girl, Cass."

"I didn't know I was being bad." The words spilling from my mouth even catch me off guard.

"Oh." the corner of his mouth curls into a knowing smirk. "You've been very disobedient lately. I think I need to remind you of who you belong to."

I want to believe what Levi is saying is true. I want to believe he wouldn't be here, pinning me against a wine barrel when no one else is around. I have to believe he wouldn't have put his mouth on me last night, sucking on my clit until I'd had one of the best orgasms I'd ever had.

Something tells me he means what he's saying. In some capacity, I belong to him. It's a foolish notion considering I've never known Levi to care for me in any capacity. But something between us has shifted these last few days.

"Show me," I tell him, allowing the words to settle between us.

His eyes move between each of mine as if he's studying them, working out what to say next.

But I'm left completely breathless when he crashes his mouth against mine. My breath falters as I try to gain my footing, allowing what he's doing to hit me.

Levi Hawkins is kissing me. Not because I'm his fake fiancée and he needs to put on a show.

We're the only ones in this entire barn. The faint rumbling sounds of laughter filter through the wooden walls, reminding us that only a few hundred feet away, we aren't alone.

But I don't care.

I grip the edge of the barrel tighter as he deepens our kiss, using more force behind his mouth. Each grain of wood digs into my fingers. I use that sensation to anchor me as Levi moves his mouth against mine. He parts my lips with his tongue, sliding it across mine. He's rushed and hurried, as if he can't get enough of me fast enough. He pulls away from my mouth long enough to draw my bottom lip between his teeth. He bites down and I cry out, the sensation it gives me shoots straight to my lower belly and between my thighs.

He pulls away, pressing his fingers against my mouth. My hot breaths pass through each of his fingers. "Like I said, you haven't been a very good girl." He places one hand on my hip, leaning into me.

"Show me," I tell him.

His cock presses against me, already hard as stone. It's straining to break free from the confines of his jeans, begging to be inside me. The silhouette of it is enough for me to grow more wet for him than I already am.

Not that I've ever imagined Levi's cock before, technically.

Well, sort of.

I'm almost to that point of begging him to move faster when he unbuckles his belt. I inhale a deep breath and hold it, anticipating what he's going to do.

"Hold out your hands for me." He slides the belt out from the loops. I hold my hands out, putting my wrists together. He weaves the brown leather between my wrists before clasping it. He fastens it enough to prevent my hands from coming apart, but not enough to where it hurts.

When he's satisfied, he moves my arms down to his hardened cock. I uncurl my fingers, stroking his length from above his jeans.

He releases a deep groan from his chest. His eyes flutter closed, and I look up at him, not believing this is what we're doing.

He wraps a hand around my wrist, stopping me from stroking him.

"Turn around," he orders me. "Put your hands on the barrel."

I do as he says and spin around. The barrel I am leaning against is pushed up near the wall. A few feet above the wall is a small window. My heart races, hoping the window isn't low enough for someone to see in if they walked by. I place my hands on the other side of it, gripping onto the top lip. My stance causes me to lean over the barrel, my hands pushing into the barrel for support.

Levi's arms reach around me, and he lifts the bottom of my dress, exposing my bare ass. He slides his entire palm across my cheek, moving it from one to the next. I opted not to wear underwear today. I look over my shoulder with hooded eyes, watching him examine me. There's a fire in his eyes, one I haven't seen until now. This is what he's truly been wanting. I thought last night was it, but this is different.

"You have no fucking idea, Cass." He pushes his hips into me. I release a hiss, the intensity of me wanting him between my legs growing.

"What?" I ask him, turning back around and looking down, attempting to keep myself together long enough to feel him inside me.

He leans forward and wraps his arm around me, spreading his hand across my breast. My entire body presses against him, my bare ass exposed to him. "You have no fucking idea how long I've wanted this."

I look over my shoulder again as he unbuttons his jeans. "You say you've always known me better than I think you do, Levi. So, show me."

My eyes meet his briefly before his fingers wrap around the waist of his jeans and boxers. He quickly slides them down far enough for his cock to spring free. It stands straight up and my throat runs dry at the length of it. I want to wrap my hands around it. My mouth. But I can't. Not when my hands are tied together with his belt.

"As much as I'm tempted for Miles to hear every sound you're about to make, I'm warning you right now to be as quiet as possible."

"Okay." I turn to face front, my eyes fixating on my hands gripping the barrel.

One short burst of air passes through my lips before Levi's hands are on me again. He lifts my dress, bends me farther forward, and centers himself behind me.

I can feel him pull back before he slides the tip of his smooth cock between my folds. It's effortless, and the moment he pushes himself in as far as he can go, we let out a heavy breath. I bend my head forward, looking down at my chest as I bite down on my bottom lip. His cock fills me completely, swelling and twitching inside me before pulling back out. His hands are on my hips, keeping me still.

"Fuck, Cass." He hisses, pushing into me again. "Your pussy is so fucking wet for me."

"Oh god . . . Levi." I tilt my head back and close my eyes. "Harder. Push harder."

He wraps his arm around me and lowers his hand, sliding his fingers between my folds, finding my clit. He circles his fingers. With him inside me and his hand stroking me, I stand on my toes, certain if he keeps this up, I won't last much longer.

My legs quiver beneath me, shaking as he pounds into me harder with every thrust. I curl my fingers, digging my nails into the wood. I want to touch Levi. I want to feel his skin beneath mine. I've spent too many years wondering what it would feel like to fuck Levi. And now that we're here, I can't move my hands. I'm completely at his mercy.

He leans forward, pressing his mouth to my back. My skin is slick and wet underneath my dress, but I'm unsure he can feel it.

One of my breasts is exposed, the collar of my dress pulled

down under it. With his other hand, he pinches my nipple, twisting it slightly.

It's then I feel every nerve in my body ignite. "Yes, Levi. God, you feel so fucking good. I'm going to come."

"Shh." He breathes out. His body tenses behind me and I can tell he's attempting to keep himself together longer. "You've been a good girl so far, Cass. Now come for me. I want to watch you writhe underneath me."

I point my toes, digging them into my sandals as Levi's thrusts move faster and his circles against my clit are more firm.

I bite down on my lip as I climax, my orgasm moving through me like an earthquake. It starts at the base of my throat, vibrating down to my feet.

Levi grips onto my hips, thrusting a few more times before he stiffens behind me. His cock pulsates inside me and the motion of it intensifies the rest of my orgasm. I roll my hips into his, letting him fully ride out his orgasm before he pulls away from me.

Gently, he lowers my dress back down and steps backward. I spin around, watching as he slides his underwear and jeans back up, buttoning his jeans closed.

I'm watching him, studying him, hoping to hell he doesn't walk away the same way he did last night. A heavy weight presses on my chest and I swallow past the thickness rising in my throat.

I know Levi and I haven't always gotten along. Not until the past few days have we been able to stand each other long enough to hold a decent conversation. But I can't help but let the fear of being used creep in.

I hope Levi isn't using me and stringing me along.

Once he's fixed his pants, he looks up, tilting his head to the side with a smirk. He steps forward and fixes the collar on my dress. He places it back over my chest before dragging his fingers down my arms.

Quietly, I watch him unbuckle his belt from around my wrists. Once he has it free, he wraps it back around his waist, weaving it into the loops of his jeans.

My heart rate is slowing down as I smooth the bottom of my dress, then run my fingers through my hair. The memory of Levi between my legs is still very present. I'm not entirely sure how I'm supposed to go back to the wine tour.

"Levi." I clear my throat, nervous to hear his answer. "Um . . ."

"I know what you're thinking."

"You do?" I quirk an eyebrow, resisting the urge to call bull-shit on him. He's always claiming to know me more than I think he does.

"I do, and trust me . . ." He lifts his hand to my mouth and swipes the pad of his thumb across my bottom lip, soothing the spot I'd bitten down on. "If you keep this up, before this reunion is over, I will fuck you on every single piece of furniture in our hotel room."

My cheeks grow impossibly pinker, heat blooming across my already heated body.

Without another word, he wraps his hand around mine and pulls me toward the barn door and back out to the table where everyone is sitting.

"I don't know about you," he says, "but now if there isn't any dessert, I'm guessing we'll have to get it back at the hotel."

Something tells me I know exactly what he means.

FIFTEEN

LEVI

I hit send before I allow myself to regret it. I drop my phone onto the table and take a sip of my beer. The bright sun shimmering across the sand of the beach and the water is muted by the sunglasses I have perched on my nose.

My phone chimes on the table before I'm able to even take a sip of my beer. I don't need to look at it to know who it is and what his message says.

I'm only doing this for Vada's sake. And maybe Cassidy's.

Only a bit.

My stomach sinks the second he turns around the corner. His smug face says it all, as if he were expecting this to happen. A time for us to meet and talk shit through. Only he's wrong. I'm not here to talk about the past.

"I must say, Hawkins . . ." Miles sits in the seat on the other side of the table from mine. He's wearing that smug grin I've gotten used to seeing this past week. "I was wondering when you were going to want to meet up. Just us two."

"Well." I grin. "I figure it's about time."

"I've talked to your fiancée more than I have to you."

I shake my head, forcing myself to smile. Anger sizzles beneath my skin any time I hear him utter Cassidy's name. "Cassidy is more outgoing than I am. She makes friends with anyone she meets."

"I can see that," he says. He turns to face the ocean. The patio we're sitting on is located on the opposite end from the pool. There's a nearly unobstructed view of the water. Miles gestures toward it. "What do you think?"

"What do I think of what?" I mutter, lifting my beer glass to take a swig.

"Of my hotel. The vineyard? All of it."

"It's nice, Miles." It's the first honest thing I've ever said to the guy. At least since we played on the same football team. At one point, our interests were the same. To win.

Now I need Miles on my side. To share his story with me.

"Nice?" He raises his eyebrows. "Just nice?"

"What do you want me to say?" I lean forward, resting my arms on the table. "You already know what I think of it."

"I do." He laughs. "It's just always better to hear others say it. Especially from someone like you."

I grind my teeth, knowing Miles is pulling the same shit he always does. Manipulating his condescending words to sound kind and sincere.

"I'll hand it to you. It seems you're doing well, considering how much you've taken on since graduation."

"I have." He lifts his hand, signaling to one of his waiters to bring him a drink. He looks down and smooths his hand across his chest, removing the wrinkles in his shirt. "I heard Zane told you I play for a professional team out of El Paso."

"He did." I grit my teeth again, this time enough to cause a throbbing ache to pulsate beneath my temples. Miles's words cut me deeper than he probably realizes. He's living the life I was meant to have. The life I promised my father before he died.

But Miles isn't only living it. He stole it.

"So," he says. "What's the real reason you asked me down here? I know it wasn't to sit here and shoot the shit. As much as I enjoy it."

The waiter sets a small glass of clear liquid in front of Miles. He takes a sip, then leans forward over the table the same way I am.

I chew on the inside of my cheek. Part of me wants to leave this entire meeting and go find Cassidy. Our dynamic is somewhat the same as it's always been and although we're still playing our parts as fake fiancés, I can't deny how it's changed. And being with Cassidy is infinitely better than this. I'm starting to think I like being around her more than I have attending this so-called reunion.

It's all bullshit in my book. Just another way for Miles to inflate his ego.

But I have a job to do. Because without my job, I have nothing. I need Miles's story.

"I'm not here to talk about the past."

Miles's usual smug expression fades. He's clearly different now than when we're in front of the rest of the team. Or Cassidy.

It's a face I'm all too familiar with.

His thin mouth thins even more and his eyebrows slant.

"I didn't think you were."

"Miles." I sigh, not buying it. "It's impossible not to be around each other and not think about what happened between us."

"You mean what you did to me," he argues, correcting me. Even if he isn't correct.

My anger spikes. "I told you. I'm not talking about this."

"Fine." He holds his hands up, pretending to concede.

"I came here to tell you my boss wants a story published."

"What kind of story?" I've piqued his interest now. His expression has now transformed into curiosity.

"This." I lift my hands in the air and look up at the hotel. "Your hotel and how you've taken over the shores of South Padre. Your life and how you got to where you are now."

He twists his mouth in thought and for a moment, I think I see a flash of worry in his eyes. But it's quickly replaced. He rakes his fingers through his hair and scratches at his chin. He stares off, his attention focused over my shoulder.

"I had a feeling you were going to ask me this," he says, leaning back in his chair.

"What?"

"Yeah." He nods. "I'm not a fool, Hawkins. When you told me you and Cassidy worked for the same paper, I had you pegged. I knew you would be tempted to write a story."

I can't tell whether he's being truthful or not. Sure, Cassidy and I came here for the sole purpose of getting a story. He just doesn't know we're faking our engagement.

"I don't necessarily need your consent to tell this story." I ignore his comment about knowing I would be writing a story about this. "I could have written it and published it for the hell of it." My frustration with him is simmering again. Every word out of Miles's mouth always feels like daggers pointed straight at me. He can never carry a normal conversation.

The longer we sit here, the more I'm regretting even telling him. I shouldn't have mentioned it. I should have let the fucking asshole find out when it appeared as a feature story on the front page.

"Huh." He nods, twisting his mouth in thought. "Are you expecting a thank you for telling me?"

"Shit, Miles." I sit back in my seat and sigh. This conversation is exhausting. "I'm simply wanting to have a normal conversation with you. I wanted to run this by you. This story will run whether or not you knew about it. But it would help to know the details. More than if I were to simply research you online."

"Okay, fine." He leans forward again, this time staring directly at me with narrowed eyes. "You want to have a civil conversation? Let's have it. I know we can talk shit back and forth for hours, so I'll get to my answer."

I sigh with relief. Not that it makes me remotely like Miles. I appreciate his willingness to agree. Not that I need it.

"I agree to writing this story about me and the hotel. I'll even give you the history about my family and the agreement it took for me to acquire both the vineyard and this new string of hotels."

"Thanks." I nod once.

"But," he adds, "I have one condition."

"Condition?"

"Well, it's more of a request since you can technically write whatever you want."

"What's your condition?" I ask him, straightening my back.

"You can write the story on my strip of hotels and my other investment properties. Fuck, you can even write about my family and all their secrets. But you leave out football."

"You don't want me to include your professional career?"

"I'm sorry, Levi. I should have been more specific." He picks at the napkin sitting underneath his glass before flicking his eyes back up to me. "You don't mention college football or our senior year."

Under the table, I clench my hands into fists. My nails dig into my palms, cutting the surface of my skin. To me, it seems Miles has a hard time letting go of the past. He's always the one who seems to bring it up. It's there—I can sense the bitterness he still holds onto.

But I know the truth. The truth is, I'm the only one who has the right to be bitter. I'm the one who lost everything because of Miles's selfishness.

Despite his ego and pride, there's weakness in his eyes. He's afraid I'll write the truth, turning the tables on him. Deep down he's terrified I'll ruin him by writing about his path to success in college.

I swallow my pride and ego. When it comes to Miles, I have a difficult time conceding. But I do it for Vada's sake. I do it for my job. And I do it for Cass.

"You have a deal."

"Great." The weakness I saw in his eyes disappears nearly instantly. "Let me know when or how you want to interview me. Is that what you want to do?"

"We can do it that way." I shrug. "Not sure what your plans are, but I can let you know."

"Maybe after dinner tonight. I thought maybe we could play a fun game of football on the beach."

"Okay," I agree, nodding my head.

Miles inhales a deep breath before emptying the last bit of his drink. He places it back on the table, the empty glass tapping against the metal.

"You know. It all makes sense to me now." He slides his chair back and stands.

I stand too, ready to head back up to the hotel room. "What makes sense?"

"Why Cassidy kept that camera wrapped around her pretty little neck this past week." The corner of his mouth curls. "I mean, I understand she's a photographer, but that woman carries that thing with her everywhere." He points to his chest. "Kind of distracting. Don't you agree? Especially at the end of the wine tour the other day. She was telling me how amazing it was that I was interested in investing into all these different properties and how I wasn't focused on one type of industry. Then she showed me the pictures on her camera and although I was distracted, it wasn't hard to tell she had some good shots."

Miles winks and it's in this moment my anger flares up once again. Only this time it isn't simmering. It's boiling.

I take a step toward Miles, steeling my eyes to make sure he gets every word I'm about to say. I grind my jaw, clenching my teeth so hard I'm convinced they might split and crack if I don't speak.

"I'm only going to say this one time, Miles," I grit out between my clenched teeth. "If you so much as talk about my fiancée that way again, I won't hesitate to beat you. I don't give a shit what's happened in the past. Just stay away from Cassidy."

Miles twists his mouth, then scratches at his chin. He takes a step back. "No worries, Levi. I didn't mean anything by it. And don't forget, I'm married now."

He says it as if it holds any merit. Not to him at least.

I haven't forgotten this little fact he so effortlessly puts out. It's the whole reason I roped Cassidy into this arrangement with me. But I don't care. Hearing Miles talk about Cassidy reminds me of exactly the kind of person he is and has always been.

A protectiveness weighs down on me, wanting to keep Cassidy far away from Miles if I can.

Even though she isn't technically mine, the thought of her with Miles is enough for me to explode. My vision turns to red, and it takes every ounce of strength in me not to retaliate.

"Good talking to you, Hawkins. I look forward to my interview." Miles grins, patting me on the shoulder before he heads inside.

I don't turn around or follow him inside. My breathing is erratic, and it takes several minutes before I'm able to move.

The realization of making a deal with Miles has me reconsidering everything. It's not that I'm completely innocent, but it feels as if I've been fooling myself ever since I sat outside the bar with Zane and agreed to come to this reunion. All of it is for the sake of this stupid fucking story.

Fear of what Miles might say to Cassidy is the only thing that makes me move from the patio.

When I make it up to the room, I find Cassidy standing in the bathroom. She's in front of the mirror, swiping lipstick across her bottom lip.

"How did it go wit—"

I stop her short when I grab onto her hip and spin her around. I slam my mouth against hers. She hums, her unfinished words vibrating through me. She drops her lipstick and wraps her hands around my neck. But that's not where I want them.

I move my mouth along hers, biting down on her bottom lip before sucking on it as I pull away. My movements are slow and meticulous. Not like the last few times I've been with Cassidy. This is hurried and rushed. I can't get the conversation with Miles out of my head. Heat and fire expand across my chest, growing more intense with Cassidy's touch. She moves her arms, lifting at the bottom of my shirt. She removes it and my mouth is back on her skin. I drag my lips across her neck while moving my hands. She's wearing a thin tank top, held only together by two tiny straps. I quickly lift it over her head, grabbing onto one of her breasts. I stretch my fingers out, fitting my entire palm around her full, soft flesh.

It's not until I pinch her nipple before moving my hand in between her legs do I realize she's completely naked.

"Fuck, Levi," she cries out, her skin bursting with goose bumps. "The way you touch me."

I pull my mouth away from her and look down at my hand, my fingers already sliding between her folds. A heavy breath falls from between her delicately pink painted lips. "Can I tell you how grateful I am that you were ready for me?"

"I just got out of the shower," she mutters, trying to explain. "I didn't have a chance to get dressed yet."

I don't need an explanation. Seeing Cassidy completely bare, dressed in nothing but her smooth, full curves is enough for me. My cock is hard as stone, straining under my shorts. I quickly remove them, pressing myself against her.

I already know we've crossed the boundaries we are meant to keep as fake fiancés. Fake fiancés aren't supposed to kiss and fuck and touch. Not the way Cassidy and I have been.

I'm moving my fingers between her folds, her back arching the faster I move. I push two fingers inside her, pull them back out, find her clit, circle them a few times. Repeat. Each time she moans against me, tilting her head back. I lean forward, my cock twitching, begging to be inside her.

I lick all the way from her collarbone to the hollow of her ear. "When I told you I would fuck you on every single piece of furniture in this hotel room, I meant it."

The only sound to escape her already swollen mouth is a weighted gasp. Her chest stills and her eyes widen, anticipating what I'm about to do. Her body hums with the excitement of it. She's silently begging for me, her eyes shining.

I grip onto her hips and guide her over to the velvet chair sitting in the corner of the bathroom. The red velvet stool in the corner. It's the one piece of furniture Cassidy brought up the first day we were here. Saying it was the most ridiculous thing she'd ever seen.

She sits back in the chair, lifting her chest. Her breasts are perfectly round, her nipples peaked just for me.

I stand in front of her and grab my cock, stroking my entire length. Her eyes fall to me, watching me.

Her bottom lip pouts and it takes everything in me not to cum all over her right here.

"Spread your legs." I hiss.

She obeys, parting her knees. She bends her legs and lifts them, displaying herself to me. "I want to see that delicious wet pussy."

Staring at her this way stirs a feeling in my chest. I think about the conversation I had with Miles downstairs. Listening to him talk about Cassidy that way. Hearing her name pass his lips.

A fuse has been lit underneath my chest, an unfamiliar feeling sizzling on the surface.

Once I'd left Miles, Cassidy is all I've been able to think about.

I'm hoping she's the remedy to the feeling inside me. I'm hoping it will disappear and I can get a grip.

I lean over her, placing one hand on the back of the chair. She looks up at me as I center my cock in front of her. I slide the tip of my cock between her folds. "Shit, Cassidy. Your pussy is already wet and I've barely even touched you."

"I've realized," she says, wrapping her hands around my waist, pulling me closer. Her breasts push together, and I don't want to waste any more time. I need to be inside her. "My pussy is wet for you every time, Levi. It begs for you to be inside me."

I raise an eyebrow and smirk, placing my cock at her entrance. The same sensation twists in my chest. Warm at first before it heats, overwhelming me. Her eyes soften as she looks up at me. A contradiction to the way I've been with her before.

I thrust myself inside of her, pushing hard and fast. She cries out, tilting her head back. Her jaw falls open and her eyes close.

"Open your eyes, Cassidy."

She opens them, moaning again as I pull out, then push back into her.

"I want you to watch me as I fuck you," I tell her. I crush my mouth against hers, breathing deeply with every push and thrust of my hips. She's warm and soft and wet. I fit so perfectly inside her.

Her mouth moves against mine in perfect tandem. We create a rhythm, both of us moving together. Her breaths grow heavier, and her moans grow louder.

"Levi." Her name passing my lips as I move inside her sparks that fuse again. I squeeze my eyes shut, concentrating on reaching my orgasm.

My cock throbs as Cassidy's body quivers and shakes underneath me. Her legs vibrate as she rides out her orgasm as I continue to pump inside her. A tingling sensation breaks out across my skin, heat swelling in my lower belly. I stop moving the second I feel myself about to come, and I pull myself out of Cassidy when I start to. I hold the base of my cock, watching as the clear white liquid spills all over her stomach and chest.

Once I've finished, I drop my head close to Cassidy's neck. There's a narrow space between us, but she doesn't break her touch with me.

Cassidy lifts her hand and places it on the nape of my neck. She threads her fingers through my hair, almost as if she's attempting to regulate my breathing, calming me down.

I sit up, not wanting her to stop, but I know I can't stay leaning over her forever. She allows her hand to drop as she drags her fingers across her belly, smearing my cum all over her. She grins, her eyes sparking with playfulness. "Looks like I'm going to need to take another shower."

A small laugh rumbles from my chest. "Looks like it."

Before I push off the back of the chair and stand, I look into

Cassidy's eyes. A silence falls between us. The air swells and contracts before it completely falls back level.

I place my lips against hers. This time it isn't because we're fucking. This time it isn't because we're in front of my old teammates. And this time it isn't out of rage for Miles having spoken about Cassidy as if she were just another piece of meat to him.

This time I don't know what it is. All I know is that it's different.

SIXTEEN

Cassidy

Tiny, minuscule grains of sand glide over my skin with each pass I make with my hand. I'm lying on my stomach, attempting to tan the back side of my body. I'm not lying on a towel, and the damp sand has managed to sneak its way into every crevice.

I'm resting on my elbows, watching the waves roll in and out, paying attention to every detail. There are only a few more days left of the reunion and part of me feels as if I haven't done much. Between the constant bonfires Miles insists on having and the single vineyard tour we've been on, I can't help feeling as if I'm missing something. It's like I haven't connected all the dots.

Levi has only mentioned vaguely about his history with Miles the night he dragged me into pretending to be his fiancée. I know Miles has to do with Levi's scheme. I just don't know how. Or why.

It's a nagging idea I've been trying to let go of ever since the start of this reunion. The distance and silence between Levi and Miles speaks volumes. He didn't tell me how it went with Miles, but I haven't worried much about it. Any time I ask Levi about his history with Miles or even their conversations, he's quick to stop me. I've simply stopped worrying about it, figuring Levi will tell me when he's ready.

I spread my fingers across the sand and fan my hand across the surface, creating a half circle. Mindlessly, I draw lines in the half circle, making it look like a rainbow.

I yelp when the strap of my bikini tied around my back is quickly pulled back and let go, snapping onto my skin.

"Hey." I laugh, half rolling over.

Levi lies down beside me, sporting his signature mischievous smile. "You think you're tan enough yet?"

"No." I laugh, rolling back onto my stomach. I continue playing with the sand. I drag my index finger through the lines. "When we go back home, I want to make sure I look like I was on vacation."

"Technically you aren't."

It's a simple statement and one of fact, but still, my stomach flips. I try not to look at Levi. Not because of regret. But because I know the feelings I've harbored for him since we were in high school are true.

It's one thing to spend years building a fantasy in your head. It's another to be living it, realizing it's in fact not a fantasy. It's true and real.

Although I'm confident, I know my feelings for Levi are real, I don't know how he feels. I won't dare ask him. Despite the fact that he's followed through on his promise of us fucking on every piece of furniture before the reunion is over and him finding the smallest moments to touch me, I'm not convinced. It's hard to break a years-long cycle of routine thinking when it comes to him.

That's the issue with Levi Hawkins. Deep down, I know he's still the same Levi I came here with. Ten days on the shores of South Padre Island, pretending to be his fiancée won't change that.

"You haven't been bringing your camera with you." Levi shifts to lie on his side, placing his hand on my back. He ghosts his fingers across my skin.

I look up, seeing Miles walking along the edge of the water. He's farther in the distance and he's distracted. He's holding his phone to his ear, waving one of his hands around dramatically.

"I don't like bringing it to the beach. Too risky with the sand and the water."

"Huh." Levi nods. "You've taken pictures down here before, though."

"I have." I can't help but smile despite the uncertainty I've been feeling lately. It's odd to be having a civil conversation with Levi. Especially when it comes to carrying my camera. A fact he used to tease me about. "It's different when I'm specifically down here to take photos. I'm enjoying the beach today."

I cross my arms in front of me and rest my head on them, facing Levi.

He does the same, lying down beside me. He's wearing a simple pair of black swim shorts. He isn't wearing a shirt, displaying his perfect tanned and toned muscles.

"It's a rare sight to see you without your camera."

"I told you before, I don't always carry it with me. There's a time and place for everything. It's a habit I've tried to break over the years. I used to carry it with me everywhere."

"I remember." His two words suspend in the air between us.

I hold my breath until I can't hold it anymore. I squint my eyes, the sun shining behind Levi. "I'm surprised you wanted to come down here today."

"Why?"

"You told me you prefer the pool to the beach. Besides, I haven't seen you touch the sand aside from when you're down here for the bonfires."

He pauses, his eyes roaming over my face. "Really, I just don't like going in the water."

"Hmm." I hum, giving him a closed smile. "We might have to change your perspective then."

"No." He shakes his head. "You don't."

"Come on." I slide my arm out from underneath my head and tap him on the arm. "You can't come down here and not get in the ocean."

"It's not an ocean, Cass. It's the gulf. Technically, it's a basin."

"Whatever." I roll my eyes. "Same thing. We live in central Texas. We never get to swim in water like this."

"It's not as if I never swam in an ocean." He points to the water. "Or the gulf."

"Oh, really?" I ask him, intrigued. "When?"

"When what?" He laughs.

"When did you swim in an ocean?"

He releases an audible sigh. "When I was a kid, my parents owned a vacation house in Florida."

"Really?" Honestly, I don't know the history of Levi's family. I don't know whether he was rich or poor. All I know is that he has three brothers. All younger than him. Until the other day, I didn't even know his father passed away.

"Yeah, my mom sold it after my father passed away, though."

"I'm sorry she had to sell it. I'm sure you have plenty of memories of spending time there."

His hand stops ghosting along my skin. He stops on my lower back but keeps his hand there.

"It's not a big deal." His voice sounds far away. As if he doesn't believe his own words.

"We don't have to go in if you don't want."

"I might reconsider it."

I stare at Levi, wondering where this version of him has been hiding all along. The uncertainty of what life will be once we return to Austin hits me like a barreling train to the chest.

All of this will disappear, and I will have convinced myself this was a fantasy. It was a fantasy all along.

I'm staring into his blue eyes, listening to the waves crashing onto the shore when my phone rings. The shrill sound pings and vibrates from under my folded towel. I kept it near me in case Jonah or my dad needed me.

I haven't heard from either of them very much since I've been on this trip.

I lift the bit of towel covering my phone, my dad's name displayed on the screen.

Levi's eyes fall to it, reading it as well.

"I, um," I tell him, "I should take this."

I sit up, grab my phone, and walk toward the water. I leave Levi where he's lying and swipe the green button on my phone.

"Dad. Hi."

"Hey, Cass. I haven't heard from you in a while."

"I know." I nod, digging my toes into the wet sand. "It's been fairly busy here."

"No, it's okay. Jonah and I are doing fine here. Just wanted to call and see how things were going."

"Oh." I smile, even though he can't see me. "Is Jonah there?"

"Yeah, hang on a sec." My dad calls for Jonah and within ten seconds Jonah's high-pitched voice has taken over the conversation.

"Aunt Cass, you'll never believe it! I've missed you so much and I have big news to tell you."

"I miss you too, buddy." I laugh. "What do you have to tell me?"

"Uncle Colton and Aunt Vada bought us tickets to a comic convention in Dallas next month."

"What? That's awesome."

"Yeah," Jonah's voice calms, but only slightly. "Uncle Colton said I can even dress up if I want to. Will you help me pick out a costume?"

"Of course, buddy."

"Great," Jonah says. "I have to go. Rory came to the door and asked if I could play. Pop-Pop said it was okay as long as I check back in with him in an hour. Are you going to be home soon?"

"Few more days."

"Awesome," Jonah yells in excitement. "I love you."

"Love you too."

The phone falls silent for a few seconds before my dad is back on it.

"That boy is fast. He's already out the door." My dad laughs and the sound of it is enough to make me feel like I'm back at home.

"Now, I promised you I wouldn't ask, but—"

"Oh, here we go again." He sighs. "Cassidy. I am doing fine."

"I'm not going to ask you specifics. I just wanted to know how things were going with Joni and physical therapy."

"Things are fine. I've taken a few sessions this week."

"With Joni?" I ask, attempting to hide my relief and hope.

"No." His voice evens out, laced with a hint of disappointment. I think. "But I told you not to worry."

"I'm not worried."

"I don't believe it."

"Dad." I laugh his statement off. "It's true. I haven't been hounding you while I've been gone. Have I?"

"You're right. You haven't."

"Good." I look up from my feet to find Levi heading in my

direction. He's about ten feet from me when I hear Miles call my name.

I turn around, catching him walking toward me from the opposite direction as Levi.

"Hey, Cassidy. I was planning on taking a few of the guys out on one of the boats later this afternoon before my wife gets here in a couple days. I asked your fiancé here if you both would be interested, but he hasn't given me an answer."

"Fiancé?" My father's stunned voice is loud in my ear.

I don't answer Miles's question, too distracted by my father.

I spin around, shielding my frustrated gaze from Miles. The blood drains from my face, hoping I can somehow explain this away.

"You're engaged?" There's a hint of hurt in my father's voice and it only gets worse when Levi stands beside me, placing his hand against the small of my back.

Levi's fingers gently press into my back. "Give us a few minutes, Miles."

"Sure thing," Miles says, backing away. "We head out in a few hours, so I'll need an answer by then." I don't miss how he keeps his focus on Levi several steps before he finally turns around.

"Um, Dad, I'll call you back later."

Levi looks down, seemingly just now realizing I was on the phone and who I'm talking to. His dark eyebrows knit, and he lifts his hand, pushing the hair from his forehead. Sand falls away, sprinkling back down to the ground.

"No, you hang on a minute," my dad says. "Don't hang up. You're engaged and you didn't tell me?"

"Dad, I . . ." I bite down on my thumbnail, trying to come up with an explanation. Any sort of explanation.

"Is that whose backpack was there when you were showing me your hotel room?" he asks.

"Um . . ." I'm panicking. The blood drains from my face all the way down to my toes. I feel like melting into a puddle onto the sand, seamlessly rolling into one of the waves rolling onto the shore. I want to disappear.

But I can't. Levi must be able to hear my dad's voice. He gives me another look of sympathy, his blue eyes softening under the bright white light of the sun. A battle of tug and war wages in my brain. On the one side, I want to tell my dad no, I'm not engaged. This is all fake and an arrangement Levi and I have while we're on this trip. On the other, I don't want to disappoint him even more. Despite the pain in his voice at the prospect I've been keeping this from him, I can sense the hope he has that this might be true. He hasn't made it clear much in the past, but I know my father has held out, hoping I've managed to build a life outside of work and taking care of Jonah. Somehow, I feel as if I've stooped down to Levi's level. I don't know his true reason for creating this fake engagement. But the wobbling sensation settling into the pit of my stomach tells me we're two sides of the same coin.

I swallow when the rope is tugged in one direction, the other side losing. My urge to tell my father a little white lie won out.

"Yes." I manage to croak out a response. "I'm engaged."

"What?" my dad asks, shocked. "Who is it?"

The pain and hurt in my father's voice are clear. My stomach flips and there's a sudden ache in my chest at the thought of disappointing him. Even if this engagement isn't real.

"It's Levi."

"Levi?" He pauses for a moment. "Why does that name sound familiar?"

Levi looks at me with confusion. Surely wondering why my dad would think his name sounds familiar.

"We went to high school together. We went to separate colleges, but he works at the newspaper with me now."

"Oh." He pauses again. "Well, then, I'd love to meet him."

"Um." I shift a worried gaze up to Levi. He isn't paying attention to my conversation anymore. His fingers are tapping quickly across the screen of his phone. "Of course, Dad."

"I won't tell you I'm not a bit hurt, Cass. I'm guessing you have a good reason for keeping it quiet."

"I do, Dad. And I promise I'll tell you all the details when I can."

"Okay." He clears the emotion from his throat. "Listen, I have to go. I'm heading across the street to help Mary repot some of her flowers."

I swallow, holding back the tears building behind my eyes. "I love you, Dad. Call me when you can."

"Love you too, Cass. Stay safe."

After I hang up, I clutch my phone in my hand, tightening my fingers around it. My heart is splitting, small at first. The more seconds that pass after ending the call with my dad, reality sets in.

Not only have I lied to the one person who has taken care of me my entire life, I've managed to crush his heart. Not break it. Crush it.

I sniff and swipe at the one tear sliding down my cheek.

"Man, I'm glad Miles walked away when he did. If he stayed any longer, he might have heard your conversation."

I stare up at Levi, with watery eyes. Tears threaten to spill. He's acting as if he doesn't understand the gravity of the rift he's put between me and my father. It was my choice to tell him Levi and I are engaged. But still, it's hard not to feel a tiny bit of resentment.

"Let's just go find Miles." I sigh, walking over to gather our belongings lying on the sand. Levi doesn't speak another word as he follows, helping me. If he notices my shift in mood, he doesn't let on.

We head in the direction Miles went earlier. Levi scoops my hand into his, intertwining our fingers. And for the first time since he roped me into this situation, I don't want to hold his hand.

The longer we pretend, the harder it's becoming to remember it's not real.

SEVENTEEN

LEVI

There's been a vacant look in Cassidy's eyes since yesterday afternoon.

I don't need to ask to know why.

She lied to her dad because of me.

I haven't exactly figured out the right thing to say to her. Technically, I shouldn't care. I haven't put any effort in the past in getting to know Cassidy or the details of her life in the past. From what I've gathered, she's close with her dad. She's never mentioned her mom or her sister. I only know of her sister through rumors I heard when I transferred my senior year. The only family she's ever spoken about are her nephew and her dad.

But the hurt has been visible in her eyes and the guilt has weighed heavily on me since. I can't get the conversation out of my head. She's been quiet and distant. Nearly retreating back to her usual interactions with me. Keeping them to ones of necessity.

I'm lying on the velvet couch, staring at Cassidy from across the room. The doors are propped open, the silhouette of her hips down to her legs visible under the sheets. The darkness of the bedroom makes it almost impossible for me to see her. I've only slept in the bed once since I've been here. Even after Cassidy and I started fucking, I still slept on this ugly couch. In a way, it made a great reminder. Maybe I was deceiving myself into believing if I didn't sleep in the same bed with Cassidy, our fake engagement would stay just that. Fake.

The ugly velvet couch has served well as my boundary.

One of my arms is dangling off the side of the couch. I pick my phone up off the floor, scrolling through my notifications and text messages. There's a text message from one of my younger brothers, reminding me he's starting his freshman year of college in a few weeks. Entering on a football scholarship, much like I did, he wanted to see if I'd gift him the cleats I'd always promised him if he made it.

After replying to his message, I open my text from Zane.

Zane: Get ready, motherfucker. I'll finally be checking into the hotel tomorrow. I'm assuming you haven't beat the shit out of Miles or else you would have called me to bail you out of jail. Asshole.

I look back up at Cassidy before responding to Zane. Cassidy rolls over, turning to her other side. The sheet slides down her body, exposing her chest. She keeps one hand tucked under her cheek, her small breaths blowing on the silk pillow supporting her head.

Me: The reunion isn't over yet. I'm not making any promises.

I drop my phone and roll off the couch, landing on my feet. I stand and quietly walk over to Cassidy.

My stomach dips as I crawl into the bed beside her. I picture her furious when she realizes what I'm doing. It's a risk to climb in with her. Especially after what happened with her father.

I imagine her turning on me, looking at me with disdain like she used to. Like the day I'd thrown it back at her that I'd helped her with her car. She owed me a favor by pretending to be my fiancée. Payback.

I lift the sheet and slide in behind Cassidy. Her blonde hair is fanned out behind her and her legs are bent. I lie silently for a few minutes, thinking this is a mistake. I've crossed a boundary I've set for myself.

This isn't who I am. I lift the sheet to climb back out when Cassidy's voice breaks the silence.

"Levi?"

"Yeah?" I pause, holding the sheet up as if I'm preparing to get out.

"What are you doing in the bed?"

Her question hangs between us like a heavy weight. Her soft, hushed voice is a contradiction to it.

"Couldn't sleep." I lower the sheet back down and turn back on my side, facing her.

She doesn't move. Every bit of her body is frozen in the same position. I lay my head on the pillow and stare at the back of her head, wondering if she's fallen back asleep.

"I haven't been able to sleep either."

Fuck. Does she know I've been staring at her all night? I'm a fucking creep.

Heat expands across my chest, up to my neck. Finally, she turns around. Her eyes catch the small, tiny ounce of light filtering through the window of our room. The angles of her face are accentuated as she moves her mouth. Her pillowy soft lips are flushed a pale pink. My cock vibrates, perking at the sight of her face.

Her eyes harden as she stares at me. The blue shade of her irises frost over, like two pieces of ice. "I want you to fuck me," she whispers into the dark. "But not like the other times. I don't want you to be gentle."

I smirk, a small laugh reverberating across my chest. "I *haven't* been gentle."

I lift my hand and drag my finger across her jaw, tucking a loose strand of hair behind her ear.

She moves to climb on top of me, sliding under the sheet. She straddles me, resting a knee on each side of my torso. She's completely naked, her warm, wet pussy presses against my skin. I release a small hiss from between my teeth, my cock swelling.

She places both her hands on my chest and starts rocking her hips, rubbing herself against me. I keep both of my hands on her hips.

I don't understand whether she's upset with me. Logic tells me she can't be if she's the one who climbed on top of me. There's a hunger in her expression as she continues rocking her hips. Everything in me is telling me she's begging me to satisfy that hunger.

"Are you sure you don't want me to be gentle?" I ask her.

She spreads both of her hands across her breasts. She massages them in her palms before pinching both her nipples.

"I'm sure."

"Okay." My grip tightens around her waist, telling her I want her to stop moving. She does.

"If you don't want me to be gentle, Cass. I won't."

She bites down on her bottom lip and slowly nods.

"Place your hands on top of the headboard." She does as I say.

She leans forward, gripping both her hands around the wooden frame. Her breasts are bent toward my face. I lift my head high enough to suck one of her nipples into my mouth. I stick out my tongue and circle it around her pebbled nipple, biting down on it before falling back onto the pillow.

"Oh." She moans, rocking her hips deeper. "Fuck, Levi."

"Before I tell you what to do next," I whisper, my cock

turning hard as stone, begging to be inside her, "I have one condition. When I fuck you, I want you to scream, baby. I want the whole fucking hotel to hear me making you scream."

Her eyes spread wide in shock as she looks down at me between her outstretched arms. My heart leaps in my chest before it rattles against my ribs. She's fucking beautiful straddling me. Her long blonde hair is framed around her face, dancing across her smooth cheeks with every breath. The perfect round swells of her breasts are highlighted in what little light is pouring over us.

"Now I want you up here. Sit on my face so I can lick that perfect wet cunt of yours."

She scoots her way up, resting both of her knees on either side of my head. Her warm pussy presses against my mouth. I reach up, separating her folds with my fingers before replacing them with my tongue. Once my tongue slides across her wet slit, she grips onto the headboard, her entire body tensing above me.

"Mmm, your cunt tastes so fucking good." I find her clit, curling my tongue around it, licking it as if I'm licking the tip of a lollipop. I smirk before placing my tongue back on it. "Even better than the first time."

She moans as she grinds herself against my mouth. Digging into the words I'm telling her.

I find her clit again, this time pinching it between my teeth. She hisses. "I told you I wanted you to scream for me, didn't I?"

I move my hands to the top of her round ass, keeping her pinned. Her breasts move as she looks down, watching my mouth working her. And then she finally listens to my order.

A cry escapes her chest. She tilts her head back as I move my tongue faster. I place both hands on her ass cheeks, pressing my fingers into her supple flesh. I keep her in place as she tries to wriggle above me. I want her to come, and I want to be the reason.

"Levi, your tongue. You . . . oh god . . ." She tries to back away again. "I'm going to come unless you stop." I know she wants me inside her. But she told me she didn't want me to be gentle. So I don't plan on it.

"Cass." I grunt. "I'm not fucking stopping." She's soft and warm, and my chest swells hearing my name fall from her mouth, time after time. She repeats my name over and over. My cock pulsates and I don't know if I can hold out. Every moan and scream she lets out only makes me want her more.

Her body tightens around me, her knees closing around my head. She stops moving and I pick up my speed. Licking and sucking, pulling her into my mouth. She tastes sweet.

"Levi," she cries out. Her body quivers above me, her legs shaking as she rides out her orgasm. I only keep my tongue pressed against her long enough to finish, and then I'm quick to move.

She moves backward, allowing her arms to fall away from the headboard. She lowers herself down enough to bring her face close to mine. I tuck her hair behind her ear and grip the back of her head, crashing my mouth into hers. I bite down on her lip, tugging on it as I back away. I wrap my hands around her waist.

Without another wasted second, I move quickly. I move her to the side and crawl on top of her. "Roll onto your stomach," I tell her. "Bend your knees and lift your ass into the air."

She does as I say, displaying herself for me. I move behind her, pressing my knees into the mattress. Into the space between her legs. I press my hand into the small of her back and lean down so she can hear me. She has her face pressed into the mattress, staring off to the side. Her body is still humming with a subtle vibration from her orgasm.

"Are you sure you don't want me to be gentle?" I ask her. I need to hear her say it. My hand and cock twitching to feel her.

But there's no way in hell I would do anything to hurt Cassidy. Or upset her more. I want to make sure this is what she wants.

"Yes." She swallows. "I want you Levi. I want all of you."

I smirk, fire sparking in my chest. "Good." Keeping one hand on her lower back, I pull the other back. Without using too much force, I spank her.

She lets out a yelp, clearly surprised. My heart skips a beat and then she lifts herself, pressing her hands into the mattress. She looks over her shoulder, her blonde hair cascading down her back. "Again," she whispers.

She's panting as I smack her on the same cheek. Her back arches and her chest shudders. Her mouth falls open, her full bottom lip popping away from her top. The sensation of my hand meeting her soft, supple flesh cracks against my palm. After I spank her a third time, I smooth my hand over her cheek. A fresh, red handprint slowly appears, much like Cassidy's photos being developed in her darkroom.

"Now I know you won't forget this, Cass." I center myself in front of her entrance. "Tell me you won't."

"I won't," she says.

I let out a low chuckle, satisfied with her quick answer.

She's on all fours, her thighs pressed around mine, waiting for me.

"I'll make sure every inch of my cock is buried inside you. I'll make sure you feel it all." I pull back my hips, guide myself to her center, and thrust myself inside her. She let out another cry of pleasure, tilting her head back. It doesn't take long before I'm moving faster than the other times I've been with her.

Every thrust is harder than the last. Deeper.

I spank her again.

She screams my name.

And then she's quivering underneath me, falling to the bed in exhaustion. I pump a few more times, reaching my own release. She reaches back, holding my hand as I keep it held onto her hip. She's moaning into her pillow as I spill my cum all over her back. My cock pulsates and throbs, finishing my orgasm. When I'm finished, I grab one of the towels I'd tossed onto the floor earlier. I wipe Cassidy's back, then fall onto the bed.

She's still lying on her stomach when she turns to me. She smiles a lazy, satisfied grin as she lifts a hand, tracing it down the side of my face. The same way I did before when I'd first woken her up.

Her eyes grow heavy, her eyelids drooping with every breath.

"I'll go back to the couch."

"No," she says, tucking her hand under her head like before. Only this time she's facing me. "You can stay in the bed. I don't mind."

Her eyelids shut and her breathing evens out.

I don't know if she feels any better than she did yesterday. But if she is, I hope I'm the reason.

Trouble #4

The game between love and hate is tough. Sometimes you forget which side you're supposed to be playing for.

EIGHTEEN

Cassidy

My mind is running in a million different directions, making it hard to concentrate on one specific aspect of my life.

My father's disappointment mingles with the knowledge that he has secrets of his own. I wanted to throw it back at him, the fact he was keeping his reason for letting Joni go away from me. But with Levi standing beside me on the beach and the mounting pressure to keep up with this facade, I couldn't ask him. It wasn't the right time.

Then there was the little problem of Levi. My feelings have been all over the place. I now realize it isn't a new feeling. I've been confused ever since he forced me to sit down in his lap and dragged his finger along my thigh at the restaurant that first night. I haven't been able to look at him the same. I've learned more about him in the past seven days than I ever have before. Despite my inability to decipher the true Levi from the fake one, I still wish for him to care for me.

I'm simply hoping it isn't a foolish thought.

And then there was the matter of finishing out this reunion. I still have a job to do.

The reunion isn't over, and it doesn't matter whether or not

I've already taken a million photos. There are only three days left and something big on the final night. Miles has kept the plans under wraps. I don't know what to expect, but then again, that's the kind of man Miles is. Or so I've figured out this past week.

I slide out from under the sheets. My feet land on the carpet without a sound. Levi is fast asleep in the bed, his back turned toward me.

Last night when he crawled into bed with me, I was shocked. More so because I wasn't the least bit close to falling into the darkness. My mind couldn't shut off. Reel after reel, thought after thought continuously played. I needed an outlet. I needed a way to shut it off. I needed to feel Levi, begging for him to give me a signal that any of what we were doing meant anything to him. I wanted him to give me the dirtiest, most vulnerable version of himself. I wanted to push him to see how far he was willing to go with me.

But afterward, even when my body was still thrumming with the memory of him being buried inside me, my eyelids grew heavy. I no longer had the strength to keep them open and focused on Levi. I fell asleep feeling no closer to deciphering the truth from fiction.

Most of the night, Levi kept one hand touching my back. Until this morning when he'd rolled to face the other way. I missed his touch and haven't been able to shut my brain off since.

I tip toe over to my bag and quickly find a pair of shorts and a T-shirt without waking Levi.

My stomach grumbles when I slide them on. I swipe my tangled hair together, twisting it into a messy bun on the top of my head. I swipe my phone and room key from the side table. I look back at Levi one more time before closing the front door to the room.

I head down to the restaurant, hoping to find some breakfast. I've only been down to it a few times, grabbing a toasted bagel before heading out to the sand or back up to the bedroom to sit on the balcony. I've enjoyed watching the sunrises here.

The lobby is already filling up, guests milling about the breakfast station or deciding to sit down for full service.

I snatch up one of the cinnamon raisin bagels and spread it open, popping it into the toaster. I tap my fingers on the counter, staring out the window. The bright orange sun pours through the window. I squint and lift my arm, shielding my half-asleep eyes.

"Is this all there is to breakfast or am I missing something?"

I turn around, following the voice coming from behind me. The man standing behind me as if he were waiting in line, looks down at the breakfast area filled with pastries and coffee machines as complicated as the one up in mine and Levi's room.

His tall frame towers over me. He lifts his hand and runs his fingers through his long beard as if he's trying to figure out a math equation. Despite his rugged appearance, he seems kind.

I halfway turn and point to the podium behind us. "The restaurant serves breakfast in there. I think they put this stuff out here if you don't want to sit and dine in."

"Huh." He nods, grabbing for one of the chocolate filled croissants. He shoves the end of it in his mouth, taking a huge chunk out of it. "I think I like this better anyway. I'm not usually a breakfast kind of guy, but I've been on the road for nearly four hours. I'm starving."

"Wow." I look at the man with surprise. "You've had an early day then."

"Yeah." He laughs around a mouthful of croissant. "I can't stand leaving for trips so late in the day. By the time you get where you're going, your day is completely wasted. You know what I mean?"

I frown, tilting my head. My bagels pop out of the toaster. I quickly pick them out and drop them on a plate. "I can see what you mean."

"Are you a friend of Miles or . . ." His voice trails off as he reaches for another croissant.

I grin, stifling a laugh. "No. Not at all."

"Nice." He winks. "Neither am I."

"You don't know him personally?"

"I never said that. I simply said he wasn't my friend." He smirks.

"Oh." I look up at him as I smear a giant wad of cream cheese onto one side of the bagel. His response reminds me of the few moments Levi has talked about Miles. Showing up to the reunion as a sense of obligation or loyalty for the team. Not Miles. But although Levi's words were painted with a hint of anger, this man's is more blasé. As if he couldn't care less whether he ever spoke to Miles again. It wouldn't bother him one way or the other.

"I'm Zane." He shoves the croissant back into his mouth with a smile.

"Cassidy." I return his smile. Other than Jimmy and Paul, he's the only one who seems interested in speaking to me.

"Zane, you asshole. I thought that was you. Almost didn't recognize you with that gnarly beard. It's about damn time you showed up." Both Zane and I lift our heads as Miles walks toward us. He holds his arms out as he weaves across the lounge space between the breakfast bar and the restaurant.

"I thought you said you weren't friends." I laugh, turning back to my bagel. I'm out of ear shot from Miles. I know he can't hear my comment to Zane.

"We aren't," he quickly mutters from the corner of his mouth, plastering on a fake smile.

Once Miles reaches us, he pulls Zane in for a quick hug and slap on the back.

"Sorry I'm late," Zane says. "My nephew was born this past week, and I stuck around to help my sister."

"No problem," Miles says with that signature fake grin of his. "The important thing is you're here now. I see you met Hawkins's fiancée. They work together at the newspaper."

I'm licking a small dab of cream cheese from my finger when I turn to look up at both men. Both sets of eyes are pinned directly on me, but both are sending completely different signals.

Miles looks pleased with himself to have pointed this little fact out. Zane looks as if he heard he would be charged one hundred dollars for the croissant he's munching on.

"You mean Levi?" Zane asks, not knowing whether to look at me or Miles.

"Of course," Miles says, laughing. "Who else would I be talking about?" Miles points to me.

"Hawkins is a fairly common last name, no?" I ask, hoping to ease the immense amount of confusion on Zane's face. He hasn't stopped looking at me since Miles said I was Levi's fiancée.

Miles shrugs his shoulder while Zane stands in front of me like a statue.

"I guess it could be," Zane says.

Then, as if the blood in his veins has suddenly started pumping again, his eyebrows dip in confusion. "You said you work with Levi?"

"Yeah, I do. I'm the photographer for the paper." The blood drains from my face, prickles making their way down the back of my neck.

My stomach flips. Something tells me Zane knows Levi

more than their other teammates. Jimmy or the other guys never looked at me in this way for this long.

I bite down on my bottom lip, inhaling a deep, calming breath. If he suspects I'm a fraud, I'm hoping he won't blow my cover right here in front of Miles.

"Cassidy is great. I've been excited for my wife to get here. She's bummed she's missed most of the reunion." Miles turns to me. "I think she'll like you. Something tells me you two will get along."

I attempt to give him my most convincing smile. "I bet." I place the top half of my bagel on the other and wrap it in a paper towel. I've never wanted to get back to the room more than I do now. I need to get away from Miles, and I need to get away from Zane's inquisitive stare.

"I'll see you both later." I hold my bagel up, pointing it toward the elevators. "It was nice meeting you, Zane." I give him a curt nod and duck my head, moving around both men.

"See you later, Cass." Miles says, behind my back. I cringe, lifting my shoulders as I shuffle my feet across the marble tile. I hate how he used my nickname.

I don't take a breath or a bite of my bagel until after I've stepped off the elevator and stuck my key card into the slot on the door.

When I step inside the room, I drop my bagel on the table. I'm not hungry anymore. I pout, disappointed with myself. Miles's hotel may be over the top, and being surrounded by dozens of retired football players may not exactly be my definition of a great time, but the bagels are the one thing I enjoyed. Well, that and Levi.

Speaking of the devil himself, after I drop my bagel on the table, I spot Levi in front of the coffee machine.

He moves swiftly in front of it, dropping the coffee in effortlessly. It's a completely new sight from the one I saw that first morning here.

He turns his head as he places his mug underneath the spout. "Hey, I was wondering where you went. Do you want some coffee?"

Simply put, it's unfair to see him this way. Reeling from my conversation downstairs and with the uncertain feeling our secret will be exposed, it's a shock to see Levi when I feel this way. I'm wondering if last night changed anything for him, looking for any sign whether he thinks of me differently.

His dark brown hair is tangled, sticking up in entirely too many directions to be considered presentable. But for him, it works. He's completely naked, the dips and planes of his abs and hips continuing on for what seems like forever. The man is covered head to toe in muscle. The orange glow from the morning sun is reflected in the bright blue hue of his irises and the stubble lining his jaw is thicker than it was yesterday.

Heat blooms between my legs, remembering how it felt to have that same stubble grating across my folds.

I'm almost wet for him again, but stop myself from taking it too far before I'll be able to hold myself back.

"No, thanks," I tell him, giving him a small smile. Small but genuine. "I'm going to take a shower."

I hate how this morning has made me feel like a fucking coward. In every way possible.

NINETEEN

LEVI

"Open up, motherfucker." Zane's voice booms across the hotel room from the other side of the door. It drifts all the way out to the balcony where I'm standing. I'm leaning against the railing, facing the inside of the hotel room, waiting for Cassidy to get out of the shower.

The morning sun is warm on my bare back. I hate to leave where I am, but when Zane's fist pounds on the door, I reluctantly move.

"I swear to god, Levi." *Boom.* His fist hits again. "If you don't open up this door" *Boom.* "and expl—"

I swing the door open before he has the chance to finish. He pokes his head inside the threshold but stays where he is.

"I thought you were going to text me when you got here?" I ask him, confused. "Why were you banging on the door and yelling? Besides, how did you know what room I was in?"

He strokes his beard several times before he slides his hands into his pockets. "I saw Jimmy in the lobby and convinced him to tell me which room you were in."

"Of course you did." I lift my hand and brush it off my forehead.

"I didn't text you when I got here because I was starving and stopped in the lobby to get breakfast," he explains. He keeps his hands in his pockets and leans back, studying me.

Creepily, his eyes move up and down as if he were examining me.

"What's wrong with you?" I ask him.

"The better question is how the fuck my best friend is engaged and conveniently forgot to tell me."

"Oh, shit." I run my hand down the side of my face, realizing I haven't told Zane about mine and Cassidy's arrangement. "Jimmy told you, didn't he?"

"No." He crosses his arms. "He didn't. Miles did, but not before I met Cassidy down at the breakfast bar." His eyes catch the bagel she placed on the table before she went into the bathroom. "She's in here, isn't she?"

"Fuck." I sigh, pinching the bridge of my nose. "Yes." I squeeze my eyes shut, trying to think of a way to explain this to Zane.

"Now, I know you're an adult man but you . . . Levi Hawkins . . . engaged?" His eyes spread wide. "I don't necessarily believe it because let's face it, I don't believe over half the shit that's ever come out of Miles's mouth. But if it's true, there better be a good fucking explanation."

"Come on." I tip my head back, inviting him into the room. Before I shut the door, I peek down the hallway, hoping no one from the team heard. The room I'm staying in is only one of two on this floor, so I'm thinking I might be in luck.

Zane follows me out to the balcony. I snatch my T-shirt from the foot of the bed and quickly toss it on before heading outside. The sun is already warmer than it was when Zane first showed up. There isn't a cloud in the sky, allowing every single ray to beam down on us. Zane sits in one of the patio chairs. I reclaim my spot, leaning against the railing.

"So," Zane says. He drapes his arm over the back of the chair. "Feel free to start."

"Cassidy is the photographer for the newspaper I work for."

"Huh." He nods. "She mentioned that when I met her."

"We also used to go to high school together." I hold my breath. It's the first time I've ever told anyone the connection between Cassidy and I. No one at work knows. None of my other friends know. It's a secret Cassidy and I have kept well hidden.

"Wait a minute . . ." Zane stops, pointing over his shoulder. His face shifts into recognition at the same time I realize I told him about Cassidy when I got hammered at a team party. I had never spoken about her after high school until then and I haven't since.

But somehow, my best friend seems to recall the story impeccably.

He has his thumb hitched over his shoulder, pointing to the room. I crane my neck to get a better view of inside, hoping Cassidy isn't out of the shower yet.

Zane's eyebrows shoot upward, arching across his forehead. "You mean, that's the same Cassidy you've—"

"Yes." I stop him from finishing his sentence, my stomach twisting into knots. "I know, I know. Don't continue with what you're saying. I got it. I remember."

He laughs. "Of course, you remember. Shit, even I remember it and it was the one night. Although, I think it's because I couldn't get you to shut up. Either way, you haven't mentioned her since. What are the odds you get a job at the same newspaper as her?"

I ignore his question.

"I was drunk that night and didn't know half the shit I was saying." It's a lie. I know exactly what I was saying. I just regret telling Zane. "By the way," I whisper. "Can you keep your fucking voice down? I'm not sure if she's out of the bathroom or not?"

"Fine." He raises his hands, whispering back. He's sitting back in his chair, looking up at me with narrowed, skeptical eyes. "I don't get it, though. Knowing how you've felt about her all this time, I thought this would be what you wanted. I mean, congratulations, man. Considering who your fiancée is, I still don't understand why you didn't tell me."

"Well . . ." I consider telling him the truth about mine and Cassidy's situation. Zane is my best friend. Has been since we first met in college. But then again, if I tell him the truth, I'm worried he won't understand.

My decision to bring Cassidy in and have her play as my fiancée was a game time decision. Born out of selfishness and pride. Born out of the ego everyone has always assumed I've had. It's a game time decision I'm quickly regretting.

But I'm only regretting it because the longer we put on this charade, the harder it's becoming to keep up with. I'm losing the ability to decide what's considered taking it too far and what's not.

Fuck. I've probably already crossed that line. I'm just too chicken shit to admit it.

I decide to go with the truth, not having the energy to keep up with the lies.

"We're actually not engaged." I toss the truth out there, letting Zane take it for what it's worth. I don't elaborate and I don't offer another explanation. I cross my arms and wait for the flood of questions that are sure to come out of his mouth in a matter of seconds.

"What?" He blinks, shaking his head. "I'm confused."

"Look." I sigh. "I don't want to explain it all right now." My head pounds. My body feels as if I've played an entire four quarters of football on absolutely zero sleep. "I will tell you that when I told my boss about the assignment, she was all for it, but only if Cassidy came along to take photographs to go along with the article. The first night we were here, I was eating dinner in the restaurant in the hotel, listening to Miles and . . . then Cassidy walked into the room. She walked into the room at the right time, I guess. I saw the opportunity, and I took it."

Even I sound like an asshole to myself as I quickly explain the story to Zane. I know my reasoning for deciding to convince everyone Cassidy is my fiancée isn't exactly justified. But that night my defenses were down, fueled by a history of competition and jealousy. I'm not the first one to admit it, but the closer I've grown to Cassidy these past few days has made me realize how weak I was that night.

I add it to the list of truths I'm too afraid to admit out loud.

I leave out the part where I've been sleeping with Cassidy, not exactly sticking to the typical rules of a fake engagement. Although I was willing to tell Zane about mine and Cassidy's fake engagement, he doesn't need to know all the details.

He doesn't question me any further. A small part of me feels relief. Only a small part.

"Dude." He shakes his head. "I'm not sure this is a good idea."

"Come on," I say. "There are only a few more days left. Cassidy and I have made it this far without anyone questioning us or prodding for more details."

"I don't know. I think you're in over your head on this one, but . . ." He considers me for a moment. My stomach wrenches again, seeing the look of apprehension written across his face. Zane usually keeps up with the appearance of being a tough, hard as nails kind of guy. But the look on his face tells me he gives the same one to the kids he counsels at his school.

He sighs, his shoulders falling in defeat. He still isn't fully convinced.

I snap my head up when Cassidy emerges from between the two open French patio doors. Her wet hair is tied up into a high messy bun, a few strands of her blonde hair framing her tan face. She's changed into a long sundress, the bottom dancing above her bare feet. Her teal-colored dress has thin straps wrapping around her shoulders. The collar dips low and there's a long string of buttons running down the front. As she crosses the patio, one of her bare legs is exposed, a slit on the dress driving all the way to the top of her thigh. Wrapped around her neck are two tiny strings. If I had to guess, she's wearing a bathing suit underneath.

"Cass." I push off the balcony railing.

"Hey." She grins, the sun catching her bright green eyes. She stops when she sees Zane sitting in the patio chair. She points to him. "Zane, right?"

"Yeah." He nods, grinning.

Cassidy shoots me a look of confusion before turning back to Zane.

"Zane is my best friend," I explain to her.

"Oh." Her grin widens as she shifts her attention back to Zane. I'm thankful he at least gave her a good first impression. Or so I can tell.

"He just got in this morning."

"I know, I heard," she says, smiling. She turns to Zane. "Congratulations on becoming an uncle, by the way."

"Thanks." Zane grins. I can see the thoughts working in his mind. He's replaying our conversation from earlier. The one where he brought up the night I couldn't stop talking about the girl from high school.

Silence falls between the three of us.

I cough, scratching at my chest. I need to tell Cassidy that Zane knows about our fake engagement. "He knows. I told him."

Cassidy snaps her head back in my direction. Surprise is written across her beautiful face.

"That we're engaged?" she asks.

"No," I say, shaking my head. "I told him the truth."

"Oh." She slowly nods her head, understanding what I mean. "Okay."

"He won't expose us." I attempt a laugh, but something in Cassidy's expression causes my chest to squeeze.

Her expression is flat, her full bottom lip pouting more than usual. The blue in her eyes darkens as she blinks several times, as if she's trying to blink the darkness away. She gives me a small reassuring grin, but I don't buy it.

"That's a relief then."

I can feel Zane's gaze bounce between us. He sighs, slapping his knees as he sits up. "Well." He puffs his chest in a stretch. "It's been a long fucking morning, and I barely checked out my room. I'll meet you both later."

"Okay." I nod.

"What are the plans for today?" Cassidy asks me.

Earlier when she was down grabbing her still uneaten bagel sitting on the table inside, Miles had texted me with a plan for today.

"Miles texted me when you went down for breakfast." I cross my arms. "He said he wants to take us on his yacht before we play another game of football. This time he wants to play on the beach before we all get together tonight for dinner."

"His yacht?" Zane asks, blowing a breath between his lips. "Why does this not surprise me?"

"Do you not know Miles?" Cassidy asks, laughing. "The man nearly owns this entire beachfront. He even took us to a vineyard he barely manages."

"That's because his wife manages it."

"He told you that?" Cassidy asks.

"Yeah, ever since I told Miles I planned on writing a story about him in our paper, he's been slowly coughing up more information."

"So you told him you were writing a story?"

"Yeah." I nod, uncrossing my arms. I take a step closer to her. "Remember the other day when I went to go down and talk to him? I told him then."

It's then I realize I never told her that Miles agreed to me publishing a story on him. I'd stopped her midsentence and crashed my mouth to hers, fucking her in the bathroom.

"That's good." She's giving me the same expression again. Darkness fills her gaze, but it doesn't last long.

"Will you text me when you're heading out for this yacht trip?" Zane asks. I'd almost forgotten he was here. "I'm going to take a nap. I'm beat."

"Sure," I tell him.

I wait until Zane leaves the patio before I close the gap between me and Cassidy.

She's still standing in the middle of the patio. A few strands of her drying hair blow in the subtle breeze. I lift my hand, tucking one of them behind her ear.

"Everything okay?" I ask her.

She hesitates, twisting her mouth. I fight the urge to crash my mouth to hers in the same way I did the day I came up from talking to Miles.

"I'm fine."

"Are you sure?" I tease, dragging my thumb down the side of her face. She sighs, her eyes fluttering shut with the motion. She opens them again.

"Yeah, I just realized you never told me how your conversation went with Miles."

"Oh, yeah, well . . ." I wrap my arm around her waist. "I was a little distracted when I got back."

"You were?" she asks, her mood lightening. She stands on her toes, bringing her face to mine. Her mouth sits on the outside of my ear, her breath blowing against my skin.

Prickles make their way down the back of my neck and spine, causing me to wrap my hand around the back of her head. My fingers thread effortlessly through her hair. "I have a confession to make." She whispers. I lean farther into her, pressing my cheek to hers. Her body effortlessly molds to mine, even when she's standing on her toes. I hold my breath, waiting for her confession.

"I was a little distracted too."

TWENTY

Cassidy

Living in denial is a double-edged sword.

I don't know how we got here. One minute Levi was looking at me as if I was the most hated person in the world. Now, it's as if he hasn't been able to keep his hands off me.

Part of me wants to know why he feels so different with me. At first, I convinced myself it was because of our fake engagement. Pretending to be fiancés made for an easy excuse to sleep with one another.

But the more he touches me and has normal conversations with me, I'm convinced there's more to it than that.

"Okay, I have an idea." Miles is sitting across from the fire pit, his strong jawline highlighted in flickering orange.

The lights from the hotel blend with the fire, keeping the beach half lit with the night life surrounding us.

I'm sitting on Levi's lap. His hands are resting on the tops of my thighs, near the bend of my hip. I lean back against him, holding my half-empty margarita glass in my hand. I swirl the half-melted liquid around before taking another sip. The sour green icy mixture slides down my throat, causing my cheeks to pucker.

"What's your idea?" Zane asks. He's sitting a few seats over from me and Levi. Jimmy sits between us, sipping on his third beer. On the other side of me is the first woman I've seen show up for the reunion. She's the girlfriend of another one of the teammates. I spoke to her for a while when we took the short trip out on Miles's yacht. She was sweet, but incredibly shy. Even more so than me. She hasn't spoken much since we sat around the fire. She's observing the group much like I did when I first met the team. The rest of the guys are circled around the fire, Miles on the opposite side.

"In the tradition of this being a reunion, especially one coming to a close, how about we play a game?" Miles asks.

Half the men groan, the other half stay silent. I look between all the men, wondering what game Miles is considering. Levi doesn't make a sound indicating whether he cares one way or the other, but his fingers twitch on my hip.

Miles's chin is tipped up, his eyes pinning to Levi behind me, as if he were challenging him.

"What's the game?" Levi asks, breaking his silence. His voice vibrates across my back, warming me from the inside out.

Miles laughs. "Truth or Dare."

"Hell no," one of the men yells.

"Are you kidding me?" another guy asks.

Levi's hand twitches again.

"Come on." Miles laughs again, pushing his blond hair off his forehead. "We can make it even more interesting. Every time someone can't act out their dare or is proven to be deceitful, they have to take a drink."

Some of the group falls silent while the others begrudgingly agree. Again, Levi stays silent.

Miles smirks. "Sounds as if the team stands undecided. What do you say, Hawkins? As former captain of the team, let's leave the decision up to you?"

I don't hear Levi give an answer, but Miles doesn't give him one.

"Or would that make it mine?"

Immediately, I feel my eyebrows knit in confusion. What is Miles talking about?

Levi's hand twitches again.

"Let's play." His voice is foreign, escaping his chest as hard as steel.

"Great." Miles claps, his body humming with excitement. He leans back in his chair and points to the group. "We all good to play, then?"

"Yeah." The group collectively agrees.

"Who should we start with?" Miles asks. He surveys the group. "This would be a lot more fun with my wife here, but you crazy lot will have to do for now." Several of the guys chuckle along with Miles.

"Jimmy." Miles points to him. "Why don't you go first? Truth or Dare?"

"Oh." Jimmy adjusts in his seat, resting his arms on the armrests of his chair. He holds his bottle of beer between his fingers. "Truth, I guess."

"Is it true," Miles asks, "you lost the winning field goal the night we dared you to eat one hundred tacos because you stayed up all night the night before playing D&D online?"

"What the fuck?" Paul yells. "Are you telling me that's why we lost?"

A few of the other men mumble and groan under their breath. I even hear Levi groan behind me. Clearly, this is still a point of contention between them.

"Whoa," Miles says. "He hasn't answered yet." There's a sly grin plastered to his usual fake grin. But this I can tell is genuine. He's eager to know the truth.

Jimmy's eyes widen as he looks at the group. With a panic-stricken look, he sighs, his shoulders dropping in defeat. "Yes."

The group immediately starts shouting, Zane kicks sand up at him. He shields himself from the grains of sand spraying him, attempting to explain himself.

"Hear me out. Let me explain," he yells, his voice turning gravelly. The group quiets down. "I was in a D&D league." The group yells again, Jimmy's explanation getting lost over them. He continues, despite the boos and heckles.

"There was a tournament that night and I couldn't let them down. I'm sorry. But I was really into D&D back then."

"Back then?" Zane asks, stunned. "It was only over a year ago. You don't play anymore?"

"No," Jimmy says, defeated. "I haven't played since that night since it caused me to lose the winning field goal the next night at our game."

"You motherfucker." Miles laughs, pointing at Jimmy. "I knew it had to be over some bullshit like that."

"Whatever." Jimmy waves him off. "Now you guys know the truth. Can we move on?"

"Not until you take a drink," Zane says.

"That's only if you can't answer truthfully," Jimmy says.

"Not in this case, Jim. You cost us the game for that shit. Drink up." Zane laughs again, shaking his head.

Jimmy lifts his beer to his mouth, and the group moves on.

After Jimmy finishes his drink, it's his turn to ask the next person. He asks Paul. He takes a dare. Jimmy dares him to go down to the edge of the water and drink a handful of it. With a scrunch of his nose and the curl of his lip, he backs out. He takes the punishment of downing the rest of his beer.

The guys move around the circle, each of the team taking their turns. Most of them opt for truth. But not the girl I'd met earlier. After she successfully accomplishes her dare, she hands her turn off to Miles, for his second. By the time it goes to him, Levi and I have yet to go.

As if he were reading my mind, Miles's gaze hardens, laser focusing in on me and Levi.

"Your turn, Hawkins," he says, tipping his chin up. "Truth or Dare?"

Levi takes his time answering. His grip stiffens on my hip. Instinctively, I place my hand over his. His rigid body relaxes only slightly at my touch. The thought of my touch calming Levi down melts the ice that once formed in my chest for him. It's as if these past few days have allowed me to see past Levi's hardened exterior, chipping away at the frozen wall he's always had between us.

"Truth," Levi finally says, curling his fingers even deeper into my hip.

"Perfect." Miles says, already sporting a satisfactory grin even before he's finished his question. "True or false? You wish you got to play starting quarterback during the playoffs of our senior year. Instead of me."

Levi's hand stiffens, this time it's noticeable. In fact, his whole body goes rigid, and his chest doesn't move. I try not to appear too confused as to why Miles's eyes seemed to brighten as he waits for Levi's answer and why Levi's grip is growing more intense the longer he holds his breath. I rotate my head far enough to see Levi's expression. His mouth has thinned into two thin lines. The muscles in his jaw tick, the movements of them highlighted by the crackling fire.

At first, I think he won't break his attention away from Miles, but he proves me wrong when his eyes shift to me. He doesn't move his head, keeping it facing forward. But his eyes shift to me long enough to send me a message.

He's using me as an anchor to keep himself from giving into what Miles clearly wants. To piss off Levi. Although Levi hasn't answered Miles, the expression on Miles's face tells me he doesn't need to answer him. The hesitation and Levi's steeled expression tells him all he needs to know.

I push away the confusion settling into my bones at the true history between Miles and Levi.

How bad could it possibly be for this sort of standoff? One man pitted against the other. Since the beginning, it's been a never-ending tale of challenges between the two men. Since day one, Levi has even been skeptical of Miles's motives in inviting him here to the reunion.

I think back to the day he'd confided in me, telling me he wasn't entirely sure why he'd booked Levi one of the second-best rooms in the entire hotel.

Curiosity eats away at me, but I swallow it down, knowing Levi isn't exactly enjoying this game of truth or dare. He's already hating the question Miles has thrown at him. I look around at the rest of the guys sitting in silence around the fire. Most everyone's eyes are on Levi, a few of the men are looking down at their hands resting in their laps. The tension on the beach is palpable. If I had a knife, I could cut through it as easily as a bowl of Jell-O.

I look at Zane. He's leaning over in his chair, resting his elbows on his knees. His head hangs low as he looks to the ground, digging his feet into the sand.

The next words out of Levi's mouth surprise me. But I seem to be the only one. The other men simply shake their heads as if they'd already known what Levi was going to say.

"True." Levi cocks an eyebrow, his eyes narrowing to two slits on Miles. "I'd trained for years to get there."

Although Levi answered Miles's true or false question, he takes a drink from his beer anyway. The mouth of the bottle presses against his lips. He closes his eyes, inhaling a deep breath through his nose. He doesn't look in my direction.

Silence falls over the group, and I'm waiting for the moment when someone calls to end the night. But they don't.

It's almost as if everyone is too afraid to speak up or stand up to Miles. Maybe it's because every word out of Miles is an indirect insult, making you question whether or not he means to be condescending.

Miles continues to sport his satisfactory grin, clearly not reading the group's sudden shift in mood. "All right, Hawkins. The only one left who hasn't played is your fiancée."

I wave my hand and shake my head. "Oh, no. That's okay, we don't have to."

"Come on," Miles says. "Everyone else got to go once. It's only fair."

I sigh, not wanting to argue anymore. Here I am, clearly as guilty as everyone else for not speaking up. I let Miles continue only for the sake of not causing a scene.

"Wow." Miles grins, cocking one eyebrow. "Two for one turn?"

"Sure." I shrug, hoping this will be quick and painless. Miles doesn't know me as well as Levi.

"Okay, okay." Miles's eyebrows straighten, creating a shelf of concentration above his deep-set eyes. They're almost menacing, in a sense. I hold my breath, anticipating what I'm going to choose. "Cass, truth or dare?"

I chew on the inside of my cheek, unsure what's the safer option. Usually it's truth, but I'm terrified of answering any question that might give Levi and me away. "Dare," I quickly mutter.

"Huh." Miles nods. "Interesting. I thought you would have gone with the safe choice and pick truth."

"Are either of the choices really safe?" I ask him.

Miles lets out a small laugh. "Point well made, Cass."

Levi's hand twitches on my hip again. My stomach wobbles

with excitement. I know it's because Miles used my nickname. Twice.

"Come on." I give him a smile. "Lay the dare on me."

Miles looks around the circle before bringing his eyes back to mine. "I dare you to kiss any of the guys here, but it can't be Levi." He smirks. "It can be on the cheek, of course."

My mouth falls open, stunned by Miles's dare. The uncomfortable sensation settling in my chest only grows the longer I stare at him. Aside from the fact that technically Levi and I aren't engaged, or even in a relationship, Miles doesn't know that. Regardless if we are in fact together, it's beside the point. Miles shouldn't be asking me to kiss anyone. Even if it's on the cheek.

"What?" I ask him, still unsure whether I heard him correctly.

He holds his hands out as if waiting for my answer. "Who's it going to be?"

Before I even have the chance to tell Miles I won't even bother taking the drink, I'll just end the game, Levi is lifting me from his lap.

Despite his rigid frame, he gently moves me aside as he stands. I gasp, unsure what he's doing.

His biceps are swollen, stretching the sleeves of his T-shirt. His hands are balled into fists and his jaw is ticking with anger. There's a fury in his normally bright blue eyes. His feet move quickly, kicking the sand up behind him with the few steps he takes toward Miles.

"Fuck you, Miles," Levi yells. "Fuck. You."

A few of the other men stand, understanding what's happening quicker than my mind is able to process. Zane is suddenly standing beside Levi, holding onto his arm.

The blood drains from my face, unsure of what to do. I'm watching Zane hold Levi back. He turns his body toward Levi, pressing his shoulder to his to keep him from walking. Levi doesn't move his focus away from Miles.

When I finally bring myself to look at Miles, the blood drains from my face. He's sitting the same way he was before. Leaned back in his chair, one leg bent and resting on the other. His eyes flickering with amusement and his mouth curled into a permanent sneer.

This was the ultimate challenge to Levi, and he knows he's already won.

I turn my attention back to Levi. He's standing with his hands clenched into two tight fists, as if he is ready to deliver a blow to Miles.

But he backs away the more Zane urges him to. I don't hear what he says to him, but within seconds, Levi's backing away, grabbing onto my hand and pulling me away from the group.

I try to keep up with him, my bare feet sliding and digging into the sand.

My mind races, trying to get a grip on the scene that unfolded in front of me. My breath is lodged in my throat and my heart is pounding in my chest, rattling to escape. I can't discern what's happening or where Levi is taking me. All I know is the group behind us is still buzzing with adrenaline. Their voices mix and mingle, growing quieter the farther Levi takes us down the beach.

I force myself to take a breath and run my tongue across my mouth, thinking of an explanation. Even if Miles's dare was innocent, why did Levi get so upset? It's not as if we're *actually* engaged or in a relationship. Why would Levi get so visibly worked up to the point of wanting to fight Miles?

"Levi, wait," I say, tugging my hand on his.

He takes my hint and stops. He doesn't immediately turn around to face me. He stands in front of me and inhales a deep breath. He looks up to the sky, working his fingers back and forth, curling them in and out.

For what feels like minutes but is probably only seconds, he finally turns to face me.

His breathing is ragged as his eyes soften the longer they stay on me. I can tell he's trying to calm down, but the blood visibly boiling under the surface of his skin says he's anything but.

"What the hell happened back there?" I ask him, letting my irritation get the better of me. I hold my arm out behind me, pointing to the group.

"I'm sorry." Levi pants, still catching his breath. He lifts both of his arms in the air, resting his hands on his head. He weaves his fingers together, taking deep breaths. He looks up toward the sky as if he's trying to come up with an explanation. "I just—I don't know how—"

He sighs in frustration.

I cross my arms over my chest. "Miles is an asshole."

Levi scoffs, as if it's an obvious statement. He's right. It is.

"But even still, I don't understand." I continue, tilting my head and staring up at his tall frame. "What happened?"

He slowly backs away from me, his eyes filling with sadness. Or regret. Or pain. I can't tell.

I've never seen Levi this way. It makes me feel as if I've never truly known who he is, despite all the times I claimed I did. My chest feels hollow, despite the way my heart is beating as if I've run a marathon.

He pauses, considering what to do. The frustration builds inside him like a pot of boiling water, threatening to spill over. He hesitates before taking a step forward. He holds his hand out, then quickly withdraws it. He takes a step back. Then another.

His eyes shift to the group and the fire behind me. Without another glance in my direction, he takes another step back.

"I'm sorry, Cass. I need a moment. I just need to get the fuck—" He shakes his head as if finishing his sentence is tough to swallow. "I don't know." He runs his hand across his mouth, exhaling a deep sigh.

I'm speechless as I watch him spin around and walk farther down the beach. I don't know where he's going. I don't follow him, and I don't stop him. My feet are heavy and weighted, as if they're sinking into the sand the longer I stare at his back. Once Levi disappears into the darkness, I turn around and start making my way back. Each step is difficult to make. I try not to glance over my shoulder, constantly reconsidering my decision to let him walk off alone. Maybe I should have gone with him. Then again, I saw the pain in his eyes.

I'm nearly back to the hotel when I stop in my tracks and stare up at the man standing in front of me.

TWENTY-ONE

Cassidy

"Zane?" I narrow my eyes, unsure if it's truly Zane standing in front of me. The light from the hotel is shining behind his shadowy figure. His entire body is covered in shadows. His beard is the only feature I'm able to identify him by.

I walk closer to him so I'm able to see him better.

"Where did he go?" he asks me. His hands are shoved into his pockets and he's looking past my shoulder, into the same darkness Levi walked into. He must have watched us head down the beach before Levi took off on his own.

"I don't know." I sigh. "He didn't tell me. I think he needs time to think."

"Yeah, I had a feeling this was going to happen. Honestly, I'm surprised they lasted this long without fighting."

The cool night air brushes across my face. A few strands of my hair fall around my face. I tuck them behind my ear as I look to where we were sitting only minutes ago, playing the worst game of truth or dare I've ever played. The fire is already put out and the space where Levi and Miles almost got into it is dark and deserted. Everyone is gone. I don't even see Miles. Zane and I are the only ones left from the group.

I ask him the same question I asked Levi. "What was that all about?" I can't help it. My curiosity is eating away at me, and I can't fight the incredible weight of sadness pouring over me. This night has turned to complete and utter shit.

Zane winces, clenching his teeth and hissing as he breathes in. "If Levi hasn't told you yet, I'm not sure I should be the one to tell you."

I take a step closer to him, bringing myself farther into the light coming from the back of the hotel. He's standing near the edge of a brick wall. The wall opens up to a small set of stairs leading up to the pool area and patio.

He leans against the wall, clearly conflicted.

Guilt seeps its way into my veins. Although Levi and I aren't technically together, I want to be with him more than I do standing in front of Zane. And although I know Levi is probably the better source of information, I can't help but want to get some sort of story out of his best friend. He must know something.

I bite down on my bottom lip and quickly scan the beach and patio surrounding us, making sure no one is around to hear us.

One of the hotel employees is off in the distance, wiping down the lounge chairs surrounding the pool. But I know he wouldn't be able to hear us from where we're standing.

"I know you and Levi are best friends," I say, "but I'm not sure if he's ever mentioned me to you before. Honestly, I don't see why he would. Even though he started at the paper not too long ago, I knew him a few years ago."

Zane doesn't move or flinch. The expression on his face doesn't change. He isn't giving me any indication of whether he already knows the history between me and Levi.

I continue anyway. "Levi and I went to school together our senior year of high school. We weren't in the same circle of friends and outside of school and football games, I never saw him. In fact, until a few days ago, he hated me."

"Oh." Again, he doesn't change his expression. Even when he moves to lean against the brick wall. He crosses one leg over the other at an angle and crosses his arms over his chest. His thick muscles strain against his shirt.

"I just wanted you to know." I swallow, unsure if any bit of what I'm saying matters. "Before we leave in a couple days." I don't know if Zane has any interest in my history with Levi, but I'm hoping by telling him the truth about me and Levi, he'll tell me the truth about his past with Miles. Or some version of it.

Zane looks to his right, where Levi disappeared. "That's assuming Levi hasn't already left yet."

"I don't think he has." I place my hand on my chest, convincing myself he wouldn't. "I don't think he would do that when this story is on the line."

Zane shakes his head and looks down at his feet in the sand. "I shouldn't have convinced him to come."

"What do you mean?" Part of me feels like Levi or Vada, fishing for a story. I hate the way it's making me feel, as if I'm digging my nose in where it doesn't belong. This is why I should stick to taking pictures.

"I was the one who told Levi about this reunion," he admits. "His invite was sent to his spam folder, so he never even saw the invite come through his email until I brought it up and told him it would make for a great article in the paper. But I should have listened to my gut when I suspected Miles's invitation."

"Why?" I ask him. "I mean, Levi told me he and Miles have a history of competition, but I didn't understand exactly what he meant by that."

He pushes his hair off his forehead with a groan. The weight of what he's about to tell me is building inside him. "We were in summer training about to start the preseason of our senior year."

Zane starts telling me the story and I hold my breath, hoping I can finally get an answer. I sit down on the step, wrapping my arms around my knees.

"Miles and—" He pauses, considering how to continue. I already know he won't be telling me the whole story. "Miles and Levi had a misunderstanding one night."

"A misunderstanding?" I ask him.

His gaze shifts, landing on me. His hardened exterior crumbles, his eyes softening. He shakes his head slightly, only once, letting me know that's how much he's willing to tell me. "It's hard for me to explain, but basically, Levi ended up getting injured. He'd broken several bones in his hand and a few in his wrist. Multiple surgeries over several weeks kept him from playing. Miles was our backup quarterback, so when the doctor told Levi his injuries were basically career-ending, Miles essentially took his place on the team. We ended up going to the state championship and winning. I think it hit Levi harder than he thought it would. I mean, it hit the team as well. But ever since we ended that season, Levi hasn't talked about football or even played. Well, until this past week." Zane's eyes fall to mine. "He told me about the day on the field."

I think back to it myself, remembering how Levi nearly flipped out on Miles after he'd gotten the cut above his eye.

My stomach aches, twisting and churning. Levi was forced to quit football. Not out of choice.

"So, he resents Miles for replacing him on the team?" I clarify.

Zane presses his mouth into a thin line and nods.

A sadness washes over me, the ache in my stomach growing.

I look up and down the beach, hoping to see Levi walking back up to meet us. My shoulders fall when I don't see him.

"He might have gone back to your room," Zane says. He pushes himself off the wall and starts heading back up the stairs. He rubs his eye with the heel of his hand.

"How do you know?" I stand, placing my hand on the railing.

"I don't." A small laugh rumbles from his throat. "It's a guess. Come on, I'll walk with you to the elevator."

I follow Zane to the elevator in silence. We don't continue our conversation from outside and we don't talk about Miles.

I have more questions, but I know my answers don't lie with Zane. They're with Levi. But after seeing the pain and regret in Levi's usual bright eyes, it's not the right time. Hell if I'm ever going to know exactly what Zane meant by a *misunderstanding*.

I replay my conversation with Zane the entire ride up the elevator. It's as if I'm trying to put together a puzzle, but all the middle pieces are missing.

Did Levi get injured during a game? What really happened between Miles and Levi?

Even though my head is still clouded with questions, there are a few that I have answers to. I now understand why Levi was hesitant to come here. The last time he'd been with the entire team was when he was overshadowed by Miles. The last time he was with them, they'd gone to the state championship without his help. And if there's one thing I know about Levi, it's that until his senior year of college, football was everything to him. Absolutely everything.

My heart crumbles thinking of the loss Levi must have felt. The pain he felt knowing he'd never fully heal enough to play professionally.

Before the elevator reaches my level, it stops a few floors down, letting Zane off.

He says goodnight to me before he steps off, disappearing

behind the doors before I have a chance to see him make it to his room.

My crumbling heart beats erratically in my chest the closer I get to my floor. I hold my phone in my hand, checking to be sure I don't have a text or missed call from Levi. But I have nothing. I figure I'll check the room first. If he isn't in the room, I'll head back down to the lobby and check around the restaurant or pool for him. Maybe even the beach.

The idea of him leaving the hotel is still a possibility. We drove separately to the reunion. My stomach flips at the thought of him leaving early, driving hours into the night back to Austin.

When I step out of the elevator, I take my time walking to the door. I don't know why my nerves are rattled. It's as if I've been shaken up inside and turned upside down. I can't keep my thoughts straight and every inch of my body is vibrating from both physical and mental exhaustion.

I know Levi and I are here for a job. He's supposed to be writing a story. I'm supposed to be taking photographs. But somewhere along the way, the lines have crossed and been drawn out of focus. I'm no longer worried about the article or getting back home, putting distance between me and Levi. All I can think of right now is finding him.

I open the door to our room, stepping into total darkness. Not a single light is on. The room is shadowed in a hue of dark blue, reminding me of the sky before the sun completely sinks behind the horizon. Only the sun has been gone for hours. There's a heavy weight of silence spreading throughout the room.

I slide out of my sandals, looking around the room. "Levi?"

I call out his name but don't hear him answer. Instead, when I step farther into the room, I find the balcony doors spread wide open. Through the course of our trip, it isn't unusual to find the doors open. But we've never left them open when we aren't here. Levi must be out on the balcony.

My suspicion is confirmed when my feet meet the concrete slab.

I find him sitting in one of the patio chairs. He's slouched, resting his back completely against the seat. He's resting both of his arms on the arm rests, staring out at the nearly invisible horizon. Storm clouds are rolling in off in the distance. Their deep gray and blue tones contrast against the pitch-black sky. Thunder rumbles in the distance as a cool breeze floats across the balcony. The wind brushes against my bare legs, separating the slit of my dress even more with each step I take closer to Levi.

"Hey." I stand in front of him and give him a weak smile.

"Hey." He looks up, moving his eyes away from the water. One corner of his mouth lifts, almost as if he's relieved to see me.

"I was hoping to find you up here." I stick my foot out, sliding it between his parted legs. I rest it on the edge of his seat and bend it. My dress falls away from my leg, exposing all of it. I'm hoping to cheer him up a bit. Tonight has been heavy, even without Zane filling in a few of the details. I'm a mess on the inside, but the sickness swimming inside me has toned down since I've laid eyes on Levi.

"You were?" The corner of his mouth that was curled into a smile grows. He's amused.

"Yeah," I say, pressing my toe into the edge of his seat again. This time, I send him a genuine smile. "It would have fucking sucked if I had to search all of South Padre for you. I don't think I'd be mentally prepared to put in that kind of effort."

"Huh," he says, leaning forward. He closes his legs slightly, keeping my foot between his legs. He wraps both of his hands around my ankle, sliding his fingers around to the back of my calf. "Are you saying you wouldn't go searching for me if I went missing?"

A slight bit of sadness spreads across his gorgeous face. The all too familiar ache in my chest returns. I hate seeing him this way.

He's changed out of what he was wearing down on the beach. His bare chest stands out against the darkness, the dips and planes of his muscles contracting with every breath. A perfect v dips down to the waist of his black sweatpants. The fabric is loose around his legs, the ends resting above his bare feet.

I watch as his fingers ghost along my leg. My eyes focus on the three scars drawn across the tops of his fingers of his right hand. Each faint line stretches from his middle knuckle to the last, connecting to his hand. I have never noticed them before.

I take in his truth, not wanting him to know Zane told me only a fraction of his history with Miles. Bringing it up now will only upset him more and although Zane didn't come close to telling me the whole story, I don't want Levi to be upset with him.

Zane was only trying to appease me.

"I'd go searching for you if you were missing," I admit. And if his question were asked in a game of truth or dare, I'd be telling the truth.

"That's good to know." His eyes shift to his hands still ghosting along my leg. His smile disappears, replaced by a frown. It's an expression I've seen too often tonight. He snaps his head up, his eyes meeting mine. "I'm sorry I left you on the beach, Cass."

"Stop." I shake my head. "It's okay."

He shakes his head fervently, keeping his hands on my leg. "It's really not. I shouldn't have left you alone."

"I wasn't alone." I shrug. "I ran into Zane on my way back into the hotel. He walked me to the elevator."

He quietly nods and his shoulders only relax slightly. I leave out my conversation with Zane.

"Levi." His name falls from my lips without effort. He looks back up at me as he slides his hands farther up my leg. He grips the back of my knee, gently moving my leg to his side.

"Come here," he says, leaning forward and grabbing onto my hip with his other hand.

I part my dress and straddle him, resting my knees at his side. My skin presses into the wood of his chair, but I don't care. I wrap both hands around the back of his head, grazing my nails across the nape of his neck. He wraps both arms around me, holding me to him. My ass is resting perfectly between his parted legs.

My chest is in line with his face and he looks up at me with widened, lazy eyes. "Cass, there are things I need to tell you."

I remove one hand from around his neck, placing my fingertips to his mouth, stopping him. "You don't *need* to tell me anything."

He closes his eyes and opens them again. He wraps his hand around mine, lowering it between us.

"I don't *need* to. But I *want* to tell you. I *should* tell you."

I replace my hand around the back of his neck. I move the other one and place it on his cheek, brushing my fingers across the arch of his eyebrow.

"We don't have to right now. I know it's been a long night and with everything going on . . ."

"Yeah." His deep, velvety voice is hidden behind his whisper. "There's so much shit, I don't even know where to begin."

His eyes search mine as if he's hoping to find an answer in me.

"Here might be a good start." I bend down, lift the corner of my mouth in a smile, and crush my mouth to his.

The salty scent of sea water and the mint on Levi's mouth surrounds me. I get lost in it as he continues to slide his hands around my waist, pulling me in deeper.

I rock my hips, pushing them into his lower stomach. He moans against me as if the longer I stay connected to him, the more I'm healing him from whatever is tearing him apart on the inside.

The way he moves his hands across my body is different from all the other times we've been together this past week. Usually, and fitting for his personality, Levi is dominant, taking charge and ordering me where to go. But tonight he's laid himself bare and vulnerable. He's completely at the mercy of my touch.

My stomach sparks with fire, knowing I'm eliciting this type of feeling out of Levi. For years, I wondered what I'd done to make Levi look at me with disdain. But now he's looking at me as if he needs me to simply stay above water.

I take it, my chest swelling at the idea.

"Come here," he says, the same way he did earlier. Only this time, I can't possibly be any closer. But when he slides his hand between us, I know exactly what he means. "I need to feel you."

His hardened cock presses against me, my bikini and his pants keeping me from feeling him slide between my folds.

I'm already wet for him, remembering what it feels like to have him inside me.

I lift myself off him enough for him to free himself through the front of his sweatpants. There's an opening in the front and it's nearly effortless on his part. His cock springs to life the moment it's free.

I lean forward, pressing my stomach against it. I crash my

lips back on Levi's. He bites down on my bottom lip and I moan as I buck my hips once again.

His chest vibrates against mine as I bring my mouth to the hollow of his ear. "I need you inside me too," I confess.

He reaches under my dress and pulls on the string to my bikini. It falls away from my hip. Then he works the other. I lift myself again and he pulls my bikini out from under me.

"Fuck," he says when I sit back down. "I don't think I'll ever get over how this feels." His eyes flutter closed as he tilts his head back.

"What will?" I breathe out, rocking my hips. His cock slides between my wet folds, but he still hasn't pushed inside me yet.

"You," he says, opening his eyes. He lifts one hand, threading his fingers through my hair as he grips onto the back of my head. "I don't think I'll ever get over how it feels to have my cock slide inside of you and to have your wet pussy surrounding me."

With his admission, I lift up and center myself over him. I slowly sit back down as his cock slides into me. When I get him all the way in and I'm sitting back down, I don't immediately lift myself up again.

I keep him inside me, feeling his cock swell and pulsate. He pins his gaze to mine. The sharp blues of his eyes shimmer against the moonlight above us. I rock my hips slowly, keeping him inside me. I don't want this feeling to ever go away. I don't want to move. I want to stay here, like this, with my arms and legs wrapped around him, his face pressed against my chest.

He presses his cheek against my chest, parting his lips along the swell of my breast. Hot breaths dance across my skin, his teeth gently grazing my flesh every time I move my hips. With every forward and backward motion, and every lift of my hips, pulling him out of me only slightly before pushing back down, I'm healing him. From the inside out.

He raises both of his arms behind my back, gripping onto my shoulders from behind. He guides me, keeping me from falling apart too quickly. We move slowly, in rhythm, listening to the sound of our breaths blending with the water down below.

Even though I'm on top of him, he's pouring every ounce of energy into me. His arms grip around me tighter, his fingers press into my shoulders, holding me close to him.

He slides his face away from my chest, pulls one hand from my shoulder. He presses his hand to my cheek. His thumb presses into my cheekbone and his fingers thread through my hair.

My skin dampens the more I move above him, but he doesn't seem to care.

Levi keeps his eyes pinned to mine. They're spread wider than usual, growing brighter with every move I make. His eyes search mine as I rock my hips harder. His cock pulses inside me and my entire body tenses. Heat spreads across my thighs and my chest expands. It's as if hot air is being blown into my chest. It bursts and disperses through my veins.

I gasp as my body tenses and shudders above Levi, reaching my orgasm. I fight the urge to close my eyes. I want to see Levi. I want him to see what he does to me.

"Fuck, Levi. I'm coming." Shaking, I bite down on my lip as I rock into him once more. Almost immediately, Levi does the same. His arms harden, his muscles tensing as he holds me in place. His cock pulsates, spilling himself inside me. If it weren't for the fact that I'm already on birth control, I'd be worried about how much I've allowed Levi to orgasm inside me. But there's something to be said about having him come inside me. The feeling is more intense and each of our orgasms lasts longer than without. Or maybe I'm saying that because it's Levi.

Levi doesn't close his eyes either. He watches me, unwavering as he orgasms. His breaths are deep, as if he's using his entire body to complete them.

Once he's finished with his orgasm, I don't immediately pull away from him. I leave him inside me.

"Cass." His eyes swell with sadness again. My heart breaks, unsure what to say. It's as if what we'd experienced has only acted as a temporary bandage. He still remembers what happened down at the beach.

I don't speak a word. Instead, my chest swells with confidence for the first time. Confidence in knowing I'm falling for Levi. And a small part of me believes he might feel the same way.

I lean down, grab onto the side of his face, pull him up to me, and slam my mouth to his.

TWENTY-TWO

LEVI

I've never felt so broken yet complete at the same time.

I'm lying in bed with my hand raised in the air, staring at the three scars permanently etched into my skin, stretching from one knuckle to the other. I flex my fingers repeatedly, convinced if I do it enough, they might disappear. But that's a foolish notion. My fingers don't even bend the way they used to. The tendons in each finger are tense and swollen, like a rubber band stretched to its limit, about to snap.

I'm stretching my fingers, thinking back to last night and Miles's stupid fucking game of truth or dare. It wasn't so much of the game itself, or the question he'd asked me. It was the dare he'd given to Cassidy.

Until last night, I'd given Miles the benefit of the doubt. I had hoped he had changed for the better over the past year, somehow believing he'd let go of what had happened between us before he'd given me the three scars I now have on my hand.

But he didn't. He'd thrown back what happened, using Cassidy in the process. And I nearly lost it. If it hadn't been for Zane and the other guys holding me back, I'm not sure I'd be lying here in bed with Cassidy.

I turn to my side, facing Cassidy's back. The sheet is half draped over her smooth as velvet skin. She smells like sand, salt, and vanilla. I breathe her in, watching as the sun catches a few of her blonde strands. They shine in the golden light. My chest squeezes, unsure of what's going to happen once this reunion is over, and we head back to Austin tomorrow.

I'm trying not to think of it, keeping my focus on Cassidy. She's the only person in this whole goddamn hotel that doesn't make me feel as if I'm losing my mind.

Her long blonde hair is splayed out behind her. I reach up, playing with a few strands. They slide between my fingers, brushing over my scars. The thought of going back home and back to work stirs in my stomach. All the times I'd brushed Cassidy off, refusing to speak to her more than necessary. All to keep her at a distance. It was my safest bet. But now, after the past eight days, I'm not so sure it is anymore.

I'm playing with Cassidy's hair when she stirs beside me. She rolls over with a groan, her eyes still closed.

She slowly cracks them open, peeking up at me. "Good morning." She grins and I swear it's the most beautiful smile I've ever seen in my fucking life. My chest explodes with a feeling I've never felt before.

I bite it back, remembering I need to sort this out before we head back to our real lives in a few days.

"Good morning."

"How long have you been up?" she asks, tucking her hands under the side of her face.

She's lying on her stomach, completely naked. The sheets slid down her body as she turned. They're wrapped around her legs, exposing her perfect, round ass.

I lift my hand and trace a finger down her spine, stopping above the curve of her cheeks. She wriggles underneath me.

"Don't get me all worked up, Mr. Hawkins," she mutters against her hand.

"Mr. Hawkins, huh?" I ask her, grinning.

"It has a nice ring to it." She shrugs, stifling a laugh.

"Don't worry," I tell her. "I already know if I get you started, I won't be able to stop either. And we have shit to do today."

"What are the plans today," she asks, a hint of amusement sparking in her eyes, "Mr. Hawkins?"

"First, I have lunch with the entire team, followed by a game of football."

She adjusts her head to face more toward me. I can see the shift in her eyes. "Do you think you're up for it after last night?"

She's hesitant to press me on what happened last night. She'd told me she met with Zane on the beach after I'd walked away. From what Cassidy said last night, I don't believe Zane told her the truth of why I'd gotten so upset with Miles. If he did, she would have said so last night.

I push through my uneasiness and remember there's only one more day left of this reunion. As much as I'm weary of popping this bubble I've created with Cassidy, I know I can survive today. I'm just hoping I don't kill my jaw and the inside of my mouth from how much I'm going to be biting my tongue and grinding my teeth to keep it together.

"I'll be fine," I tell her, hoping to ease her worry. "I'll be with Zane and Jimmy. If Miles says any more shit to piss me off, they'll have my back. But I need to go if I'm hoping to get more info out of Miles for this story."

"You still plan on interviewing him?"

"I have to. I'm a journalist. We get the story no matter how we feel personally," I tell her. "But you don't have to worry too much, I'm keeping my interaction with him to a minimum. Luckily, I got the bulk of my notes this past week."

"Okay." She sighs, her shoulders relaxing. "Do you need me to go?"

"Not if you don't want to. We're mostly going to be talking and playing football. Nothing new." To be honest, I'm dreading our little game of football. Until last week, I hadn't played since before my injuries. Not a full structured game anyway. It's different when I've tossed the ball in the backyard with my brothers. Playing with my old team is on a completely different level. Thankfully, we aren't playing for points.

I wrap my arm around her back, bringing my face close to hers. "But I will want you with me tonight."

She turns, pressing her body to mine. Her breasts push into my chest, and she hitches one leg over mine. I slide my hand all the way down her back, to the curve of her ass, down to the back of her thigh. I grip her flesh, keeping her leg hitched over me.

"What's tonight?" she asks.

I curl my fingers around her thigh, pressing them on the inside of her leg. "A dinner."

She gasps, her eyes fluttering shut. "A dinner?"

"Yes," I tell her, not moving my hand. She told me not to get her started. My already swollen, hard cock is telling me otherwise. But I ignore it, knowing I need to be getting ready soon. "Dinner at the restaurant."

"Oh, where this all started then?"

"Yeah." I laugh. "I guess so."

"Wow." She rolls her eyes. "I love how Miles had talked up this reunion so much, but we've done pretty much all the same stuff. He hasn't shown us much of the city."

"I agree." I laugh, loving she's able to see through Miles's bullshit as easily as I do. It makes me feel better to know I'm not the only one in this world. "Then again, my expectations have never been high."

"Great," she says, giving me a playful snort with a roll of her eyes. "Now what am I supposed to wear to this dinner? Is it casual or fancy?"

"If it were up to me," I slide my hand back up to her soft cheek, "you'd be naked." I grip onto her flesh, then snap my hand back, popping my hand onto her skin. She yelps, shocked I've given her a light smack.

"But since it's not . . ." she says, her eyes lighting with fire.

"Since it's not." I smirk. "I'd say a dress should do."

"Hmm." She hums. "Maybe I should go out while you're at lunch and see if I can find something new. I've worn all the dresses I brought with me."

"Sounds like a plan," I tell her, flipping onto my back. I pull her with me. She straddles me. Her knees press into the mattress on either side of me. Without a second thought, she slides my cock inside of her. She slowly starts rocking her hips back and forth, lifting herself. I don't move, allowing her to take the lead.

"I thought you said to not get you started."

"Looks like you already did," she says. "Now when you go to lunch, you won't be able to stop thinking about this. And me."

Her breathing gets louder and deeper with each thrust.

"It would be impossible not to," I tell her. "Just promise me one thing."

"What?"

"That when you go out shopping in town"—I swallow, fire igniting in my lower belly, my cock sliding easily in and out of her—"you'll come back to me."

"I promise, Levi. I promise I'll come back."

Trouble #5

**Falling in love with someone you hate is the hardest
fall of all.**

TWENTY-THREE

Cassidy

I type the address into my GPS and put my car in drive. It's been forever since I've driven my car. Any time Levi and I have gone anywhere, he's insisted on driving his truck. I don't think he wanted anyone to see we'd driven separately or speculate why we would.

But now that I'm in my own car, I'm missing his company. Admitting to myself that I miss Levi is an intimidating idea.

To be away from him feels foreign, as if a piece of myself is missing. It's a stark reminder of what it will feel like to drive home tomorrow. I'm still unsure of where we are or where we stand.

Surely, our fake engagement won't extend beyond this reunion. It isn't part of our deal. But then again, neither was sleeping with each other.

Right?

If we continue this, will we officially be together? Will I want to introduce him to my dad? Will *he* want to meet him?

Each scenario I bring up only makes my head spin even more.

Maybe finding a dress and grabbing some lunch by myself

will help clear the fog that's clouded my brain over the past few days.

Like a photograph being developed in a dark room. At first, the image is out of focus before it all comes together.

My stomach twists and flips with uncertainty.

"Fuck, I need to get out of here," I mumble to absolutely no one. I consider calling Vada or my dad, but decide against it. I need this time to think. Breathe and think.

The GPS takes me to a shopping center a few blocks from the hotel. I pull into the parking spot outside the small brick building and check my phone.

There's a text from Levi. I've only been gone for fifteen minutes and he's already texting me.

World's Best Fiancé: Any chance you can send me photos of you trying on dresses?

Me: No. I didn't bring my camera.

World's Best Fiancé: Normal people don't take photos like that with their fancy cameras, Cass. I meant with your phone.

I let out a laugh, considering going back to the hotel. I'm sure Levi wouldn't mind.

Me: Maybe.

World's Best Fiancé: Don't make me beg . . .

My chest burns and my stomach flutters.

Me: Hmm, I think I'd like to see you beg.

World's Best Fiancé: Fuck, Cass. You're making me regret going to this lunch without you.

Me: Why's that?

I'm playing with Levi. From the sound of his text and with how quick his replies are, I already know why he's regretting it.

World's Best Fiancé: I'm sitting at a table surrounded by the entire team and my cock is hard as a fucking rock for you.

Me: Oh, no. You should probably take care of that.

World's Best Fiancé: Turn around, come back to the hotel, and take care of it for me. Right now.

Me: I'm not sure that's such a good idea. I need to find a dress for tonight.

World's Best Fiancé: Fine. But try to be a little faster. I won't stop thinking about you the entire time you're gone.

Me: I think you'll manage.

I don't wait for a reply from Levi. I lock my screen and drop my phone in my purse. I inhale a deep breath before stepping out of the car. The conversation with Levi has caused me to go wet between my legs. I can already feel it soaking through my panties. Knowing he's sitting at a table of over twenty of his former teammates, thinking of me with a persistent erection turns my insides to mush. I'm melting from the inside out.

Once I've calmed my heart and cleared my head enough to step out of the car, I head inside the store. It's a small boutique. Bathing suits and beach cover-ups hang from tall silver racks outside the store. The breeze blowing in from the shore causes the pieces of clothing to sway in one direction. The hangers clang against the metal rods.

When I step inside, I welcome the cool air. Even though it's a small boutique store, likely owned by a local to South Padre, the inside of the store is bigger than I expected. The brown cement floor gleams against the black walls. Outside the store offered beachwear. The inside is covered in wall-to-wall dresses.

I start on one side, a bright teal dress catching my eye. I sift through the dresses, eventually making my way to the floral patterns when a woman moves to stand beside me. At first, I think she's an employee. Until I get a better look at her.

A large pair of black sunglasses are perched on her head, pushing back her near perfectly straight long blonde hair. It's a few shades darker than mine, several chunks of brown woven in with her highlights. Her lips are painted a pale shade of pink. They're nearly as shiny as the concrete floor we're standing on.

"This place has the best dresses," she says, picking one of the teal ones I was looking at when I'd first made my way over here.

I give her a sheepish grin, grabbing a floral one and draping it over my arm. I absentmindedly grab a yellow and black one as well. "That's what all the reviews said."

She grins, displaying blindly white straight teeth. This woman seriously looks like she stepped directly off a runway. Her long, flowing red dress wraps around her small frame. She's tall yet thin. Her dress slits down her left leg, displaying a single toned tan leg. Her feet are wrapped in a simple pair of wedge heels.

"Seriously," she says, waving her hand, "my husband picks on me all the time for coming here. But when you have as many charity balls, business meetings, and functions as we have, you have to keep your options open. Know what I mean?"

There's a slight southern twang to her voice.

A small, humorless laugh escapes my throat. I give her a weak smile. "Yeah."

I don't get what she means. This woman reeks of money and entitlement. Even if she looks similar to my age.

I set aside my first impression of her. To be honest, despite the slight bit of snobbery in her southern drawl, she's been kind to me.

"Are you from around here?" she asks. She stops sifting through the dresses and turns toward me.

"No." I shake my head. "I'm from Austin."

"Oh, I love Austin." Her eyebrows shoot across her forehead. "I used to visit quite a bit when I was in college. I'm originally from Houston, though."

"Nice," I tell her, unsure of what to say. I settle on the

handful of dresses I have draped over my arm. "I've always wanted to visit Houston, but I haven't had the chance."

"Girl, you aren't missing much. I'm so glad my husband brought us out here after we were engaged and started opening his chain of hotels. I think I could stay here for the rest of my life." She frowns, tossing her head back and forth in thought. "Actually, I kind of have to at this point. Or else my farm will go to shit."

"You own a farm?"

She waves me off with a lilted laugh. "I call it my farm, but it's a vineyard."

"Wait," I say. "Is your husband Miles Deacon?" My stomach quivers, silently hoping I'm wrong. Not that this woman isn't sweet. But the idea that I've been standing here chit-chatting with Miles's wife is mind blowing. What are the odds?

"Yes." She beams. Her smile broadens, spreading from one ear to the next. "Do you know him?"

"Oh." I shake my head, trying not to sound disappointed. I don't want her to know I think her husband is an asshole. "Yeah, I'm staying at the hotel right now."

"Really?" Her eyebrows knit, her brown eyes glittering under the lights. "How do you know him?"

"My fiancé is part of the reunion." I leave out Levi's name, not knowing if she knows him. I don't want to cause more problems than necessary.

"You're engaged?" she asks, shocked. "Congratulations."

"Thank you." I nod once, finding myself grinning more than I probably should, considering I'm a liar.

Her eyes fall to my hand, holding onto the dresses. "Do you not have an engagement ring?"

Her face falls with genuine curiosity, as if she's disappointed in not finding my finger adorned with an egregiously gigantic rock. Like the one on her finger.

I look down at my hand, spreading my fingers. "Not yet." I blush. "He only asked me a few weeks ago. It was a spur-of-the-moment kind of thing and we haven't picked one out yet."

I justify my lie, knowing not all of it is false. Our engagement was spur-of-the-moment.

She opens her mouth, but I stop her when I lift my arm. The one covered in dresses. "Anyway, that's why I'm here. I'm looking for a dress to wear tonight for the dinner at your vineyard."

"Oh my gosh." Her grin has returned, her curiosity about who my fiancé might be has dissolved. She sifts through the dresses on my arm, picking out the flat red minidress and the one covered in gold sequins. "Well, in that case, I think these would look stunning on you tonight."

"Really?" I ask her, biting down on my lip. Normally, I don't put much stock in what I choose to wear. But tonight is different. This reunion has been spent with an incredible amount of effort on mine and Levi's part. I want to make sure I look my best.

"Absolutely." Despite her enthusiasm, I at least find it genuine.

"I normally don't wear red, but I figured since tonight is a special occasion, I might try something different. That and my fiancé might like it." It's funny how the lie has so effortlessly rolled off my tongue. Almost as if I'm speaking the truth.

"It will, and I'm sure *he* will." She clasps her hands together. Her gold purse bounces off her hip as she leads me to the dressing room.

The woman working behind the counter sees us heading in that direction. She pulls out her key and unlocks one of the doors for me. She grabs the two dresses from my arm and hangs them on the two hooks inside.

I stand outside of the room, holding the door open.

Miles's wife doesn't follow me. She stays just on the outside of the rooms. "I can't stay long," she admits. "I technically only came in to grab a new clutch for tonight and got distracted. I've been standing here long enough, and I know if I don't get over to the vineyard, the caterers will be lost without me."

"I thought the dinner was at the hotel," I say, confused. Maybe Levi had gotten the location wrong.

"It is." She grins. "But all the wine and appetizers are being brought over from the vineyard. Or so Miles says."

"Ah." I nod. "Sounds great. I had a bit of wine the other day when Miles took us on a tour of your vineyard. It's a beautiful place, and the wine was delicious."

"Thank you." She grins in appreciation.

"I guess I'll see you tonight, then." I half shrug.

She laughs, adjusting the strap of her purse on her shoulder. "Absolutely." She starts to turn around but stops, holding up a finger. "Oh, shit. I didn't mean to be rude. I didn't catch your name."

"Cassidy," I tell her.

"It was nice to meet you, Cassidy. I'm Lindsay." She grins again. "I'll be the one holding onto Miles's arm all night. That's if he can break me away from the caterers and staff." She laughs before spinning on her heel.

She's headed toward the front where all the purses and clutches are displayed.

I close the door behind me and step out of my clothes, knowing that if all else fails tonight, I'll at least know someone other than Levi and the rest of his old team.

TWENTY-FOUR

LEVI

I've always fucking hated parties.

It didn't matter if they were high school parties. College frat parties. Even my boss's farewell party a couple weeks ago. Every party I've ever been to has been dreadful.

The only thing giving me the motivation to leave our room and head down to this party is Cassidy.

She's the most beautiful woman I've ever seen in my fucking life. I've known it since the moment I laid eyes on her the first time she'd stepped onto the field our senior year. The same camera she'd had that day is clenched in her delicate fingers. But she's grown from the girl I'd seen that first day.

Tonight her long blonde hair is curled around her face, a few strands near her temples pulled back and braided. It cascades down her back, the ends dancing across her bare shoulders. Her lips are colored a bright red. The same shade to match her dress.

She's a mix of elegance and sexiness, all wrapped into one.

"We should probably head out." She crosses the room, heading toward the front door.

"No one will miss us." I stop her. I lift my hand, ghosting my fingers along the edge of her jaw. Her bottom lip separates from her top, creating a small gap wide enough for her to inhale a small gasp. A fire sparks inside me whenever I see her react to my touch. It fucking turns me on.

"Yes, they will." Her eyes flutter closed, her black eyelashes rest on top of her cheeks. She opens them again, this time she pins her eyes with mine. "Are you sure you're okay to be around Miles?"

"Yes." I roll my eyes, giving her a small reassuring smile. "I told you I would behave. I did earlier when we were at lunch and at the game."

It's true. I didn't ask Miles any questions for my story. I didn't need to. Miles has always loved to hear himself talk.

At this point I'd gotten all the details and background I'd need to write Vada and the paper a killer story. All while avoiding the history between us.

As far as the game went earlier, I'd only managed a few plays before my fingers grew tense and the familiar pain shot through my joints. After that, I'd happily sat on the sidelines and cheered Zane on, along with some of the other guys. All the while, I'd ignored Miles's sneering expressions and muttered comments.

He hadn't said much to me after last night and part of me hoped he wouldn't for the rest of our trip.

"Where did you eat lunch?" Cassidy asks. We haven't spoken much about the details of today. I assume she hasn't asked me in fear she'd spur on another conversation about Miles, and I know she'd rather avoid it. Especially after last night.

"We ate at this little pub farther down the beach after we played our game."

"I thought you were eating lunch at the vineyard," she says.

"We were, but a few of the guys convinced everyone to eat there instead."

"Huh," she says, nodding as she walks over to the table near the front door, grabbing onto her purse. "Well, I think we should get going before the others notice we're late."

"Either that," I say with a laugh, "or Zane will kill me for leaving him alone down there."

"I'm thinking that would happen first." She giggles.

I lead her out of our room, letting the door click shut behind us. I keep my hand wrapped around hers the entire way to the elevator until we step inside, and I click the button for the lobby. The doors slide shut.

I can't help it. I stare at Cassidy in the reflection, my eyes roaming across her body. All the way from her eyes down to the tips of her toes peeking out from the bottom hem of her dress.

"I thought I pegged teal as my favorite color on you, but I think I might have a new one." I slide my hand across her bare back, feeling her smooth skin. The dress is similar to the ones I've seen her wear on this trip, but it's not quite the same. It's long, flowing down to her ankles. A long split in the fabric drives all the way up to the top of her thigh. The back dips down dramatically, stopping just above her curves. It's as if she's upgraded her usual casual beach dress.

"I normally don't wear red, but I like the way it fits. A woman at the store suggested it for me." She adjusts the top hem around her chest and looks down.

I reach across and grab onto her chin, turning her head to face me. "You look beautiful."

"Thank you." She sighs, the corners of her mouth curling into a smile. Her bottom lip spreads out, and I fight the urge to press my mouth to hers. "You clean up pretty well. How did you sneak a suit in that tiny ass backpack of yours?"

She reaches out and slides her hand down the front of my

forest green tie. She wraps her fingers around the end, pulling me toward her. She quickly pulls me down to her, crushing my mouth against hers. Her move takes my breath and when she pulls away, it takes me a moment to regain my composure.

"I may have snuck off to a store myself after lunch."

"Ah." She wraps her fingers around my tie again, pulling me down to brush her lips against mine. "Well, I think I like this look on you. Are you ready?" A small chuckle vibrates against her chest.

"Not really." I sigh, not entirely sure if she's asking if I'm ready for the party. Or if she's asking if I'm ready for this trip to be over. There's still a sea of unknowns floating around in my head. Although I know how I feel about Cassidy, I'm uncertain how much it will affect us when we get back to our normal lives.

I don't know if we can continue this back home.

She releases my tie and wraps her hand around mine again, threading our fingers. "It doesn't matter whether you're ready or not."

"Why's that?" I ask her, my eyes moving from her eyes to her mouth.

The corner of her mouth curves as her eyes shoot up and to her left. "Because we're almost to the lobby and the doors are about to open."

I snap my head to my right, looking up at the number one displayed on the screen at the top of the button panel as the doors slide open.

My stomach wobbles and the blood drains from my head, prickles making their way down my neck.

Cassidy's hand on mine is holding me together. I didn't expect to feel this way stepping out here. But when we follow the signs, directing us toward the back patio, my nerves seem to knot even tighter. Something about tonight feels final.

This reunion has opened old wounds for me. Stirred up memories I've been foolishly hoping to forget for the rest of my life. But being out of college for over a year was plenty of time to rip them open. Although the wound has been open, I'm still stupidly hoping I leave this place without throwing salt onto it.

At least then I can recover and move on with my life.

Cassidy and I follow the signs until we step through two open patio doors leading to the enormous, paved patio. All the tables and chairs that are usually scattered across the area have all been removed. They're replaced with small round bar height tables. There are no chairs surrounding them. Each one is decorated with a white tablecloth and a single candle situated inside a lantern.

"Wow." Cassidy looks around. "We are in the same hotel, right?"

"I think so." I scratch my chin, looking for Zane. The entire back patio and beach are filled with the hotel guests. This isn't just our old team. It's Miles's entire guest list and then some.

Several servers are weaving in and out of the tables, small silver trays perched on their hands. Some are carrying drinks, others little bits of food. They don't even look big enough to take in more than one bite. A few servers are carrying bottles of wine with the Deacon name on it. Wine from Miles's vineyard.

"Let me know if you see Zane," I absentmindedly say, scanning the crowd for him.

"Are you kidding?" Cassidy laughs, pulling onto my hand as she lifts her chin and attempts to stand on her toes. "I can barely see over their heads."

I smile, finding it cute how invested she is in finding Zane. A warmth spreads across my chest.

"Come on." I tug on her hand. "Let's see if we can find them over by the pool."

Cassidy and I shove our way through the crowd. The closer we get to the pool, the louder the music gets. A band is set up on the opposite side of the pool, playing music that seems to fit the beach theme going on. The sky is pitch-black, the lights from the hotel sparkling across the surface of the water.

"I think I see him." I stop, following Cassidy's eyes.

Zane is standing near the hot tub, talking with a few people I don't recognize. He has a glass of wine in his hand, but from what it looks like, it appears he hasn't touched it yet.

Once we make our way over to him, he looks up with a grin.

"You know, I was worried you two wouldn't show up."

"Why would you think that?" I ask, trading glances between him and Cassidy.

"Aside from the fact I've been here for an hour already, Miles has circled back over to me about three times, mentioning he hadn't seen you two yet."

"Why does he care so much?" Cassidy asks.

Zane shrugs, leaning on the table with his elbow. "Fuck if I know. Why does that man care about anything?"

"He's a cocky bastard, that's why," I mutter, grabbing two glasses of wine as one of the servers passes me.

I hand one to Cassidy.

She playfully slaps my arm, smiling against the rim of her glass. "You're the worst."

"I'm glad to see your opinion of me hasn't changed." I take a sip of wine. It slides down the back of my throat, warming my empty stomach.

Zane looks between me and Cassidy, confused. I haven't told him about Cassidy and me sleeping together. I can already hear his voice, urging me to tell her the truth. But I can't.

Because even now, when I've felt Cassidy's touch the past ten days and felt her mouth press to mine, it's all been for show. It's all been a ruse.

Even if I told her, I doubt it would change the situation we're in.

Zane shakes his head with our comments and inhales a deep breath. "Miles's wife is supposed to be here tonight. Maybe that's why he's been hounding me, asking about you."

"Why?" I ask. "So he can rub it in my face that he's married? So he can show me he's got the upper hand by snagging a wife before me?"

The words stumble from my mouth before I could even consider taking them back. Even if I wanted to, I know I can't.

Cassidy turns to face me, an expression of confusion immediately filling her gorgeous face.

She knows Miles and I have always been competitive. That much I've shared with her. But the curiosity about my comment tells me she's wondering if there's more hidden under the surface.

I ignore her apprehension for now.

"I thought she was already supposed to be here. A few days ago."

"She was, but she got held up at a few out-of-town business meetings," Zane explains. "I heard the receptionists talking about it at the front desk."

"Have you met her yet?" I ask him.

He shakes his head, but Cassidy's answer has me turning my attention to her.

"I did, earlier."

"Really?" I ask her, stunned. My eyebrows arch across my forehead.

"Yeah." She shrugs, nonchalantly. "I met her when I went shopping earlier. She seemed nice."

I swallow again, wondering why Cassidy didn't mention it until now. Maybe she didn't think it would be that big of a deal.

But the longer we stand here, the more I notice her avoiding my gaze. She brings her glass to her mouth again, taking a large gulp this time.

"You talked to her?" I ask, trying not to seem too eager to know details. Honestly, it's none of my business and I shouldn't care about Miles's life or who he marries. But the familiar feeling of envy for the life he built settles in my bones the same as it did my first night here.

"Yeah," Cassidy says. "She was sifting through the dresses next to me. Eventually, we got to talking, and she told me who she was." She looks down, gesturing toward her dress. "She helped me pick this dress out, actually."

"Huh." I nod.

"Is that okay?" Cassidy asks.

I immediately place my hand on her back, reassuring her. "Of course it is. I'm just surprised you didn't mention it until now."

"I didn't think it was too big of a deal. I figured you'd see Lindsay at the dinner anyway."

"Lindsay?" Zane asks, his back straightening as he pulls himself to a stand.

My eyes widen and I swallow, hoping to hell I misheard Cassidy.

"Yeah," Cassidy says, not understanding our reaction. Her eyes shift to something over my shoulder, behind me. I turn around, following the direction she's looking. "In fact, she's over there."

And as soon as the words fall from Cassidy's mouth, it feels as if the wind has been knocked out of me.

Walking down the steps leading to the patio is Lindsay, her arm wrapped around Miles's.

I swallow the sickness rising in my throat, my body betraying me. There's nothing inside for me to give. My stomach is empty, yet every vein in my body seems to be void of any substance. It all seemed to evaporate in an instant. And then I'm left with nothing.

See, I've always fucking hated parties.

TWENTY-FIVE

Cassidy

Like a deer caught in headlights.

The way Levi's expression has suddenly changed is the way I feel on the inside. I probably should have told him sooner. That I'd met Miles's wife. Now that I'm witnessing his reaction, I'm regretting not having done it sooner. But deep down, I truly didn't think it would be a big deal.

Apparently, I'm wrong. Severely and sorely wrong.

Lindsay and Miles catch sight of the three of us standing by our table. They make a beeline for us, not stopping on their way.

At first, I'm focused on Levi, wondering why his face has paled at the sight of the couple.

But it isn't Levi's expression that has me the most confused. It's Lindsay's.

Her eyes are spread wide and by the time she's reached the pool area, she hasn't blinked once. She glances around, seemingly nervous. At first, I'm thinking she's nervous about speaking to us or for Miles to introduce us, but it almost looks as if she's planning her escape route. It's almost as if the moment she laid eyes on us, she no longer wanted to be here.

I can relate.

Miles and Lindsay stand in front of our table and Levi's hand finds the small of my back. Again. A habit of his he's developed since we started playing future Mr. and Mrs. Hawkins. But I haven't complained. He gently presses his fingers to my flesh, urging me to curl into him. I sidle next to him. He holds his breath.

"We were wondering when you both would be down here," Miles says once he reaches our table. "Didn't we Lindsay?"

"Oh." She clears her throat. "Yeah."

Her eyes fall to mine, and they soften with the tiniest bit of relief. Until now, I've watched her body stiffen. She looks like a Barbie doll. Her long arms are rigid and unmoving. Her mouth is set into a thin line. Her chest is barely moving, as if she hasn't taken a breath. It's as if I've become some sort of lifeline for her without understanding why. Our silent exchange is brief and short-lived.

"You remember, Lindsay, don't you Hawkins?" Miles gestures toward Lindsay.

Levi doesn't speak a word, and neither does Zane. Their silence is loud enough to hear the band playing the same song I heard them play nearly twenty minutes ago.

I almost get lost in the song before Miles's question hits me. He's implying Levi would somehow know Lindsay. His wife.

My stomach sinks. Everything about this week crashes together, coming to a head all at once.

The miscommunication between Miles and Levi. The anger that has seemed to carry through their relationship this past year. And the competition between them.

My intuition tells me Lindsay is the center of it all. I just don't understand how yet. I hold my breath, anticipating what will come out of Miles's mouth.

Lindsay and Levi don't bother acknowledging one another,

even with Miles's question. They leave it unanswered. Miles doesn't care.

"We should go make a few rounds, Miles. We haven't seen everyone yet." Lindsay turns to him, moving to walk around him. But he stops her. Her attempt to escape fails.

"Hang on a minute, sweetheart," he says, pulling her back to her original spot beside him. "I didn't introduce you to Levi's fiancée yet."

Levi's hand slides across my back the way it did when we were in the elevator. By the time he curls his fingers around my waist and pulls me closer, I'm already noting the differences between his touch then and the way it is now.

His fingers are more tense, pressing into me harder than usual. He's protective, keeping me as close to his body as possible. His body goes rigid beside me. Hard as stone. The same way it did last night when we were playing truth or dare.

"This is Cassidy." Miles gestures toward me.

A slow smile grows on Lindsay's pink painted mouth. She's wearing a long black dress, the fabric clinging to her every curve. She's as pretty as she was when I first met her. But the light I saw on her face in the store is now dim.

It isn't fear I see in her soft brown eyes. It's awkwardness for the situation we're in. I can practically hear her screaming on the inside to get out of here.

"It's nice to see you again, Cassidy." Her eyes bounce between me and Levi. "You didn't mention Levi was your fiancé. Congratulations."

"Thank you." I acknowledge her response, unsure how to digest it or respond to it.

She wraps her hand around Miles's arm, tugging him away from us, but he still doesn't budge. "You two met already?"

Lindsay pauses, nervously swiping her tongue across her

lips. "Earlier, when I went to the boutique a few blocks away to grab my clutch." She turns over her clutch, showing Miles.

"Wow. What a small world." Miles looks between the two of us. He's impossible to read.

Despite the odd reactions from Miles and Lindsay, it's Levi's stare I feel the most.

I turn to face him. His face is expressionless.

"You didn't tell me you met Lindsay," he says. His voice is unwavering. Confusion is written all over him.

"I didn't think it would be a big deal." I shrug, narrowing my eyes. "Is there something I should know?"

"Oh," Miles says, pointing between us. "Wait a minute."

We snap our attention to him.

He wags his finger back and forth. "You haven't told her about Lindsay yet."

For the first time since Miles and Lindsay joined us, Levi leaves my side. I feel the absence of his touch immediately. He's quick to circle around the table. He stops directly in front of Miles, only giving him the slightest margin of space.

Levi's square jaw ticks, the veins on his neck popping in anger.

Zane moves to stand behind Levi, carefully. I can tell he's preparing for what Levi might do. Or what Miles might say to set Levi off.

Confusion settles in the pit of my stomach. I feel more sick the deeper we get into this conversation.

"What is there to tell?" I ask both men, not caring that Levi's hands are clenched into fists at his sides.

Miles sets his beer down on the table and curls his fingers into his fists the same way Levi's are.

"I've always known you were a pussy, Hawkins." Miles seethes.

His comment catches me off guard. I step back with a gasp.

"Miles," Levi warns between clenched teeth, "don't do this."

"Miles," Lindsay pleads, hoping she can pull him away or somehow deescalate the rapidly growing situation, "please don't do this."

"Don't do what?" I ask. Again, my question goes unanswered.

"No," Miles growls, not moving his eyes away from Levi. "I've been waiting for this moment for the past year. I've been waiting to let this motherfucker know I haven't forgotten."

"He knows, Miles. He sees that we're married and that we're happy," Lindsay says.

"Is that why you brought her here?" Miles says, shifting his eyes in my direction, ignoring Lindsay once again.

I take a step back, wondering how I'm suddenly pulled into the mess of an equation.

"To show her off?" Miles continues. "You thought you'd had the upper hand, didn't you?"

Miles snaps his head in my direction, fury in his eyes. They're burning red at the edges.

My heart is beating in my chest at an alarming rate. It's about to burst from my chest, leaving me standing here on the patio, hollow and empty. The blood drains from my face and my skin tingles with nerves.

"First, he's the team's favorite player. Then he takes my girl. Fucks her in the bathroom of my frat party a week before summer training. Then he expected to get away with it." He snaps his head back to Levi. "How's the hand, asshole? I hope it didn't hurt too bad while we were playing this week. In fact, I'm surprised you bothered playing at all."

"What?" I trade glances between Levi and Miles, too stunned to focus on one person. My eyes are watery, my vision blurring.

"You were with Lindsay?" I ask him. Not because I'm jealous. How is it possible to be jealous of a relationship you've never been in? It's not as if Levi cheated on me.

It's hard to have your heart broken when your heart was never involved in the first place.

"No." Levi sighs, rolling his eyes to me. His body has relaxed somewhat, as if he's remembering who he's talking to. "It wasn't like that."

It's not until I swallow the tears welling inside me do I see the crowd around us has turned silent. They're all staring at us. Most of them appear as confused as I am. The others are the teammates, they're faces still and pointed. As if they've been waiting for this moment like a grenade with the key pulled. It's only been a matter of time.

"Then what was it like?" I ask him, my breath shaky. Every word out of Levi's mouth barrels into me. My chest vibrates with a hollow echo. It feels as if the wind has been knocked out of me. "Is that why I'm here? To show me off to fucking Miles and his wife?"

"No," he says. "I told you, it wasn't like that."

"Are you sure, motherfucker?" Miles asks. His words clearly cut Levi deeper. "Because with you, I never know what's true. But I had to invite you here. I had to see you for myself and to show you Lindsay is mine. Always has been."

"If you don't shut the fuck up . . ." Levi seethes.

"What?" Miles asks, squaring Levi up again. "What are you going to do? Hit me?"

Levi doesn't answer Miles.

Miles cocks an eyebrow. A humorless chuckle rumbles out of his chest. "Wouldn't want your fiancée to think you're a pussy, now would you?"

"Miles!" Levi yells, his face turning red and his jaw clenching tighter. "I swear to god, shut the fuck up."

Tears well in my eyes as I shake my head in disbelief. I need to get out of here. I need to walk away before I vomit all over Miles's expensive stone patio. "No." My voice is shaky. "I'm not doing this."

"Cass, please," Levi begs, turning away from Miles long enough to face me. But I can't stand here anymore. I don't care that we're surrounded by his old teammates. I don't care we're surrounded by strangers. The humiliation is already suffocating me. It couldn't possibly get much worse than this. And I won't stand here any longer and listen to Miles and Levi fighting.

Despite my shaky footing on the stone patio beneath them, I move away. "No," I say through a shaky breath. "I can't."

I wave him off and push through the crowd. Every single eye follows me, and every single stare feels like a knife to my back.

I used to think I'd never feel as humiliated as the day I'd heard Levi utter mean words to me down the hallway of our high school before a pep rally.

But this is worse. Levi has topped that feeling, shoving it in my face.

The tears slide down my cheek the second my feet hit the sand. I have no idea if I'm being followed. I don't know if anyone cares enough about me to follow me. Either way, I don't know where I'm headed. I keep walking, my feet kicking up the sand behind me.

"Cass." I hear Levi's voice in the distance, calling after me. But I don't stop. My steps slow, but I don't stop. My dress blows in the breeze coming off the water. It's salty air slams against my skin.

How can we be somewhere so beautiful yet feel the way I do on the inside?

"Please, stop."

With my ragged breathing and my slow and silent sobs, I

stop. My body is already exhausted. Exhausted from ever believing I could be anything more to Levi than a pawn.

I slowly turn around.

"I thought you were tired of playing this game," I say to him, my voice wobbling with the tears welling inside me. With every second that passes, it becomes harder to breathe.

"What game?" he asks. He takes a step closer. I take a step back.

He notices, his eyes falling to my feet.

"This." I gesture between us. "Where you use me. Where you shit all over me, pretending as if I don't have feelings or that I don't, or won't, care what you say to me. I shouldn't be surprised, but somehow I am."

"Cass, I can explain."

"Please do!" I shout, gesturing toward the hotel. "Please tell me how you didn't use me for some sort of fucking revenge, Levi."

We're the only ones in this area of the beach, but I'm sure some guests on the outer edges of the crowd can hear us. In the distance, I can make out the shadow of Zane making his way down the stone steps from the pool.

"Okay." Levi blows out a heavy breath. He lifts his hand, shoving his windswept hair off his forehead. He's fucking perfect standing under the moonlight and I curse the way I remember how it feels to have him stand close to me. To touch me.

"Yes," he says. "It's true that's why I asked you to pretend to be my fiancée."

Just when I thought I couldn't lose any more oxygen, I do. Levi's confession dangles in front of us on a string, swinging back and pummeling me in the gut. I want to bend over, realizing despite how he's treated me this past week, he's still the same cocky asshole I knew in high school. My throat seizes, pushing back the vomit I'm sure is about to come up.

"That's why?" I ask him in disbelief. "You asked me to pretend to be your fiancée to get revenge on your old college rival? Your ego must be so fucking fragile for you to pull this shit."

He blinks, clearly surprised by my anger. Usually, I'm quiet and reserved. Come to think of it, I don't think I've ever felt this much anger coursing through my body. It's anger and hurt and pain all rolled into one. A cocktail of heartbreak I wasn't prepared for.

"Yes." Levi stumbles over his words, trying to come up with a decent explanation. "It's true I asked you because I wanted to get back at Miles. He took everything from me." His voice shakes, vibrating up his throat. "No, in fact, he stole everything from me, Cass. You have no idea what he's done."

"What happened with Lindsay? Did you fuck her back in college when she was with Miles?"

"No." Levi shakes his head, quickly dismissing me. "It was a stupid misunderstanding that night. It's true I went to a party that night. Miles used to be in a fraternity, and they were throwing a party before summer training started. I was in the bathroom taking a fucking piss when Lindsay barged through the door. She was insanely drunk. She was stumbling over her words. Her eyes were half shut and swollen. Luckily, I caught her before she'd tripped and hit her head on the sink." He shakes his head again, taking another step closer, pinning his stare on mine. I take a step back, still unsure of what to make of his story. He continues. "When I caught her, and she fell into my arms, she looked up at me, mumbled some nonsense, then kissed me. I was already pushing her away from me when Miles shoved the door open and caught us. Miles was in such a rage, he'd punched me. A few of his frat brothers must have heard because they were there in a second, trying to pull him off me. But it was no use. I'd fallen back into the bathtub, and he was on top of me. He delivered blow after blow. I'd tried to hit him back, but when I did, I hit the side of the ceramic tub, shattering several bones in my hand. When the guys could finally pull him off me, I'd already passed out. I woke up in the hospital with a concussion and a shattered hand. My career was over after that. He became the starting quarterback, and I turned to journalism. That's why I was shocked when Miles invited me here. I guess now I know the reason."

I inhale a deep breath, trying to understand. I feel terrible Miles had beaten Levi to the point of ruining his career. But the hurt I feel from him using me still pains me.

Another tear slides down my already wet cheeks. "I just"—I swallow—"don't understand why."

"I don't either." He shakes his head. He can see the pain in my eyes. He reaches out, trying to grab onto my hand.

"No, not about that." I sob. "I still don't understand how you could use me this way. I don't know what I expected when you begged me to put this whole charade on. I knew there was a reason. But this? You used me to get back at Miles, thinking it would give you the upper hand. But you want to know what makes it even worse? I don't understand how you could fuck me, knowing you were using me."

The sadness in his expression transforms to one of anger. His eyes narrow and his jaw clenches tight. I've struck a nerve, but I don't fucking care. I want Levi to feel all of my anger and hurt.

"It wasn't like that at all."

"The thing is"—another tear sheds, spilling over my eyelashes—"it was. It always has been. Like football, I've always been a game to you."

"Cass." He pinches the bridge of his nose. "You aren't and have never been a game."

I squeeze my eyes shut, not wanting to hear another excuse. Another sob rolls through me. It catches in my throat, and I attempt to breathe. "I told you when we came here that I had a life, and you were keeping me from it. I've been here for you, Levi. This whole fucking time. And all you've done since I've been here is string me along on some little game of yours."

"I told you." His blue eyes narrow and darken, creating a perfect storm, aimed straight for me. "You aren't a game."

"Then tell me what I am." I hold my hand to my hollowed-out chest. "Because I can never tell the difference with you, Levi. I can never tell the difference between a truth and a lie. I don't know what's fact or fiction. You hate me. You don't hate me. It's all too much." I pause, my decision to tell Levi my truth wavering. Deciding I have nothing to lose at this point, I tell him. "The problem is, Levi. I've been in love with you ever since the first day I saw you through that camera lens out on the field."

His electric blue eyes widen, reflections from the boardwalk lights sparkling and blending in.

A cry lodges in my throat as another tear falls. "But the same moment I fell in love with you was the same moment I realized I would never be good enough for you. Your ego and your pride always stood in the way of seeing anything past your-self. And as I suspected, not a single ounce of you has changed since then. I'm just angry with myself for foolishly believing that it had."

I back away, my feet sliding in the sand with every step. Levi starts to walk toward me, but I hold out my hand.

"Please don't follow me, Levi." I sob again, knowing I have to truly let him go this time. I have to let go of the idea of me and Levi, knowing we can never change for one another. "This engagement." I stop myself, realizing this was never a real engagement to begin with. Despite how real it felt. All it has ever been to Levi was a game. A game of exacting revenge on an old college rival. I choke on a sob. "Or fake engagement. Whatever this fantasy was . . . it's over."

As much as it pains me to leave Levi on the beach, I force myself to walk past him.

He doesn't reach out to stop me. His hand doesn't pull on my arm, forcing me to stay for him to convince me this was anything more than what it was. He doesn't bother convincing me what I'd felt and what he'd felt were the same.

The more distance I put between me and Levi, the more I realize this fake engagement has always been one-sided. I'm the only one who believed it was real.

My heart cracks and shatters when I make it up to the room to pack my bag. By the time I've tossed my bags into my car, and I've typed in my home address into my GPS, I feel even worse than when I believed Levi simply hated me.

Because at least then, I wasn't being played for a fool. I'd simply had a crush on the boy I knew I could never have.

TWENTY-SIX

LEVI

I don't follow Cassidy back up to our room.

The hurt in her eyes was enough to shatter me from the inside out. I've never felt as much pain as I do now, knowing I'm the reason her tears were shed in the first place.

"What the fuck, man?" Zane yells as he stalks toward me. His feet kick up the sand behind him and the wind blows his shirt against his monstrous frame. He holds his hand back, pointing to the party still in full swing.

"Zane." I hold my hand up, stopping him. "Don't."

"You couldn't just fucking tell her," Zane says.

Shame hits my gut, and the blood drains from my face. I should have told Cassidy the truth. The entire truth.

"No, I couldn't," I say, unable to look my best friend in the eye.

"Why?" Zane steps closer to me. "Why couldn't you just fucking tell her."

Anger surges through me. My heart hammers in my chest and I feel like I'm about to explode. I grip onto Zane's shirt, fisting the fabric of his shirt. His eyes widen but only for a second. He knows I'm not angry with him. He knows I'm in pain. The same pain Cassidy felt when she'd left me here on the beach.

"Because I'm a fucking coward!" I yell. I push Zane away from me and step back, struggling to catch my breath. I shove my hair off my forehead and stumble in the sand. I bend over and rest my hands on my knees, feeling sick. "I couldn't," I swallow, no longer yelling. "I couldn't tell her the truth because her truth was clearly written across her face."

"What?" Zane asks, clearly not understanding what I said.

I pull myself to a stand, raking my fingers through my hair again. "I couldn't tell her I'm in love with her because I saw the hatred in her eyes, Zane. She was looking at me the same way she always has. She hates me and I knew nothing I could say would change that."

"You don't know that," he says, gesturing toward me. "You can't say that because you've never told her."

"It doesn't fucking matter." I shake my head, feeling defeated. "It doesn't. I came for a story and that's what I did." I inhale a deep breath and move to pass Zane. "Now it's time to go home."

I don't know whether Cassidy is still at the hotel or if she's already on her way home. I don't know where she went from here. Either way, I know that even if I saw her, it wouldn't fill the hole that's dug itself inside my chest.

"The reunion doesn't end until tomorrow," Zane says, causing me to turn around. "Stay tonight. You can drive home in the morning when you've had some rest."

"Seriously, Zane?" I ask him, the realization of my regret hitting me. "I don't think it matters whether or not I leave. In fact, I don't think it ever mattered I was here. To anyone. And the more I think about this bullshit with Miles, the more I realize I never belonged here. I haven't been a part of this fucking team in years. I never should have come."

I turn my back to Zane and lift my hand in the air, too hurt and tired to care whether I give my friend a proper goodbye. "I'll text you when I get home."

Then, even when I get to the room to find all of Cassidy's bags gone, I know Zane was right. I should have told her I've been in love with her from the start.

TWENTY-SEVEN

Cassidy

"These are stunning." Vada clicks through my camera, quickly sifting through my seemingly endless number of pictures I took over the past ten days. She nods, scrolling from one photo to the next.

"Thanks," I mutter, attempting to give her my best fake smile. Ever since I got home two days ago, I've become an expert at putting on my mask.

Today has been the first time I've seen Vada since Levi and I had our video chat with her near the beginning of our trip.

I'm sitting on my couch in my living room, listening to the sound of Jonah's pounding footsteps upstairs in his room. Vada dropped him off after he stayed with her and Colton for the weekend.

"Did Jonah have fun at the amusement park?" I ask her, hoping simple conversation will take my mind off Levi. Talking about my nephew is usually a surefire way to help.

"Are you kidding?" She rolls her eyes, dropping the camera in her lap. She holds it between her hands. "He had a blast. Colton somehow got a sunburn." She laughs, wiping at the corners of her eyes. She waves her finger in front of her eyes. "You should see him. He has a burn line in the shape of his glasses."

"No." I lean back, dropping my jaw.

"Yeah." Vada laughs, holding her hand over her stomach. "Poor guy. I think he was also more afraid of the rides than Jonah was. But I think his favorite part was the bumper cars, though."

"Really?" I ask her, attempting a smile. "Out of all the roller-coasters and water rides, Jonah chooses the bumper cars?"

She shrugs, a small laugh escaping her chest. Her curly blonde hair is tied up into a high messy bun. She's swapped out her usual corporate wear for a plain T-shirt and leggings. It's the way she used to look when she would help serve at her brother's restaurant, Dallas's Barbecue and Brew.

It's nice to see her this way.

"Yeah." She laughs again. "I love seeing those two together. Sometimes when I see them standing beside each other, I can see a bit of Colton in Jonah."

"It's the eyes." I nod. "Lyla's were brown, so I knew his eyes always belonged to his dad's side of the family."

"I agree," Vada says, giving me another small smile. She picks up my camera again and clicks through the photos. "Wow, I'm serious Cassidy. These are beautiful."

I don't say another word, the emptiness of the week settling back into my bones. Our side conversation about Jonah was short-lived.

"How was it?" Vada asks, setting down the camera again. "You haven't said much about the reunion itself. I'm sure it must have been hard being surrounded by a bunch of football players you don't know."

I bite down on my bottom lip, considering telling Vada the truth. I never told her the connection Levi and I share. Our past.

As far as she's concerned, she simply sent her best reporter and photographer on an assignment.

Tears well in my eyes. As much as I want to shove them away and not let Vada see, I can't stop them. A tear spills over my eyelashes and slides down my cheek.

"Is everything okay?" she asks, setting the camera aside.

I hold my breath, wondering how Vada will take the news of Levi and me playing fake fiancé's while on an assignment she'd given us. "I never told you about me and Levi."

"What do you mean?" Vada asks, her perfectly sculpted brows knitting between her eyes.

"Levi and I knew each other before he started at the paper. We've just never spoken about it."

"Really? How?" She adjusts herself on the couch, tucking her legs under her. She places her elbow on the back cushion and rests her head on her hand.

"In high school." My voice is shaky, and I inhale a deep breath, forcing myself to get the words out. "Actually, he didn't transfer to my school until our senior year. He was the quarterback of the football team, and I was the yearbook photographer. He hated me. He never outright said so, but he always treated me as if I were some sort of outcast. When we graduated, I was relieved. But then last year he was hired at the paper, and it was as if nothing changed."

"What?" Vada presses her hand to her chest. "I never knew you both knew each other that way. Much less hated one another."

I wince, suppressing my nerves. Even though Vada is being the concerned friend right now, I'm unsure when her boss mode will kick in and she realizes this might be a conflict at work.

"We never told anyone." I sniff. "Levi and I did a pretty good job of hiding it. When you wanted me to go on this assignment with him, he wasn't exactly thrilled with the idea."

"Oh my gosh." She reaches out and places her hand over mine. "I can only imagine how it was at the hotel when you got there."

I lay out the entire play-by-play of the reunion. Starting with our first night there. Everything from how we were only booked for one room and then the night when I'd walked into the restaurant and Levi roped me into playing along with pretending to be his fiancée.

By the time I tell her about our final night and how I'd found out the truth about Levi, the tears are continuously flowing down my cheeks. They haven't stopped.

Vada says, "I don't know what to say."

"I'm so sorry, Vada." I shake my head, squeezing my eyes shut, hoping it will clear away the tears.

"For what?" she asks.

"For not telling you about the history between Levi and me. For not telling you about what was going on at the reunion. The last thing I'd want to do is let this interfere with our work."

"For one," she says, dipping her head down to pull my gaze up to hers, "you and Levi have done a pretty good fucking job until now about keeping this a secret. I mean, you both hated each other and came into work every day pretending as if you didn't." She pauses. "Second, I don't know what you're talking about. Aside from this whole mess, you both haven't let it affect your work. Levi has already turned his article in, and you have a million pictures taken. I won't even know where to begin on choosing the best ones." She gestures toward my camera.

"He already turned in his story?" I gasp, struggling to wrap my head around the fact that Levi has already written and submitted his story. We've only been back for two days.

I haven't heard from Levi since I left him standing on the beach. Not that I expected to. But the fact he could write and submit his story only reaffirms the notion I meant nothing to him at all.

"He did." Vada nods, the corners of her mouth curling into a grin. "He emailed it to me this morning. Honestly, he killed it. It's a really good story."

"Oh." I nod, biting down on my bottom lip.

"It's okay, Cass," she says. "I just wanted to tell you, so you didn't think it interfered with your work."

Relief washes over me. When Vada took the position of editor in chief, I didn't want our friendship to interfere with work. But at this moment, I'm thankful to have her as my friend. I'm thankful she understands.

"Yeah, but what do we do now? How do we go back to work after this? I'm so confused."

"Do you want to take a few days off to think about it?"

"No." I shake my head. "I told you I didn't want this to interfere with work and I think that would only do the exact opposite." I inhale a deep, shaky breath and turn to face the sliding door leading to my backyard. "I'm not sure how I'll feel when I see him again."

"Are you sure?" she asks, her eyes softening. "It's okay to take a few days for yourself now and then."

"You're one to talk." I snort. I muster up enough energy to curl the corner of my mouth.

She rolls her eyes, tilting her head even more. She smiles and we sit in silence for a few seconds before it fades. "I know you said you hated one another. But from what I know, hatred doesn't look like this."

"What does it look like, then?" I ask her, not understanding.

Both of our heads snap up to the familiar creak of my front door swinging open. My dad walks through, carrying a small plastic bag of groceries. He gives us a small wave before he limps his way into the kitchen, leaning on his cane the whole way.

"I don't know," Vada says, once again pulling my attention back to her. Her round eyes widen, glistening under the sun pouring in through my back door. "But I think hatred is often used as a disguise for the truth. Sometimes, it looks the same as love."

TWENTY-EIGHT

LEVI

The longer I sit at my desk, unable to gather the courage to look up and chance a glance in Cassidy's direction, the more I realize I was right when I told Zane I was a coward.

Fear has been a weight bearing down on my shoulders since the ripe old age of five. Until this morning, I haven't thought about my father and the way he shaped my life, telling me there was no other option for me. Every afternoon and every weekend, he used to force me to go to football practices, scrimmages, and games. No day was off limits. Right before I'd head out to the field, he'd stand behind me with his hands on my shoulder and whisper into my ear.

"This is your only path, Levi. The Hawkins name depends on you."

My father's words never hit me until a few months before he'd died, when I learned exactly why he'd pushed me so hard growing up.

Not only had he played in college, but he'd also been drafted to play professionally by one of the major NFL teams directly after graduating. Until he'd broken his ankle on a game winning play. It ended his career after that.

I always believed my father and I had a great relationship despite the constant pressure he'd put on me and my brother's. He was a good man in all other ways.

But I can't help the bit of resentment settling in the bottom of my stomach. The fear my father had instilled in me has now seeped into every other aspect of my life.

Cassidy.

My fingers fly across my keyboard, typing up my next story. I'd finished the one of Miles and the reunion as soon as I'd gotten back from South Padre Island. I didn't want to waste any more time thinking about the fucking asshole who'd ruined my life. Both then and now.

I was determined to let it all go. The first step was to write the story I'd came there to tell. And that's what I did.

I didn't include anything about my history with Miles or the way I'd fabricated an entire relationship and engagement with Cassidy.

The article stayed fairly neutral considering the circumstances.

I stop typing and bury my head in my hands, attempting to catch my breath. It feels as if I've been holding it for days, waiting for the moment when I can catch some air, relieving my lungs from the burning sensation that's made a home behind my ribs.

I lean back in my chair and chance a glance around the office. I sit up and peek over the top of my cubicle. The newsroom is buzzing, a typical Monday morning for us.

The hushed clicks of fingers running across a keyboard. The voices of the other reporters on the phone or having conversations with one another.

"Hawkins. Meeting in the conference room in five."

I snap my head up to see Vada passing my cubicle. She taps her fingers on the top, shooting me a look. Her eyebrows are arched even as she passes me. It's an expression I'm becoming familiar with. She's about to speak to a selective group of staff.

"I'm on my way," I tell her, even when she's moved onto the next desk.

I grab my pad of paper and my favorite pen, crossing the news floor to our conference room. The room is surrounded by floor to ceiling glass and a few of the reporters have already gathered inside. Several other staff members are filing in ahead of me. Including Cassidy.

I stop walking, watching as she reaches for the door handle in front of her, swinging the door open. In one hand, she's carrying a stack of photos. In the other, her fingers are clasped around her camera. She stops just inside the door, deciding to sit in a chair at the end.

Her back is turned toward me as I enter the conference room. I stop in the same way Cassidy did, looking for an open seat.

The only one left is the seat directly across from Cassidy.

She doesn't chance a look in my direction, keeping her focus down on the photos placed in front of her. I recognize the one on top. One of the beach at night.

I slide my chair out and sit down, slowly breathing out. I shove the sleeves of my white button-down shirt up to my elbows and rest my arms on the table. I'm focusing on my blank pad of paper but look up to Cassidy, watching her.

She's dressed differently today than her normal outfit at work. She's wearing a long sleeve lightweight pullover. The color is a muted blue tone, matching the color of her eyes. The sleeves are pushed up the same way mine are, displaying the bracelets dangling from her wrists. Small, thin gold rings are wrapped around three of her fingers on each hand. One is on her thumb. I swallow, remembering how those very hands have touched me. She clears her throat and shakes her head. Her blonde hair falls away from her shoulder, displaying her perfectly smooth neck.

I gnaw on the inside of my cheek, silently willing my dick to calm down. Cassidy was no longer mine to touch. But then again, was she ever really?

I clear my throat and shift in my seat. Thank fucking god there's a table blocking everyone's view of my swollen cock.

Everyone stops talking the moment Vada walks through the door.

"All right, everyone, I trust you had a good weekend." She stands at the end of the table with one hand on her hip. She glances around the table before picking up one of the sheets of paper in front of her. "I called this meeting to go over articles we're set to publish tomorrow as well as some I want to gather this week."

Although I'm listening to Vada, I haven't been able to pull my attention from Cassidy. She's only sitting a couple feet away from me.

I look down at the pad of paper in front of me and pick up my pen. My heart races in my chest and my stomach clenches with nerves.

I scribble out a quick message.

I'm sorry.

I swiftly tear the paper as quietly as I can and turn it over before sliding it across the table in front of Cassidy.

Her attention is pinned on Vada until she sees my hand place the paper in front of her. She still hasn't looked in my direction. Her eyes dart to the right, landing on the paper.

And for the first time, she acknowledges me. Well, not so much as acknowledges *me*. Once her eyes land on the paper, she closes her eyes and inhales a deep breath. Her full lips part as she creates the perfect opening to release her breath.

Then, with reluctance, she picks up the paper and places it in her lap. She reads it.

She reads over it for a few seconds, Vada's voice the only sound in the conference room.

A tiny bit of excitement flurries inside me when I see her reach up and grab her pen from the table. Her hand moves, then she slides the paper back over to me.

I look at either side of me, hoping none of our colleagues are watching. They aren't. They're too focused on Vada's explanation of the article I'd written about Miles's hotel chain.

I try to dampen my shaky fingers when I pick the paper up and read what Cassidy wrote.

I don't care.

I pick up my pen again. *Come on, Cass. Please. All I need is five minutes.*

I pass it back to her. She rolls her eyes again. This time she seems even more annoyed.

If she weren't trying to stay quiet, I could swear I hear a groan rumble from her chest as she picks up her pen. She scribbles in her lap again. Passes it to me.

No.

I write back. *Cass, please.*

She writes back. *Levi, just stop. Stop pretending you ever cared about me. It's exhausting.*

I reply. *I did care about you. I do care about you. I really am sorry.* I slide it back to her.

I hold my breath as she grabs the paper once more. It isn't until she reads my messages do I see the tears lining her eyes.

Slowly, she picks up her pen again and slides it back over to me. I pick it up and read it.

Keep telling your lies to your big fat ego, Levi. Just leave me out of it.

I snap my head up, Cassidy's words hitting me like a

battering ram to my chest. The blood drains from my face when I find her staring directly at me. One tear slides down her cheek before she gathers her camera and photos, shoves her chair back, and quickly leaves the conference room. I stare at her empty seat, swallowing the pain I feel all over.

When I'm finally able to pull myself together, I look up and catch Vada's eyes bouncing between Cassidy's empty seat and me. At first, I'm nervous Vada caught our note passing session and is angry for not listening to her. But instead, her expression is sad, as if she knows what's going on between me and Cassidy.

As if she knows the pain I've caused her friend.

I clear my throat as Vada picks back up, moving on to the next topic.

Feeling empty inside, I don't look back up from my blank paper until the meeting is over.

💔

"I feel like fucking shit, dude." I watch my best friend from the other side of the table.

He picks up his half-eaten burger, shoving another huge bite into his mouth. A glob of barbecue sauce drips onto his beard. He doesn't notice as he chews. He picks up his napkin and wipes his fingers. "You should have gotten something to eat. Maybe take it with you. I'm going to have to cut lunch short."

"Why?" I ask him, frowning as I drag my nail across the table.

"Ugh." He groans. "Preseason football is about to start, and the principal wanted me to join the team out on the field for their first practice. Last year our school almost went to state in our conference. I guess she wants me to make sure all the students are prepared mentally. In case any of them want to talk. But the practices are at one of the college stadiums. The principal made a deal with them to use their larger field."

It's the first time I've heard Zane talk about his job. He usually keeps his personal life and work life separate. I don't blame him, considering the nature of his job. I'm sure he has to keep information confidential.

We're sitting at a table outside Dallas's Barbecue and Brew. Although I have no desire to eat since the morning I had with Cassidy, I'm sitting with my best friend on my lunch break. I'd agreed to meet Zane, hoping he'd get my mind off Cassidy. I haven't stopped thinking about her since I saw the tear slide down her cheek, the pain in her eyes so intense I thought I might disintegrate right there in the conference room.

"I talked to Jimmy the other day," he mumbles around a mouthful of food.

"Oh." It's the only word I have enough energy to say. It's not that I don't care that Zane has talked to Jimmy since the reunion. I still consider Jimmy a friend. He had absolutely no involvement with Miles or the scheme he cooked up to get me to go to the reunion. I know Jimmy's intentions were genuine.

I don't have the energy to ask him to elaborate on his comment because it doesn't fucking matter. The only opinion that matters is Cassidy's and I've fucked that up.

But I don't need to ask Zane for the details. He offers them anyway.

"Yeah." He nods. "He said he had no idea Miles asked you to the reunion for some ulterior motive. In fact, none of the team did."

"I didn't think they did." I sigh, frustrated where this conversation is going. If I couldn't possibly feel any worse, this conversation has topped it. "Miles usually works alone when it comes to destroying someone's life and humiliating them."

"I agree. Are you sure you don't at least want some onion rings?" Zane asks, pointing to the nearly empty plate in front of him. "You should eat something. Sweet tea doesn't count as food."

I scrunch my nose. The idea of eating when I feel this way sounds like the worst possible idea right now. "No, thanks," I mutter.

"Fuck, man." Zane shakes his head, talking around another mouthful of food. "This woman has you fucked up."

"No kidding." I sigh, sitting back in my chair. I shove my unkempt hair off my forehead, watching as Dallas, the owner of the bar, steps outside to clear off one of the tables. He gives me a quick wave when he sees me before he heads back inside.

"You know the owner of this place?" Zane asks.

"Yeah," I say. "He's my boss's brother."

"Really?" he asks, his dark bushy eyebrows arching.

I nod. "I went to his wedding last fall. He's a nice guy. So is the other guy that owns this place. Colton."

"Huh." Zane grins as he wipes his mouth with his napkin. "I didn't know that. Small world, I guess."

"Yep." I lean forward and rest my elbows on the table.

"You've got to do something, man," Zane says, leaning back in his chair. "I can practically see how torn up you are."

"What am I supposed to do?" My throat swells. "I told you about this morning in our meeting. She doesn't want to talk to me."

"Dude," he says. "I don't know, but ever since I've known you, you've always been in love with this woman. You talked about her as if she was this unattainable thing. As if you never stood a chance at being with her. But the thing is, I don't think you ever gave *her* the chance."

"What do you mean?" I ask him, finally gathering up enough energy to turn and face him.

He's finished his plate and his soda is nearly gone. "I saw the way she looked at you. The expression on her face when she talked about you." He shakes his head. "I don't know. From my experience, that's not the expressions of someone who hates you."

"Well, I think it's different now. If she didn't hate me then, she does now."

"Has she said that?" he asks.

"No. But I know from the pain in her eyes, there's no going back. I shouldn't expect her to forgive me."

"You shouldn't expect it," Zane says, looking me in the eye. "But if you love her enough, you sure as fuck can show her."

TWENTY-NINE

Cassidy

I've never experienced true love. The closest I've ever come to it is the act of falling. I say *falling* because to me it's a different concept than actually being *in* love. Two different levels of love.

When you're in love with someone, your love is reciprocated. It's two people loving with their whole hearts. Day in and day out, putting in the effort to make sure the other is happy and fulfilled.

For ten days, I believe that's what I had with Levi. Or at least he put on a good show of what life would be like if we were in love. But now, since I left him standing on the beach, I've come to the understanding I will perpetually be *falling* in love with Levi Hawkins.

My love for him has never been returned, continuously running on a never-ending loop of misery. I've been in a constant state of falling, never knowing where I might finally land. I've never known whether I would ever find the path to no longer being alone, or if I would fall flat on my face, realizing Levi could never love me in return.

Understanding my love would never be reciprocated has been a hard pill to swallow. And that same pill became lodged in my throat last week when Levi passed me a note in our meeting.

I did care about you. I do care about you. I really am sorry.

Lies. All fucking lies.

The image of Levi's handwriting scribbled across that piece of paper has been stuck inside my head for the past week. Even as the days pass since that day in the conference room, I'm convinced the pain will never go away. I will forever be stuck falling in love with Levi.

"Hey, baby girl. Do you mind grabbing me the baking powder?"

I'm sitting at the kitchen table, reorganizing my camera bag, when I look up to see my father standing on his toes in front of one of the cabinets.

"Dad, come on." I rush over to him, moving him aside. I reach inside the cabinet, grabbing onto the small silver can of baking powder.

"You shouldn't be straining your knee like that. It'll only make it worse." I hand him the baking powder and stalk back over to the table.

"I'm fine, Cass. My knee hasn't even been bothering me lately."

I sit back down in my chair at the table, bending my leg. I rest my heel on the edge of my seat and place my chin on my knee as I sift through my memory cards. I slide them into their compartments, trying to think of anything other than Levi. It's been an impossible task.

"Are you still doing your physical therapy?" I ask him. We haven't spoken much about my dad's health. Aside from the fact that I've been distracted by the mess I've made with Levi, I haven't asked him about it.

It's a subject I've been careful to broach with him.

"I am." He nods, tossing a scoop of baking powder into the

bowl he has set in front of him. "Hence why I said it hasn't been bothering me."

He looks up from his bowl long enough to give me a knowing look. I've opened the floodgates. My question about physical therapy has now opened up the possibility for him to ask about Levi.

My stomach aches and twists, my chest squeezing like a dagger has pierced it. I bite down on my lip.

"Are you going to tell me why a woman who is in love and engaged hasn't mentioned her fiancé once?" he asks. "Or are we going to pretend it never happened?"

I absorb my father's last question, allowing it to burrow into the crevices of my fractured heart. His question hits a little too close to home. He just doesn't know it.

"I don't know," I whisper. "There's so much to tell, Dad."

"Well." He sighs, dropping his measuring spoon. He sits down across from me. "I have some time."

With a wobbly voice and a quivering chest, I tell him everything. I leave out the parts my father has no business knowing about his nearly twenty-three-year-old daughter. The parts where I feel Levi gave me the closest version of himself. His most vulnerable self.

When I'm finished telling him, he sits back against his chair and shifts his focus to the window. He keeps his eyes trained on the backyard, his bottom lip quivering.

"I don't think I've given you enough credit, Cass."

I tilt my head to the side, confused.

"I will always love both of my daughters. Even though Lyla chose to leave the way she did, I will always love her. But you amaze me, Cassidy. I know you said he roped you into pretending to be his fiancée, but I can't help wondering if you hadn't truly been in love with him, if you would have gone along with it."

"I went along with it because—"

"You love him." My dad cuts me off.

I shake my head and sigh, the familiar pressure building in my chest, squeezing what remaining oxygen I have left inside. "It doesn't matter if I love him or not, Dad."

"Why?" he asks, genuine concern in his expression.

"Because for a man like Levi, there is no such thing as the concept of love." My voice wobbles and my chin quivers as I attempt to stifle my sobs. I've done enough moping around and crying. I don't want to cry in front of my dad, especially when it comes to talking about men.

My father frowns, bringing his focus back to the window. His eyes swim with thoughts. He's clearly trying to come up with the right words to say. All my life, my father has been anything but a man of few words. He's filled to the core with wisdom. He isn't afraid to call anyone out. He isn't afraid to ask questions or even offer advice.

The corners of his mouth are curled down into a frown when he finally speaks. "I don't think that's true."

"You would feel differently if you'd met him." I swipe at the tear running down my cheek.

"Not everyone shows you who they are on the inside, Cass. There are people in this world who spend years putting up walls and barriers, protecting their hearts. People spend so much time hiding their true selves behind masks, sometimes it even becomes unrecognizable to them."

I tilt my head as the tears continue to spill over my lashes. I blink them away, knowing my father's words come from a place of experience. I'm just not entirely sure how.

Either way, I get what he means.

In a matter of ten days, Levi played his part of the loving fiancé.

But over the years, he's been playing another role. The role of someone who keeps others at a distance. Never allowing himself to be in love. Remaining in a state of perpetual falling. Like me.

My heart cracks as I stare at my father's aging eyes. Becoming a grandfather in the past seven years has aged him. Lyla leaving has aged him.

He reaches across the table and wraps his hand around mine.

"You've spent the past seven years taking care of me and Jonah. Have you ever asked yourself what it is that you want?"

"No." I shake my head. "I told you before, Dad. Taking care of you and Jonah is all that matters. Levi doesn't love me the same way I love him. In fact, he never did, so that's beside the point anyway."

"Cassidy Anne," he scolds. His southern accent rises through his throat at the use of my middle name. A name he hasn't used in *years*. "There is no way that boy asked you to go to that reunion of his and dragged you into playing as his fiancée if he wasn't in love with you."

I bite down on my bottom lip, the image of Levi's face on the beach that night clear in my mind. Electric blue eyes and his windswept hair. Regret seeping into every pore on his body.

I'm just not sure if it's regret for falling for me, or regret for our fake engagement ending before the reunion was even officially over.

Another tear slips down my face. I sniffle and shake my head. "I don't know."

"Maybe for once," my father says, bringing my attention back to him, "you should tell him what you want instead of moping around here like some sort of zombie."

I find my mouth curling, a laugh clawing its way up my throat. I don't know if I'm going to take my dad's advice on telling Levi how I feel.

I think back to last week when I'd seen him in the meeting, sliding his note across the table. I refused to hear any more of his excuses, and I'm not sure I can hear them now. Even with my father's advice.

Seeing Levi at work has been torture. It's impossible not to look at him and want to melt into his arms. I want to accept his apology, even if I risk learning it's only for his own benefit. Levi is known for doing things simply for his own benefit and no one else's. It's the reason I got into trouble with him in the first place.

I look over his shoulder and gesture to the mixing bowl sitting on the counter. I'm changing the subject with my indecision on what to do. "Who are you making cookies for, by the way? I don't think I've ever seen you bake."

My father looks over his shoulder and pulls himself out of his chair. "Oh, right." He wags his finger in the air as he stalks his way over to the bowl, speaking over his shoulder on the way. "They're for Joni."

"What?" I swipe my hand across my wet cheek, hoping my damp skin will somehow make me feel less zombie-like. As my dad put it. "Why?"

My dad picks up the whisk, mixing the baking powder into the flour. He shrugs. "Because I love her."

His words fall from his mouth so effortlessly, acting as if he didn't drop a bomb into our conversation, setting off an explosion. My heart sinks into my stomach. "You love her?" I blink several times. "We are talking about the same Joni, right?"

"Yes," my dad says, dropping his whisk. He stops stirring and halfway turns toward me. "I'm in love with Joni. Have been for the past year. That's why I've asked her to stop being my physical therapist."

I struggle to find the right words. "I don't understand."

But when my dad reaches for the sugar, digging the

measuring cup into the container before he dumps it into the bowl, I realize I do understand. I understand it all.

"There's not much to it." I'm still in shock he's speaking about his feelings for Joni so casually. "When she was first assigned to be my physical therapist after the surgery, I couldn't stand her. She'd push me further than I was willing to go, and she was always so damn happy." He laughs under his breath, shaking his head with the memory. "But after a while, I got used to her and looked forward to the days she would come. Eventually we grew closer, and it wasn't until a couple months ago when I asked her to meet me outside of my appointments. Well, I asked her if she wanted to meet for coffee. But she told me she couldn't pursue a relationship with me if she continued as my therapist. So, I asked her if she'd be willing to quit as my therapist. I didn't want her quitting her job altogether, I simply wanted her to transfer so she would be comfortable pursuing this between us."

A large lump has formed in my throat. Emotion wells inside me. Not because I'm upset about my father keeping his relationship with Joni a secret. It's because I've never seen his face light up the way it is now. The light flickering in his gaze and the constant smile spread across his mouth is enough evidence he's telling the truth. He's been in love with Joni since he met her.

"That's why she called me upset, you were telling her you didn't want to be her patient any longer."

"Joni loves me too," he says. "She wanted what was best for me and was willing to sacrifice the possibility of us for the sake of my therapy. But eventually, we both decided it was worth her transferring."

"Oh my god." I set my elbow on the table and rest my head in the palm of my hand, cupping my cheek. "I can't believe I didn't know."

My father pauses, then reaches inside the refrigerator,

pulling out two eggs. He holds one in his hand as he turns to look at me. With watery eyes, his expression softens as he gives me a knowing look. "I told you, baby girl. Some people spend years creating layers of masks to hide what they truly feel inside. I kept my feelings hidden from Joni for too long. I was foolish enough to believe that the further I pushed her away, the easier it would be to let her go. When in reality, it only made me want her closer. And the same goes for you. I kept my relationship with her from you because I'd spent many years dedicating my life to you and Jonah. I didn't know how I would handle telling you both, and I didn't know how you would react."

He uses the side of the bowl to crack the egg. He drops it in before tossing the shell into the trash behind him.

I manage a weak smile, happiness for my father and Joni swelling inside me. "I'm happy for you, Dad."

"Really?" He stops mixing his dough and tilts his head as he looks at me with relief.

"Of course I am." It's the truth. I've only ever wanted my dad to be happy. Especially after all the people who have walked out of his life. Out of our life. First my mother. Then my sister. "I'm sorry you didn't think you could tell me, but I understand why. No one deserves love more than you do," I tell him, standing up from the table. I stand beside him and grab the wooden spoon from his hand. He lets me, moving aside to watch me.

"We may agree on most things, baby girl. But that isn't one of them. You deserve love too." He clears his throat and passes me a box of chocolate-covered cherries. He sets it down beside the bowl. "Now be sure to chop those up and toss them all in there. They're Joni's favorite."

THIRTY

Cassidy

Levi hasn't shown up to work today.

I'm staring at his empty desk as the hollow sensation in my chest grows. I'm disappointed. But why?

It's been almost two weeks since we called off our fake engagement. But nonetheless, it hurts the same as it did the second my feet slid across the sand as I walked away from him. I've had time to think this past week, especially after the talk I had with my father. Learning about his relationship with Joni has me rethinking my whole life. It's as if I've spent my life standing outside of a store, peering through the glass window, making assumptions as to what's inside.

I've never been happier for my dad to have found someone he loves, but it's left me with this cloud over my head.

The truth is, falling for Levi has been the hardest fall of all, and I'm not entirely sure how I'll ever make the emptiness go away.

My love for him simply doesn't disappear overnight.

My hope was I would get that answer today when I saw him sitting at his desk. Over the past two weeks, I haven't gathered the courage to speak to him. But today I had gathered up the courage to at least try, hoping the sting of my anger toward Levi had waned.

By the time lunch rolls around, my disappointment remains the same.

He hasn't been in the office all day. Figuring he must be out gathering information for a story or conducting an interview, I grab my purse and sling it over my shoulder. Before I reach the elevator, I catch Vada walking out of her office.

She's holding a stack of papers, but stops when she sees me. "Hey, Cass."

"Hey." I grin. "I was just heading out to grab some lunch. Do you want anything?"

"Actually"—her shoulders sag with relief—"that's perfect. I'm kind of stuck going over this article with Joey in the politics department. I ordered some food from Dallas's. Would you mind picking it up for me? If it isn't too much trouble."

"No." I shake my head. "That's not a problem. I'll grab a sandwich or something from there while I'm at it."

"Thank you." She hums, her mood lightening. "Tell my brother to add your order to my tab." She lets out a small laugh. "He loves when I do that."

"Will do." I grin. "I'll be back in a bit."

I leave Vada and head down to Dallas's restaurant. It doesn't take long before I'm pulling into a parking spot outside of the restaurant. The familiar sign of Dallas's Barbecue and Brew hangs above the door. The weather is mild today. All the windows lining the front of the dining room are open. Loud pulsating country music pours out of them and the propped open front door.

I step inside, lifting my glasses off the bridge of my nose and sliding them back on top of my head.

The bar and dining room aren't nearly as busy as I've seen

them in the past. With only a few guests inside, I don't have to elbow my way over to the bar.

I slide onto a barstool near the middle of the bar as Dallas, Vada's brother, emerges from the back. He pushes through the swinging door, recognizing me almost immediately.

"Hey, Cassidy." He grins, walking over to me. He spreads his arms out and leans on the counter, gripping the edge. "What can I get for you?"

"Well, I'm here to pick up Vada's order. She got stuck with one of our reporters, so she asked me if I wouldn't mind picking it up for her. I figured I'd put in my order as well."

"Great. I have her order in the back." His smile hasn't wavered. I don't know much about Dallas, but from what I've been told, he's changed this past year. I think it mostly has to do with his wife, Sloan. "What can I get for you, though?"

"Um." I twist my mouth, deciding what I'm in the mood for. My appetite hasn't exactly been the greatest lately, considering how I've been feeling. But I figure I need to try to get out of my slump. "I'll take the chicken fried steak on Texas toast."

"Good choice," Dallas says, spinning around. He says that every time, regardless of what anyone orders.

He enters my food into the computer, then disappears into the back. A bartender hangs out at the other end, distracted by what's playing on the TV.

"Grabbing some lunch?" A familiar voice behind me causes me to spin around on my barstool.

When I turn around, Zane is climbing onto the barstool beside me. He looks the same as he did the last time I'd seen him. His long beard still hangs above his chest. I tilt my head, wondering what he would look like with it shaved. Would I have recognized him otherwise? Probably not.

"Yeah." I nod, feeling myself gather up enough emotional strength to smile. But I can't deny seeing Zane instantly makes me think of Levi. A pinching sensation tugs at my heart. I clear my throat, shaking it off. "I'm just waiting for my order before I take it back to my office."

"Oh," he says, nodding absentmindedly. He eyes the counter, staring off at nothing in particular before he swings his gaze back up to mine. "How have you been?"

I knew this question was coming. I wince. "I'm okay. It's been tough getting back into normal everyday life. Being away from home for ten days has been hard, and well . . . you know." I allow my words to drift off. Zane knows exactly what I mean. Or I at least trust he does.

"Same. I mean, who has a reunion for ten days? That's a long ass fucking time, and I wasn't even there for all of it."

"Right?" A small laugh escapes my chest. "That's exactly what I said to Levi."

It feels like it's been forever since I've said his name. It's ridiculous. It's only been two weeks since we broke off our fake engagement. Despite the warmth his name brings to my body, a cold and empty sensation follows it.

"Have you eaten here before?" I ask him, changing the subject. I don't want to spend my time talking about Levi. If I had it my way, I'd end up talking about him or at least asking Zane how he's doing. That's the last thing I want to do.

Only because I'm terrified of his answer.

"I have." He grins. "The school I counsel at isn't too far from here."

"Oh, that's great."

"Yeah." He takes a deep breath.

Dallas emerges from the kitchen, two bags hanging from his fingers. He eyes Zane sitting beside me before setting them down on the counter.

"Here you go, Cass. Your lunch is on the house."

"Good," I tell him. "Vada told me to add it to her tab anyway."

He rolls his eyes. "Of course she did."

"Thanks." I slide off the stool and grab the bags. "I'll see you later, Zane." I want to get out of here and the food is the perfect excuse.

Sitting beside Levi's best friend is becoming increasingly difficult.

"Cassidy, wait." He stops me. "I don't know if you're busy, but I was wondering if I might ask you for a favor."

I swallow past the lump in my throat. "Sure."

"Well, I told you my school isn't too far from here, but I'm currently counseling the football team while they're in summer training over at the university. My school got permission to use their practice field."

"Huh." I bite down on my bottom lip, unsure where this is going.

"I was wondering if you might swing by and take a few pictures for the team. Since I'm a counselor, I'm working on building a motivation board for them. I think it'll do great for the students if they can get a visual of what they look like when they are a team."

"Like a vision board?" I ask him.

"Yeah." He grins, gesturing toward me. "I know it's probably a stretch and I can pay you if you want—"

"No." I shake my head. "I can do it."

My resolve at keeping Levi's best friend at a distance completely crumbles.

"Thank you." His shoulders fall in relief. "Do you know where it is?"

"I do." I nod. "It's where I went to college."

"Cool." He swings around on his barstool, facing the bar once again. Dallas has disappeared but the bartender watching the TV earlier walks in our direction. "I'll be there until six, so stop by whenever you're free from work."

Making sure I have both bags in my hands, I leave Dallas's Barbecue and Brew hoping my favor for Zane doesn't turn out the same as the last favor I'd done for someone. Left me with nothing but a broken heart and the promise that the one person I've only ever wanted can never be mine.

***

THE DAY MOVES SLOWLY. Mostly because I still couldn't help staring at Levi's desk, hoping he'd walk in. After a few hours with him not showing up, I figured it'd be better if he were here. Only in the hope it would feel like ripping off a Band-Aid.

But the Band-Aid remains snug, clinging to me as if it's permanently glued to me.

Once I'm finished with work, I say bye to Vada and a few of the other staff members before heading out to the practice field.

When I pull into the parking lot of the university's practice field, I wonder if maybe I'd misheard Zane earlier at lunch.

There are absolutely no cars here. The entire lot is empty.

Zane could have possibly parked elsewhere. Along with the rest of the team.

The afternoon sun beats across my face as I step out of my car. The sky is painted a red, orange, and purple hue. The sun, combined with the practice field, takes me back to the days I'd spend on the high school football field, just as the team would come roaring out of the tunnel at the start of a game.

The university's practice field is nowhere near as large as their official field. There is no stadium surrounding the perfectly kept green turf. Instead, each side has maybe twenty rows of basic metal bleachers. The field is made of regular grass littered with mounds of dirt, kicked up from the players as they scrimmaged against one another.

I push through the small chain-link fence dividing the lot from the field, considering turning around and leaving.

But I stop when I see a familiar man standing at the opposite side of the field, leaning against the goal post. He tosses the ball into the air. It spirals, spinning perfectly before landing back on his large palm. His fingers clamp around it. He does it again. And again.

My heart instantly thrashes against my bones as his electric blue eyes notice me walking toward him. He pushes off the goal post and takes a step forward, but stops.

I hold my breath, and I see his shoulders stop moving. He's holding his breath as well.

I swallow, nervously glancing around, wondering why in the hell Levi is here but no one else is. Not one single student or football player. Not even Zane.

I cross yard after yard, putting more distance between me and my car. Less between me and Levi. I can already feel the tears welling behind my eyes even before I meet him under the goal post.

I stop when I'm within a few feet of him. My camera is dangling from my shaking, curled fingers. My palm is clammy and damp, clearly sensing my nerves.

"Levi," I say. "What are you doing here?"

"Hey, Cass."

Hearing him say the shortened version of my name hits me just as hard as the first time. Falling.

Falling.

Falling in love with Levi.

It's a vicious, delicious never-ending cycle.

THIRTY-ONE

LEVI

If I were to combine all the nerves I've felt over the years before the start of every game, they still wouldn't amount to ones I'm feeling now.

Every single ounce of blood pumping through my veins is electrified at the sight of Cassidy walking across the field.

The sun is shining down on her in all the right places. Her face and body are tan from the beach even though it's been two weeks since we were last there. I've obviously seen her since then, around the office, but she looks different today. She looks different when there's nothing above her except an orange cloudless sky. Her blonde strands reflect against the sun. It's as if the sun is glowing around her.

She's wearing a bright pink button-down shirt tucked into a black leather skirt. The tight fabric stretches across her thighs as she walks toward me, her black ankle boots digging into the dirt field.

I'm fucking nervous. After Cassidy's last note she'd written to me, I wasn't entirely sure I'd be able to ever get her in a place to hear me out. In fact, I wasn't sure she'd ever speak to me again. But Zane's words the other day flipped a switch in me. For the first time since I became a reporter, words were only going to fail me. I needed to show Cassidy my love for her. I needed to show her I've always loved her.

I figured the best place to do that was in a place similar to the one where it all started.

My nerves dissolve the second she meets me. There's an expression of confusion on her face, but I expected that.

I clear my throat and step closer to her. This time she doesn't move back like she did on the beach.

"Levi," she says. "What are you doing here?"

"Hey, Cass." It feels like it's been ages since I've heard her voice. It shoots straight to my chest, bringing me back to life like those fucking life-saving paddles they use in emergencies.

She looks around, her eyebrows arched with confusion. Her camera is dangling from her hand, the strap wrapped inside her clenched fingers. "Where is everyone? Where is Zane?"

"They aren't here."

"What?" She snaps her head in my direction. She glances around once again, searching for anyone here besides me. "But I thought—"

"It's just me," I tell her. Before she has a chance to respond, I spit out the words I came here to say. The words I've held in for the past five years since I first saw her on our high school football field. A field almost identical to this one.

"Four years ago," I say. "UT versus Abilene Central."

"What?" She blinks, tilting her head.

I take another step toward her, rolling the football in my hands. I pass it from one to the next. Then back again. She's watching me carefully.

"UT. Your school." I point the ball toward her. "Was playing Abilene Central." I hold the ball to my chest. "My school."

She clears her throat. "I didn't know you went to Abilene Central."

"I did." I smile, inhaling a deep breath. "Like I said, Cass, I don't think you know me as well as you think you do."

Her bottom lip pops out. She frowns and the sight of it is enough to make me want to lean forward and crush my mouth to hers, wanting to erase it. But I need her to hear me out. I need her to hear my truth. The one I've kept secret for the past five years.

Her eyes have already started to well with tears. They're glassy and sad, as if she's been holding those tears in for the past two weeks. The way she looks is exactly how I feel.

"It was a clear night my sophomore year," I say, telling her the night just how I remember it. The night she'd pieced me back together yet shattered my heart all in one night. "Hot and sticky as Abilene usually is in the fall. It was the end of the second quarter. We were in a time out and my coach was quickly running me through a play on the sideline. But I stopped listening when I caught sight of this gorgeous flowing head of blonde hair from the corner of my eye. I looked up and narrowed my eyes, convinced it wasn't you. It couldn't be you. I mean, the last time I'd seen you was nearly two years before that. It could have been anyone, but then I saw your camera and that familiar strap." I point to the one she's holding in her hand. "At first, I wasn't sure if you were real or if I was imagining it because I hadn't seen you after graduation. But there you were, walking down the sideline on your team's side with that fucking camera in your hand. I thought after graduation, that was it. I'd never see you again. But there you were." A small laugh vibrates from my throat. I take another step closer, lowering the football between us.

"You saw me?" she asks.

"Cass," I say, wanting her to know everything. Every word

and feeling I've kept to myself all these years. I want her to hear them all. "You have no idea what seeing you did to me that night. It fucking wrecked me."

"I saw you."

Her three-word confession nearly knocks me off my feet like a linebacker tackling me on the field.

"You did?" I ask her.

"I did." Her bottom lip quivers. "It wasn't until I was about to leave that night after the game was over. I'd seen your last name on the back of your jersey. I'd convinced myself to go despite the risk of seeing you. But I'd also convinced myself that even if I did see you, you wouldn't care. I mean, I guess in a way I was right. You didn't talk to me that night." Her statement is hushed and there's pain laced in her words. As if she's checking off another box on her list of all the times I've hurt her. The thought of me willingly not speaking to her. It feels as if a knife has wedged itself between my ribs, twisting with the reminder of how often I've hurt her.

"There are many things I regret in my life, Cass. And not talking to you that night is definitely in my top five regrets." I shake my head. I remember exactly what happened that night, the image of Cassidy wrapping herself around someone else who wasn't me clear in my mind. "As much as I wanted to go over to you right away, when I saw you, I couldn't. I was forced to play out the rest of the second quarter. But once the clock had run out and my team headed back into the locker room for half-time, I went the other direction. I made it about halfway across the field when I'd taken off my helmet and I saw you. I stopped, watching as one of the UT football players wrapped his arm around you and kissed you."

Another tear spills down her cheek.

"Levi," she says, pressing her hand to her chest. "I've never had much time for dating. Between my dad and Jonah but Hunter was the only person I dated in college. I say dated, but that was only one of two times I'd ever spent time with him."

"You don't have to explain it to me, Cass. I get it. Obviously, you had every right to date or be with anyone. I wasn't in your life and technically, I never was. I just wanted you to know that considering the way I have always felt about you, it rocked me to my core." I'm sincere. I mean every word. "My entire world flipped upside down watching you, Cass. I wanted to be happy for you, but I couldn't. Jealousy was running rampant through my veins. I couldn't be happy for you. Not when I saw another man placing his hands on you. Kissing you. Not when I'd spent our entire senior year convinced it would never work between us, even if I told you I was in love with you."

"Wait, what?" she asks, blinking rapidly. "Our senior year?"

"Cassidy," I say, taking the final step between us. She tips her chin up, matching my stare with hers. "I've been in love with you since the moment you stepped out onto our high school football field and pointed that camera lens at me."

"But that doesn't make any sense," she disagrees, unconvinced.

"It makes perfect sense."

"You've hated me from the start."

I fervently shake my head. "I'd spent the first few years of college actively trying to forget you, Cass. I was a dumb and foolish eighteen-year-old who'd fallen in love with a girl who had despised me. I mean, you had a hard time even looking at me. And every time, it gutted me. But still, even then . . . the worse I treated you, the more it made sense to me. At the time, at least. I had moved to Austin my senior year of high school and my dad had just passed away. I told myself there was no way I could string you along in the mess that was my life. My father's plan for me was to always go off to college to play football. There was no room for you, and I spent way too long believing it. I spent entirely too long believing that's what was best. When in reality, it was at the expense of my happiness. Year after year passed, even after that night I saw you on the field, where I knew I would never see you again. But then when I'd landed the job at the paper. There you were. The day I walked into that newspaper and realized I was hired to work at the same newspaper as you was one of the worst things to ever fucking happen to me. It was also the best. I regret asking you to be my fake fiancée. If only for the fact it made it impossible to keep you at a distance. The way I had for years. And it's only made it more difficult not to completely fall in love with you."

"Levi." Her voice breaks, thick with emotion. She squeezes her eyes shut, inhaling a shaky breath. When she opens them again, the pain is still there. "I was doing just fine with you hating me. I learned to live with it, knowing the possibility of you and me could never be. You hated me and I hated you. That's the way it was. That's the way it was supposed to be."

"But it's not, Cass, and I'm sorry I've spent so long making you think it was," I whisper. "I'm so sorry. I never hated you."

A tear slips from her eye and I step forward again. She doesn't move. I lift my hand and press the pad of my thumb to her cheekbone, swiping it away.

"I *never* hated you." I repeat myself, gripping her chin and pulling her gaze up. I need her to not only hear my words, but feel them. I keep my fingers on her chin as she stands on her toes.

"Well." She sighs, her bottom lip quivering. "I hate you, Levi."

A sob breaks through her chest, and my stomach twists with her confession.

"I'm sorry, Cass." I shake my head, digesting her words. "I never meant to hurt you."

"Why didn't you tell me?" Her breath is shallow as another tear falls.

I shake my head, unable to give her an answer worthy enough. When I think back on all the time wasted, it sounds ridiculous.

"No reason I give you, Cass, will ever be good enough. But I think I was mostly afraid," I explain, swallowing all my reasons. "At first, I blamed timing. What good would it do to fall in love with you when we were set to graduate? I couldn't break your heart. I guess after graduation, it was easier to convince myself you were better off without me. You had moved on in your life and I would only throw a wrench in it. I'd already shown you a version of myself that you had learned to deal with all of senior year. But I swear to you, I never meant to hurt you." I swallow again, catching her watery eyes. "I never should have used you to get back at Miles. He was never worth any of it, and I'll regret it for the rest of my life. I guess you were right. I kept telling lies to my big fat ego."

Her expression remains the same, unwavering by my confession. For a moment, I believe my worst nightmare has come true. She hates me even more than she already did.

"No." Her voice is stronger, filled with conviction. She grasps onto my shirt with her free hand, fisting the fabric between her clenched fingers. Tears continue to flow, sliding one after another down her cheeks. I can't tell if she's angry with me or not. Either way, I can see every thought and emotion she's ever had toward me spill out of her. "I hate you, Levi. I hate that I've loved you from the beginning, despite all the trouble you've caused since that moment I saw you through my camera lens. I hate that I've loved you ever since. I hate that despite all the times you brushed me off, were rude to me, and guilted me into pretending to be your fake fiancée, I'm still completely and insanely in love with you. And I hate that I spent those ten days on the beach with you in silent agony, wishing they were true."

"They were." I reassure her, ignoring the way doubt has started to creep in. I push on, determined Cassidy knows the truth. Regardless of how she feels. "Every touch was real." I drag the pad of my thumb across her bottom lip, savoring the way her pillowy soft flesh feels against my skin. Every single word falling from her mouth soothes the parts of my soul that believed she would and could never love me back. "Every kiss," I say, bending my face toward her. I brush my lips against hers, every nerve in my body exploding as she leans into me with all her strength. "Every second of our fake engagement wasn't fake. It was real. It's always been real."

Her gaze shoots straight to mine. They flicker back and forth as if she's quickly trying to read whether my words are true or false. It's tearing me up inside to see her crying, but they've transformed to ones of relief the longer we've been standing here out on the field. "It's always been real?"

"Yes," I tell her.

"It's always been real for me too, Levi." Her eyes flutter shut as she leans into my touch.

I slide my hand from her cheek, gripping onto the back of her head. I thread my fingers through her long blonde hair, the orange sun catching her eyes before she closes them. I slam my mouth to hers, tasting her for the first time, as mine. Not as my fake fiancée.

She parts her lips, inviting me in, fully. A loud thud pounds to the ground beside our feet. I don't have to pull away to know Cassidy has dropped her camera onto the ground. She lifts both hands around my neck, dragging the tips of her fingers against my skin. A prickling sensation spreads across my body, shooting straight to my chest.

I let the football drop to the ground beside Cassidy's camera.

Then, just as it had the night I slammed Cassidy down into my lap, announcing to all my old teammates she was my fiancée, I'm left completely breathless.

THIRTY-TWO

Cassidy

Levi Hawkins has been nothing but trouble from the start. But despite the trouble he's caused over the years, I still love him as much as I ever have. Impossibly, I think I love him even more.

His hand is wrapped around the back of my head, keeping me pressed against him, and I don't think his touch has ever felt more real than in this moment. I can feel his truth and his love pouring into me like a radiant heat. It seeps into my skin and bones, expanding and filling inside me like a hot-air balloon. All the pieces of my heart and soul that have been fractured are glued back together.

I feel whole.

"Oh, fuck," Levi mumbles against my mouth. He hasn't been able to break our kiss long enough to make a coherent sentence. "I fucking love you."

I laugh, smiling against his lips. My chest is bursting with happiness. A happiness I haven't felt in forever. At least, nothing like this.

"Why are you laughing?" I can feel his mouth stretch across mine. He's grinning.

"Because"—I giggle—"you keep trying to talk . . ." He kisses me. "And kiss me . . ." He kisses me again. "At the same time."

Both his hands are now cupping my cheeks, his fingers pressed against my temples. He finally pulls back long enough to stare at my whole face. His eyes are bright, and he hasn't stopped grinning. He's deliriously happy. Like me.

"I'm sorry." Quick, heavy breaths cause his chest to expand and contract. "It's just that you're finally mine and I can't believe it. It feels as if I've been holding my breath this whole time, my lungs slowly withering away without oxygen. But you've brought me back to life."

"You don't have to apologize," I tell him, wrapping my hands around his wrists. His hands are still on my cheeks. I press my hips into his once again. "I love you."

He presses his mouth together, blowing one resolving breath through his nose.

He leans forward, bringing his mouth to the hollow of my ear. I clench my thighs together, savoring the way it feels. It's familiar and exhilarating all at once.

"You have no fucking idea how much I love you." He pulls back and I turn my head only slightly.

"Show me." It's a challenge. It's a dare. It's whatever you want to fucking call it.

I know I can't stand here much longer without feeling Levi. All of him.

Levi takes my challenge almost immediately. The familiar look of hunger that has yet to be satiated washes over his face. His jaw ticks and his eyes light with a fire that shoots straight to my core.

"Come on." He quickly wraps his hand around mine and starts to pull me from the field.

"Wait," I say, tugging on his hand. He stops and I jog back the few steps, picking up my camera.

Levi wraps his hand up in mine again, continuing to pull us in the direction he initially started to go.

"Where are we going?" I ask him, looking around.

"There's a locker room back over here." He points to a large white painted brick building.

My heart hammers and thrashes in my chest, as if Levi's wrapped a string around it, attempting to tug it free of my body. Every move and sound he makes causes my body to hum with excitement.

He's pulling me in the direction of the locker room in such a hurry, my boots skid across the dirt. Clouds of misty brown dust kick up behind me as we reach the door to the locker room.

The white brick building is small. The door is painted a deep dark blue.

Levi pushes through it and holds it open long enough for me to follow him in.

He doesn't bother stepping in more than necessary before he's spinning me around and pinning me against the door.

My back hits the painted metal. The sound echoes inside the empty locker room. We both laugh, hunching our shoulders as if we might get caught.

The excitement and thrill Levi has been giving me this whole time shoots straight between my thighs. I'm already soaking wet for him.

He snaps the dead bolt behind me and presses his large frame against me. It molds to mine. His hips press into my stomach as he towers over me. He rests his arm above my head and looks down. I tip my chin higher, resting my head back against the door. The tips of Levi's dark brown hair drift off his forehead, creating a shadow over his blue eyes. They're sparking with fire and electricity. Every color combination I've ever seen in them is there now. I swallow the lump in my throat, knowing I'm fucking hopelessly in love with him.

Our breaths are ragged and heavy, as if we ran the entire length of the field and back.

He lifts his hand and rests his palm on my collarbone, wrapping his fingers gently around my neck. His fingers are resting on my throat, likely feeling the rate of my pulse. I place my hand over his, unable to take my eyes off his.

"I love the way you look at me." The words fall from my mouth so effortlessly. And aside from telling Levi I have always been in love with him, I don't think I've ever spoken more true words than those. It hasn't been easy forgiving Levi, but I realize in this moment, I forgave him days ago. Because my love for him is stronger than any anger I might feel toward his reasons for stringing me along as his fake fiancée.

A burning sensation ignites in my lower belly, and I rub my thighs together, begging to have Levi between them. I want to feel his cock slide into me, swelling inside my warm folds.

I don't realize I'm still holding my camera in my other hand until Levi takes it from me and places it in one of the cubbies lining the wall beside us.

I have no clue where we are or what this room looks like. For all I know, someone could be in here and we have been too wrapped up in one another to notice.

It's a risk I'm willing to take. Like the night at the pool. When Levi tasted me for the first time. Remembering that night brings the realization that Levi loved me even then. He was showing and doing things to me he's always wanted to do.

As if he's reading my mind, he presses the pad of his thumb against the base of my throat. The pressure isn't too much, just enough to make my heart skip a beat.

Without wasting another second, his mouth crashes to mine. This time it isn't gentle. He doesn't take it slow. He ravishes me. This kiss is the kiss I've always imagined. The kind where Levi is staking his claim on me, making it known I'm finally his. I'm only his.

He moves his mouth against mine as if he can't get enough. And I do the same. I stand on my toes and slide my hand under his shirt. I rake my fingers against his tightened abs, pulling him impossibly closer.

Heat is already spread out across his skin. I lift his shirt over his head and toss it aside. He does the same with mine before he slides one hand to my back, unclasping my bra with two fingers.

I gasp, the warm damp air grazing across my already peaked nipples. Pulling me away from the door, Levi wraps both arms around me, spinning us until I'm walking backward. One of his hands is around the back of my head, the other cradling my lower back.

"I love you," I say against his mouth.

"I love you, Cass." I don't think I'll ever tire of hearing him use the shortened version of my name. It's a name reserved only for those who love me.

Levi keeps walking us farther back into the locker room until the back of my legs hits the edge of what feels like wood. He pulls back, keeping his arms on me.

"Lie back," he orders.

I glance over my shoulder, spotting the long glossy wooden bench behind me.

I do as he says until my entire body is lying flat on the bench. I spread my legs, parting them over the bench. Each foot is resting on the floor. My breasts fall slightly to the side, but I don't care. I gather both of them in my hands, massaging them and pinching my nipples as Levi removes the rest of his clothes. He quickly slides his jeans and boxer briefs off in one move.

"Fuck," he grits out, a loud vibrating grumble moving up his throat. "I'm going to fucking come right now simply watching you do that."

"You like it?" I ask him, heat rising in my cheeks. If I wasn't already wet before, I am now. I can't wait for Levi any longer.

He bends down and places one of his hands above my head. He uses the other to wrap around the back of my knee, bending my leg and centering himself in front of my wet folds. I'm still wearing my leather skirt. It slides up my thighs, bunching around my waist.

I'm not wearing any underwear and Levi notices almost immediately after he looks down.

"Holy shit, Cass." He runs his tongue across his lips, a heavy weighted breath exhaling from his chest. "Of all the fucking times I've imagined fucking you in the locker room, I never imagined you like this."

"You've imagined fucking me in a locker room?" I ask him. My curiosity is piqued.

"Oh," he grits out, driving himself inside me. I tilt my head back and gasp for air as he fills me. He leans down and presses his mouth to mine as he pulls out, then thrusts himself back in. I gasp again, arching my back. "You have no idea the places I've imagined being with you."

I move myself in tandem with Levi, pressing my hips harder and deeper into his with every thrust. He pulls out, then pushes in, filling me.

I keep my eyes in line with his, watching how they fill with love for me.

Sadness. Regret. Pain. Lost time. Inflated egos. Our history. Our secrets. Old college rivals. Fake engagements.

All of it is rolled into this moment. Every thrust, every touch, and every kiss is an apology.

His hips buck against mine harder. My back slides against the smooth glossed benched. Levi wraps one arm under me, gripping onto my shoulder to keep me in place. His thick frame moves above me, and I wrap my arms around him, holding him against me as my legs quiver around him.

"Come for me, Cass." He breathes out, moving his hips harder. "I want to fuck your pussy until you have no choice but to come. I want to watch that beautiful face of yours fall apart at my touch."

"Oh." I moan. "Levi, I'm coming." I tighten my legs around his waist, holding him against me as my body pulses with my orgasm. I can feel myself contracting around him, riding it out.

I relax enough for Levi to move above me. He thrusts his hips back and forth, his cock sliding in and out of me. My orgasm has lit a fire under him. I bite down on my lip, watching his muscles flex and contract with every move he makes.

I wrap my hands around the back of his head, pulling him down to me. He keeps his eyes on mine as I hold his face only inches above me. "I love you, Levi. I always have."

"Fuck, Cass." He moves only two more times before he stops and his cum spills inside me. His cock throbs and pulsates as he rides out the rest of his orgasm. His hand is pressed against the bench, holding himself up. His arm shakes above me, exhaustion settling into the fibers of his muscles.

With his other hand, he traces his finger along my cheek, down to my jaw. The tears I cried earlier have now dried. I have no idea how I look, but I don't care. Apparently, neither does Levi.

He grins, displaying his near perfect teeth. I melt inside when three creases form in the corners of his mouth. "Do you want to know something?"

"Sure," I say, tilting my chin back up to meet his gaze. He keeps himself inside me, unmoving.

"I've always loved you, Cass."

I giggle. "I already knew that."

"No," he says, his smile fading. But it isn't replaced with

sadness. It's replaced with a fervent need to remind me of his truth. "I don't care how many times I say it. I will remind you for the rest of my life if I have to. I've always loved you, Cass."

"Sounds good to me." I lift my head and place my mouth on his.

When I pull back, he grins, finally pulling himself out of me. I feel the absence of him immediately.

Even though he's no longer inside me, he doesn't move. He studies my face as if it's the first time he's ever seen it. My chest bursts with love for the only man I've ever truly loved. I'm no longer falling in love with Levi.

I'm in love with him.

"We shouldn't stay here too long," he says. "I don't want to get in trouble. Zane and the team should show up soon."

"Are you kidding, Levi?" I ask him, biting my lip, resisting the urge to laugh. "You're lucky I've been in love with you all this time."

"Oh yeah?" he asks, pressing his lips to mine. He pulls back with a devious smile. "Why is that?"

"Because"—I kiss him back—"you've always been trouble."

EPILOGUE

Cassidy

Three months later

"Put your fingers here." Levi spreads each of my fingers across the white stitching. I grip onto the leather, feeling more awkward the farther he spreads them.

"What?" I ask, wincing.

He's standing behind me, holding my back against his chest. Even though he's trying to show me how to hold a football properly, I haven't been able to stop thinking about how his breath keeps grazing the hollow of my ear. My skin tingles with goosebumps as they spread across my body like the sand on the beach.

"Place your fingers here." He repeats. I can feel him grinning behind me.

"You're laughing at me." I groan, rolling my eyes.

"I am not," he says, grabbing onto my hand again. "Okay, maybe I am."

"My hand is too small. This ball is fucking huge, Levi."

"It's a standard size ball, Cass." He clears his throat. He keeps his hand over mine, moving the ball back and forth as if he's simulating a throw. "It's important to hold it this way so you get the perfect spiral. It's the right way to hold a football."

"Well." I giggle. "If this is the right way, then I'd rather be wrong."

"Is that right?" he asks. His large hands grip my waist and spin me around. He pushes me gently down to the ground. My back lands on the sand. I squint against the harsh rays of the sun beaming down on me through the cloudless sky.

Levi lands on top of me, his gorgeous face blocking the sun.

After my father and Joni eloped at the courthouse over a month ago, Levi and I haven't had time alone until now. Even with my father's limited mobility, they took a small trip for their honeymoon. They had spent a few days in San Antonio. Levi and I were happy to take care of Jonah while he was away, sharing our time with Colton and Vada.

I've been grateful for the help from them, and I've never been happier for my dad. Seeing the way he loves Joni reminds me of my relationship with Levi. The way it's evolved over the years, turning from denial to anger to acceptance. It's horrible to put up a wall between you and the one you love. But still, if Levi and I hadn't gone through our fake engagement, we might never have ended up where we are now.

After my father and Joni returned, Levi surprised me with a do-over trip to South Padre Island. This time I didn't bring my camera. This time I'm not under the false pretense we're here for a story. And this time we are nowhere near Miles's hotel or his vineyard.

Levi booked our own room at a completely different resort. I guess this was his way of making it up to me and making a new memory of this beautiful place.

I can officially say, this time around, is infinitely better than the last.

Levi's tan sand-covered body hovers over mine. He crushes his mouth to mine, breathing me in. He smells like the coconut sunscreen I sprayed all over him earlier.

He pulls away from me, looking into my eyes. The hot sun creates a halo around his head, his blue eyes shining even in the shadow.

"Truth or dare?" he asks me.

I narrow my eyes, still smiling. I place my hand against his damp cheek, a dot of sweat streaming down his temple, disappearing into my skin. I arch an eyebrow.

"Truth," I say, playing along.

"True or false?" he asks me. "You would rather be my real fiancée than my fake one."

"What?" I ask him. All the oxygen I had left in my lungs escapes through my parted lips. I swallow, massaging my fingers against Levi's temple. His blue eyes stare straight into mine. I know exactly what he's asking me.

The gravity of what he's asking barrels into me. It wraps around me in the same way Levi is right now.

I've spent too many years going from secretly loving Levi, to hating him, to falling in love with him all over again. Now all I'm left with is his love. His full, complete love and I wouldn't want to be anywhere else.

"True or False?" He repeats. "You would rather be my real fiancée than my fake one."

I tip my chin even higher, my head digging into the sand. I wrap my hand around the back of his head, pulling him closer. The tip of his nose brushes against mine as I whisper.

"True."

The End

**Want to read more from the Heartbreak Series?
Read a Bonus Epilogue HERE**

Wow! First of all, I want to thank you, the reader, for reading Cassidy and Levi's story! If you've read all the books in the Heartbreak Series, I couldn't be more grateful. Even though I'm a bit sad this series is finished, I'm thankful to have it completed. And what a better way to finish than with Cassidy and Levi. They have been my absolute favorite couple to write. Their hate for each other came easy and their love for each other was even more easy to write. They made me laugh and they made me cry. I hope they did the same for you!

If you have a chance, I'd love it if you'd be able to leave a review. They mean so much to me and I am always grateful!!!

Cassidy and Levi's story gave me inspiration for my next series! I can't say too much about it just yet but if you'd like to stay in the loop and be the first to hear all about it, be sure to sign up for my newsletter! That's the best place to stay connected.

Sign up for my newsletter HERE

Again, I want to thank each of you for coming along on this journey in the Heartbreak Series. Everyone at Dallas's Barbecue and Brew is grateful! LOL

Thank you from the bottom of my heart for giving this series a chance and hopefully falling in love with all the characters just as much as I have!

XOXO Brittany

STAY CONNECTED

Website
Newsletter
Amazon
Instagram
Reader Group
Facebook
BookBub
TikTok

THE WRONG PITCH

Chapter 1
Ophelia

Today is quite possibly the worst day of my life.

Moving in with my younger brother at the ripe old age of twenty-two isn't exactly what I had envisioned at this stage of my life. I always imagined living in a high-rise apartment in the center of New York City, owning my own fashion design company. I wouldn't rely on anyone other than myself, and my success was all owed to the work I'd put in the past four years.

I was well on my way there. My path was free and clear. Nothing stood in my way.

Until I woke up this morning and my life was catapulted in a completely different direction. It feels as if within the matter of a few words, my life came to a screeching halt, and now I'm left with next to nothing.

I'm walking down a lonely, dark road, headed to my brother's house with nothing but the clothes on my back and the suitcase trailing behind me. The eerily quiet street is deafening, sending chills down my spine ever since I stepped off the bus half a mile back. But I was left with no other options. My life dissolved before I'd even had an opportunity to realize what was happening. Between work and school, I hadn't taken the time to invest in buying a car, which led me here. Forced to book a last-minute bus ride from New York City to the tiny town of Eden, Maine.

My hometown. The last place I ever wanted to return.

I'm dragging my suitcase behind me, the small plastic wheels beating against the asphalt. Every now and then I run over a few pebbles. The constant bumps cause my suitcase to wobble, including the sewing machine resting on top of it. I refused to leave it behind in New York. The only thing that could make this day worse is if I were to lose it.

I grunt in frustration and grab onto the handle of my sewing machine. I wrap my hand around it and my suitcase handle. Hopefully it'll stabilize it more as I march down the long, deserted road. Normally, I wouldn't complain about being dropped off one block away but considering it's nearly midnight and there are only two streetlights on this road, I'm annoyed. Irritated beyond belief at the circumstances leading me up to this point.

Chills prickle their way down the back of my neck. It's silent. Uncomfortably quiet. Something I'm not used to, coming from a city such as New York. I pull my phone out from the back pocket of my jeans and call my best friend. At least she can keep me company while I head toward Reed's house.

"Ophelia?" Claire whispers into the phone. Her voice is low and gravelly, as if she's trying to sleep. Or she was on the verge of falling asleep. "What's going on? Did you make it to Reed's yet?"

"Claire, shit." I place my hand against my forehead and wince, remembering the plans my best friend had gushed about non-stop earlier. "I didn't interrupt your date, did I? How did that go?"

"No." She snorts, her voice clearing slightly. She groans. "I'm in my bed. The date was going great until the end when he asked if I was interested in a foursome."

"No," I say, stifling a laugh. It's a contradiction to how I was feeling only moments ago. But this is exactly why I called my best friend. "He didn't."

"Hey," she's quick to defend. "Still nowhere near as bad as the one guy who asked me what wine I drank at dinner, and when I told him I liked white, he still proceeded to order a one-hundred-dollar bottle of red. Then by the end of the meal, claimed he left his wallet out in the car and didn't even offer to go get it. Worst and biggest waste of two hundred dollars I've ever spent."

"Oh my god." I grin. "I do remember that."

"I'm telling you, Ophelia. Dating fucking sucks."

"Tell me about it," I mumble. "At least you're going out on dates. I'm currently walking down a creepy dark road all by myself. Not to mention, I'm moving in with my little brother."

"It's only temporary, Ophelia."

"Doesn't feel like it." I sigh then inhale a deep breath, hoping it'll make me believe my own words. "Or at least I hope it's not."

"It's not," she reaffirms. "Besides, it's a good thing you took that self-defense class a couple years ago when we joined that sorority freshman year. I can't believe you have to walk."

I nod, even though she can't see me. She's right.

Claire's been my best friend ever since I met her in one of those speed dating sessions our college organized. I was only nineteen at the time. I didn't have any intention of finding my soulmate or my future husband, but apparently, she was. She has been for as long as I've known her.

I don't know where she gets her drive from when I decided to give up a long time ago. Not that I haven't dated over the years. But I haven't been dead set on finding my perfect match.

As far as I'm concerned, love is for the birds.

"It's a good thing I still remember some moves," I tell her. "I guess joining the sorority wasn't completely useless."

"You're right," Claire mumbles, her words dragging into one another. "Are you almost there? Why exactly are you walking by yourself? Reed couldn't pick you up?"

I groan, still trudging down the street. Reed's house comes into view. There's a light turned on the front porch, but otherwise, it looks dark. All the windows are pitch-black.

"He had to work tonight. Shouldn't surprise me, though, considering he's always working. Working or playing baseball."

"None of his other roommates are home?"

"No. I don't think so." I sigh again, knowing my luck hasn't been the best this past week. "I'm not really sure where they are. Reed told me one of them had to work. I guess the other is out training or something."

"If no one is home, how are you going to get in without a key?" Claire asks. "I'm guessing he didn't leave the house unlocked for you."

"No, I hope not anyway." I snort. "Reed told me he left the spare key under the doormat."

"Good," Claire says.

I survey the neighborhood, gauging the kind of environment I'll be living in for the foreseeable future. Well, at least the time it takes me to find another place to live.

"I don't get it. This is supposed to be a college town," I tell Claire. "The school is only a few blocks away, but I've never seen a college town so... dead."

"Didn't you grow up there?"

"Yeah," I say, laughing. "But I didn't grow up around this neighborhood. Our house was on the outskirts of town, and I never had a reason to come over here. I didn't go to college here."

"Well." Claire sighs. "It's not forever, right? You're only there for a few months."

The hope in Claire's voice is enough to bring tears to my eyes. Warm liquid wells behind them, and I sniff, attempting to keep them at bay. I look down and kick at a few pebbles dotted along the street.

"I don't know to be honest." I bite down on my bottom lip. "I'd like to go back to New York City, but I don't even know how I'll be able to do that. It sounds impossible right now."

A silence follows my words, and I know exactly what Claire is thinking.

She reads my mind. "I'm sorry you couldn't stay with me."

"You've already apologized." I shake my head.

"I know, but it still fucking blows that I couldn't even take in my best friend. My roommate isn't moving out for another six months, and there's no room here. There's barely enough room for the two of us as it is."

Take in.

Hearing Claire use those words only makes me feel worse. Like I'm some sort of stray begging for a place to stay. As if I have no home.

"Seriously, Claire. I get it. Renting in the city is next to impossible and well, add in no job on top of it, I get it. I was barely scraping by as it was. I didn't expect you or anyone else to have a place for me to stay on demand. None of us saw this coming." I pout. I can't help it. I still haven't gotten over how drastic my life has changed in the past three days.

The worst two days of my life.

Day one. Get laid off from my coveted internship. Day two. My roommate inexplicably disappears, doesn't renew our lease, and I find an eviction notice taped to my door. I begged my landlord to give me time, but she wasn't hearing a word. She stood in the doorway only long enough to allow me to pack whatever I was able to take with me. My sewing machine and my suitcase.

She offered for me to come back and pick up the items she was going to leave out on the curb, but at the time, the task seemed impossible. My life was crumbling quickly. I couldn't think straight.

Bad circumstances usually happen in threes.

At this rate, I'm worried the saying is true.

Claire's voice softens. "I'm still shocked they pulled the rug out from under you the way they did. Is it even legal?"

"It is." I tilt my head to the side, pressing the phone harder against my ear. "Everyone I talked to says they had the right to lay everyone off. I was just the start, apparently. Interns usually are. It was all in the hands of this shareholder company anyway. They control everything. Andrew Turner had the largest slice of investment in Travis Sterling's design firm. He pulled his funding and immediately the funding was pulled. Travis panicked and immediately started laying everyone off. With no warning."

"Shit."

"Yeah, well, money talks. I never met Andrew, but I've seen enough pictures of him to know the kind of person he is. Fucking asshole." I bite down on the side of my cheek. The familiar sickness I've been experiencing all day returns. Landing the internship at Travis Sterling Designs in New York City was a fucking dream come true. I'd dropped practically everything in my life to work there. Only to have it stripped away from me in the most brutal way.

Andrew Turner is now considered my number one enemy.

Claire offers me nothing but her silence in response. She

knows I'm right about the money and she doesn't bother trying to convince me. My entire situation is bullshit.

"It's fine." I inhale a deep cleansing breath, willing myself to believe the words I'm speaking out loud. So far, it hasn't helped. "I'll figure something out."

Uncertainty ebbs its way into my bones, burrowing deep inside me and making a home there.

"I know you will," Claire reassures me.

I look down. I kick at the rocks again. They fly out in front of me, skittering out several feet.

"Is there anything I can do for you?" Claire asks.

I abruptly stop, leaving Claire's question unanswered. I'm only a few houses down from my brother's but I can't move. I yank on the handle to my suitcase, but it won't budge. The bottom corner is stuck in a small pothole, and the wheel has popped off. It rolls down the street, landing a few feet away from me.

Maybe I'm wrong. Maybe bad circumstances happen in fours. Not threes.

"Shit." I groan, still holding my phone to my ear. "Could this night possibly get any worse?" I let go of my suitcase, gently placing my sewing machine case on top of it and walk to pick up the wheel. I want to laugh. I want to cry.

My body can't decide which emotion to feel. My throat swells, yet I find the urge to laugh. At how different my life is in this moment. I swallow down the tears I know are threatening to come and move to pick up the wheel.

"What happened?" Claire asks, but I don't answer her.

I'm mid pick-up, bending down to grab the wheel. An unfamiliar sound stops me. A quick secession of pounding comes from my right. It gets louder as if it's growing closer to me. It's a noise I haven't heard aside from my own feet and the wheels of my suitcase grinding the pavement with every step. It's the rhythmic beat of another person's footsteps on an otherwise desolate street. The air catches in my throat. I look up to see someone charging in my direction. He's running at full speed. Directly at me.

His face is covered in shadows and darkness. The hood of his sweatshirt is pulled up and over his head, hiding himself from me.

My heart races in my chest, and the blood drains from my face. My neck prickles with nerves, and my stomach flips.

His footsteps grow louder. I use every instinct in my body when he reaches me.

I immediately let go of my phone and drop it onto the street. I have no idea where it lands. All I hear is a loud smack, the sound of crushing metal hitting asphalt. I have no clue if Claire is still on the other end. I lift my arm, stopping the man before he has the chance to attack me. He stops, his eyes growing wide, realizing I'm prepared to fight back. I haven't been able to see them until now. Not until he's inches from my face, realization replacing his determined expression.

Not today, asshole.

I wrap my hand around his wrist. With my other hand, I grip onto his bicep and push him backward with as much force as I can muster.

His yell echoes across the otherwise empty street. The deep guttural growl that erupts from his chest as he slams back onto the street shoots straight through me. Adrenaline immediately courses through my veins. I tackled him. I *actually* tackled him to the ground.

I kneel over him, pressing my knee into his chest, holding him there and pinning him to the asphalt. He begs for me to get off him.

"What the fuck?" he grits out.

He tries to grab my knee with his one free hand. I have the

other held down on the ground. His hood has slipped back and off his head, exposing his face. The one streetlight above us highlights his features, and I immediately make a mental list of all of them. You know, in case I need to call the police afterward. If my phone still works.

Dark-brown hair cut short on the sides, long strands at the top falling back away from his tan forehead. His thick eyebrows are knitted. He opens his eyes. They're a bright shade of green with golden flecks, igniting with anger. His near-perfect sculpted jawline is clenched tight.

My heart continues to hammer in my chest. I bend my head down, bringing my face closer to his.

"What is wrong with you?" I ask him.

He stops moving, still grunting against my knee pressed into his chest. His eyes spread wide and he inhales a sharp, tight breath.

"What is wrong with me?" he asks. "What the hell do you think you're doing?"

"What did you think, huh?" I ask him, my eyebrows arching across my forehead. "Did you think I was an easy target? Woman walking alone in the dark?"

"What?" he asks, frowning. Shock is written across his regrettably gorgeous face. I hate admitting it to myself, considering the man tried to snatch me off the street. "I wasn't trying to attack you."

"Yes, you were."

He groans, squeezing his eyes shut before he opens them again. "I was not," he insists. "I was running. Like I do every night. *You* were the one who attacked *me*."

Normally, I wouldn't pause to consider an attacker's excuse. But the softness in this man's eyes urges me to listen. It's not that I immediately believe him, but I take my chances anyway.

Aside from the fact that his skin is covered in a thin film of sweat and his hair is equally just as drenched, there is one white earbud into his ear, the other sits on the concrete beside his head.

The distant, faded sound of drums and guitar flow from the one small plastic bud. I don't move my stance, but I glance over my shoulder at his feet. He's wearing a pair of worn running shoes. Printed in the corner of his black t-shirt is a baseball with a patriot hat on top of it. The same logo as my brother, Reed's, baseball team.

I realize none of this equates to proof he wasn't intending on attacking me. The man was clearly headed in my direction, but my intuition urges me to give him the benefit of the doubt.

He rests his head back on the concrete as soon as I loosen the pressure on his chest. I move my leg and let go of his arm, pulling myself to a stand. I'm cautious, moving slow. Just in case.

The man bends to pick up the lost earbud. He fishes inside his pocket and grabs his phone. He taps the screen, stopping his music.

My heart is still pounding and my cheeks warm. The man catches my eyes with his. He hasn't changed his expression. There's a permanent scowl written across his impossibly gorgeous face. If we didn't meet in this way and if I didn't think he was trying to snatch me up on the street, I might have immediately fallen for him. It'd be impossible not to with a jaw cut like his.

I don't let my guard down. Even if I might catch myself staring at him longer than I should.

I swallow the heat in my throat and take a moment to steady my breath.

"What?" The man asks, impatient with my silence. The anger inside him is now spread across his gorgeous face. "Are you going to tell me why you thought I was attacking you? I think you at least owe me that much."

I place my hands on my hips, biting back the tears behind my eyes. I can feel them, swelling and threatening to spill at any second. My chin quivers. Today is quite possibly the worst fucking day of my life.

"The wheel to my suitcase broke off." I gesture toward it, resting on its side in the middle of the street. The wheel sits along the curb several feet away.

The man turns to look where I'm pointing. He sighs then slowly walks over to the wheel. He bypasses my suitcase and picks up the wheel.

"So," he lifts it up and holds it between two fingers. "This is your justification for attacking me?" He frowns, glancing between the wheel and me. He rolls it over his hand several times. "Who knew a wheel could do so much?"

Anger boils to the surface, keeping my sad tears at bay. My cheeks enflame and I tighten my hands into two fists. "I was bending down to pick it up when I saw you charging at me. What else was I supposed to think?"

My teeth grind together, and the side of my head pulsates. I just want to leave this man, grab my suitcase and get to Reed's house.

The man steps closer, narrowing the space between us. My suitcase is still several feet away from me.

I still keep my guard up. The man could be bluffing. He could be pretending to be innocent, placing all the guilt on me. Maybe he suspects I will fall for his charm and allow my defenses to fall long enough for him to attack me again.

I take another look around the neighborhood, checking to see if anyone else has come out in the time I tackled the man to the ground to now.

There's no one. It's just as silent as it was before.

The stranger extends his arm, holding the wheel out to me. I slowly open my hand, never taking my eyes away from his.

The corner of his mouth curls into a sly grin. For a moment, I think he might tell me he understands why I thought he was attacking me. For a moment, I'm naïve, thinking we would trade apologies then go our separate ways. I'm silently hoping this stranger will see the exhaustion and defeat in my expression. My feet are throbbing, and my head is pounding as if it's been beaten against a wall. Honestly, my body aches in places I didn't know existed.

But the second he opens that mouth of his, I realize I am wrong. He isn't sympathetic toward me.

"Maybe you should have bought a better suitcase." His eyes narrow and the muscles in his jaw harden.

The anger from earlier boils up again. Only this time, the tears from today's events stay. They don't waiver. One spills over my lashes, sliding down my cheek. I quickly swipe the warm liquid away, not wanting this stranger to see how his words have affected me.

He doesn't flinch. He places his hood back over his head and backs away, leaving me standing in the middle of the street holding a single broken suitcase wheel. I stand there with my feet bolted to the pothole ridden asphalt, watching until the man has disappeared back into the shadows.

Welcome to your new home, Ophelia.

Want to keep reading this college sports, roommates to lovers romance?

Continue reading The Wrong Pitch HERE

ACKNOWLEDGMENTS

I'm going to keep this one short although the amount of people I have to thank never runs short. It only grows with each book I write.

As always, I send never-ending gratitude to my husband and my kids. I wrote this book at a rough time in our lives. It's been a hard year and at times, I didn't think I'd get this one done. But you three stood by me as always. I'll love you forever.

To Lisa and Dani, thank you for our morning Fam-Bams. They kept me going and were the glue that held me together.

To my beta readers, Amy, April, and Nadine. Thank you from the bottom of my heart for being the first to lay eyes on Cassidy and Levi. Your feedback is invaluable.

My editor, Kimberly Hunt. Thank you so much for whipping my words into shape.

My designer, Amanda. Where do I begin with you? Thank you for designing the entire Heartbreak Series, including One-Time Secret. Every single graphic has been absolute perfection.

To Sara, thank you for the late night sprints. Even on the nights you weren't writing with me, thank you for sitting in as my timer. Those sessions might be the biggest reason I finished this book on time.

To my author bestie, Ashley. You will always be my favorite person to message at any time of day. Thank you for being my best friend and cheerleader.

And to you, the reader! Without you, I wouldn't be here. I know it sounds cliché, but I really couldn't do this without you.

XOXO

ABOUT THE AUTHOR

Brittany is a New Adult, Contemporary romance author best known for writing steamy, heart-clenching love stories, pulling out all the feels. She resides in Maine with her two sons and husband. She loves reading and writing spicy romances and is a Starbucks addict.